#1
IN A NEW SERIES FROM THE AUTHOR OF
Bloody Murdock and *Murdock for Hire*

ROBERT J. RAY
The Hit Man Cometh

"The plot is littered with a full complement of dead bodies and live Newport Beach arrivistes, including a stunning rags-to-riches bitch Spyglass Hill resident and a sexy *Orange County Register* reporter. Branko, Ray's Volvo-driving, tennis-playing protagonist, is believable. . . . We can look forward to more Frank Branko."
—*Los Angeles Times Book Review*

"Ray begins a new series with a fortyish, attractive Newport Beach homicide cop, Frank Branko. The absorbing, complex plot puts Branko on the trail of Benny Rubidoux, a hit man. . . . Consistent prose, graphic sex, and plenty of violence add to the entertainment."
—*Library Journal*

"Branko [is a] likable hero. . . . Along with plenty of action and a satisfying resolution, Ray offers an engaging cast of good guys and bad."
—*Publishers Weekly*

Also by Robert J. Ray

Merry Christmas, Murdock
Murdock for Hire
Bloody Murdock
Cage of Mirrors
The Heart of the Game

THE
HIT MAN
COMETH

A Frank Branko Novel

Robert J. Ray

A DELL BOOK

Published by
Dell Publishing
a division of
Bantam Doubleday Dell Publishing Group, Inc.
666 Fifth Avenue
New York, New York 10103

ISBN: 0-440-20466-6

Reprinted by arrangement with St. Martin's Press

Printed in the United States of America

Published simultaneously in Canada

November 1989

10 9 8 7 6 5 4 3 2 1
KRI

This one is for my brother,
Frank B. Ray,
whose talent keeps me inspired

ACKNOWLEDGMENTS

My thanks to Jean Femling, Jay Styron, and Lorraine Zimmerman, good pals who read the manuscript of *The Hit Man Cometh* and gave me telling advice.

VIDEO GAMES

CHAPTER ONE

BENNY felt edgy about the hit, so he ducked into the Fun Zone photo booth to have his picture made. Benny was an Arkansas Baptist. He'd never whacked a preacher before.

Under the brown jacket, the Kevlar body armor felt thick as a cowchip. Normally, Benny wore a size-forty jacket. This suit, a hundred and seventeen biscuits from C&R in North Hollywood, alterations extra, was a forty-three, bought big to hide the bulk of the Kevlar.

The booth smelled of popcorn and reefer smoke and kids' Double Bubble gum. Black-and-white photos cost a buck. Color went for two-twenty-five. Benny took off the wraparound shades, sat in the metal scoop seat, and chugged in nine quarters. The camera made a clicking sound and Benny smiled for Mama and Aunt Phoebe Rubidoux, back in Little Rock. The fake mustache tickled and his scalp felt sweaty under the black hairpiece.

With a final click the camera finished its work. A mechanical voice said: "Wait sixty seconds for processing, please. Thank you. And have a pleasant day."

The time was 2:52 when Benny stepped out of the booth. Inside dope said the target's Fun Zone ETA was 3:00 P.M. Eight minutes until the hit.

He checked his photo as he cruised by the Fun Zone Ferris wheel. The Santa Monica tan showed up terrific. Shrewd eyes, easy surfer's smile, what they called the laid-back look. Shit, he loved talking Californian.

Benny rolled his shoulders, enjoying the feel of the new shoulder rig, twin holsters, one for each side, gray nylon, three hundred bucks from Consolidated Police Supply, in Whittier. For Benny's line of work, the Velcro quick-release rig was best. The barrel went in straight, muzzle pointing behind you, gun butt hanging down, where you could reach it easy.

He put the photos into his left-hand coat pocket with the speed-loader for the S&W. If the shoot went according to blueprint, he wouldn't need the extra loads. The sun was hot on his back and shoulders. It was the last Friday in May and the Balboa Fun Zone was packed with young stuff. Music piped out from the ferris wheel, an oldie, he couldn't remember the words. He whistled when a skater slid by, blond hair flying.

"Grrr," Benny said. Her skates had red wheels, hot, whirly, summer sizzlers. Benny wet his lips. Her legs were long, sleek, toasty tan. They flowed like magic out of tight pink shorts and swept down to trim dancer's calves. Imagining those legs around his waist made Benny grin. Squeeze a guy to death, whoo-boy. She was wearing a silver bikini top and pink Walkman earphones and a purple sunshade that said Fila Sports.

Benny wiped his forehead. Too bad he was working. "Hey, baby," he growled. "Flick my bic."

The skater slid around the corner and Benny followed, leaving the music behind. This was Cortez Alley, the hit zone, packed with shops for the tourist trade. Angie's Curios, Sweets-N-Things, From Balboa, The Alley Florist, Suits for Cutes, Just Bikinis, and Fun Zone News, a narrow-front bookstore. The time was 2:55.

The skater turned a neat figure eight with the Inn of Cortez as a backdrop. The Inn, a battered beach hotel, spanned the block along Balboa Boulevard. The getaway Honda was parked in front of the flower shop on Cortez, across the street from the Inn. Benny figured ten minutes left on the meter. The Beard, Benny's shotgun, was inside the Inn, casing the place for security.

So far, there was only one uniform in sight, old Square Face, standing near the front entrance to the Inn. His black-and-white police unit was parked heading east. Square Face stood in the shade, thumbs in his gunbelt, staring around like Clint Eastwood. Square Face was the Beard's responsibility.

The skater reached the far end of Cortez, where it dead-ended into Balboa, and the target came into view, heading up his procession of blue-hairs. They were singing "Onward, Christian Soldiers." The target was chunky, five-ten, with wavy blond hair and a round face that was always smiling.

Benny had studied the target all week. He lived in Newport Beach, number 7 Singapore Circle, a cushy pad worth maybe six hundred grand, five bedrooms, a Spanish tile patio, brick sidewalks, a swimming-pool-and-hot-tub combo, and palm trees everywhere. In the morning, between eight and nine, a white church limo would pick the target up and drive him to Promontory Chapel, a whopper of a steel-and-glass church on the Back Bay. He'd be inside for a couple of hours, reading his Bible, praying, taping a sermon asking for donations. Around eleven-thirty, the target would come out, climb behind the wheel of a beige Mercedes, and drive to lunch at a snappy eatery in Newport Beach. Monday, it was the Meridien. Tuesday, it was the Marriott. Thursday, it was back to the Meridien. Friday, it was the Ritz. Wednesday, the preacher skipped lunch for a sweaty nooner in Dana Point, at Pirate's Cove Motel, room 113, overlooking the blue harbor.

His lunch date on Wednesday was a bottle-blond hooker, sweet tushie, smooth Acapulco tan, named Michele. From Benny's Caddy window, through the Army surplus field glasses, Michele looked like Jail Bait City. Up close, she matured some, twenty-four, twenty-five, a working girl from Eugene, Oregon, down to hook the Disneyland area for the winter season. "Honey," Michele had said, "it rains like be-Jesus up there. All that H-two-oh, a girl's skin turns to oatmeal." For a hundred biscuits and two ounces of Colombian Gold, Michele had told Benny all about the preacher. For another hundred, she'd driven the red Caddy back to L.A.

In the afternoons, after "lunch," the preacher surveyed the construction at Ministry Beach, USA, a theme park in the beachfront hills between Corona del Mar and Laguna Beach. Specs for Ministry Beach included a 700-room hotel, a church, a water park, and an open-air shopping mall.

After visiting Ministry Beach, USA, the reverend took to the campaign trail, shaking hands, kissing babies, begging for votes.

This coming Tuesday was the primary to decide who'd run for Congress in the big one in November. Politics was crap. The client, Mr. No-Name, wanted the hit today, Friday, four days before the primary. Benny'd wanted to do the job earlier in the week, catch the target in room 113 at the motel, take some candid camera photos, fill his fat Republican butt with rock salt. But, nooo, Mr. No-Name had said, Friday, a hit in the leg, small-caliber, in a public place, lots of shocked eyewitnesses.

The Balboa Hit Zone. Friday at three.

Benny was a specialist. Being a specialist paid top dollar. He worked in close, ten feet, fifteen feet, *blam*, see the whites of their eyes, yeah, the open mouths, that yuck surprise, and then dance out of there like a quarterback on Super Bowl Sunday. He'd taken targets down in bathrooms, in bed, in limos, in the office, in parks, in movie lines, in the exec washroom at the plant. One guy, a bird-colonel in the Air Force, he'd whacked near a base in Texas.

The dollars were piling up. This Fun Zone hit, for example, would go down for twenty-five big ones. The Beard got three for riding shotgun. Dixie wanted two for the boat. That left twenty for Benny.

The target came up the street toward Benny. He was wearing a three-piece suit and his smile flashed in the hot California sun. Inside dope said he kept the tan smooth with a sunlamp. The target could sing, voice booming, "Christ, the royal master, leads against the . . ."

Two steps behind the target was his old lady, Sister Winona Lee, in a floor-length blue dress with a white collar. Her face was like granite, the eyes like ball bearings. Sister Winona Lee was not a big woman but she moved with purpose, striding along, singing off-key. According to inside dope, Sister Winona Lee had no weaknesses. The smug look on her face reminded Benny of his Cousin Mercedes Rubidoux, an old-maid school-teacher in Fort Smith.

Walking with Sister Winona Lee was the target's bodyguard, Old U.S. Army Retired, a Vietnam vet in his fifties who kept peering around like he was Secret Service guarding the president. A shoulder harness was visible under his gray coat.

Behind the target and Sister Winona Lee came the troops, a gang of eighty born-again oldsters, the trifocal crowd. They carried signs that said DOWN WITH CRIMINAL PORNOGRAPHY and CHRISTIANS AGAINST SENSELESS SMUT and CASS NEEDS YOU! JOIN TODAY!!!

The skater zoomed by again and Benny spotted a black dude about twenty people back in the line of marchers. He was wearing running shoes and a bright orange jacket and white pants, and carried a sign that said REVEREND WILLIAMS FOR CONGRESS. He was hefty, with a wide shiny face and bright teeth.

It was 2:58 when the target stopped to make his speech. The blue-hairs circled around. A couple of teens on bikes wheeled past, grinning. With her blue dress shimmering, Sister Winona Lee toddled inside Fun Zone News.

"My friends, thank you for coming. God has given us a beautiful day and we are gathered here together to witness . . ."

The Beard came out of the Inn of Cortez, passed behind Square Face, and pressed the button to change the traffic signal. A horn sounded on Balboa. Benny's heart started thudding.

The preacher had just sucked a tittery laugh out of the assembled blue-hairs when Sister Winona Lee jetted out of Fun Zone News carrying a stack of magazines. Behind her marched three stern-faced ladies and four geezers, also with magazines. The preacher kept on talking, but people were watching his wife and not him as she dumped the magazines in the street. Her soldiers added to the heap. Someone giggled. Her movements were tight and bony.

"Winona Lee—?" the preacher called.

Eyes bright, Sister Winona Lee reached into her purse and pulled out a can of Texaco barbecue starter. Then she soaked the magazines. The pile was half a foot high. Benny moved closer. He could see *Playboy, Penthouse, Club, Oui.* What a waste.

The Beard blew his nose in a Kleenex and kick-started the Honda. Sister Winona Lee struck a match and lit the magazines. Her voice grated on Benny's ears. "Burn, you filth! Burn your way back to Hades!"

The preacher rushed over to his old lady. She stared at him, head thrust forward. He spoke to Sister Winona Lee and she

7

shook her head and pointed at a man in the door of Fun Zone News. Two more blue-hairs brushed by the man in the door and came out into the street with their magazines. *Whump*, onto the fire.

Square Face was leaning into his black-and-white, talking on the radio. Benny felt the need to piss. He coughed, turned his right shoulder toward the target, and reached under his C&R coat, casually, to caress the butt of the S&W.

Inside dope had said speechifying but nothing about a bonfire.

A little lady in a blue pants suit tossed on a paperback book and giggled. A woman in a yellow sun dress tossed on two magazines. The time was 3:02. Burn the books, Benny thought, but save the girlie mags. The Beard nodded. Ready.

It was your typical Southern California beach crowd, sandals and Reeboks and jams and Bermuda shorts and monogrammed T-shirts and here and there a business suit. The average age of the members of CASS—that stood for Christians Against Senseless Smut—was sixty, sixty-five, on the grave's dark lip, as his Uncle Groat Rubidoux used to say. The civilians were nodding to each other, Yeah, yeah, Save the World From Smut, yeah, Burn It.

Square Face had replaced the radio mike and was starting across the boulevard. The skater swirled by again, her buns going *snick-snick* in those hot pants. Benny's eyes tightened as he neared the target.

Three-oh-four. The target was talking, sweating, working the crowd. "This is a symbolic gesture, my friends, a holy fire. And we know we are in the right. This merchandise is paid for by hard-earned dollars. Right is on our side. We haven't stolen a thing. For this holy fire, we—"

"Reverend Williams for Congress!" a man shouted. "Let's send this man to Washington!"

"Williams for Washington!" a woman cried.

Gold rings flashed on the preacher's fingers.

The Beard was catty-corner from Fun Zone News as Benny came up on the target. He was wearing a white tennis jacket, size extra-large, with an alligator on the left lapel and white pants. He weighed two-fifty and half of it was beer gut. Under the jacket the Beard had on Kevlar body armor.

Benny was twenty feet away when he saw it—a quick flicker of movement from a second-floor window of the Inn. Three rooms overlooked the Fun Zone. The movement in the window took only a second, the curtain rippling as if the sea breeze had sucked it out and then shoved it in again. Benny saw a hand, half of a face, and a shadowy movement. The movement made him sweat harder. That was the Beard's job, casing the frigging rooms! Then the curtain settled back. Benny shook his head. Earlier in the week, he'd thought about changing styles, using the room, using a rifle with a scope. But the rooms with the best view of the hit zone had been reserved. And Benny liked working closer to the target, liked seeing their eyes go wide when the muzzle covered them and they knew they were getting it. Rifles were chicken-shit.

The Beard unzipped his tennis jacket as the target raised his arms to the sky. People stared at the flames. Sister Winona Lee was back inside Fun Zone News, probably buying more magazines. The fire smoldered up in spirals of blue smoke, sputtering.

"Hey, Reverend!" Square Face called out. "Cut that out now. Let's douse the fire, okay?"

Benny was fifteen feet away from the target. Feeling smooth now, he eased past three blue-hairs, hand on the butt of the S&W. The target turned to look at Benny. Square Face walked with his big arms held out by his sides, like a weight lifter.

It was time.

"Excuse me?" A voice said behind Benny. "Could you move aside for this shot? We're from the *Trib*."

The voice belonged to a pretty redhead with blue eyes and a fine set of cheerleader's teeth. She had a yellow PRESS badge pinned onto one lapel of her tan jacket. On the other was a NOW button. She was carrying a mini tape recorder. The photographer, a big old boy in a leather jacket, was at her elbow, his camera aimed at Benny.

That made four targets. Goddamn.

"Get the fire, Josh." The redhead stared past Benny, framing the scene. "I don't believe this!"

The S&W slipped out of the Velcro and into Benny's hand. Benny shot Leather Jacket in the gut just as the camera lens went *click*. Little .22, wouldn't hurt more than a bee-sting.

The S&W had a silencer, German-made, from Bundes-Werke way over in Stuttgart, so the only sound was a soft *splfft*. The photographer went down. Benny grabbed the redhead around the throat and pumped one round at the bodyguard and one at the target. The bodyguard was set up perfect, with the Fun Zone News behind him for a backscreen. The target crumpled to the ground, clutching his leg. Sister Winona Lee, emerging with a new stack of girlies, screamed and grabbed her face with both hands. The magazines fell in a stream of bright colors. The bodyguard took his hit like a trooper and dropped out of sight behind a gaggle of blue-hairs. Benny holstered the S&W and brought out his backup piece, a Colt .357. *Boom*. Now he had firepower. A plate glass window shattered.

"Get down!" someone yelled. "Hit the dirt!"

The blue-hairs panicked and Benny, excited now, zigzagged for the Honda. Square Face was down. Score one for the Beard. The redhead smacked Benny from behind with a big leather purse. "Goddamn!" Benny swiped at her with the barrel of the .357, and she went down.

The suckers were really screaming now. Benny ran broken-field through them. Super Bowl City.

He dodged a baby carriage. The baby was wearing a blue sun hat. The mother, fear in her eyes, fell, dumping out baby. The carriage crashed over. Benny kept moving.

"Come *on*!" the Beard yelled.

Without missing a stride, Benny shot out a tire on the police cruiser. As the tire blew, the cruiser sagged down like a lame rhino. Shit, with moves like this, he should try out for the Rams. He was ten feet from the Honda when the shots came from behind him. He turned to see old U.S. Army Retired, up on his knees and holding a .45 military-issue with both hands. Blood ran from a wound on his head. The muzzle of the .45 looked like a howitzer. To his right was the black dude in the white pants. He'd dropped his sign and was holding a short-barreled automatic. Undercover fuzz, not part of the plan. "Police!" he yelled.

"Jig!" Benny yelled back. He squeezed off a round at U.S. Army Retired, then one at the fuzz. The Beard revved the

10

Honda. The fuzz fired as he went down and Benny felt something tug at the outside of the Kevlar. As the Honda roared up
beside Benny, a surprise shooter opened up with a rifle from that
second-story window in the Inn of Cortez. Goddamn. Benny
heard three sharp cracks as the bullets sliced the air.

The first shot from the window nailed the fuzz. Number two
nailed the old bodyguard. The blue-plated .45 skittered across
the sidewalk. Sister Winona Lee cowered behind a parked car.
The target was crawling toward Fun Zone News, his wounded
leg dragging behind him. Material for your Sunday sermon,
preach. Number three knocked out the florist's window. Who
was that shooter?

Benny swung on behind the Beard. The Honda revved like a
Saigon hooker on speed, burning rubber, and zipped across Balboa toward the pier. Up ahead, over the Beard's right shoulder,
Benny saw the skater, between the Honda and the pier, bran-
dishing a fishing pole in both hands. "Shoot!" the Beard yelled.

Benny fired a round and saw wood splinters tear off the railing
behind the skater. Teeth gleaming, she slid aside like a lady
bullfighter as the Honda swerved past. Benny saw a bright
flickering movement as the fishing pole arced, then caught the
sun. The body armor shielded his back, but he felt the pole whip
his bare neck, just below his left ear. The wraparound shades
flew into space.

"Fucking bitch!" the Beard growled.

And then they were past, charging out over the boards with
the beach below them on both sides and the ocean straight
ahead, toward Ruby's Diner. The pain from Benny's neck radi-
ated up to his left ear. He grabbed at the pain and his hand con-
tacted fishing line. The skater had hit him with a fish hook,
caught him like a fucking catfish. He took three turns of the
clear plastic line with his hand, looping it to get some slack. The
line cut into his hand. Someone yelled as the Honda roared past
Ruby's. Civilians scattered. The Honda slid to a stop at the edge
of the pier. Benny's ear was on fire.

The Beard grabbed his arm and grinned. "Hey. Charlie Tuna."

Benny tugged on the line, jerking it forward. The skater was
on her knees, forty yards back down the pier. The line ran from

the hook in his neck to a fishing pole on the pier. His left hand was bleeding. "Jesus H. Christ! Get this out!"

The Beard flicked open his yellow switchblade and cut the line. "Go, Charley!" Benny jumped off the pier. He landed on the orange rescue air bag that said LBFD. Dixie pulled him off the bag as the Beard sailed down, landing with a soft *whump*.

"We're behind schedule." Dixie was wearing yellow shooting glasses and a Budweiser cap.

"Well, move this crate." The Beard aimed his piece at the railing above them and fired.

The power boat, the *Belinda II*, cranked around with Dixie at the wheel, making white water. Benny hunkered down behind the gunwales, checking for pursuit craft. When none appeared, he yelled at the Beard, "Do something, man!" He pointed to the hook.

The Beard cut away the last bit of fishing line, then probed with the switchblade. "I seen more blood come out of a mosquito bite."

"My ass." Benny covered the bleeding wound with a handkerchief embroidered with the initials *BR*. He sat huddled in a blanket, his back propped up against an orange boat cushion, biting back the pain.

The *Belinda II* hugged the coast, heading northwest. They flew past white buildings and palm trees. Newport Beach was behind them, Huntington Beach coming up. He could see cars crawling along Pacific Coast Highway. Every bump of the boat on a wave seemed to drive a twenty-penny nail into his neck. The excitement was over. All he wanted was his money, a Bourbon and Coke, a woman. In that department, Michele would do, Michele from Eugene. His hands shook. The sun slipped behind a patch of dark clouds, holding off summer. Grinning, the Beard poured coffee from a red thermos and handed a cup to him.

"Backup shooter, Charlie. You should of told me."

"Don't call me Charlie." The coffee tasted like rich folks, with booze.

The Beard grinned, showing bad teeth. "I want another two grand, Charlie."

"Our deal was three, not five."

"I hate surprises."

Benny glared at him. "It was your job, checking the rooms."

"I checked, man. That one was empty."

"Did you go up there? Or did you just sit at the bar blowing your nose and checking out the stray pussy?"

"I went up, Moby. Onliest person up there was a maid and a gal in high heels and a pretty dress. I cased it. No security. Not a roofer in sight. This was big time, Charlie. Could have got our butts shot off."

Benny shook his head. "No way."

"Dixie wants another grand."

"Dixie can blow it out his ass."

The Beard swung his big body around. There was a dark stain on the front of the white tennis jacket. It blotted out the alligator. "You didn't know, either, did you? About the shooter?"

"A grand more for you. Five hundred for Dixie."

The Beard grunted. "You'd deal your mama out of wood for the cookstove."

"Leave my mama out of this."

The Beard sneezed and reached for a Kleenex. "Okay. I'll talk to Dixie. You better get through to that goddamn General Moneybags."

The Beard had been in the Army in Vietnam. He thought the client, Mr. No Name, was ex-Army. It didn't mean much. He thought everyone was ex-Army. "You still dealing with that Mex?"

"Yeah."

"Where's the meet?"

"None of your business."

"Ask the Mex about the bonfire, while you're at it. That crazy wife was something else, wasn't she?"

Benny remembered Sister Winona Lee's ball-bearing eyes as she soaked the magazines with barbecue starter. "I knew about the bonfire."

The Beard laughed. "You were set up, Charlie."

They were closer to shore as the *Belinda II* eased into Huntington Beach. The traffic was thick out there, but no sign of any fuzz. Benny kept his seat until Dixie tied up. Then the three of them left the stolen speed boat and walked fifty feet across the dock to a second boat, the *Circe*. This one had sails. The Beard helped Dixie with the canvas. Dixie wanted his five hundred before he cast off, so Benny counted out five bills. By the time the first Coast Guard cutter steamed into view, the *Circe* was turning north at Paso Robles and Rolling Hills, heading for El-Ay City.

It was darker now, with clouds boiling up gray on the water. Benny used the time to clean his guns. He hated being set up.

CHAPTER TWO

BRANKO was winning.

He was up 5–4 in the third set against crafty Spider Longo, the head pro at Le Club of Newport Beach. They were battling on Court One, sweating and grinding before a Friday afternoon crowd of a hundred members and guests. The sun was hot. The men in the stands had their shirts off. In between points they talked stocks, bonds, takeovers, development deals. Snazzy women with slick society faces sat barefoot, their elegant California legs propped on chairs as they sipped cool drinks from the bar.

Smart money was riding on the Spider. In matches with Branko, he led 14–4. But today, by God, was different. Today the Spider's drop shots were falling too deep in the court, his angled overheads were sliding off his strings into the doubles alley, and his creative line calls hadn't upset Branko. Today, Branko's big serve was cooking, smoking across the net and landing six inches inside the line. Also, the spectators in the end zone were keeping the lid on the Spider's creativity. When he made a bad call, they hissed and whistled.

Spider had won the first set, 6–1. Branko had clawed his way back to win the second set, 7–6, taking the tie breaker at 10–8. Now he was ahead in the third set. One good serve would do it.

At the right liquor store, twenty-five bucks would get you three cases of Miller's.

Frank Branko was a forty-three-year-old homicide cop on the Newport Beach police force, lean, lonely, tenacious, and good at his job. Spider Longo was a professional tennis hustler, thirty-six, smug, arrogant, and full of himself. Branko drove a '79 Volvo. The Spider drove a red Maserati. Branko was lucky if he played tennis once a week. The Spider, who'd won the U.S. Junior Singles title when he was seventeen and the French Open doubles when he was twenty, got to hit every day because that was his job. The Spider was five-eleven, narrow-shouldered, with thin arms and hairy legs that bordered on being spindly. His teeth were large for his face. Rumor around the locker room had him hung like Secretariat. Bored society ladies lined up to climb into bed with him. His not-so-secret nickname around the courts was Spider the Sword.

The Spider was also a superior shot-maker. He could hit hard or drive you crazy with junk. His backhand overhead smash, the trickiest shot in the game, was used as a model in tennis textbooks. He was a lousy teacher, however, joyless, sarcastic, and unsympathetic. He had the top job at Le Club because of his world-class trophy from Paris.

The Spider, in short, was a creep, but he'd played the circuit, and Branko loved tough opponents because they made you dig deep, probe yourself, brought up the best tennis. The Spider was world-class. He was younger and craftier. Branko was a warrior, an aging gladiator. His weapons were the big serve, the sharp volley, and tenacity. Branko knew how to hang on.

That was what it was all about, hanging in there when you had a headache and a bellyache and your shoes were worn through and you owed fourteen grand to the credit union.

Because tennis allowed you to forget.

The score was 5–4, 40–30, Branko's serve. One sweet speedball would do it. His toss hung in the air, the yellow-green sphere shadowed by the sun off Newport Bay. The stadium was hushed, no glib society chatter. A gull honked overhead. Outside, along Pacific Coast Highway, traffic wheezed to a crawl in preparation for the upcoming California weekend. Across the net, the Spider waited, big teeth gleaming ravenously. Branko could feel the ace coming as his racket swung back and down and around in a graceful arc.

Just as the strings made contact with the ball, his police beeper screamed.

Ah, shit.

The serve zoomed by the Spider, hole in the racket, a perfect ace.

"Play a let, Branko," he called, grinning.

But Branko knew it was over. The police beeper sliced into the afternoon, cutting the legs out from under his day off. In the stands, people stirred. What is it? What's going on? Branko was already jogging for the pro shop and the telephone. As he left the court, he noticed Mrs. Susannah Maxwell watching him. She was sitting alone, legs crossed, her pale blue eyes tracking him. Mrs. Maxwell was a tennis legend at Le Club. Like the Spider, she'd played the big time, Forest Hills, Longwood, Wimbledon. She'd battled names like Billie Jean King and Margaret Court and Evonne Goolagong. Around the club, the word was she could have turned pro but had decided to get married instead. She was too good for the women at Le Club, so she played men. In her matches with the Spider, Mrs. Maxwell was about forty-sixty, better than Branko. She did it with control, craft, percentage tennis, never giving anything away. Branko admired that. But he was a power player. Percentage tennis was not his style.

A siren wailed somewhere across Newport Bay on the Balboa Peninsula. Branko could feel the pavement through the worn green soles of his Rod Laver shoes. Time for a trip to Second Sole. There was just one problem—payday was nine days away.

In the pro shop, Miguel Ortega, the assistant pro, took one look at his face and handed him the phone. Branko dialed the Newport Beach station. He got a busy signal and dialed the emergency number.

"What's the score out there, Panchito?" Miguel, a solid Latino dressed in spotless LaCoste tennis whites, was draping a pea-green tennis dress carefully on a silver hanger. The dress was made out of sheer material, filmy stuff, like a nightie. The price tag read $450. Upscale.

The phone was ringing. "I had him at match point when the beeper went off. Had an ace on the strings."

"*Pobre* Francisco." Miguel didn't like his boss.

The phone was answered on the sixth ring. "Newport Beach police. This is Officer Brazelton." Molly Brazelton, traffic division, sounding stressed and out of breath.

"Frank Branko, Molly. What's up?"

"Oh, Frank, where are you?"

"Playing tennis. It's my day off. Or was."

"There's been a shooting on Balboa. In the Fun Zone. We've got an officer down."

Branko felt a sudden chill. "Roscoe?"

"Not on my list."

His buddy Roscoe Smith was working as undercover security for the speedball reverend, a television preacher who had his eye on a congressional berth. It was Branko's day off, so Roscoe had been assigned by Lieutenant Archer. Friday night was Sirloin Night at Branko's place. He still had to buy a steak. "Who's down?"

"Randy Whitson."

"What happened?"

"During the speech, someone started burning magazines in the street. A photographer was shot taking pictures. Then the reverend and Officer Whitson. That's all I have. The killer got away on a motorcycle."

"Have we got roadblocks up?"

"Sergeant Osterhaus is coordinating, Frank. He's working on a description of the perp. We've got a call in to the chief, in Sacramento. That convention thing."

"Where's the lieutenant?"

"Lieutenant Archer took some personal time. We're trying to raise him." There was a pause. "Could you hold, Frank. It's the chief. We have reports of heavy weather in Sacramento."

"Sure." Branko motioned to Miguel for pencil and paper. The pro handed over a pale-green Le Club notepad and a ball point with a gold cap. The club logo was a pair of crossed tennis rackets. Quickly, Branko jotted some notes:

Balboa hit, Rev Williams, preacher.
Tuesday primary, politics. Motive!!!
APB on the perp.
Roadblocks.
Security for reverend. Hospital?
Witness interview team.
Who's REV running against?
SWAT guys, crowd control.
Roscoe?

He wrote *Lt. Archer!!!*, then drew a heart with an arrow through it. He was suddenly aware of perfume, a shadow in the door, a shift in the vibrations of the room, and turned to see Mrs. Susannah Maxwell entering the shop. Snazzy lady, money, class, a big, fat-cat house on ritzy Spyglass Hill, servants. She shot skeet and played top-class tennis and got her picture in the society pages. She took a good picture but looked even better in person, here, today, in close-up. Yum. She nodded at Branko. "You had him."

"Yeah."

At the counter, she said, "Miguelito, are we on for Sunday?"

"Si, si, Mrs. M. You betcha. Only I'm slowing down. This week, you gotta spot me a couple games."

"You devil, Miguelito. Show me that creation with the daring décolletage."

She leaned her hip against the counter, the right leg slightly bent, a model's pose, sending a ripple through the pleats in her white tennis dress. Her tan was deep, golden, smooth. Her hair was ash-blond, medium-length, then swept up over the right side like a surfer's wave. She was wearing silver earrings. Her arms were lean from exercise. The legs were show-stoppers, sweet and long, like a Las Vegas showgirl's. Her husband had died around Christmas and left her bongo bucks. Branko had seen her in three different vehicles—a Jag, a Mercedes, and a BMW. Probably owned a Lear Jet and an Onassis yacht and a posh condo in every jet-set spot on the globe. People around the club said the view from her house on Spyglass was worth six million, easy. "Tell you the truth, Francisco," Miguel Ortega had said, "I play her on Sunday morning, I watch the old booze level Saturday night. That one is a tiger."

Mrs. Maxwell's gaze was knowing, full of irony. Her face was long, Nordic, with prominent photogenic cheekbones. The mouth, which was too wide, kept it from being perfect. The imperial nose was almost too long. Today, he noticed she had an overbite and a tiny gap between her front teeth.

She regarded Branko through slanted blue eyes. "You're very brave."

He could feel her eyes, the irony. "How so?"

"Going up against him with no backhand."

That made him grin. "My coach used to say the same thing."

She nodded and turned back to examining the dress. Branko figured her age to be mid-thirties; height, five-ten; weight about a hundred and thirty.

Tommy Osterhaus came on the line. Tommy was a sergeant on the Newport Beach police. "Frank? Tommy here. I've got a profile on the perp."

Branko turned away from Mrs. Maxwell. "Shoot."

"Okay. Late twenties, five-ten, sharpshooter who could really move. Had to be an ex-jock. Thick black hair and a matching mustache. Nothing distinguishing about the face. Wore a brown suit, drab socks. Someone remembered a tie. Two pieces, both revolvers, one small-caliber, the other sounds like a Magnum. He hit the reverend from fifteen feet away, the bodyguard from farther off. He did a running shot and blew a tire on Whitson's unit. He had backup from a big bearded monkey on a motorcycle. After the hit, they rode the bike out to the edge of the pier and then jumped into a powerboat. Frank, this was planned. It's a twenty-foot drop out there. They landed on a fire department air-rescue bag from the Long Beach Fire Department. A fisherman on the pier remembers the boat hanging around the area. The boat headed north."

"Did the fisherman get the registration?"

"No—too good to be true. Coast Guard's been alerted. And the departments along the coast."

"They could have doubled back, headed south."

"We've alerted Oceanside and San Diego."

"A buck says it's stolen."

"You already owe me five, for that last Laker game."

"Don't rub it in, Tommy. What about registration on the bike?"

"It's being checked." Papers were riffled on Tommy's end of the phone. "Something just coming in. Damn."

"What is it?"

"Roscoe Smith. He's been hit."

The hairs rose on Branko's neck. "How bad?"

"It doesn't say. He's being transported to Seaport."

Branko had to get down there. "Tommy, I'm leaving for the area. I'll radio in from the car."

"Sorry about Roscoe, Frank. He'll be okay."

Branko hung up and headed for the door. He was worried about Roscoe, so he only caught a glimpse of Mrs. Maxwell as she pivoted away from the counter toward the mirror. She was holding the filmy tennis dress in front of her, angling for a look at herself. Branko collided with her hip, felt her foot under his. He danced lightly away to take the weight off. She stumbled but held onto the dress. Branko smelled a whiff of perfume.

"Sorry, ma'am."

"I owe you." She was inches away, her startling blue eyes angry. Behind the eyes, a sarcastic smile.

"Sorry."

Then he was out of there, running for Court One. The Spider was flirting with two pretty Newport wives while he waited. "Don't tell me, Branko. It's a default."

"Shooting. My partner's been hit."

The Spider's expression changed. "You serious?"

"Catch you later."

"Under the circumstances, we could start at one set all."

Branko said nothing. Tennis was over. Death squatted outside Le Club, laughing like a maniac. He stuffed his racket into his bag and ran toward the parking lot.

Susannah Maxwell reached the parking lot as the policeman was driving off. Man in a hurry, she told herself.

His car was a vintage gray Volvo, six or seven years old. On the roof over the driver's seat was a little red police light, turning and turning. Susannah walked to her car, a maroon Jaguar XKE, unlocked it, and got behind the wheel. She inserted the key in the ignition and turned it. The Jaguar starter whined, but nothing happened. "Blast!" Susannah pumped the accelerator and tried again. The Jaguar's engine coughed, then caught. Cursing all mechanics, she wheeled out of the club parking lot.

Traffic crawled weekend thick on Pacific Coast Highway as she headed southeast, toward Spyglass Hill. It was almost 3:30 on a Friday, not Susannah's favorite hour. Her foot ached slightly where it had been stepped on by the policeman. The toe of his right shoe was worn through, from dragging on the serve. The soles were threadbare. She remembered how it felt to be poor.

The policeman was tanned and angular, with pale blue eyes and a mustache. His eyes had a haunted look, probably due to his work, hunting criminals or associating with low-life beach bums and riff-raff. His presence was an unexpected anomaly at Le Club of Newport Beach, whose members were either old money or nouveaux riche. Susannah had watched him play, studied his game, the way he constructed points. His serve was a cannonball, hard and flat and merciless. When it was on, he was on. He never played percentages. He followed his serve to the net and made a dive for the volley. He was one of the few players at Le Club besides herself who could come close to beating the Spider. When she played the Spider, Susannah used craft and guile. That was not the policeman's way. Percentage was everything, in tennis and in life. She was curious about the policeman. He'd won a tournament back in December, just before Jordan had died. Susannah had not been playing then.

The Jaguar slipped past Reuben's and up the hill without a single cough. It was Jordan's car. He'd bought it from an Iraqi on Lido Island—how long ago? three years, four? The car had not run well since his death.

A sign advertising Ministry Beach reminded her that Jordan had sunk ten million dollars into the church camp for adults. If he were here, Ministry Beach would have been completed. Now Susannah was paying for it.

The Jaguar was for sale. So was the house on Spyglass Hill. The next payment, to TexAmerica in Houston, was due on the tenth, $81,000. She would have to sell off another block of securities. Fear rose in her throat.

She passed Fashion Island off to the left. Andre was keeping a dress for her that needed alterations. It was half past three. She turned the radio on, to a music station. The cellular phone rang as she was approaching the Jamboree intersection and she answered as the Jaguar slid to a stop. The windows were up. In the car beside her, to her left, a teenaged girl with blond hair and a vivid mouth leaned across to give her boyfriend a lazy Friday afternoon kiss. To Susannah, the girl's move looked calculated. The boyfriend, lost in a maze of lust, would never suspect otherwise.

"Hello," Susannah said.

"Hello? Is this here Nightingale Enterprises?" It was Roberto Devane, ex-Foreign Legion, ex-colonel of Special Forces, present King of Devania.

"Roberto. Don't be naughty."

Devane chuckled. "How's the weather over to the beach? My weather service predicts rain and fog and two days of California winter."

Susannah clenched the wheel with her left hand, the phone with her right. Making her sweat was part of Roberto's strategy. She loosened her fingers on the phone, urging her body to relax. Contact from Devane made her think of the promissory note he held on her house. When she spoke, her voice was suggestive, the role he liked her to play. "It's a beautiful day, Roberto. Lots of sun and seagulls mating in midair. Teenagers copulating on the golden sand. A regular Garden of Eden. To what do I owe the honor of this call?"

"Thought I'd invite you over tomorrow, Suze. Eat a bite of lunch. Pop a wine cork. Celebrate my victory."

"The primary's not until Tuesday, Roberto. You're awfully eager for your money."

Devane laughed. "Well, shit, come to lunch anyway. We can chat about Reverend Lard-Ass and Washington society."

"I have the party, Roberto. Much to do."

"Come early, kiddo. You can slip in here for some rumpus and be back home in La-La Land by one-thirty."

Devane's idea of fun was red wine and fast Cro-Magnon sex. Once, a long time ago, she hadn't minded it rough. Those days were over. Now she detested his desire to control her. "I loathe that drive, Roberto."

"Loathe? Where do you find the words, Suze?"

"You could drive this way for a change."

"Can't do it, Suze. Too much cooking out this way."

She knew he was running military contraband through his little narrow-gauge railroad. She didn't know the specifics—guns, explosives, whatever—but she knew he was making a fat profit selling to ugly little men in Asia and Africa and Central America. How could she use that against him? Susannah, spy entering the cold. "Well, what about next week? Wednesday or Thursday."

"Be better if I saw you tomorrow."

"It's impossible, Roberto." Susannah wiped the sweat off her forehead with her wristband. Devane had the confidence of a military man who might lose a battle but would always win the war.

"Got your radio on?"

The light changed and cars honked behind her. Traffic was moving again. Susannah took her foot off the brake and the Jaguar slid forward. "Yes. A music station."

"See if you can find the latest hit single from Balboa."

There was a crackle on the line. "What?"

Instead of answering, Devane shifted subjects. "Got to sign off, Suze. Long distance from Tokyo. That invite for lunch is still open, in case you change your mind."

"Roberto, the party."

"Got a new case of Plymouth gin. And the limes are sweet and green."

"I hate it when you pressure me."

"Call you later. See if you change your mind."

"I won't."

"Remember the Palmer House, kiddo. Chicago in 'seventy-three. This is the colonel, signing off."

The connection was broken. Susannah let out a long breath. Ugh.

She turned left off Pacific Coast Highway and headed toward Spyglass Hill. It was the end of May and the June primary was right around the corner. The temperature had been in the eighties all week and Susannah's tan looked sleek. She smoothed the pleated skirt over her thighs. Being tan was a major part of her packaging of herself. The world was owned by men and she was a commodity, a package. An attractive package—if nicely wrapped—was worth more in the marketplace. She was thirty-four. How much longer could she hold her value?

She aimed the Jag up the hill, thinking of Roberto Devane and the wager she'd made with him two weeks ago. . . .

They'd been sitting in the stark, Spartan living room of the hacienda at Devania, in the Santa Ana Mountains near Lake Elsinore. Susannah remembered being tipsy on gin. Gin got her going.

"How on earth could Reverend Williams win? He's a romantic and a fool. Ministry Beach is stalled. They owe ten million to the contractors. The wife is an evangelical zombie. The children are like orphans. The reverend has no war record."

"Shit, Suze, he's a circus clown. Give people a choice, they'd choose a clown over Jesus Christ or Dwight D. Eisenhower. Your late hubby saw it. That's why he backed old Lard-Ass."

"Impossible."

"Want to bet?"

"Jordan was wrong." Susannah finished her gin. "It could not happen, even in Southern California."

"Put your money where your mouth is."

"He's behind in the polls. No one in his campaign thinks he can win."

Devane snorted. "Polls are bureaucratic bullshit, Suze. Once the vote's counted, polls are yesterday's news." Devane held his glass up and studied the color of the wine against the light. It was one of his few civilized gestures, this liking for red wine, a developing taste made possible by the permanence of Devania. Before coming here and building the compound, he'd lived in tents and trenches and temporary barracks. He'd slept on the

24

ground, in the mud, in hot sand, in cold snow. Susannah had heard all the stories.

When he took a trip into civilization, Devane wore a sober blue suit, tailored for him on Savile Row in London. But here in the foothills of the Santa Ana Mountains, he dressed the way he had most of his life, in the plain olive-drab combat fatigues of the professional soldier. He wore paratrooper boots with a high black sheen and a fatigue cap decorated with a colonel's insignia. He could cook and sew and doctor his own wounds. A pale white scar ran from his hairline down across his forehead to his left eye, a trophy from his days with the French Foreign Legion. His eyes were pale blue, wintry. He claimed to be fifty-one. Susannah knew he was fifty-five, perhaps a year older. He walked with a slight limp and kept in shape with daily calisthenics.

There was no telling how many people he'd killed. Or ordered killed.

According to Jordan Maxwell, Devane had money stashed in banks all over the world. He had hoarded gemstones, gold coins, gold bars, silver. He'd boasted to Jordan about the gold bullion buried somewhere on the compound grounds. Devane could have lived in Paris or Rome or Tahiti or Chamonix or New York. Anyplace. Yet here he was in a perpetual military-dugout situation in the bare and dusty hills of Southern California near the tourist village of Sierra Monte, around the bend from Lake Elsinore, living out a fantasy that was both absurd and expensive. In town, they called it "the Colonel's Outpost." Privately, Roberto referred to it as "Devania."

Devane leaned forward, his pale eyes glinting, voice growling with telltale male superiority. "Listen up, Suze. In seventeen months, I put four wogs on four goddamn thrones in countries that didn't have spit for breakfast or a pot to piss in. One wog had a British education that made him uppity as a lord. One had a Harvard degree that made him a bona fide political horse's ass. He got himself off on boys and three kinds of dope, for Christ's sake. The other two couldn't copy their own name in block letters if the Holy Whore of Hamburg held their hand and guided the pencil. If I can put a blackamoor on a straw throne in Africa, I can sure as shit plop Reverend Lard-Ass the Boy Lifeguard into a leather chair in Washington. Give me some credit, Suze. He's a white man. This is still a white man's country. And Bobby Devane knows how the engine works!" He tapped his temple and smiled.

"How would you engineer this, Roberto? Machine gun the ballot boxes?"

"Leave the tactics to me. You're the college gal, the poli-sci major. You're theory and I'm practice. You want to make this bet or not?"

Susannah yawned. "What are the stakes?"

Devane leaned back and grinned. "You win, you get that paper back, the one old Jordy signed. I win, you spend your weekends with me."

A typical Devane offer, primitive control, the iron military grip, and Susannah sweating. He was an outsider, a sociopathic renegade who lived in a perpetual bush landscape of his own imagination. She knew him. But she never knew exactly what to expect. With Devane, she was always off balance. Maybe that's why she kept returning. The idea, on the face of it, was ludicrous. "My weekends? Here?"

"Yeah."

"For how long?"

"Say a year."

Fifty-two weeks times two. A hundred and four days, gone. She crossed her legs. "Could we put up drapes, Roberto?"

He laughed, then sat back in his chair. "Hell, gal, whatever you want. Drapes, new rugs, soft furniture, whatever."

"Picture windows?"

The grin wavered. "In some of the rooms."

"Would I still have to use the tunnel?"

He stared at her without blinking. "Maybe. Maybe not."

Susannah sipped her gin and looked around at the Spartan hacienda. They were in the living room, on brown Naugahyde chairs that belonged in a planter's club in Nairobi in the twenties. There was no sofa. The tables were metal or black plastic. The windows were narrow, four-inch slots three feet high, built securely into walls eighteen inches thick. In case of attack, each window was equipped with a sliding metal shutter that narrowed the opening and provided a square hole to shoot through. The windows had been modeled on windows from a castle in Carcassonne, one of Roberto's favorite towns.

The walls of the living room were covered with maps. The front door was five-inches thick. It was held secure by two dead-bolts. There was no back door, no second story. There were other rooms—a library, a large master bedroom (Roberto called it his Rumpus Room, for making rumpus), a well-equipped kitchen, a lovely cool wine cellar, guest rooms, storage rooms, and, at the center of the hacienda, the War Room.

Inside the War Room were computers and surveillance cameras and high-powered radios and at least a dozen telephones with lines to stock exchanges and weather services and news agencies scattered across the globe. Susannah had been into the War Room several times to view new pieces of electronic equipment. Over the door was an absurd brass plaque, with a motto etched into the surface:

> Let us not hear of generals
> who conquer without bloodshed.
> —VON CLAUSEWITZ

There was only one chair in the War Room, a wooden swivel chair with a high back that had belonged to Roberto's grandfather—Daddy L.B. "Buck" Devane—a circuit judge in Big Spring, Texas. Today the War Room door was shut, locked up tight. It was always off-limits to everyone except Roberto. Susannah viewed the War Room as the quintessential technological center for the ultimate male fantasy—destruction through penetration.

When she visited, Susannah entered through a tunnel—a cob-webbed, dank shaft that led from Devane's walk-in closet in the Rumpus Room to an emergency exit built into a shelter of rocks and scrub pine and pepper trees in the shadow of a small hill north of the main house. She knew she was not the only visitor to use the tunnel. For Roberto, the tunnel served three functions. First, visitors would not be seen by his men, who he referred to collectively as "the Cadre." Second, the Cadre would not be seen by visitors. Third, it provided him an escape route, a secret back door that few people knew about. He had a marvelous story about using a tunnel to escape from the Vietnamese in 1954 in the fortress at Dien Bien Phu. "Dien Bien Phu was the end of the French in Asia," he often said, "and the beginning of Robert Emory Devane in the goddamn world of poly-ticks and high finance."

Susannah got up, wobbling slightly, and walked into the kitchen to build herself another drink. The gin was Plymouth. Roberto kept it stocked for her. There were limes from trees in an orchard on Lake Elsinore. She carried the gin back to the living room.

"Time's up, kiddo. Spin the wheel."

"The answer, Roberto, is no. It's a silly bet."

"Then you think he can win, too."

"The thought of spending my weekends here . . ." She shook her head. "You always want absolute control."

Devane leaned forward, elbows on his knees. "Jordan's been in the grave six months. I like you around. That house in Newport is a white elephant like I never saw. You rattle around in there. You need to sell that sucker and make some changes yourself."

"It's on the market."

Devane grinned, causing the scar in his forehead to whiten. "Any bites?"

Susannah was uncomfortable. "A few. The season's right around the corner."

"It's a five-million-dollar property and you're trying to get six million for it. Maybe you haven't heard about Arab oil."

"It's still my house."

"According to Jordan's paper, it's one-fifth mine."

"One-sixth."

"You're a bitch."

Susannah stood up and walked to a window. Outside, near the warehouse, she saw men of the Cadre loading wooden crates onto a railroad handcar. Ants, they looked like, wearing combat fatigues. To the left of the warehouse, she could see the rotors and part of the fuselage of a helicopter. To see more, she'd would have had to move to another window. "Pluto and Proserpine," she said.

"How's that?"

She turned to face Devane. "A slice of Greek mythology. Pluto raped Proserpine and carried her off to Tartarus, the Greek Hades. He kept her there six months of the year."

"Those goddamn Greeks. They knew a bunch. Why'd he do that?"

"Cupid shot him with an arrow." She pointed to her heart. "Here."

Devane laughed. "Spooked you, didn't I?"

Susannah made her decision. "The reverend's a born loser. I'll bet you a thousand dollars."

"A thousand it is. Shake on it?"

Susannah touched her glass to Devane's. The paper he held on her house on Spyglass Hill was a promissory note from her late husband for a million dollars. As she stared into Devane's pale-blue eyes, Susannah did some arithmetic in her mind, trying to balance a year of weekends against the million-dollar piece of paper. The idea made her shiver. She didn't like coming to Devania. She was invited—more like ordered out—every weekend. When she did come, she stayed only a few hours. It was not her idea of Shangri-la. She kept hoping Roberto would tear Jordan's note up, rip it to shreds before her eyes. So far, that had not happened. Now Roberto was dangling this idea in front of her. A year of weekends—an eternity.

Where did he keep the note? Had he taken it to his little man, Byron Foxcroft, at the bank in town? Was it in a safe-deposit box in New York or Zurich or Hong Kong? Or was it here, in this thick-walled, all-male hacienda at Devania?

So they had clinked glasses for a thousand dollars and Susannah had put the matter out of her mind. The house was up for sale. If she could get her hands on five million eight hundred thousand, she could pay off the bank in Houston and retire the note held by Roberto. If things got tricky, his man Foxcroft could block the sale. If. If. If. She was angry at Jordan for leaving her in this mess. . . .

It was almost four by the time the Jag climbed Hill Road to

her house on Spyglass Circle. Tomorrow's party would be catered. The reverend had a crush on her. What a laugh.

Near the crest of the hill, she turned off the air conditioner and opened up the sun roof to let the sunshine stream in. Clouds were gathering over the Pacific, but the sun still gave off its lovely baking heat. If she hurried, she could still do some nude sunbathing, work on her packaging.

She drove into the garage and parked the Jag with a sharp squeal of tires between the silver Mercedes and the black BMW. She walked upstairs and tried the automatic ice-maker. No ice. She called Julio, who squeaked in alarm.

"I come, missy," he said. "I bring ice."

Her world was falling apart, but her tennis game had never been better. Earlier today, at Le Club, she'd taken a set off Ernest Mako, who'd played at Wimbledon and Paris. She wondered how she'd do against the policeman. She was sure she could beat him playing to his backhand.

Julio arrived with ice from the downstairs ice-maker. He promised to call the repair people. Julio was her only full-time servant these days. A year ago, they'd had a gardener every day and a live-in maid. He mixed Susannah's gin and tonic and left, silently glowering.

Susannah stripped off her tennis dress and untied her shoes. She knew she was drinking too much, had been drinking too much ever since Jordan died. Gin was her weakness. Damn Roberto Devane and his phone call. Damn the reverend. Damn Jordan. Damn Ministry Beach and Arab oil petrodollars and especially Roberto Devane.

She took a sip of gin—ah, that was good. She unsnapped her halter and tossed it on a chair. She kicked off her pale yellow panties. The skirt fell free.

Barefoot and naked, she walked to the French doors that led to her terrace. She opened the doors and stepped out. The terrace faced the Pacific. Thank God for the sun.

The pebbly surface was warm on her bare feet. As she spread on the Ban de Soleil, she wondered why Jordan had waited so long to tell her about his deal with Devane. Two days before he died, Jordan had held her hand and apologized with tears in his eyes. Now Devane was pushing at her, jabbing her from different angles, testing for weak points in her defenses. She hated to see the tenth of the month roll around. She hated to pick up the phone, thinking it might be Devane. Each month, she felt the noose of poverty tighten around her throat. There had to be a way out.

What if she told the police about Roberto's little railroad?

She finished anointing herself, then lay down on her chaise longue facing the sun, closed her eyes, sipped her drink, and thought about nothing as she felt the heat on her skin. She visualized a hundred police cars converging on Devania, the dust, the rattle of Hollywood gunfire.

They would get Roberto. But would she be able to retrieve Jordan's promissory note?

That wasn't quite the right scenario. But it was a start.

Smiling, she ran the iced drink over her forehead and opened her legs to the sun.

CHAPTER THREE

BRANKO used the red police light to bulldoze his way northwest along Pacific Coast Highway to the Lido overpass, zigzagging through the Friday traffic and leaning on the Volvo's horn. As he turned right onto the overpass, he looked up the hill at the heavy gray ramparts of Seaport General, the windows of the hospital tower reflecting the bright afternoon sunlight. A white ambulance groaned up Newport, roof light flashing.

For a long moment, he wanted to swing left instead of right, follow the ambulance, and check on Roscoe. But going up there wouldn't help. He'd just end up standing around in a chilly corridor with his hands in his pockets, feeling helpless, waiting for the medics to do their thing. Branko hated feeling helpless. Roscoe's fate was in other hands for the time being. Branko felt a lump in his throat. Good luck, buddy.

The Volvo crept onto the overpass. To Branko's left, sailboats slid across the water of Newport Bay like royal swans on a silver mirror. A beach kid in an orange Ford pickup braked to let Branko pass. He high-signed the kid a thank you and eased forward two car-lengths. The radio was on search mode. It was too early for news of the hit, and he could only get music. Hard rock. Easy listening. Classical from Los Angeles. Country. Gospel. Latino mariachi. A melting pot of song, but no news from the Fun Zone.

The traffic signal turned green, and as Branko moved forward a bird flew at his windshield, bumping the glass with a flurry of gray-brown feathers. Stunned, the bird hovered for a moment before flying off with a steady beating of wings. Even the birds were crazy today.

He watched the bird get smaller against the blue California sky and suddenly he was remembering a time in the lunchroom in junior high school in Beloit, a lush spring day, green buds sprouting out of the only recently frozen Wisconsin earth, bright sun, birds singing. He was fourteen that year, his mind on a career in professional baseball, his heart set on a date with Annette Berg, a brunette with silver braces, a straight A average, and fantastic legs. Times were tough in his dad's butcher shop. Lunch was bologna sandwiches and dried apricots that made your mouth pucker.

He was sitting across the lunch table from Annette, listening to her recap of third-period English. The subject that day had been the derivation of *halcyon*, from a poem he could not remember, by Keats, Shelley, somebody, and Annette's eyes were glowing with excitement as she explained Halcyone and Eryx and nesting on troubled waters when a girl screamed from across the room and Branko saw the bird.

The sliding glass doors were standing open for the first time that spring and sunlight streamed in. There were two hundred kids in the room, eating, talking, arguing. And against the plate glass windows, a small trapped bird flailed its life away. Miss Waggoner appeared and tried to restore order. Mr. Gottshalk yelled advice, but nothing happened. Most of the kids backed away, giving the bird room to commit suicide against the hot glass. Terry Figler, a football guy, stood ten feet away, munching an apple.

"Frank!" Annette Berg grabbed his arm. "Do something."

"What? What can I do?" The sound of wings, drumming on the glass, drumming in his mind.

"Do something. Herd it toward the door."

Some jerk had closed the door. Branko stood up, his heart flapping in time with the bird's frantic wings. Annette stood up, the light shining in her eyes, her chest heaving with excitement. She gave him a look that said *You can do it, Frank Branko.* She hurried to open the door. Branko approached the mad bird. "Hey, Branko," Terry Figler called. "What's up that comes down?"

Branko said nothing. The window panes of the lunchroom were four feet wide by eight feet tall, separated by stout pine beams. The bird could see the sky but not the glass. Each charge toward freedom slammed the bird up against the invisible barrier, *whump*, and sent feathers flying. The pine beams formed a confusing cage around the bird.

He heard Mr. Gottshalk's voice behind him. Annette stood at the door, hoping. Branko was within four feet of the bird, when *whump*, against the inexorable glass, fluttering wings getting weaker now and the bird falling to the carpet, one fearful eye on Branko. Zow, he thought, it knows me. The bird retreated then, toward the door.

And that gave him the idea.

He snatched a notebook off a lunch table and popped it open and then popped it closed. The bird responded to the sound by moving four more feet toward the door, where Annette waited.

"Hey, Birdman!" Terry Figler called. "Hey!"

Another pop of the notebook, but the bird was weaker now, flailing out with its spindly legs, and stopped moving. A third pop only made the bird shudder. "Frank—?" Annette said. Shut up, he thought, and let me think. Old Mrs. Sheen, Branko's next-door neighbor on Park Street, was a bird-watcher. She caught birds with a silky green net, banded their legs, and wrote stuff about them in a ledger. Mrs. Sheen, who looked like a bird and fed them suet from a wooden feeder. She'd offered to teach

Branko about birds, but his first morning out a bird had crapped on his sleeve, a sudden nervous blast of bird shit, splat, making Mrs. Sheen titter nervously. "Frank?" Annette said again.

Hell, if Mrs. Sheen can do it, I can do it. He set the notebook down, took a deep breath, and reached out for the bird, touched it, felts its wild heart. Beware the bird shit, Branko. His hand touched the feathers, gray-brown, not a pretty bird, too bad. There were yellow markings on the bird's face and terror in its tiny eyes. His hand closed around it, there was a slight struggle, and then the bird stopped everything, shut down, like a switch had been thrown, turning off the engines.

My God, he thought, I've killed the damned thing.

Silence then as Frank Branko walked, knees trembling, to the lunchroom door. He saw Annette's face, the wonderment, her mouth, those shiny braces, as the crowd parted into a corridor lined by kids. Terry Figler whispered, "Is it dead, Birdman?"

Outside, in the sun, the bird's eye opened, its heart fluttered, a faint pulse. Annette was beside him, a neat feeling, as he held up both hands to the sky and released the bird. His own heart sank as the bird fell. There was a collective moan from the kids behind him, clustered in the sliding door, and then its wings flapped, catching the air, and the bird soared off, toward freedom.

He remembered the taste of metal and the hot hum of a hero's reward as Annette Berg kissed him on the mouth. "How was it, touching that poor thing?"

"Nervous. I was afraid it died."

"You were so strong," she said. "And so gentle."

Her long lovely body, pressing against his. Zow.

Terry Figler christened him Branko, Birdman of Beloit. The name stuck. At ball games, whenever he hit a homer, they'd cheer, "Birdman, Birdman, Birdman . . ." Now, Terry sold insurance in Janesville and Annette Berg was married to a pediatrician in Madison and the Birdman of Beloit was a Newport Beach homicide cop who hated wearing a gun. . . .

He radioed the station. Roscoe Smith was enroute to Seaport, along with Officer Randy Whitson. Tommy Osterhaus was coordinating the crime scene by phone while acting as liaison with the chief in Sacramento. Branko could take command when he arrived on the scene. There was still no word from Lieutenant Robert Archer, the exec. Lieutenant Stan Plotvik, SWAT commander, was leaving the station now with a van and six SWAT team personnel.

"Frank," Molly said, "Officer Duncan says there was a third shooter."

"Where?"

"It was a backup man, shooting from a window of the Inn of Cortez."

"Have they sealed the room?"

"I'll double-check."

"Okay. The third shooter get away on the boat?"

"She didn't say."

"Who's in charge down there?"

"Don Taylor, from Traffic."

"Don's a good man. See if you can borrow half a dozen deputies from the Orange County sheriff."

"Ten-four, Frank." The radio crackled. "What's your ETA?"

"Three-forty. Lido traffic's like Fourth of July."

Branko signed off. The Porsche in front of him swung out of the way and he moved up three car-lengths. Ahead, at the supermarket intersection, he saw a second white ambulance. The traffic signal changed and he eased the Volvo forward. The ambulance passed, siren winding down in a low, dying moan. On the side was the logo of Seaport General. He hoped Roscoe Smith was inside.

The first news came at 3:31, on KQZ, the all-news station, old Red Satterwhite reporting from the Orange County Bureau. Red's voice was gravelly and ironic:

"Unconfirmed reports are filtering in about a commotion on the Balboa Peninsula in Newport Beach, folks. There was a parade scheduled by CASS—those letters, in case you didn't know, stand for Christians Against Senseless Smut. Reverend Terry Williams, pastor of Promontory Chapel in Newport Beach, was making a speech about the upcoming primary election, which takes place on Tuesday. In the primary, voters will select candidates to fill the party ticket for the November election. The reverend is battling incumbent Jimmy Sherwood for space on the ballot. On Balboa, we have a report of an alleged burning of books and newspapers, still unconfirmed at this time, and printed matter alleged to be obscene, also unconfirmed. Witnesses report hearing gunfire and police are on the scene. Our man Harry Beaver is en route to the area. Stay tuned to KQZ, ten-eighty-three on your dial, for an update. Now, we switch you to Barry Kravitz, on the floor of the Pacific Stock Exchange in downtown Los Angeles. . . ."

Balboa Boulevard was two lanes in and two lanes out, with a concrete parking divider in the center. Last summer, the department had tallied four hundred and fifty-three accidents caused by this curious parking strategy, mostly because drivers couldn't learn to parallel park on a left-hand curb.

As he passed the Newport Pier, Branko made radio contact with Officer Timmy Farris, who was in a traffic unit on Newport, a half mile away. "Farris, this is Sergeant Branko, Homicide. I want a roadblock at Seventeenth and Balboa, just west of the Surf Shop. All incoming traffic, turn 'em around. Official vehicles only, going toward the scene. Outbound traffic, check them out. We may have to leave one lane open for ambulances and official vehicles. You have descriptions of the perps?"

Farris paused. "Short guy, black hair, black mustache, brown suit. Big guy, white jacket and a beard, on a bike. Word was they made it on a speedboat."

Branko rubbed his forehead. A headache was starting. "Let's button it up, Farris, seal it off."

"Ten-four, Sergeant."

Branko signed off and racked the radio mike. Outbound traffic was moving steadily, fifteen miles an hour in both lanes. Branko saw an open space and cranked the Volvo up to fifty. The Inn of Cortez was three blocks away. He could see light bars turning on two police cruisers. People in bright beach colors milled around the area. How many were witnesses? He slowed down for a knot of pedestrians. A kid in a blue swimsuit pointed at the light on the roof of the Volvo. Two cyclers wheeled by, heading west, legs pumping in muscled precision. Both wore crash helmets and long black Tour de France biker's shorts. As he pulled up beside the nearest police cruiser, he radioed Officer Farris to remind him to check cyclers. It wasn't a bad way to escape.

He could feel the eyes on him as he climbed out of the Volvo. Officer Frederich was tying off a yellow crime-scene ribbon. Words on the ribbon, printed in heavy black, read POLICE LINE, DO NOT CROSS. The crowd stood three deep on the edge of Cortez Alley, where Louie Gardino, face beaded with sweat, held his arms up, easing them back from the ribbons. Over the heads of the crowd, Branko saw a white ambulance. Gardino spotted Branko and came over. They shook hands. Gardino was dark, with brown eyes and beautifully barbered hair. He was a second-year man, a local boy who'd grown up in Tustin.

"You worked that crowd like a sheep dog, Louie."

Gardino grinned and started his briefing. Branko changed out of his damp tennis shirt and slipped into his Adidas warm-ups. There was a breeze off the water, and the temperature was dropping. Two blocks west, Branko saw a black-and-white unit from the sheriff's department. He listened to Gardino carefully, making mental notes, and decided to leave his .357 in the trunk.

"What's the manpower situation?"

"We've got two units on the scene, Sergeant, and one on the other side, checking the ferry passengers. Sergeant Taylor's over at the Inn, setting up a command post. The merchants are mad as hell already. One guy took my name down, said he was pals with the mayor."

"Where's Officer Duncan?"

"I saw her with the ambulance, then heading over to the Inn. Did you hear, Sarge? She got the perp with a fishing hook?"

"Good work. Where?"

"Caught him in the neck, right under the ear."

"What about the third shooter? Which room?"

Gardino pointed out the room, a window on the second floor overlooking Cortez Alley. The sheriff's vehicle stopped and two deputies got out and came over. They were heavy-shouldered men, with razor haircuts and dark green uniforms. California peace officers were always ready for the television cameras. When you lived fifty miles from Hollywood, your brain hummed with star-crossed hope. One deputy gave Branko's warm-up suit a long look.

"Thanks for coming, guys. This is a dirty one. We could use some help lining up witnesses. If you unearth a hot one, route him or her over to the Inn. We've got a command post working." He turned to Gardino. "Any spent shell casings?"

Gardino shook his head. "Haven't had time to look."

Branko attached his shield to the left pocket of his warm-up jacket. "We need hard evidence on this. Three shooters, maybe more. A planned getaway. We've got one dead, at least three wounded. Two of the wounded are policemen. Let's move on this before it cools."

The deputies nodded and their eyes grew hard. Clutching their notebooks, they followed Gardino toward Cortez Alley.

Traffic slowed heading west as drivers gawked at the police barrier. As soon as more help arrived, Branko would assign someone to handle the intersection. Right now, witnesses were priority. He jogged across Balboa, passing the black-and-white that had been driven by Randy Whitson. The left front tire was totally flat. The windows were open. The departmental riot gun was locked in place.

Branko stopped at the entrance to the Inn and scanned the Balboa Pier. Dark clouds rolled across the sky over the Pacific. People in beach clothes were standing in small groups, talking. A man in shorts and a tank top swept his arm along the route taken by the shooter on the bike. Officers were needed on the pier.

Branko went inside.

The exterior of the Inn of Cortez was Spanish-colonial, pale stucco, red tile. Potted palms flanked the wrought-iron gate that guarded the entryway. Cool in here, thanks to the afternoon shadows, Branko figured. He blinked to adjust his eyes to the light. There was a short corridor of red Mexican pavers and the walls were whitewashed and decorated with two posters of Manolete. A sign on a desk said CONCIERGE. Behind the desk, a woman in a business suit was trying to calm down half a dozen excited guests. The woman stared at Branko, eyeballing his shield. Another angry merchant. Branko introduced himself,

38

told her the police would be around all night, and asked if he could use the copy machine.

The concierge gave him a bright, bitter look. "This is killing our business."

"Sorry. We'll be out as soon as possible."

He found Officer Jamie Duncan in the Sea of Cortez restaurant, interviewing an old party in a blue blazer and ascot. She was wearing a gray police department sweatshirt, but her legs were bare and tanned and coming out of tight shorts. A pair of skates with red wheels and high white tops lay on the floor, next to her service revolver. She was barefoot. Her feet were tanned.

Sergeant Don Talor sat across the room, talking to three women with varying shades of blue in their carefully coiffed hair. In a booth against the windows, Freddy Lyle, from Narcotics, took notes while he listened to two teens. A dozen more witnesses sat around, staring at the floor, sipping coffee, whispering as they waited to be called. Two waitresses in short skirts and mesh stockings stood near the kitchen door, looking bored. Things were under control here.

Branko spoke briefly to Sergeant Taylor, a balding heavyset man in his forties. "Good work, Don. Glad you're with us on this."

"You hear about the third shooter?"

"Yeah. Have you been upstairs?"

"Just a quick look."

"You got a man up there?"

"Romero."

Officer Jamie Duncan was finishing up with her interview when Branko walked over. He shook hands with the old party, whose name was Tevis Underwood. Mr. Underwood, a member of CASS, had brown eyes too close together and a smile made happier by dentures. Even as he shook hands, he cut his eyes toward Jamie's bare legs. Branko asked him about the book burning.

"It was a surprise to me, Sergeant. A complete surprise."

When Mr. Underwood was out the door, Branko turned to Jamie. Her eyes were red from crying. One strand of blond hair straggled down.

"You okay?"

"I missed him, Frank. I had the perp hooked. All I had to do was reel him in."

"What happened?"

"I stumbled. It was those damn skates. I tripped and lost the damn pole and by the time I was on my feet again they were on a boat heading for L.A."

"Where was your weapon?"

Jamie indicated her costume. "In Randy's unit. Roscoe was my backup. No one expected anything like this."

Branko handed her the keys to his Volvo. "Shag out to my car. There's sweat pants in the trunk. Put them on before your next interview. Mr. Underwood was devouring you with his eyes, okay?"

Jamie blushed and looked down at her bare legs. "Sorry. I forgot. There's been so much . . ." Red in the face, she took the keys and hurried out the door.

Branko borrowed paper and a ruler from the concierge. Using his broad-nibbed fountain pen, a gift from his grandfather back in Wisconsin, he sat at a desk and drew a rough diagram of the crime scene. Cortez Alley here, forming a T where it intersected Balboa. Question marks for Shooters One and Two. Inn of Cortez here, running along Balboa. Arrow pointing to Shooter Three's window. Main Street here, reaching out to the pier. Getaway boat here, at the end of the pier, tied up for twenty minutes. Ferris wheel here, at the other end of Cortez Alley. When he was finished, he xeroxed fifty copies on the copy machine and handed them to Don Taylor.

"Let's nail everything, Don. Names of witnesses, where they were, what they saw, what time it was. I want angles of sight, colors, smells, sounds. If they need to get hypnotized, we'll call in that hypnotist from Laguna."

"The lieutenant will love that, departmental funds for a hypnotist."

"I'll be upstairs if anything pops. What's the room number?"

"Two-ten."

"When Forensics comes, send them up."

At the main desk, Branko checked the Thursday and Friday

registration for room 210. Mr. and Mrs. Ralph Gordimer, an address in San Bernardino, a phone number with a San Bernardino area code. The sign-in card showed precise handwriting, small letters, neatly formed. The Gordimers had checked in Thursday evening. Check-in time was not shown on the card, but the surly desk clerk, Lance, said it had to be before six because there was no credit-card guarantee.

"So they paid cash?"

"Must have."

"Did you get the car license?"

Lance was a beach hound, tanned, mid-thirties, dark suit, an oily smile. "Nothing written here. Sorry."

"What does that mean?"

"Like in a taxi?"

"Who was on the desk yesterday?"

"Um, ah, that was Candy. Candace Woodmere."

"Where can I reach her?"

"She's off mañana. And she's on"—Lance checked a typed schedule—"she's on Sunday, noon to eight."

"What about a home phone?"

"I think she'd weekending in Rosarita."

Branko tapped Lance on the lapel with his forefinger. "The number, or I take you in for questioning."

Lance thumbed the Rolodex and came up with a number. Branko was writing it down when Jamie Duncan came back, wearing Branko's gray sweat pants. She handed him the Volvo keys and Branko walked upstairs to the shooter's room. Jamie, still barefoot, went back to the interview room. Joe Romero recognized Branko. They shook hands. Romero was a young cop, married, easygoing, with a friendly smile. He unlocked the door of room 210 and Branko walked past the NO ENTRY sign into the room.

It was an ordinary hotel room. An open window looked out across Balboa Boulevard to the Fun Zone and Cortez Alley. There was no screen on the window. The Ferris wheel wasn't turning. On the water beyond the Ferris wheel, Branko could see the Balboa Ferry chugging across to the island. Another possible escape route. People were still crowding the police barriers at the crime scene. A bald man in a muddy brown shirt was talking to Officer Gardino, pointing at the hotel window where Branko stood. The SWAT van was parked behind Branko's Volvo and he could see Lieutenant Stan Plotvik deploying his men to help with crowd control. An ambulance pulled away from the scene just as two officers on motorcycles wheeled to a stop. A television truck from Channel 3 in Los Angeles was parked fifty feet behind the SWAT van. A cameraman was photographing the scene.

The bed was queen-sized, with a white coverlet. There was an easy chair turned toward the television. Branko switched the set to Channel 3. Linda Calderon and Thomas Spenser, two well-groomed anchorpersons from Los Angeles, were updating the viewers of televisionland about what had happened on Balboa. Calderon, resplendent in a red blouse and a tasteful gold necklace, read from the television monitor with a throbbing excitement:

"The Channel Three news van is on the scene behind a police barrier at the Fun Zone on Balboa Peninsula in Newport Beach. As you know from earlier reports, a multiple shooting has occurred. One person has died as a result. We are waiting for a report on Reverend Terry O. Williams of Promontory Chapel in Newport Beach. Reverend Williams, an evangelical minister, is a conservative candidate for the Republican ticket in Tuesday's primary. The reverend was shot by an unknown assailant while he was in the act of allegedly setting fire to some newspapers. There is some speculation that the motive for the shooting was political, due to this alleged act."

Branko shut off the set and started his search. In the drawer of the bedside table he found a matchbook from a nightclub in Chicago named Rip's. The surface was shiny enough to take a fingerprint. He left it for Forensics. The closet was empty. There was a Gideon Bible in the top drawer of the dresser. In the bathroom, he found a bobby pin and two long hairs that looked blond.

He went to his knees to check the floor. The shell casing was underneath the skirt of the easy chair. Branko did not touch the casing, which looked like a .223, from an M-16.

There were voices in the corridor outside and Aaron Friedberg came in, carrying his forensics kit. Aaron was short, bald, and paunchy. He had a degree in psychology from a university back East. He'd left a job with a pharmaceuticals firm because his kids loved the surf and he loved warm winters. Aaron shook hands with Branko and opened his kit. Branko gave him the envelopes and told him about the shell casing.

Aaron heaved a heavy sigh. "Dale's across the street, collecting his blood samples."

"How soon can we get a report?"

"Tomorrow morning, if we get lucky, Frank."

"We want to move on this, Aaron."

"Hell, don't I know it?"

Friedberg went to work while Branko phoned Seaport General. Outside the window, two girls in Day-Glo bikinis skated along the Main Street sidewalk. From this spot, the shooter had had a perfect sweep of the area. The hospital answered. Branko identified himself and talked to a floor supervisor. Roscoe Smith and Randy Whitson were in surgery. The reverend was in Recovery. The bodyguard, Mac White, had been dead on arrival. At this time, there was no report on the progress of the two officers. Branko thanked the supervisor and hung up. He left Friedberg shooting photos of the room and walked back downstairs, thinking of Roscoe Smith.

Downstairs, Branko picked up a fresh copy of his diagram of the area, and he and Jamie went outside. Jamie carried a canvas purse slung over her shoulder. The purse contained her weapon. The wind had picked up off the ocean and the clouds were darker. Branko asked questions, turning over one rock at a time.

"Where were you when the shooting started?"

"Right about here, Frank. Breaking up a fight between two kids."

"What made you grab a fishing pole?"

"My piece was in the unit. It was an instinctive thing, something to reach out with. I thought I could slap the bikers going by. The fact that the hook grabbed something was pure luck."

"Did they fire at you?"

"One round."

"You were lucky, Jamie."

She shivered and hugged herself. "Oh, God, Frank. I know."

They walked out to the pier, where the officer on duty was clearing the last gawking spectators. The door of Ruby's Diner had a Closed sign on it. "This is about where they jumped," Jamie said.

"Did you get a look at the boat?"

"It was low and very fast, blue, with white markings."

Walking quickly, they left the pier, passed the Inn of Cortez, and made it across the street to the yellow police barrier in sixty-eight seconds. He figured thirty seconds on a fast Honda.

The SWAT officer passed them under the barrier when he saw their shields. Stan Plotvik was standing in front of Fun Zone News, arguing with the man in the muddy shirt. Stan's uniform was spit-and-polish military, gray battle dress with a sharp crease in each trouser leg. Stan was six-two. He stared down at the man through yellow shooting glasses.

Near a green city trash can was a heap of ashes and the charred remains of half-burnt magazines. Dale Cartwright, the assistant forensics man, was on his knees putting objects into a plastic evidence bag. A blond woman wearing shorts worked in the blown-out window of the flower shop, tossing pieces of glass into a yellow bucket. The woman met Branko's eyes, then went back to work. He could hear the faint clink of glass hitting glass.

Branko brought out his diagram and his fountain pen. "Anything to add?"

Jamie paused for a moment, then pointed to a spot in the middle of the street. "There was a reporter with the photographer. She had red hair and wore a lovely khaki suit."

"Which paper?"

"Had to be the *Times*. Or maybe the *Trib*. That suit was definitely big time. A witness said she tried to slug the perp with her purse and he pistol-whipped her. I saw her leave in an ambulance. Her cheek was bandaged."

Branko printed REPORTER on his diagram, then walked over to talk to the forensics man. Dale Cartwright was a pale-faced scholarly type who loved his laboratory. He held up a battered camera, case split open, lens shattered. "Finished."

"Any film?"

"Ruined."

"Get what you can, okay?"

"Always do, Sergeant." The forensics man returned to his work.

Stan Plotvik waved Branko over. "Sergeant, this is Mr. Sternberg, the proprietor of Fun Zone News. He's threatening to sue our city for restraint of trade."

Sternberg had a round face and dark brown eyes. His teeth flashed in his mouth as he turned to Branko. "Those crazy nut-ass Christians. Think because I'm a Jew they can come in here and torch my merchandise and walk off singing hymns. Hell, if somebody hadn't shot that fat-ass preacher, I'd have done it myself."

Branko waited a couple of beats. Sternberg was angry and scared. The smell of burnt paper lingered in the air. "Mr. Sternberg, the Newport Beach Police Department regrets any inconvenience. If laws have been broken, we'll enforce the laws. Meanwhile, we need your version of what occurred here today. You're a citizen. We need your help."

"I already gave a goddamn statement. Twice. That wife of his—Sister What's-her-hame—she is one crazy old lady."

Branko motioned Jamie Duncan over. "Officer Duncan here will take down your statement. How about going inside your store."

Sternberg's eyes lit up when he saw Jamie. "Hey. You're the one on skates, right?"

Jamie took Mr. Sternberg under the elbow. "Let's go inside, sir. I'd love to take your statement."

There was a commotion over by the alley entrance, a flurry of voices, people moving aside, and Lieutenant Robert Archer stepped forward. The lieutenant was a large blond man with a handsome head of hair and piercing blue eyes. He was the department's snappy dresser, three-piece suits, hand-made Italian shoes, neckties starting at a hundred dollars. His nickname around the department was Robin Hood, or just the Archer.

Now the Archer strode forward, his blond mane of hair rippling, his shoulders straight, stage smile pasted in place, eyeing

Branko's warm-up suit. "Who authorized the Special Weapons unit?"

"I did, sir."

"We're over budget on SWAT personnel, Sergeant. Did you read my last directive?"

"We needed the SWAT people for crowd control," Branko said.

"The crowd is under control." The Archer turned to Stan Plotvik. "Disengage, Lieutenant. Get your people out of here."

Plotvik snapped a military salute. "Yes, sir." He spoke into his walkie-talkie.

The Archer poked a finger close to Branko's chest. "Change your garb, Sergeant. First chance, do you read?"

"Yes, sir."

The Archer smiled. "Image is all, Sergeant. This is a bigee, as the saying goes. It promises to grow like veritable wildfire and every agency from Los Angeles to San Diego wants a piece. Now hear this. Until the chief arrives back, you'll both report to me. The Feds are breathing down my neck. The FBI's sending a crack team down. So is Treasury. They think this action could have national ramifications and they're talking anti-terrorism, bringing in experts. The CHP wants in on it, and the sheriff. This man Williams is a pillar of the community. It's going to take some clockwork liaison here and I want support from you and your personnel. The media will be watching hungrily, waiting for us to drop the ball. Let me make myself perfectly clear. I want no ball dropped on this playing field." The Archer paused to stare at Branko. "Sergeant, where is your wea—"

And a raindrop hit him in the eye. The eyelid fluttered in reflex. The Archer glared up at the black sky. His hands clenched as if he would strangle God. More rain began to fall, the drops pelting down suddenly, forcing the Archer to take hasty cover under the awning of Fun Zone News. Gawkers behind the police barrier headed for cover. A woman in a red dress popped open an umbrella.

"Where's your command post, Sergeant?"

"The Inn, sir. In the lobby."

The Archer liberated a newspaper from the outside rack, positioned it to protect his haircut from the weather, and then hurried off toward the Inn of Cortez. As he reached the boulevard, his driver met him with a large black umbrella.

Branko grinned to himself. "He forgot to pay for the paper."

"Consider it a donation." Plotvik grinned at Branko. "Where *is* your weapon?"

"In the car. I hate wearing that goddamn thing."

"Regs, Frank. Regs."

Branko checked his watch. Five-fifty-eight. The rain would screw up the crime scene. Whatever evidence they didn't already have, they wouldn't have. "If Tommy Osterhaus arrives, tell him to meet me at Seaport."

The SWAT commander nodded. Jamie Duncan came out of Fun Zone News and walked with Branko to the Volvo. He unlocked the door and held it for her.

"Thanks for the sweat pants. I don't suppose you've got shoes, ladies' size eight-and-a-half?" He fished a dry pair of socks out of his tennis bag and Jamie put them on. "God, that feels good. My feet were freezing."

He started the car and turned on the heater. It took five minutes to have official vehicles moved so he could back his way out. Traffic was knotted up ahead of them. He stopped at Seventeenth to check on the roadblock. Officer Farris reported only tourists from the beach, no shooters. It took another fifteen minutes to reach Jamie's home, an apartment at the upper end of Newport Peninsula. Branko pulled up at the curb. Jamie opened the door a crack and looked at Branko over her shoulder. "Like to come in, Frank? You could scrub my back. I could scrub yours."

"I better get to the hospital. But thanks."

"Remember last spring? Just after your wife split? We had some fun then."

"I remember, Jamie. It was great for me. You saved my sanity."

She touched his hand. "I'm not seeing anyone now. You?"

"No. No one."

Jamie's eyes misted over. She nodded. "Thanks for the ride, Frank."

"Take care."

"Call me sometime, okay?"

"Sure."

He watched her run through the pelting rain to the door. She moved like a jock, smooth stride, hips tucked in, shoulders runner-straight. At the door, she turned and waved. Branko tapped his headlights off, then back on, signaling good-bye. As he headed up Balboa toward the coast highway, his headache got worse. He needed coffee to keep him alert. On his way to the hospital, he checked with the station. Tommy Osterhaus was en route to the Fun Zone. The boat had not been sighted by the Coast Guard. The killers were on the loose.

He wanted them. Bad.

Heavy rain slicked the windshield as he headed up the hill toward Seaport General.

CHAPTER FOUR

T HE reverend wanted his mama.

He could feel the pain, a Pentecostal tongue of flame knifing along his left thigh where the track of the bullet lay and through his vitals, making him moan and his eyes water. He tried to push it away. What was God doing to him?

A figure in white appeared above him. It was the Angel of Death. She was wearing white and smelled of grim hospital disinfectant and Juicy Fruit gum. She hovered above him, humming off-key. It sounded like "Strawberry Fields," an old Beatles tune. The reverend was a gospel-singer with perfect pitch. He hated people who sang off-key.

"It hurts," he said.

"There, there, Reverend. I'll get you something."

The Angel of Death floated away and a figure with golden hair passed between him and the yellow light. She was wearing a pale blue dress. Was it Helen? Beautiful Helen of Troy, sitting in a bar in Hollywood smoking a cigarette while he sang his heart out? Is that you, Helen? He clutched the metal rails of the bed, fighting the pain. "This should help, Reverend." The Angel of Death was standing at his bedside, fussing with a transparent plastic tube that led from a vein in his arm and connected him to . . . what? He felt sick to his stomach. White dress. Blue dress. "Helen?"

"I'm Nurse Greenfield, Reverend. You're in Recovery. Your wife is right outside. And your daughter. Everything is going to be just fine."

"How's Mac White? He was—" The reverend paused. "He worked for me."

"Doctor will answer all your questions."

Already the wall of pain was backing away, receding, leaving his vitals as cool as ice, the five-tongued fire of the Pentecost fading away. *Pentecost* was a Greek word. He remembered that from his days as a seminarian, studying for his mission with the Lord. "But I will tarry at Ephesus until Pentecost," he whispered.

"What's that you said?"

"Nothing."

The Angel floated out of sight. He was alone.

The term *Pentecostal fire* was one of Mama's. She said it a lot, even though she didn't know Greek. Mama knew Italian because of her opera arias. Daddy knew Greek because he'd gone to Harvard College, out East. Daddy also knew Latin. *Vitals* was one of Daddy's words. With his eyes closed, the reverend could hear Daddy's voice. . . .

"Vitals, Sergeant Chub. Comes from the Latin word *vita*, meaning life. Viva vitalis, the hair oil for Hollywood slicks. Fred Astaire used Vitalis on that film we made together. Rudee Vallee did not. Viva vitalis, vitamins, vitals! Hear it, Sergeant? Hear the subtle Latinate underpinnings of the word? Those old Romans could screw you with words, screw you to the wall or the Cross, whichever was handier in the Forum. Vital victuals, as my grandpap used to say before he rode off to fight the Yankees. Now there was a man who could sit a horse proper, as the pundits say. *Vita* is Latin for life. *Bethu*, Sergeant, is Irish for life. Take Lord Bethu farther down the road of words and you've got

Usquebaugh, which is Irish for whiskey. Christ on the Cross, I'm thirsty. Pour me a dram, there, Sergeant. And no whiffing at the bottle. A half-inch more, Sergeant. There. You can join me next year, when you jettison those schoolboy knickers. Did I ever tell you you look like Peck's bad boy?"

"Yes, sir."

"Yes, Captain. Remember your manners, Sergeant."

"Yes, Captain."

Vitals was one of Daddy's words. Mama would go to work and Daddy would sit at the kitchen in the white clapboard house on Fourth Street in Glendora with the pistol on the table and drink Ballantine's Scotch whisky while he talked about his vitals. Daddy wore white suits and white shoes with little ornamental holes drilled in the toes. He had a Southern accent and fourteen hats. In the summer he wore hats made of Manila fibers. In the winter he wore felt hats, like Humphrey Bogart, with a feather in the brim.

"She's gnawing at my vitals, Sergeant Chub," Daddy would say. "Her teeth are as sharp as a Mississippi river rat's and she's on her forepaws inside my gut gnawing at my very vitals!"

His daddy called him Sergeant Chub and his mama called him Terry O. His middle name was Odell, and Odell was Daddy's first name.

"Odell Macaulay Williams, at your service, sah! Bring me the Vitalis, Sergeant, and let's you and me plaster our forelocks like Caesar invading Gaul."

Daddy was a Harvard man who could play a beautiful piano and tap dance and sing up a storm. He'd been a captain in the Army and he loved barking orders. In the Army, Daddy said, everyone yelled at everyone. He'd brought his family to California because of a movie job, playing piano for a dancer named Fred Astaire. Daddy could dance better than Fred Astaire, but he didn't have the name, he said, so they set him playing piano.

Mama was a Mississippi girl with the voice of an angel. She had taught music in the Glendora public schools east of Los Angeles and everyone who heard her sing said she should have been on the stage in Europe and New York City, singing grand opera. Mama's rendition of *Butterfly* was enough to make you cry.

Mama sang in the church choir at the Fourth Street Baptist Church and Daddy played piano at Dinty's Rubicon in Hollywood and waited for the studios to call.

Sundays were bad for Daddy because Dinty's Rubicon Lounge was closed and he had no place to go. On Sunday, Mama really gnawed at Daddy's vitals. "If I could get my commission back, Sergeant, I'd sign up every Sunday for a shooting war, mark my words."

His mama called him Terry Odell because she liked the ring of it, the music, the rhythms. His daddy called him Sergeant Chub, trying to make him laugh because he was a tad overweight.

Mama liked it when Terry Odell sang in church. He made the ladies cry. He did his mama proud. Daddy liked it when Sergeant Chub sang in Dinty's Rubicon. Daddy would introduce him and bring him up on the little stage with a ripple from the piano, under the bright angled spotlight and the tiny dust motes that swam in the air. The drunks in Dinty's Rubicon would applaud and toss quarters and dimes and folded-up dollars. Some afternoons he made two dollars, three. He was saving for a red bicycle. He could earn a fortune by singing, Daddy told him. Rudee Vallee had done it and his voice quavered.

Terry Odell Williams felt good when he sang in church. He felt holy and blessed, with all the eyes on him and his boy soprano voice trilling up into the rafters, right into the arms of God.

But when Sergeant Chub sang in the afternoons at Dinty's Rubicon, he felt . . . rich. He got paid for singing and he loved to sing and he came to associate singing with money. When he had money he could buy things and then he didn't feel poor, which Mama said the family was. He liked the drunks at Dinty's better than he did the mournful, sad-eyed worshippers at the church. He liked the bartender better than he liked Preacher Mortimer, who was always asking for money. Mama made him give a tithe to the church.

"The poor will get to Heaven long before the rich," Mama always said. "It is God's will that you tithe."

A tithe was ten cents on the dollar, minimum.

Two other things happened to him at Dinty's Rubicon. He drank his first beer before he was legal. And he fell in love. The two events were connected, the beer and the falling in love. He was eleven and the object of his heart was blond and beautiful, with red lips and amazing eyes and perfume that drove him crazy. Daddy called her Helen of Troy and one day when it was raining outside Sergeant Chub sang "O Danny Boy" and Helen gave him five dollars tucked into his shirt pocket and a kiss on the mouth. He stammered out a thank you, ears burning, heart on fire.

"You've flustered the Sergeant, Helen." Daddy's eyes gleamed in the light from the bar. "You've made the boy all hot and bothered in his manly parts."

"That was beautiful, Terry." Helen sat at Daddy's table, sipping on a gin drink. She was wearing a pale blue dress with a neckline like a V, looking like a picture in *The Saturday Evening Post* called "The White Rock Girl." "You have a beautiful voice."

He hated himself for being a fool. He hated himself for not being able to talk, to tell her how he felt. Helen laughed and reached out for him and pulled him close. He smelled her glorious perfume. He was aware of soft skin, the pretty freckled softness above her pale blue frock, and the tingle of face powder on his lips and fine blond hairs at the back of her neck. Helen of Troy's eyes were shining as she kissed him. He swooned.

"Why do you call her Helen of Troy, Daddy?"

"Because her face has launched a thousand ships, Sergeant. And because she does not gnaw at my vital core, my viva vitalis. Pour me another dram, there."

And Sergeant Chub would pour. And Daddy would stare at the pistol on the kitchen table with sad eyes.

Now, lying in bed, the reverend needed a drink.

Helen of Troy had been too old for him, but he fell in love anyway. She was a woman grown, as Daddy explained, and he, Sergeant Chub, was a stripling, a green-eared youth, a moppet on the edge of adolescence. "Relish your musk, Sergeant. Explore your burning id until your little gonads pop like firecrackers on Jeff Davis's birthday! It's all we've got, we cursed menfolk, to keep us sane amidst an army, a veritable army I say, of rat-toothed gnawers!"

Helen of Troy vanished when he was twelve. One day she was there, sitting at the table, looking beautiful, smiling at Daddy as Sergeant Chub sang "We'll Go No More a-Roving." The drunks disappeared for a moment, and there was only Helen, smoking a Phillip Morris cigarette with her elegant legs crossed and the heel of her shoe swinging.

The next day, Helen of Troy was gone. And the next. The days stretched painfully into a week, then two weeks. When he asked Daddy about Helen, Daddy smiled and shook his head. "Sailed into the sunset, Sergeant, as behooves a female of cal-iber. She was drifting and so she perched her magnificent bosom on the prow of a Viking ship and cast off for Tahiti and her golden boat sails into a perpetual golden sunset. How about a sip of beer before you sing, old Sergeant Chub."

The beer was bitter. "Helen is very beautiful, Daddy."

"Yes," Daddy said. "She is."

The pistol was in the study closet, unloaded, on the top shelf in the house at 7 Singapore Circle. The house was owned by Promontory Chapel, a corporation controlled by church elders. Daddy was dead. Mama was in a rest home up near Santa Bar-bara. Jordan Maxwell was dead. Ministry Beach, USA, was going down the tubes. And the reverend at forty-five was still in love with Helen of Troy.

She had been the perfect woman. Romantic. Unattainable. Blond. Serene. An image drifting across the Technicolor screen at the forefront of his fevered mind. He searched for her face in his congregation. He searched for her in airport departure lounges, in the crowds at South Coast Plaza, in the faces of the shopgirls in the department stores. He searched for her at Dis-neyland, where he took his children for songs and innocent fun. Sometimes he saw her image at garden parties in fashionable and seductive Newport Beach, where he stared through the Cal-ifornia haze at the distant and disdainful Susannah Maxwell, who bore a resemblance to his memory of Helen. Sometimes he found her on Harbor Boulevard, a biblical vestige of the moral fallout from Disneyland, where the whores of Babylon strolled to the music of the spheres on the dark side of the Garden. . . .

The Angel of Death reappeared. She was not Helen of Troy. "Reverend? We're ready to take you to your room. Your wife's right outside. There are policemen everywhere. You must be a very important person."

He stared at her. Her face was in shadow, but he could smell that Juicy Fruit. "Now I am." The reverend needed a drink. He wished to God he could pray.

Branko parked the Volvo near a mobile truck from Channel 15 and took the back entrance into Seaport General Hospital. The lobby hummed with journalists eager for a story. Several people called to him. He recognized Pete Whisner, from the L.A. *Times*, but he did not see the redhead in the khaki suit mentioned by Jamie. He had to wait several minutes at the information desk before he found out that Roscoe White and Randy Whitson were still in the operating room. The reverend was in Recovery. The nurse, a harried brunette with rouge on her cheeks, could not find any information about a *Tribune* photographer.

"You don't have his name? I can't find anything without the patient's name."

"He was shot down on Balboa. He should have been brought in with the others."

The brunette stared at him. "It's been a terrible night for us. He could have been taken to the UCI Medical Center. Get me a name and I'll try again." She directed him to the waiting area outside the operating room. Mrs. Whitson, Randy's wife, was coming out, holding a handkerchief to her face, which was red from crying. The distraught woman canted sideways, as if shoved by a strong wind. A nurse had an arm around her waist. When Mrs. Whitson saw Branko she turned away, sobbing.

The waiting room was empty. Roscoe Smith had a girlfriend, a flight attendant named Marcie Deegan, but she was on a layover in the Midwest. Branko drank a cup of hospital coffee from a machine. It tasted of wet paper.

He went over his notes, keeping an eye on the clock. Roscoe Smith had saved his life once, in West Jetty Park, by clobbering two bikers. Roscoe had helped him through those first grim days after his wife had left for New York. He could talk to Roscoe. Don't let him die, he prayed.

It was after seven when Tommy Osterhaus sat down beside him. Tommy was wearing a Burberry raincoat and his umbrella dripped with rain. He took off the raincoat, displaying a tan jacket of light tweed, a pale tan shirt, a brown tie, and tan slacks. Tommy was the second-best dresser in the department, after Robin Hood Archer, but he did it with more studied class and less flash. Tommy was fifty-three, with a mind like a computer, and he kept thousands of criminal dossiers in his formidable memory.

"Any word?"

"Nothing."

"How long have you been here, Francisco?"

"About an hour. You been to the Fun Zone?"

"I left everything in the capable hands of the lieutenant."

"If they make him captain, I'm going back to Hollenbeck."

Tommy smiled, crinkling the corners of his eyes. As a young man, he'd had red hair. It had since turned a silvery-gray. He pulled his notebook out. "If he makes captain, I'll go with you. They found the boat."

"Where?"

"Huntington Beach. It's been traced to San Pedro, to an insurance man named Krantz. It was a Saber, California registration, reported stolen this morning."

"Are they going over it for us?"

"The usual cooperation between friendly police forces. We'll be lucky if they let us look at the boat."

"Any blood spots? Jamie hooked that perp in the neck."

Tommy shook his head. "I doubt it. It had just started to rain here when I got word on the boat. It had been raining in Huntington for fifteen minutes."

"Crap."

Tommy took notes while Branko filled him in on events at the Fun Zone. Tommy wrote with a Cross pen, gold-plated, shaping his letters carefully. At seven-thirty, a doctor in green surgery scrubs opened the door and came out. His stomach needed situps. When he took off the green cap, his bald head gleamed in the light. His name tag read GRIMES. He sat down with a sigh but did not shake hands. "You're the police, right?"

"This is Sergeant Osterhaus. I'm Sergeant Branko. How are they doing?"

"I'm Simon Grimes. The reverend will live to preach many sermons. Small-caliber wound, left thigh, about six inches down from the scrotal area. He thinks he's hurt worse than he is. Both officers are in Recovery now. The black officer is critical at this time. The other man, a husky fellow with a lot of native vitality, has an excellent chance."

Branko's voice was tight. "The black officer—Roscoe Smith—is my partner. How do you read his chances?"

Dr. Grimes shook his head. "It's a waiting game now. He was hit pretty bad, one here"—the doctor pointed to his chest—"severed some vessels."

"When can we see them?"

"Couple of hours. If you're counting on statements, don't."

"Dr. Grimes," Tommy said, "we're interested in the slugs you took out. Any chance we could have a quick look?"

The doctor hesitated. "I suppose so, as long as it's official." He pushed himself out of the chair and walked heavily back through the swinging doors of the operating room. He returned in a few moments carrying some plastic zip-lock envelopes. Each envelope had a label. The door opened to reveal Judy Whitson, Randy's wife, still holding the handkerchief. The nurse was still with her and Branko guessed the wife had had a sedative.

"Sergeant? Doctor? Is my husband . . ."

Branko left Tommy with the envelopes and walked toward her. Judy Whitson was a dreary woman who got drunk at department parties. She worked as a computer programmer at an industrial facility in Los Angeles. The drive, fifty miles to work and fifty miles back, kept her fretful. Branko sat with Judy while the doctor explained what had to be done to get her husband well.

When he had finished, she turned to Branko. Before she spoke, she blew her nose. "He's going to resign from your damned police force, Frank Branko. I've had it with worry. I've had it with excuses and hero crap. I'm going to write his resignation for him and move his hand across the paper. And then I'm going to sue the damned city of Newport Beach for a million dollars. Damn you, Frank Branko! Damn you and all the white knights of Newport!"

The doctor whispered something to the nurse, who helped Judy Whitson to her feet. Branko watched them leave the waiting room. The doctor shook his head. "Hysterical females, what a crock." He left the policemen together.

Tommy had the four envelopes lined up on a small Formica table. Each envelope was labeled with the name of the victim— Breitman (photographer), Williams (reverend), Smith (detective), Whitson (uniformed officer). There was no envelope for the bodyguard, Mac White, who had been taken to the coroner's office. "I'm still working out the hit sequence, Francisco. From what we've got on your crime-scene diagram, here's my thinking so far. The photographer took one hit with a small-caliber round. Looks like a twenty-two. The reverend took one hit also. His bullet looks about the same size. The bodyguard was shot, but his bullets have to wait on the autopsy. Roscoe took three hits that we know of. This one here looks like a three-fifty-seven. This one I can't tell about. And this third one here reminds me of my Army days."

"You think it's a two-twenty-three?"

Tommy's eyes gleamed with insight. "Could be. Opens up some curious possibilities—disgruntled vets, et cetera. Randy Whitson was hit twice. Once with the alleged two-twenty-three, the second time with this whopper."

"Could be a forty-five."

"Or a forty-four," Tommy said. "If the coroner proceeds at his usual speed, we could be Monday or Tuesday on the bodyguard."

Branko stared down at the four plastic envelopes. "You thinking of taking the exam?"

"No. I'm thinking of retiring, spending my days on the water."

"You retired once already, Tommy. Why do it again?"

Tommy Osterhaus had pulled his papers for retirement two years ago, but had been called back to help out when Captain

D'Agostino became chief. It was well known around the department that Lieutenant Robin Hood Archer wanted the captain's job. If he got it, his lieutenant's slot would open up.

"This is my last case, Francisco. Once this is over, I'm heading for Australia and blue water."

"You'd make a great exec, Tommy. The guys like you. You can cool it and get things moving."

"You take the exam, Francisco. I like the sound of Lieutenant Branko."

Branko stretched. His headache was worse. The coffee had made his stomach jumpy. "Not for me. What's your guess on the weapons?"

"One small-bore pistol, revolver so the casings wouldn't spew out. One Magnum, same M.O. One horse pistol, matched with the big guy on the Honda. Then we've got a rifle, military-issue. Could have been a Galil, maybe a Heckler and Koch, a Colt M-Sixteen. Who else made those?"

"Armalite."

Tommy wrote it down. "Lots of firepower. Could have been a massacre."

"I've been thinking about that small-bore pistol. What if they wanted to wound the reverend? Not kill him."

Tommy looked up. "Good idea. It's four days before the primary. They rush out to burn books. The reverend gets shot in the leg. Maybe they were aiming for his ass and the muzzle dropped a fraction of an inch."

"Inside job?"

"Interesting idea."

"That means an inside man."

"Or woman."

Branko clasped his fingers behind his neck and leaned back in the chair. "Let's make a list of suspects."

They started with Congressman Sherwood, then added Lonnie Chevron, the Democrat from Laguna Beach. Tommy, who followed local politics, added several politicians and Harrison Wakefield, the campaign manager. "There's a guy named Cade on the reverend's team. Accountant, I think. Or controller. I know the name, but I've never seen him."

"Hell," Branko said. "Add Cade's name."

They left the waiting room and checked with a nurse. Roscoe Smith was still in Recovery. Randy Whitson was about ready to be wheeled to his room on the fourth floor. Branko and Tommy rode the elevator to four. Ted Forney was on the reverend's door. He spoke to them briefly, letting them know things were under control. Mrs. Williams was inside with her daughter. They looked in on Randy, who was in a double room with a window. The room smelled of industrial-strength disinfectant. His wife was sitting in a chair at the side of the bed. She left the room in a huff when she saw them, handkerchief pressed to her tear-streaked face.

"Hey, Sarge. Hey, Sergeant Osterhaus." Randy's voice was weak. He tried to smile.

"You're mending already, Randy," Branko said. "Looking good."

"How's Roscoe?"

"Doing great."

Randy Whitson stared past Branko at the ceiling. "I blew it out there, Sarge. There wasn't shit going down and then the old lady starts a fire in the street, so I call it in thinking, hell, maybe they've got a permit and can't find the beach, and by the time I finish up the fire is really going, so when I step across the street to do something about it this ding-dong opens up with a piece. The next thing I know I've been sandbagged from behind and people are screaming and Roscoe is down. . . ." There were tears in his eyes as he stopped talking and tried to clear his throat. "Shit," he said. "I really blew it."

The two sergeants did their best to reassure him before leaving the room. Whitson's wife stood just outside the door. She glared at them as they went past.

Outside, in the corridor, Tommy flipped through his notebook. "I'll get back to the station and collate those diagrams. That was a good idea, Francisco. You stay here and interview the good reverend and the photographer."

"Right."

"And Mrs. Williams, if she turns up. She was at the shooting."

"Right."

"Ask Mrs. Williams what kind of starter she used on the magazines."

Branko laughed. Tommy flipped to another page. "I'll double-check with the Berkeley police. Maybe they've located the son."

"What's his name?"

"Terry Williams Junior."

"Figures."

"We're using six officers on security for the family. Roche is out sick. Trevino is still on vacation." Tommy changed subjects. "When you talk to the reverend, ask him how come they use the Maxwell place for parties."

Branko was surprised. "*The* Maxwell place?"

"Yeah. The late Mr. Maxwell was a big mover in the Ministry Beach park. I hear they're having money troubles."

"How come you know all this stuff, Tommy?"

"I read the papers, Francisco."

The two policemen grinned at each other and then Branko shook Tommy's hand and watched him walk to the elevator. They made a good team. Branko was a hunch-player who relied on luck and intuition. Tommy was a detail guy who gathered more information than he needed.

Branko asked for the photographer, Breitman, at the nurse's station. He was directed down the hall to room 415.

He knocked at the door to 415. A woman's voice said to come in. Branko pushed open the door. A big bearded man lay in bed. The television was going, volume on low. A woman with red hair sat in a chair by the bed, making notes on a yellow legal-size pad. She was wearing a khaki suit, pale yellow blouse, and brown shoes with a medium heel. Her legs were crossed. She had neat ankles. When she turned her head, Branko saw that her left cheek was bandaged. The bandage did not hide the fact that she was pretty. Her eyes were direct, intelligent.

"I'm Sergeant Branko, Newport Beach police."

The redhead stood up to shake hands. Her name was Lissa Cody and she was from the *Orange County Tribune*. She wore a NOW button on her lapel. The man in the bed was Josh Breitman, her photographer. "He's not ready for questions, if you don't mind."

The man in the bed lifted his hand weakly but did not speak.

Branko spoke to Lissa Cody. "We were hoping he got some photos of the action."

The photographer shook his head. Lissa Cody answered for him. "Josh was about to click the shutter when he was shot. He was extremely lucky. The bullet missed his liver by inches."

"That's something to be thankful for. My partner was hit, too. He's still in Recovery."

Her eyes fluttered. "I was just leaving, Sergeant. I'll walk out with you."

Branko waited outside while Lissa Cody said good-bye to Breitman. When she came out, she pulled a tissue from her purse to blow her nose. "He's really hurting," she said.

The light was better in the corridor and he got a good look at her. She was five-seven, perhaps five-eight, trim, with dazzling green eyes. Her skin was fair and she had a bridge of freckles across her nose, just where the bandage started. Branko felt a ripple of attraction. It certainly seemed to be his day with the ladies. First, Mrs. Maxwell, the Queen of Spyglass Hill. Now Lissa Cody, girl reporter and feminist. He wondered how old she was. Late twenties, he guessed. Or early thirties. She wasn't wearing a wedding band.

She didn't say much in the elevator going down. On the ground floor, he steered her past the clamoring journalists to the rear entrance. He had the feeling he'd seen her before, a year or so ago. He could not remember where.

"I'd like to talk to you, Ms. Cody, get your version of the shooting today, but I need to wait here and check on my partner. Is there some way we could meet later? Maybe at your office? You're a trained observer and you could really help us out."

Lissa Cody's eyes narrowed. "Have you found anything?"

"The boat. It was stolen in San Pedro. They docked at Huntington Beach and either took another boat or a car."

She nodded and stared out at the rain. "I'm tired. I'm very angry. My emotions are all jumbled about things. And meanwhile I've got a damned story to write. Can't we make this tomorrow?"

"Sure. It's just that we'll have a task force going by then and the Feds will be crawling all over my work space and it will be tough for me to get free of the machinery. Tonight would be better for me." He ran a hand over his face. "I'm tired, too."

She looked directly at him and sighed. "Have you eaten, Sergeant?"

"Not since breakfast."

"What if I phone you around ten? We could meet for a sandwich. I could fill you in. You could reciprocate."

"Reciprocate how?"

"By leaking a few police tidbits before they become public."

"That's against departmental policy."

"That's the best I can do. It's a tough, dog-eat-dog world." She handed him a card. "Good night, Sergeant."

She popped an umbrella open and walked into the rain. Branko watched her go. Ambitious lady. The card had black letters on a tan background. Lissa Cody, *Orange County Tribune*. He liked the way her hips moved in the khaki skirt, even if she was a feminist.

Winona Lee Williams stood at the window, back ramrod straight, staring out at the ocean. Delia Sue Williams, the reverend's daughter, sat in a chair thumbing through a magazine. Delia Sue was dressed in her usual punker style—black Reeboks, tight white leggings, a pair of black leather shorts adorned with chains and buckles, and a Superman T-Shirt that showed the Man of Steel flying through the air with his left fist clenched and his arm out straight. Delia Sue's left eye had a black circle painted around it, creating the effect of a perpetual Magic Marker bruise. Her hair on the right side was purple. Her hair on the left was blond, like her dad's, and spiked. Neither of his children looked like Winona Lee.

"That was insane, Winona Lee, burning those magazines."

"It was a warning, husband, to the purveyors of filth. We had our chance. We seized the day."

"Do you have any idea how this will appear in the media?"

"I have no control over the media."

"Why today?"

"The time was ripe for plucking."

"You planned it, didn't you? You engineered the CASS parade and you pre-planned the burning."

"It was high time. The man sells filth. The neighborhood is rife with minors and juveniles."

"Did you have to use barbecue starter?"

"It did the job."

"You could have waited, until after the primary."

Winona Lee turned to face him. "The burning was God's will. The primary is not, certainly not your part in it."

"I wish you'd stop saying that."

Her voice came out of the shadows. The sound was sepulchral. "You are out of touch with God, husband. You have lost your connection."

The reverend stared at her, standing there with her back straight and her head thrust out on her skinny neck. In this light, with the shadows playing across the planes of her face, Winona Lee looked like his mama. Her stern Puritan's eyes measured him, pinned him, sputtering, on a white mat. He felt like a helpless butterfly about to be mounted.

Winona Lee was from Marlin, Kansas. She'd been a seminary student in St. Louis when the reverend had met her twenty-two years ago. Her maiden name was Peet; her father owned Peet's Mercantile, and she claimed to be descended from a line of Peets who had come to the New World from Bristol, England, and spent the next two hundred years in New Bedford, Massachusetts. Through family Bibles she could trace her lineage back to 1512, and she was fond of telling people that Massachusetts in the year 1659 had passed a law against celebrating Christmas that remained in effect for twenty-two years. Winona Lee loved that story. When she told it, she smiled a narrow, slitted smile. Her point was that the New England colonists were made of stern stuff. She was fond of contrasting the piety of New England in colonial days to what was happening today in California. To her, California was a Western Babylon roiling in a deep trough of sin, and she had been sent here to save it. Winona Lee was a Pentecostal Christian who spoke in tongues. Her voice was clipped, no-nonsense, packed with fervor and condemnation. She spent three hours a day in prayer, three more reading her Bible. When she read, Winona Lee moved her lips, muttering the words. Sometimes, she uttered low moans. More than anything, she loved putting the fear of God into sinners.

"God gave me a green light," the reverend said. "He wants this primary."

"You have not spoken to God since you took up this abject quest for power." She leaned forward, her eyes flickering. "I smell it on you, husband. I smell the stench of the world in your clothes, your hair. I smell Mammon. I smell Babylon. Today you received a sign from God. Heed that sign, I abjure you!"

The door opened and Nurse Greenfield popped in. "Doctor's here, to check your injury, Reverend."

The reverend was relieved. His wife glared at Nurse Greenfield. Winona Lee had a low tolerance for Jews.

The doctor was a large man wearing a long white coat that reminded the reverend of the cowboy saddle coats worn in westerns. His head was bald, with a thin fringe of hair over the ears, and his eyes were too close together, making him an unattractive fellow. He nodded at Winona Lee, took a long look at Delia Sue, and shook the reverend's hand. He listened to the reverend's chest through a stethoscope while Nurse Greenfield took the reverend's blood pressure. Then he flipped the blankets back and checked the dressing on the wound. It was the first time the reverend had seen the bandage, which covered his left leg from knee to crotch. Blood had oozed through it. The reverend felt sick. In a quick flash of memory, he saw the gunman aiming the pistol and firing. Rage filled him. Was Winona Lee right? Was it a sign from God? A red light so close to the election?

Impossible.

"One-sixty-eight over a hundred, Doctor."

"Got to come down. Do you exercise, Reverend?"

"Not lately. I'm running for office. Perhaps you'll vote for me."

"I'm a Sherwood man. Sorry."

When Dr. Grimes touched the wound, the reverend felt a spiraling wave of nausea.

"Heart's steady enough, but that pressure needs to come down. How are you feeling?"

"I have had better days. When can I leave the hospital?"

"Ten days. Maybe a week. You want to stay off that leg, take it easy, get some rest."

"I've got an election to win. Tuesday is the primary. Sunday is doorbell day."

Dr. Grimes nodded. "You'll have to skip Sunday and the doorbells. Sorry this came at a bad time. Most of the people in here feel the same way about their ailments. Very damned few people I know get sick on schedule."

Winona Lee's dress rustled. "There's no need to use profanity, Doctor."

Dr. Grimes swung around to look at Winona Lee. "Sorry." He turned back and gave the reverend a thin smile as he pulled the blanket back up. It was hospital blue and felt synthetic. "You've had a shock, Reverend. A gunshot's not like something else. The bullet carries an extra load of human venom. Were you ever shot before?"

"Never."

"Well, a bullet seems impersonal, just a chunk of lead, but it's loaded with hate, an emotional charge that goes with the air speed and velocity. A bullet gets in you and tears you up in both body and spirit. You've lost some blood and we don't want infection to set in. Relax, Reverend. You can run again."

The reverend knew that wasn't possible. "No. This is my only chance. I must win on Tuesday. Or not at all."

"Sit tight, Reverend. Get well. Go back to your preaching. Do what you do best." It was clear from the doctor's attitude that he did not consider the reverend a serious candidate.

Winona Lee smiled at him from behind his back. "Thank you, Doctor," she breathed. "Thank you for that."

"I'll check on you later. If you need anything, just buzz Greenfield here. She's gotten patients up off their death bed. Good evening, ma'am."

Winona Lee followed the doctor out and the reverend looked at his baby girl. She was now sitting with her heels on the edge of the bed, legs out straight, reading a magazine. "You all right, honey?"

"Um."

"I'll bet you're having trouble understanding what happened to daddy, aren't you?"

She looked at him over the top of the magazine. "You got whacked."

"That's putting it rather baldly."

Delia Sue answered with an elaborate shrug. "It's our own hostage situation, right here in Newport Beach." The gum snapped as she chewed. "Violence has arrived, daddy. It's in the Bible. The four horsemen and all that."

Where did she get these ideas? "Delia Sue, sometimes you amaze me."

"Thanks, Daddy. I'm glad you're doing better. You looked pretty beat coming in here."

The door opened and Winona Lee came back in. "There's a policeman who wants to see you. He has assured me measures are being taken to ensure the safety of my son."

She meant Terry Junior. "Good."

"He also wishes to speak to me."

"And me?" Delia Sue swung her Reeboks down from the edge of the bed.

"Not you, young lady. You're being sent home, to bed."

Delia Sue stood. "Can I give a statement to the press? I could talk about how it feels to be the daughter of a wounded preacher?"

"Shush." Winona Lee eyed her daughter and turned to the reverend. "Are you feeling up to the police?"

Anything would be a relief from his wife, from her stern, militant rigidity. "A short visit, perhaps."

"I'm asking Jasper to schedule the funeral services for tomorrow evening. For Mackenzie White."

"That soon? I wish you'd wait, Winona Lee. He might have family that—"

"There is no family."

"I wish you'd wait."

"You are out of the church, husband. It was your wish to be out so that you could pursue this quest in the wilderness. If you wish to return to the church, your voice will be heard again."

She was digging at him, gnawing at him, gnawing at his vitals. Daddy had warned him about Winona Lee, before they had married. How long had it been, more than twenty years now?

Daddy was gone. Winona Lee had sharp teeth. She was looking more and more like Mama.

"Jasper will say the words. You can tune him in on your set."

"Winona Lee—"

"The police have provided protection. A Mexican policeman for me. A female body-builder for our daughter. These are blasphemous times. I am glad my poor father is not here as witness. It would have driven him insane." Winona Lee took Delia Sue by the arm. "Come, Delia Sue."

"Good night, Daddy."

"Good night, dear."

Winona Lee walked out with his daughter. The reverend waited for the policeman. When he didn't come, the reverend picked up the phone and called Susannah Maxwell, at her home on Spyglass Hill. He knew the number by heart, from his connection with Jordan Maxwell. As the phone rang, he made up stories about what he would say if she answered.

"Hello." It was Susannah's voice, low, vibrant, thrilling through him.

He tried to speak but his mouth was dry. He hung up the phone, feeling foolish. His palms were sweating and the dizziness returned in a rush. One day he would speak. One day soon. Sometimes just hearing her voice was enough. His courage was building. Life was short. A bullet could cut you down in midstride, as it had Mac White. The shooting today reminded him that it could all end in an instant—a mad gunman, a bullet speeding toward your vitals. Who had hired the killers? Sherwood? The Democrat Chevron? Winona Lee? Someone in his own camp? A lunatic from the congregation?

He switched off those thoughts, closed his eyes, and brought Susannah back. What would she be like to make love to? She was beautiful, and yet she seemed cold. If she had lived a past life, as the Buddhists believed one did, it had probably been as a royal courtesan. The reverend pictured her in Rome, wearing a white toga, the white stunning against her golden skin. One day soon, he would tell her about his Roman vision. Daddy would have liked Susannah. Was he going crazy, like Mama?

The door opened and the policeman came in.

CHAPTER FIVE

S USANNAH Maxwell hung up the phone with a tight smile and stared out the window at the dark Pacific. There were five telephone lines into the Maxwell home on Spyglass Hill, left over from Jordan Maxwell's days of doing business. Four of the lines had unlisted numbers. The Heavy Breather always called on line two, so he had to have been an acquaintance of Jordan's. The one number that was listed was handled by an answering service in Costa Mesa.

The Heavy Breather had been calling now for three months. He never spoke. Sometimes he stayed on the line for a minute. Sometimes he hung up right away. He called at all hours, morning, afternoon, evening, night. Susannah was no stranger to obscene phone calls. She'd been getting them all her life. They did not make her afraid or even nervous. From men, she expected much worse.

She was certain she knew the Heavy Breather.

She was sitting at her desk in her private study on the second floor of her three-story home on fashionable Spyglass Hill, in fashionable Newport Beach, sipping a very fine French cognac and going over the numbers that held the key to her future. The television was on, a picture but no sound. The screen displayed the umpteenth replay of the shocking events of the afternoon on Balboa. An attractive anchorwoman from Channel 3 was speaking earnestly into the camera, no doubt providing an intense transition from the Los Angeles studio to a camera crew at the crime scene along Balboa Boulevard. The camera recorded roadblocks in the rain, a policeman in a yellow rain jacket, people standing on the sidewalks staring around at a place of death. In college, Susannah had thought about television as a career. Wear a snazzy trenchcoat and sexy cavalry boots. Barge around the video waves looking beautiful with your microphone thrust out archly like a weapon. Make a name for yourself. Marry a movie star or a producer. Dig for the truth. Win the Pulitzer for journalism. Replace Barbara Walters with "The Suzie Novak Show." Interview celebrities. It was too late now.

Umbrellas dotted the scene on Balboa. Safe in her house on Spyglass Hill, Susannah closed her eyes and pictured herself as television journalist Suzie Novak interviewing mercenary Roberto Devane on the pier in Balboa:

SUZIE: So, Colonel Devane, when did you conceive of the Balboa strategy?

DEVANE: Couple weeks before Christmas. Had me one of them visions.

SUZIE: Do you think of yourself as a religious man, Colonel?

DEVANE: Only when I win a battle. When I lose, I'm a goldang atheist.

SUZIE: What do you hope to achieve by having an innocent man shot?

DEVANE: No one is innocent, hon, especially preachers.

SUZIE: What did you pay your assassin for this hit?

DEVANE: Did you know, pretty lady, that the word *assassin* comes from the same word as hashish?

SUZIE: Colonel, you're being evasive. This is an important primary election. People want to know the truth.

DEVANE: Shit, sweetheart, people wouldn't know the truth if it slammed them in the left ear with a two-by-four. The first assassins—*hashshashin*, they called themselves— were a secret order of Moslems who whacked Christian Crusaders. Hell, it's still going on today, only now we call them terrorists and put 'em on TV.

SUZIE: How did you make contact with the Balboa killers?

DEVANE: Honey, ever' time you cross them legs, this old heart of mine skips two beats. You ever work the Palmer House, in Chicago?

Susannah opened her eyes to a deodorant commercial playing across the television screen. A checkbook lay open on the desk, showing a balance of $7,800 at the Newport Bank. Since the first of the month, she'd spent $15,400. She had to cut expenses again. She examined some printed check stubs from a manila folder labeled ASSETS and INCOME. Last month, the oil leases in north Texas had paid only $27,000. She'd made $5,198 off her stocks. A real estate investment trust had brought in $4,200. Last month, she'd made only $36,000 in income. Her worst month yet.

To make the $81,000 mortgage payment, Susannah would have to instruct her broker to sell off more stock. She leafed through some spreadsheets. At today's prices, she had $330,000 worth of AT&T, $68,000 worth of GM, $73,000 worth of Sumitomo, $1,590,000 in Ministry Beaches USA, and $156,000 in Kruger Gold Mines. The Ministry Beaches was worthless. In the safe downstairs, she had $16,000 in cash, a nest egg she hated to touch. There was $24,000 in the Capital Preservation account and another $18,000 in the T. Rowe Price Tax-Free Account. She had her diamonds, which might bring $20,000. The Jaguar was a classic. If she could get it to run for an hour without coughing, she might get $13,000 for it.

The mortgage payment of $81,000 haunted her. She sipped her brandy.

The condo in Aspen was up for sale. So was the time-share in the Bahamas. Nothing was moving.

She had to sell the house.

It was Jordan's house, the one he had bought to thumb his nose at the world. Jordan had grown up poor in Oklahoma, in a town called Guthrie. He had been a gunnery sergeant in North Africa during World War II and he knew the value of a gallon of gas. He had made money during both the Korean and Vietnam wars, brokering oil, and his plan in life was to buffer the discomforts of the world with carefully chosen possessions. "F. Scott Fitzgerald was right," Jordan had always said. "But his motto needed a twist. Living well is not only the best revenge—it's the *only* revenge."

So the house on the highest part of Spyglass Hill was a buffer. And the cars and the condos in Aspen and the Bahamas were buffers. And the apartment in Paris and the penthouse in London.

And herself. She, too, had been a buffer for Jordan. He had set her beauty up as a defense, paraded her at parties, used her sexuality as a distraction in business deals. "Dress the part, my dear. Dress the part and let the symbolism of dreams do its work. Dreams are all."

He had used her and she had used Jordan and now he was dead and she lived in a thirteen-room Newport Beach showplace where the automatic ice-maker refused to produce ice for her gin and tonic.

So she drank brandy. Only the brandy was running out.

She sat back and gazed around the room. It was her favorite spot in the thirteen-room house. One wall was lined with books. A second sported a cozy fireplace, useful in the chilly coastal winters. A third wall was hung with paintings by Degas and Monet and Mucha. The fourth wall was windows—floor-to-ceiling glass—with French doors opening in the center to her balcony.

The chair was a man's swivel chair, made of fine-grained leather. It tilted back, and when she was thinking, Susannah would play corporate executive and rest her heels on the edge of the desk. The desk was massive, a gift from her husband, who had bought it at an auction in New York City before he had met her.

Susannah closed the assets folder and opened one labeled HOUSE. She owed $5,285,000 to the TexAmerica Bank in Houston. When he bought the house, Jordan had dealt with a Texan named Larabee, negotiating a gentleman's loan with no down payment and thirty years at sixteen-and-a-quarter percent. The interest was a write off. Larabee had died last September and TexAmerica was having cash-flow problems because of a portfolio heavy with energy loans. Rigs stood idle. Texans cursed Arabs. To pay off the bank and leave some breathing room, she had listed the house on Spyglass Hill at $6,200,000. The appraiser sent by a local bank had brought in an absurdly low estimate of $5,100,000, not even enough to pay off TexAmerica.

In addition, there was Jordan's promissory note to Roberto Devane for a million dollars, another gentleman's agreement.

71

Susannah had seen the note in February, when Roberto had flashed it at her in one of his power moods. She had recognized Jordan's bold scrawled signature and the round number, $1,000,000. She had never seen a penny of the money, but Jordan told her in that week before he died that it had gone for expenses. At $81,000 a month, she was beginning to understand the reason for the loan.

Her lifestyle was bleeding her dry.

She was worried about TexAmerica. If it went under, it could block the sale of her house. Once she sold the house, her next move would be to negotiate with Devane. How about a dozen weekends, Roberto, in return for the note? She had no choice. She must deal with Devane, who held one of the keys to her future. The trick was to deal with him on her turf, where she had the leverage. Devania was his turf.

If only Jordan had refinanced before he'd died last December. If only he hadn't put so much capital into Ministry Beach, USA. If only. If only. In February, with her husband dead and her lonely grief under control, she'd consulted Harrison Wakefield about refinancing the house at a lower rate. Wakefield, an ex-banker, had examined her portfolio and told her it would be impossible. Her income was from passive instruments, rents and royalties. Jordan had left her with a monstrous debt load. This year, she would net $140,000 less in total income than last year. Jordan Maxwell had died broke and his widow was headed for the poorhouse.

Susannah had been born poor. She'd scrimped through a grubby childhood in South Chicago while envying the rich kids from Evanston and Kenilworth. She had hated looking rich but being poor. It made her feel ugly.

She was writing Julio a check for $1,500 when the phone rang. Line two calling. She answered it. Maybe it was the Heavy Breather again. Maybe he'd like to come over for a drink. Maybe the Heavy Breather was a closet millionaire with enough money to bail her out.

"Hello."

"Suze?"

"Roberto. How long it's been."

"You know how to cut a guy down, Suze."

She stared at her checkbook. "I was just thinking of you."

"Change your mind about my invite?"

She waited. Her brandy snifter was three-quarters empty. It was the next to last bottle of a case of cognac Jordan had imported from France. The bottle was half empty, or half full, depending on your point of view. She took a sip. The brandy problem reminded her that it was time to negotiate. Robert was holding the cards. "Not really."

"Too bad."

Susannah stretched, arms above her head. "I'm busy, Roberto. There's that party. I have a mixed-doubles match scheduled."

"Lady of leisure, Suze. What you always wanted."

"Yes."

Devane paused before going on. "Remember that old boy in the bank. Byron Foxcroft?"

Susannah stared at the television. A camera in the lobby of the hospital caught the lean figure of the policeman from Le Club. He was wearing a blue warm-up suit as he walked quickly past the lobby where a deputy sheriff stood guard. "Who could forget Byron Foxcroft?"

"Byron paid a visit to your lender, down Texas way."

Susannah felt goose bumps rise on her arms. "Oh?"

"Yeah. They had to sell off some paper. Byron picked up a portfolio at eighty cents on the dollar."

Susannah was sitting up straight now. "What are you saying?"

"One of the loans he bought was yours."

"This is not amusing, Roberto."

He chuckled. "Ten days, or a couple of weeks, your paper will be as snug as a bug in the portfolio at the Bank of Sierra Madre. Bankers are as slow as Arkansas molasses, but by July you'll be writing a check to them for Jordy's mortgage. How much is it running now?"

A toothpaste commercial filled the television screen.

Susannah felt sick to her stomach. "If your man bought the paper, you know the answer."

"Eighty grand or thereabouts?"

"You bastard, Roberto."

"Change your mind about that invitation? Lunch? A little rumpus?"

He wanted her on his turf. There, he gained power and she lost it. Merlin of Devania, magic in reverse. "Absolutely not."

"Because you're a friend of mine, an old friend from way back, I could chat old Byron up some. Ask him to ease off for a couple months. Maybe you and me and Byron could have lunch sometime. He cottons to pretty gals. Wear a low-cut blouse, lean over for him, the way you're so good at, Suze. That's what they do in New York and Hollywood. Get gussied up and have lunch and lean over for the corporate boys. Give them a whiff of paradise."

Now Susannah was afraid. "You're a bastard, Roberto."

"Come on out for lunch. You and me got things to talk over."

"You know how I hate to be manipulated."

"Suze, you're a filly that needs breaking once a week."

"Damn."

"It's an effort, Suze. But you're worth it."

If she lost confidence, her power would fade away. "Let's say I do show up tomorrow. How serious are you about talking with your little minion?"

"You scratch my back, I scratch yours. I could see my way open to talking to old Byron. Shit, I'm fifty-one years old and could die any minute. Just keel over on the parade ground with the whole Cadre watching."

Devane had been fifty-one for four years. With an effort, Susannah shifted her tone to sultry. "The last time I saw you, Roberto, the only death I witnessed was the metaphorical Little Death."

"Suze, talking with you makes me wish I'd killed four years of my life getting a college education from a passle of Ivy League pansies in tweed coats and button-down collars. When can I expect you?"

Susannah did some quick calculations. It was an hour over the mountain to Lake Elsinore, if there was no fog, and an hour back. Negotiating the tunnel took ten minutes, perhaps more. She could leave the house at nine, give Devane what he wanted, and be back in Newport by one-thirty or two. Once she faced him, she might be able to better her position. Somehow, she had to find a way to break his hold. "Shall we say ten?"

"Ten it is. I'll shut down the alarms and leave the door open."

Susannah finished the last of the brandy. She was thinking about her wardrobe for tomorrow—khaki slacks and the blue blouse, or perhaps the skirt with the buttons—Roberto liked buttons better than zippers. Buttons tore.

"Got a call coming in from overseas. Popeye to Olive Oil, over and out." Devane hung up.

Branko sat in a green plastic chair, taking notes as he asked the reverend a few questions. His right ankle was resting on his left knee. The television flickered above him, to his right. After the reverend, he had an appointment with Mrs. Williams—Sister Winona Lee—at Promontory Chapel. After Sister Winona Lee, he had a tentative meet with Lissa Cody. He still had to see Roscoe Smith. The long night stretched ahead, cosmic payment for his day off.

The reverend lay propped up in bed, talking easily, a real man of words. His eyes lit up in his tanned face and he used his hands to illustrate and underline and emphasize. The face was round and boyish. His shoulders were meaty underneath the blue hospital gown, adding to the impression of heaviness and gravity. The reverend, Branko decided, was carrying too much beef to be really healthy. His nose was red beneath the tan. Could be the sunlamp. Could be booze. His voice was a rich baritone that flirted with the rhythms of poetry and song. If he hadn't been a preacher, he could have sold cars on television. Or furniture. His hair was blond, not a trace of gray. Branko's information put the reverend at forty-five. His face could have passed for ten years younger.

"How's the leg?"

"It hurts. I have been given the requisite painkillers by an astute Nurse Greenfield. She hovers. I would go on my knees to escape pain."

"I know what you mean. Ever been shot before?"

"Heavens, no. I sprained my ankle when I was a youth. My worst injury was a charley horse when I was lifeguarding."

"When was that?"

"My college days. I worked on the beach at Santa Monica."

"Near the pier?"

"Yes. Those were lovely days. Perpetual summer. I felt if I could stay there, on that beach, I would never grow old."

"You've kept your tan."

The reverend beamed a smile at Branko, the teeth flashing like a chrome car bumper at high noon. "Around the church they call me Reverend Sunlamp. Not to my face, of course. It's an elementary joke, and I take it as such. There was backbiting amongst the followers of Jesus, I am sad to say. The curse of bureaucracy."

"Were you in the service, Reverend?"

"No. I escaped that and sometimes I'm sorry not to have shared those brave moments with the men of my generation." The reverend swung his head toward Branko with a look of profound sympathy for all mankind. The guy was a real ham. "And you, Sergeant? Were you in the service?"

"Yeah. I was Army. My grandparents spoke Serbo-Croatian around the house and that made me a linguist. I had a year at Monterrey, at the Army Language School. Three guys I knew in high school were killed in Vietnam. I spent time in Germany and had a year in the jungle."

"You killed other men, then?"

"When I had to." Branko made a note. *Rev. Wms., no military service.* "Who dislikes you enough to have you shot, Reverend?"

"The name that comes to mind is James Benton Sherwood."

"He's the congressman, right?"

Williams let out a deep sigh that sounded staged. "Yes, alas, for the past twenty-four years. This is his thirteenth try and if I were a superstitious man and not a Christian, I'd think that fate might take a hand in throwing him out of office. After all, we are fellow Republicans."

"Have you two met?"

"Only briefly, at party functions. He refused to accept my challenge for a debate on the issues. The man has barely campaigned. His excuse is that he is needed in Washington."

Branko nodded. "What about internal jealousies? Someone in your camp? Maybe in the church?"

The reverend answered with a frown. "Impossible and outrageous. Whatever gave you that idea?"

Branko tried going deeper. "How about your wife? You two getting along?"

A look of incomprehension crossed the reverend's wide tanned face. His eyes dimmed with feigned shock. "What do you mean?" The golden voice had lost its mellow tones.

"Just joking." He wrote *Wife?* and flipped to a new page in his notebook. "Give me a rundown on the shooting from your point of view."

"With all that's happened, I've forgotten to ask about the policemen. Officer Smith, I believe, and the other man."

"Whitson's okay. Officer Smith—he's my partner—is listed critical. He was pulling some overtime working security for you."

"I must admit I saw no need for security. Until today, that is. How wrong one can be." He turned away from Branko and stared out the window. Then he went through his version of the shooting. "It was very sudden. One moment we were joined in song, and the next moment I see this gunman aiming a pistol at me. I was petrified and I am not ashamed to admit it. He fired two or three times. At first, I thought he had missed. Then my leg collapsed and I felt this searing pain, this tearing, ripping pain. I cried out for God. I heard Mac White calling. It did not occur to me that Mac was wounded. But he had served his country as a soldier and knew what to do when under attack. People were screaming. There were more gunshots. Someone told me to stay down. Mac White was trying to shoot the gunman when he lost his life. It was all over almost before it started. I fainted. The next thing I knew, Winona Lee was at my side and I could hear screams of terror."

"Where was your wife during the shooting?"

"Near the bookstore. Yes. Near the entrance."

"Whose idea was the fire?"

"I beg your pardon?"

Branko looked up. "The book burning. Whose idea was it?"

"Is this relevant, Sergeant?"

"The fire distracted my officers. Did you know about it?"

"No. I did not."

"Who did?"

"The fire was started by members of CASS."

"Is CASS connected to your church?"

"Only in an informal way."

"What does that mean, 'informal'?"

"Members of CASS can be members of the Promontory worship effort. And vice versa."

"We have reports that your wife doused the magazines with lighter fluid. One report says it was Gulf barbecue starter. Two people say it was Texaco."

"Your reports must be wrong."

"You didn't see your wife start the fire with fluid from a red can?"

The reverend's hands were clenched on top of the blue blanket. "I saw nothing of the sort."

"When were you aware that people from CASS were going to burn books?"

"When they started burning."

"How did you react?"

"I remonstrated with them."

"Remember their names?"

"Yes. Bill Fiddler. And old Mrs. Quintus."

"First name of Mrs. Quintus?"

"Grace, I believe. Or Faith. I do not know her personally."

"How many in the congregation over at Promontory?"

"Our rolls number thirty-seven thousand souls. We can count on approximately ten thousand for a Sunday morning service."

"What does the chapel seat?"

"Ten thousand."

"Tell me about Mac White."

The reverend ran a hand across his brow. He had lost some of the ruddy color in his face. "Poor Mac. What would you like to know?"

"How long he'd worked for you. Where you met. What kind of guy he was."

"He'd worked for me since last autumn, when the decision was made that I run in the primary. He was brought in by Jordan Maxwell, who was a major force in my campaign decision. They had known each other in Oklahoma. As a person, Mac was steady, efficient, taciturn. He did not smoke and his drinking did not impinge on the lives of others. He had been a career soldier and ran his own private security business."

"Where's it located, do you know?"

"His offices were in Houston."

Branko wrote down the names *Maxwell* and *White*. "Did Mac White have a sense of what was going to happen out there today?"

"If he did, he did not see fit to inform me."

"How much of the day was he with you?"

"He was there mainly to help with the crowds. If there were crowds. He didn't hang around the office while I did my work, if that's what you mean."

"Have you got a campaign headquarters?"

"We were using offices in the Tower."

"That's the big six-story building, right? The one next to the big chapel?"

"Correct. We call it the Tower."

"Who's there besides you?"

"Harrison Wakefield. He masterminds my campaign. Douglas Cade. He's the financial wizard who keeps the bank off our necks. There's an office for the support people, the secretaries, and the phone marketeers and volunteers."

The list was growing. "How many people, overall, work for your campaign?"

"Sixteen salaried. A hundred or so volunteers."

Branko flipped back a couple of pages. "What about Mr. Bill Fiddler and Mrs. Quintus?"

"What about them?"

"Do they work as volunteers for the campaign?"

"They might have. Harrison Wakefield handles that, or he delegates it. I'm not awfully good with numbers."

"You were on the city council for how long?"

"Four years. I remember we achieved a nice cost-of-living increase for our police and firemen."

"I remember, too. Can you still work as a minister while you're campaigning?"

"I have resigned as minister of Promontory Chapel. My place has been admirably filled by a younger man, the Reverend Jasper

Gilroy. The church has donated office space. It is not against the law, Sergeant. James Sherwood has all the accrued benefits of public office. In effect, he campaigns with public funds raised from his tenured position."

"Where did you meet Jordan Maxwell?"

"Playing golf at the country club. He had in his collection some ancient scrolls from a trip to the Holy Land. I was most interested in them, for scholarly reasons. We became friends. He had been raised a Baptist, as had I. He had left the church, but he held no malice or ill feelings toward people and their religions. He was a very wealthy man, but extremely troubled in his spirit. It is that, I feel, that killed him. He was in his early fifties."

"What do you think killed him?"

"A troubled spirit."

"So you know Mrs. Maxwell?"

A pause. The reverend's jaw tightened. "Not well. We see each other at parties. She allows us to use her home for fund-raisers. She is quite generous, a charming person. It's in the spirit begun by her late husband."

Branko stood and rolled his shoulders to loosen them. "What about Ministry Beach?"

"I beg your pardon?"

"Jordan Maxwell was a big investor, wasn't he? In the Ministry Beach park?"

"Yes."

"How's the park going?"

"My wife is overseeing construction, as I have been too busy."

Branko moved to the door. "Thanks for the interview, Reverend. We've locked up security on your family. There's a man on your door, around the clock, and we've got officers stationed in the hospital."

"I sincerely hope your people come out of this intact, Sergeant. I regret terribly that they were hurt on my behalf."

"Thanks." Branko opened the door halfway, poised for his exit line. The reverend's hand was on the remote control for the television. "How does your wife feel about politics, Reverend?"

"What?"

Branko did not raise his voice as he repeated the question.

"How does your wife feel about your going into politics?"

"Winona Lee is behind me, Sergeant, one hundred and ten percent."

"Great feeling, isn't it?"

Before the reverend could answer, Branko opened the door and walked out.

CHAPTER SIX

A T the nurse's station, Branko learned they were bringing Roscoe up from Recovery. He would be arriving in five minutes. Branko waited outside the room for seven minutes. When his partner still hadn't arrived, Branko used the phone to call Candace Woodmere, the desk clerk who'd been on duty at the Inn of Cortez Thursday evening, when the Gordimers had checked in. There was no answer.

He was hanging up the phone when they wheeled Roscoe in on a gurney. Branko followed the gurney into the room. His partner's face was as gray as death. His eyes fluttered open. "Hey, Pancho." Branko felt a wave of helpless anger wash over him. The nurse, a sturdy woman with black hair, gave directions while the two Latino orderlies lifted Roscoe onto the bed in a practiced motion. Then they hooked him up to monitors. Branko counted five wires and four tubes. A green computer screen began its silent watch, the white electronic blip sliding across, left to right, looping back, left to right, metering out the pulse of life's heart beat. The orderlies finished and left the room, wheeling the gurney out with them.

The nurse wore a name tag that said BENO. "You're not family," she whispered.

"I'm his partner."

"Is there family?"

"Back East. He's got a girlfriend. They've been trying to call her."

"Three minutes," Nurse Beno said. "Then you're out of here, Sergeant."

Branko nodded and Nurse Beno left the room. Roscoe's eyes came open. A bandage covered his left shoulder. The other wounds were hidden by the blanket. "Did you nail his ass yet?"

"We're working on it. Can you tell me what went down?"

Roscoe tried a weak smile, but it faded. "How's Randy?"

"Okay."

"Don't tell Marcie. Screw up her weekend."

"She needs to know, man."

"What time is it?"

"Eight-thirty."

"What day?"

"Cut the crap. It's Friday."

"Whoo, man. I feel like shit warmed over."

"Don't talk. Save your strength."

"Want to tell you what I can, man." Roscoe ran a tongue over his lips. "Damn stuff they give you for pain . . . makes your head lolly-wolly. Okay. Three shooters. Two on the street, one in a window behind us. They timed it with that cookout fire. I was rapping with Mac White, the bodyguard, when this mother-fucker in a brown suit opened up. Small-caliber, with a silencer. I saw the reverend fall and then Mac. I didn't think he'd made me as a cop, but there were civilians all over. Just as I hollered who I was, I saw the big guy on the bike, a Honda I think it was. He took Randy Whitson out. I got one off at him, but he was quick, Pancho. Prick shot me cold. I was about to nail him when the shooter opened up from the—" Roscoe came out with a weak cough. The monitor above his head began its electrical beeping. "Shit."

Nurse Beno entered the room in a flurry of hospital efficiency. "You'll have to leave, Sergeant. We'll take it from here." A doctor appeared in the doorway behind her. Branko looked at his friend. Roscoe's eyes, full of fear, were staring at the ceiling as Branko walked out.

This was Winona Lee's Tower. She had built it to reach up to God. She had built it against the wishes of her husband and against the advice of architects. She'd wanted a tower of thirty stories, but had had to settle for six because of the building codes.

Her name for it was the Tower of Jezreel, from II Kings, 9:17, because she loved the line about the watchman. Her husband had disagreed, saying there were better verses, better-known names. Winona Lee knew her Bible. She was a Christian and she assumed that all Christians knew their Bible, too. That had been a bitter fight, over naming the Tower. The plaque quoting the scripture was downstairs, on the elevator. Winona Lee thought it was unnecessary. The fight had launched her into the dark garden.

Winona Lee loved to sit in her Tower and study the landscape and do her figuring and think about all the unsaved souls out there. Since her husband had decided to waste himself in politics, she had spent more time in her office, reading, praying, talking on the phone. Someone had to run things. The meetings never ceased. And she ran a better meeting than her husband, anyway.

The office was decorated in her favorite colors, yellow and purple. The carpet was purple. The drapes were bright yellow. Her chair was yellow taffeta, matching the yellow pens and pencils on the desk. The nameplate on the desk was yellow letters on a purple background. Her name, Winona Lee Williams, was etched on her wastebasket, on her Cross pen and pencil set, and on the front of her Bible.

She spent an hour studying the diagrams of the construction work at Ministry Beach. Douglas Cade, the fussbudget accountant, said they were running out of money. So did Jasper Gilroy, the assistant pastor. Jasper did not have the calling. Winona Lee had to bring her husband back to the pulpit. Revenues last year for Promontory Chapel had topped a hundred and fifty million. It was the end of May now, and collections had dropped off thirty percent. Mail-order was down. The phone banks were underused. Just this week three contractors had stopped work on Ministry Beach. Ministry Beach was Winona Lee's dream, a campground for Christians. If Terry did not come back to do God's work, the gross could drop to below a million this year and they would lose Ministry Beach to the developers. She had to get him out of politics. She had to bring him back.

Winona Lee had always loved numbers, ever since she was a little girl. She loved their feel and their exactitude. In her world, two and two was always and forever four. In her hope chest at the house on Singapore Street she had a collection of arithmetic tests saved from her school days and notebooks filled with columns of numbers. She could add and subtract in her head up to eight digits, nine. She knew the multiplication tables up to twenty-five. She scorned computer spreadsheets and hand calculators. The only concession she had made to the industrial revolution was an ancient Underwood adding machine inherited from her father, a shopkeeper in New Bedford, Massachusetts.

She sat in her chair in her office on the sixth floor of the Tower of Prayer, cranking the handle of Papa's machine. Her office was between her husband's and the one assigned to Douglas Cade. It was 9:01 and there was no one on the floor except the Mexican policeman assigned for her security. God was her security. She had no need of Mexican policemen.

Winona Lee bent low over the last column on the ledger and entered her total. Promontory Chapel had $543,000 in money-market instruments. Collections past due totaled $257,000. If her projections were accurate, the chapel would make an offer next week on the KRNG television satellite station in Kansas City. That would make number nine in the growing network of Promontory sister stations. The word would spread even farther.

But she had to get her husband back into the fold.

Winona Lee finished adding her columns and smiled a thin smile of subdued satisfaction. The totals on the machine checked precisely with the totals made by her careful pencil. For ledger work, Winona Lee used a yellow number-four lead, from Vendome Stationers. She kept the pencil sharp with Daddy's old crank sharpener. It had sat next to the cash register for thirty-seven years.

She tore the tape off the machine and closed the ledger and spent five minutes speaking with God. She prayed for Terry to heed the sign from the Fun Zone this afternoon. She prayed for her children to see the light. Any moment, and the world would end. Armageddon.

"What do you wish for me, O Lord?"

Winona Lee held her breath, but there was no answer. She turned and twisted in her chair, still with her hands clasped, but heard only the wind on the windows of the Tower of Jezreel. Shivers slipped up her spine.

Winona Lee opened her eyes and unclasped her hands and made two phone calls. The first was to her son's fraternity house in Berkeley. The young man who answered sounded under the influence. Winona Lee had no truck with alcohol or drugs. They were a weakness of the flesh that she did not tolerate. Terry Junior was not at home yet. There was a police car outside, for his protection. She scolded the young man briefly and instructed him to have her son return her call.

Her second call was to the home of James G. Sherwood, the Republican incumbent in Fiftieth District and her husband's opponent in the Tuesday primary. Mrs. Sherwood answered. Winona Lee knew Mrs. Sherwood. They served on a parents' committee that advised the school board. Mrs. Sherwood commiserated with her on the events of the afternoon. The congressman was not at home, Mrs. Sherwood continued, but would call Winona Lee at his earliest convenience. Winona Lee thanked Mrs. Sherwood and hung up.

At 9:08, the buzzer on her console rang. She answered. It was Hodgson, the new security man on the door downstairs. The policeman was here.

"He's late."

"Yes, Sister."

"Send him up. Have him wait in Mr. Cade's office."

"Yes, Sister."

Winona Lee made one last call, to her husband at Seaport General. The nurses put her through. But the line was busy.

Branko was waiting in an office on the sixth floor of the Tower. From here, he could see the parking lot and the Back Bay beyond. Across the bay were some lights, which he presumed to be his apartment complex, Rugby Arms. The shoulders and back of his warm-up were damp from his run in the rain, and he closed his eyes and did some deep breathing and whispered a mantra to himself: "You won't get sick and you won't catch cold and you won't get sick and . . ."

The office belonged to Douglas D. Cade, who was the treasurer for the reverend's campaign. His desk had three things on it—a telephone, a calendar with tear-off pages, and a photograph of a woman and two children. The woman was in her thirties. The two kids—a boy and a girl—looked to be ten and twelve, or maybe eleven and thirteen.

The family photograph was the only personal item in the room. An IBM computer sat on a desk against one wall. The computer keyboard was hidden in a sliding drawer beneath the desk and the drawer was padlocked. The central terminal of the computer had a lock on its left side. There were wires leading from the back of the computer to a jack in the wall. A large floor safe sat in the corner, next to the computer. The room seemed empty and sterile, a way station on the way from somewhere to somewhere else. Branko had an itch to try the drawers, to try to get a reading on this man Cade from their contents, the way a gypsy fortune-teller would read your tea leaves at a carnival.

He was standing at the window, looking out at the rain, when the door opened. Mrs. Williams stood there, her face in shadow.

"Sergeant Bronco?"

Close enough. "Yes, ma'am. Thanks for seeing me."

"Please sit down."

Moving like a jagged charge of electricity, she strode into the room and took the chair behind the desk. Her dress was dark blue, floor-length, with a nun's white collar at the neck. Now that he'd had a close up of the reverend, Branko decided that Mrs. Williams looked at least ten years older than her husband. Where he was chubby and boyish, she was lean and spare, all sharp edges. Her gray hair was cut short and worn close to her head, doing little to soften her features. Her face was unforgettable, drawn with the harsh lines and fierce planes of the religious zealot. Maybe the wife was the driving force; maybe she kept the machine going, the torch high.

She sat with her shoulders straight, head inclined backward, staring at Branko. Her eyes did not move as they looked down her nose, boring into him. Her presence was formidable. The nose was sharp and added to the shrewd intelligence of her eyes. Branko couldn't see what color the eyes were in this light. Gray, he guessed, gunmetal gray. "I've had a terrible day, Sergeant. My husband almost killed. My children in jeopardy. Could we proceed?"

Branko brought out the diagram of the crime scene and handed it to her. She spread it out on the desk and peered at it, then looked up at him, a question on her features.

"I know this is painful for you, Mrs. Wiliams."

"Sister, if you please."

"All right, Sister. Where were you when the shooting started?"

"Here." She pointed to a place in front of Fun Zone News. "My husband was here."

"Near the burning books?"

"Yes."

"Whose idea was that anyway? To burn the books?"

"It was a sign from God."

"Who got the signal?"

"It was sent to me."

"Any idea why?"

Her voice was sepulchral. "The armies will be joined and the world will end in fire. Revelations, Chapter sixteen. 'Go ye, and pour out the seven bowls of the wrath of God into the earth.'"

Branko paused. "Mr. Sternberg is suing you."

She laughed, a derisive snort. "It is too late for that. Seven angels, seven vials."

"How old is CASS?"

Her eyelids fluttered. "It was founded three years ago."

"You were the founder?"

"CASS began as a protest against filth, against all slime. Society is helpless. Flocks are attacked by wolves. . . ." Her eyes zoomed in on him. Her face was bright with zeal.

"How many members have you got?"

"Three hundred and eighty-one." Sister Winona Lee smiled. "Do you believe in the Word, Sergeant?"

He hadn't read the Bible in years. "Not lately." He pointed to the position of Shooter One. "Did you get a good look at the assailant?"

"A tool of Satan. He was medium height, of medium build, with black hair and heavily darkened glasses. His face was evil, the eyes—"

"Did you see his eyes?"

"Yellow," she said, "with a fire burning deep within."

He decided not to mention the dark glasses. "Just a couple more questions, Sister."

She nodded without speaking.

"This was a paid-for hit. People in this line of work start at five thousand and go as high as twenty. Who might want your husband dead?"

"The world waits for holy redemption. When Christ returns, all shall be well in the Garden."

Branko waited. "Your husband mentioned his opponent as a possibility."

"Congressman Sherwood?"

"That's right."

"My husband must have been hallucinating."

"Do you know the congressman?"

"We have met. I am acquainted with his wife."

"What about someone from the church who might hold a grudge?"

"My husband is well-liked, Sergeant, and well-loved. He has no enemies." Sister Winona Lee stood up. The interview was over. "Good night. There is much work to be done."

Branko held the door open for her. Her eyes gleamed like metal. They walked down the corridor to the elevator. Sister Winona Lee produced a key, which she used to call the elevator. A bell gave off a soft bong when the elevator arrived. The doors opened. Branko stepped into it.

"God be with you, Sergeant."

Branko held the door open, his hand on the rubber bumper. "How do you feel about your husband going into politics, Sister?"

For a moment, she did not answer. Her face was working now, showing revulsion, as if she had a bad taste in her mouth.

"The will of the Lord." Her hand went to her throat, a protective gesture.

Branko nodded and let the door go. "Good night, Sister."

She turned away without speaking, a swirl of floor-length dress. The door closed and the elevator started down.

Colonel Bobby Devane thought best over a glass of red wine. He'd been a beer-drinker until he hooked up with the Foreign Legion, *La Légion Étrangère*. The Legion had taught him about women, the joys of *vin ordinaire*, and how to curse in Legionnaire's pidgin French. When he'd said good-bye to soldiering and come back home to build his hacienda, he'd scouted out sites in wine-growing regions—expecially Northern California—all because of *vin ordinaire*. He'd had this dream of growing his own grapes at Cadre Vineyards, and he'd even found some sweet acreage in the hills outside Calistoga. In the end, however, he'd decided against the wine country because he knew the grapes would distract him from his major purpose in life.

Tonight, Devane had eaten supper with the Cadre in the barracks near his heliport. Now he was in his War Room drinking a Napa Cabernet and eating chocolate Hershey's Kisses. Kisses were his vice. He'd started on them in Africa, twenty years ago, where they'd been flown in on ice from the States. Each kiss was wrapped in foil. The taste never varied. Hershey's little foil-wrapped kisses helped stabilize a world in perpetual chaos.

He used a direct line to his broker in London to buy gold when the market opened on Monday. Today, gold had closed at $417.05. The news of the Balboa hit should jockey it up seven or eight dollars, maybe even ten or eleven. An ordinary shooting didn't put a ripple into the market. But when you jabbed a needle into the heart of politics, the shit hit the fan. Devane already had $52 million in gold, some of it buried here in the compound, the rest of it in Zurich and Singapore and Dallas and down in the vault at the bank of Sierra Monte. The problem with gold was its weight. You needed a half-track to haul the shit around.

His London broker was asleep, voice groggy with dreams. Tough titty. Devane placed his order, $5 million in gold bars, and told the broker to go back to sleep.

There were seven computer screens in the War Room at the center of his hacienda at Devania. They were arranged in a semi-circle on a wooden console shaped in a half-moon and they were all hooked to a mainframe IBM housed in a room around the corner. The computer room was air-conditioned because the goddamn machine ran hot. Devane hated air-conditioning. He'd spent half his life in the bush. Air-conditioning was for women and corporate assholes and government bureaucrats and sissies.

His favorite chair was here in the War Room. It was a wooden chair on wheels with a tilt back. Devane had inherited it from his granddaddy, Judge L.B. Devane, who'd spent his life before the bar in Odessa, Texas. The Judge had used a green seat cushion, but Devane liked the seat bare. Although Bobby Devane was fifty-five, he kept his weight down, by sweet Christ, and his ass trim. Have to watch them Hershey's Kisses.

He left the Zurich screen and wheeled the chair to the left so he could monitor what the cops were doing in Los Angeles. The manhunt for his shooter was on, the APBs rolling out to all peace officers in Southern California. The speedboat had been found in Huntington harbor. There had been no trace of the killers found after that. A composite of the drawing of the killer would be sent by FAX machine to all cooperating agencies. Devane's boys down in Sierra Monte had installed a FAX machine at the sheriff's office, with an override connection to Devane's computer in the War Room. He called the sheriff and talked to a deputy named Moseby and asked for a copy. Within thirty seconds, Devane's own FAX machine was printing a composite picture of the killer, fake mustache and all.

When the FAX machine finished, Devane opened a file folder labeled RUBIDOUX, B. and compared the photos he had to the police composite. The resemblances were faint. The eyes on the FAX composite were too far apart. The hair was too heavy. The artist had failed to capture the young-buck look, the confidence that came from a pair of hot young buck gonads. Devane inserted the FAX composite into the Rubidoux folder and ate another Hershey's kiss.

He scanned a computer printout on Benny Rubidoux. High school jock—football, track and field, a first in the hundred-yard dash in a state meet in Arkansas, a couple of second-place medals in the 440. Picked up for car stealing, suspended sentence. Picked up a month later for dope dealing, released for lack of evidence. Junior college to major in police science. Arrested by campus police for dope dealing. Reported to dean for having a girl in his room. Dropped out of school. Three days later an attempt was made on the dean's life with a handgun. Served time in Arizona, Illinois, Michigan. Known ties with underworld figures. Tried his hand at dope smuggling across the Texas border. Finally began killing people for a living, hiring out to Mafia guys as an independent contractor. He had used Benny Rubidoux on three jobs. The fucker was crazy. He loved danger and thought he was Billy the Kid. The man had served his purpose. Tonight, Devane had to decide when to eliminate him.

Sipping the Napa Valley Cabernet, Devane put in a call to his mole inside the Los Angeles Police Department. He kept a cop on retainer on the police forces in the larger major cities—Miami, Houston, Los Angeles, New York, San Diego, Chicago, Denver, San Francisco, Dallas, Washington. He paid them a thousand a month to keep him informed. The information they gave him was packed into computer files. Devane recorded each connection on cassette. The mole inside the LAPD was code-named Phoenix, a careful dude who never said more than he had to. Devane recorded him anyway.

"Crap Shoot, GHQ. Sign in."

"This is Phoenix."

"Anything on Operation Scumbag?" Devane asked.

"APBs are out," Phoenix said. "But no reports of any sightings. Have you made your decision?"

"Not yet. We still got time."

"I'm on hold here, waiting for your signal."

"I'll let you know."

After hanging up, Devane pressed a button on his remote-control device to start the videotape machine. The tape showed some footage of a bush campaign in the African pisspot kingdom of N'Gamba, Devane's last coup before calling it quits. There were shots of the headquarters tent, where Devane was going over attack strategy with Otto Bettleheim and Serge

Rankelovich. Rankelovich was dead, buried in a deep grave on the N'Gamba Plain, but Otto was here in Devania, acting as Devane's exec. The scene shifted to the attack, a night assault on the palace of the N'Gamban king. Devane watched for twenty minutes as his mercenaries laid down fields of fire, taking out the key guard posts. Then there was a big explosion as the police barracks blew. Enemy troops were falling, falling. There were shots of Devane directing the attack with a walkie-talkie. One shot showed him firing his M-16. He looked cool and professional. He remembered the photographer, a kid named Filsinger. He estimated accounting for seventeen of the enemy, personally, in three hours' time.

Watching himself on the screen, Devane thought he didn't look much older. The N'Gamban coup had taken place five years ago. No. Six years ago. He'd made $8 million dollars after paying off his soldiers. Final tally, 310 enemy dead, 38 wounded. One of Devane's mercenaries had been wounded, one dead. There was a final shot of the men celebrating around a campfire. There was no sound, but you could tell the men were singing. Good times, Devane thought. Good times.

They'd continued the celebration at a bar in Cairo, and then another bar in Rome, and then a bar in Paris, where Devane had tried without luck to find a woman named Clothilde, and then at a bar in London.

Clothilde was blond and sexy, like Suze Maxwell.

Good good times.

It was after ten when line eight buzzed and Devane answered. It was his broker in Los Angeles, Hector Mendoza. "You're late, Sergeant."

Hector Mendoza was a native of the Los Angeles barrio. He'd served with Devane in Vietnam. After the Army, Hector had worked as an enforcer for the mobsters in Los Angeles and Reno. He'd graduated from enforcer to connector. His job now was putting clients in touch with hit men. His nickname was Hector the Connector. He still spoke with a barrio lilt. "He is there, *mi colonel.*"

"There" meant Cosmo's Cosmos, a night spot on La Cienega. The clientele was mostly Los Angeles hoods and their women.

At Cosmo's you could dance and drink. You could get some steam or a massage. And after your steam you could waltz into a gambling parlor wearing only your robe and a pair of Korean flip-flops and mix with Hollywood stars and tourists in evening dress. Cosmo's was a favorite spot of Benny Rubidoux.

"Scumbag comes to roost."

"*Si.* Correcto."

"Did he get the hook out?"

"*Si, mi colonel.*"

Devane chuckled. "Is he alone?"

"A woman is with him. A *puta* with sunburned arms and hair the color of corn."

"You were always a poet, Sergeant."

"*Muchas gracias, mi colonel.*"

"How'd you like to make fifteen grand?"

Hector the Connector paused before answering. Fifteen thousand was the amount he was supposed to deliver to Rubidoux. "I am no longer in that business, *mi colonel.*"

"Okay by me, Sergeant. Are you still in the connecting business?"

"Yes."

"Then here's what I want you to do. . . ."

Devane gave Hector his assignment. He'd always been a solid soldier. No imagination, but a lot of stick-to-it and brute strength. When he was finished, he had Hector repeat it back. Devane made a couple of corrections and Hector said he understood. Devane signed off.

Devane hung up the phone, left the War Room, and walked through the big living room to his kitchen. The troop on kitchen patrol had policed the area, and the room was filled with the smell of coffee, fresh-brewed. Devane pulled a clean mug off his wall rack. The rack held a hundred and two mugs, all breakable, souvenirs from Devane's life as a soldier of fortune. They came from Africa and Central America and Asia and Europe and Texas and Alabama and Utah and Arizona. They symbolized the fragility, the frailty of human culture. They also symbolized man's resilience, his ability to endure. And they symbolized simple pleasure.

He chose a brown mug from a bazaar in Nairobi. He remembered that time in Nairobi because he'd shacked up with a Swedish girl with long forever legs and a set of tits right out of *Playboy*. They'd spent two days in bed, had breakfast, and gone back to bed for another day. He could remember her legs but not her name.

As he poured, he examined the long scar running along his right hand from the index finger across the big vein and vanishing under the sleeve of his fatigue blouse. He'd come close to losing his hand on that one. Devane walked to the fridge, an oversized GE, opened the door, and pulled out the can of Pet Milk. He measured out his normal portion, watching it swirl into the coffee. Since building the hacienda, he'd tried regular milk, but he always came back to Pet for his coffee. Field habits were hard to break. He was closing the door to the GE when the red light lit up on line three of his kitchen phone. Devane took a sip of coffee before answering.

It was Otto, Devane's exec. "Hazzard has made a discovery, Colonel."

"Christ, can't you handle it?"

"He insists on speaking with you."

"Send him over."

"Right away, Colonel."

Devane reached into a drawer and pulled out his Bren Ten Special Forces automatic. It was a 10-mm piece, weight just over two pounds, silvered, with a four-inch barrel. He'd carried it ever since Vietnam. The weapon was always loaded, eleven rounds. He strapped on a shoulder holster. Around his men, Devane went armed.

He waited in a chair on his veranda in the heavy darkness, away from the rectangle of light framed by the front door. The rain fell in a fine drizzle. Lights burned in the barracks building across the way. The sound of music from a radio floated on the air. The fog would get thicker now that the rain was stopping. In the valley below, it would be like pea soup. He still wanted to put in a polo field between the hacienda and the helicopter pad. He liked horses, and polo ponies were the best horses he'd ever ridden. Devane was a good rider and he missed it.

He heard bootsteps on gravel and Hazzard called from the darkness. "Colonel Devane? It's Hazzard. Permission to approach?" Hazzard only said "sir" when he had to.

"Permission granted."

Hazzard came onto the veranda, rain dripping from his poncho, and delivered a sloppy salute. He was a lean kid in his mid-twenties, his face pock-marked from adolescent acne, with cold eyes, a prison record, and a perpetual sneer. He'd served time for fire-bombing an abortion clinic in San Francisco. A real trouble-maker, he worked as a motel clerk in Havasu City during the week. His family was back in Missouri, and he spoke with a redneck accent. He was a gold brick on labor detail, spending too much time smoking in the latrine.

"Well, what the hell is it, Hazzard?"

"A breach in the perimeter."

"A breach in the perimeter, *sir*."

"Sorry." Hazzard's voice was sassy, cool. "I meant a breach in the perimeter, sir."

Devane knew what that meant. "Can you be specific, soldier?"

"A tunnel, I think. It looks like an old abandoned mine shaft. I followed it part way. Seems to leave some rocks up near the national forest and head right under the compound."

"Who else knows about it, Hazzard?"

"Only the exec. And me."

Devane shoved the chair back as he got to his feet. The wounded leg was bothering him and he did not look forward to getting out in the rain. "Wait here. We'll reconnoiter."

"Yes, sir!"

Devane went back into the house. In the War Room, he shut down the alarm mechanism on the main gate. Then he walked to the library for his infrared light. With it, Devane could see but could not be seen from the barracks. He unlocked his gun case and brought out an M-16 automatic. He ejected the clip of live shells and shoved in an empty clip. Then he pulled on a green jacket with a hood and screwed a silencer onto the muzzle of his Bren Ten. Around his waist he strapped a webbed belt that held a canteen and an Army shovel with a folding spade.

He walked through the house to the front door, where he handed the M-16 to Hazzard along with the infrared flashlight. Then he locked the door. The two men set off into the dark, boots on packed earth, toward the main gate. Once there, Devane opened the lock with a key from his key ring. He and Hazzard passed through and Devane relocked the gate. The main road was gravel. There would be no footprints.

They hiked up the road toward the rocks. Ahead, a mile away, was the Cleveland National Forest, which was mostly not forest at all but rocks and horned lizards and California fire ants. Still, it had its own beauty, especially in the spring. In the fall, the sonofabitch was a tinderbox ready to catch fire. The cloud cover tonight was heavy, blocking out the moon and stars. The infrared light showed the ground in front of them for about six steps.

"There was a clearing," Hazzard said. "And what looked like tire treads."

"Goddamn," Devane said.

When they came to the rocks, Devane felt a great sadness, a heavy melancholy like a sack of wet sand on his neck and shoulders. He asked Hazzard to show him what he'd discovered earlier. Hazzard found the camera that had been built into the rock. It was covered with a mottled-gray rock-colored plastic that failed to change color when it was wet. Hazzard was excited as he showed Devane the tunnel entrance. The kid weighed a hundred and ninety. He was too heavy to drag around as dead weight.

"Good work, soldier. You've earned yourself a bonus."

"I think we should follow the tunnel on down. See where it goes."

Devane played the light over the entrance in the rocks. He could see steps going down. "Not yet." He handed Hazzard the light. "Show me where the vehicles were parked."

"Over here." Hazzard waggled the light and threaded his way through the rocks. Devane's boot sank an inch into the soft ground. If he could find the right spot, it would make for easy digging. His hand touched a rock; it was slick with moisture.

"Right here, Colonel. There's enough room, I figure, for three vehicles. Maybe four. From here, they can shinny up those rocks and look right down on the compound."

"Good work. Now let's look at that tunnel."

They retraced their steps. Devane told Hazzard to lead and the soldier started down. He stopped at the bottom and played the light around the walls. His voice echoed in the darkness.

"This is something, isn't it?"

"Yeah. You did great, Hazzard. What's that noise?"

"What noise?"

"Up ahead, in the tunnel." Devane pointed with his left hand and pulled the Bren Ten out with his right. Hazzard angled the light into the tunnel, then followed with the muzzle of the unloaded M-16.

At that moment, Colonel Robert Emory Devane executed him by shoving the silencer against the back of his head, beneath his right ear, and pulling the trigger. There was a muffled pop. The pistol was angled up toward the top of Hazzard's skull and the round took half his head off. The M-16 clattered to the ground. Devane reholstered his Bren Ten and stood the M-16 against a rock. He took one of Hazzard's boots in each hand and counted his steps as he dragged the body into a narrow side tunnel. Visibility was terrible and he had to count his steps, stop, shine the light, and start over again. He stopped at a dozen steps. The infrared light revealed several mounds of earth, causing him to think of all the troops he'd buried, down through the years.

Devane felt his eyes go as moist as a schoolgirl's as he stripped off Hazzard's uniform. He unlaced the boots and pulled off the socks. He unbuckled the belt, then unzipped the fly. Devane had undressed dead soldiers before. You lifted and hauled, lifted and hauled. When Hazzard was buck naked, Devane propped him up against the wall. While the body sat there, Devane went to his knees, where he unhooked the shovel from his belt and adjusted the head to ninety degrees. Then, using the shovel as a short-handled hoe, Devane scraped out a shallow grave. It took him fifteen minutes to chop through the loose rock and shale. The light was bad, so he kept feeling with his hands, measuring with the length of his arm. His knees ached and the leg wound was burning and he remembered his *first* years in the Army as a dogface EM. Those were good years. When he was down to elbow-depth, he stopped digging, jabbed the blade of the shovel into the dirt, and rolled Hazzard into the grave. His head pointed north by northwest.

Devane was sweating hard by the time he put the last shovelful of dirt in place. Hazzard's mound was bigger than the other mounds. For now, it would do. It was better down here, darker.

He folded Hazzard's uniform up into a makeshift pack around the paratrooper boots and slung it over his shoulder. He stumbled once going up the stairs and his bad leg felt weak. Before heading back to the hacienda, he paused for thirty seconds to mutter a soldier's prayer.

When he reached the hacienda, he got his exec on the line.

"Hazzard's on special assignment in La-La Land. He'll be gone a week. Find someone to take over his watch. And notify those people at his motel."

"Yes, Colonel. At once."

Devane bolted his front door, stripped off his wet garments, put on slippers and a robe, and poured himself a glass of red wine. He toasted the wall.

Tough titty, kid.

No one fucks with the escape tunnel of Bobby Devane.

No one.

CHAPTER SEVEN

As he approached the doors leading outside, Branko felt the steady throb of a heavy bass instrument, magnified by some kind of powerful electronic sound propulsion gear. A plaque on the Tower elevator read:

And there stood a watchman on the tower in Jezreel, and he spied the company of Jehu as he came, and said, "I see a company." And Joram said, "Take an horseman, and send to meet them, and let him say, Is it peace?"

A security guard in a three-piece suit stepped out of the shadows. "Hey, Sergeant. She said you were coming down."

"What's the music?" Branko asked.

"That's the Archangels," the guard said. "Tuning up for Sunday."

A horn cut in above the bass, high and jagged, carrying a strange, ugly melody.

"That's Roy Prospero. He's the leader. Great lip. Want to check it out?"

Branko had never been inside the Great Cathedral. "Why not?"

They came to the end of the corridor. To the left was the main door that led to the parking lot. The door was closed and a second security guard with a tanned face and a build like a linebacker's lounged in a brown plastic chair. The heavy, weighted sound was coming from the right, where, a hundred feet away, there was a door leading into the big glass cathedral that had made Promontory Chapel famous. The door leading inside was arched and twenty feet tall. One half was open, beckoning.

"The Archangels?" Branko asked.

"Yeah. They got their own style. Some folks call it Jesus Rock."

The arched door was wide enough for two big semi trucks to pass through side by side. The music started to scream, to wail in anguish as they stepped through into the Great Cathedral. Branko saw a panel to his left. It had ten buttons on it, like a telephone console. He assumed it was a locking device for the door.

The guard led the way. The music swept around the high ceilinged room in wild and jagged menace. The Archangels were ranged along the center stage, near a pulpit draped with a shining gold cloth. The metal gleamed in the strobes.

"What do you think?" the guard asked loudly.

"It's like a disco," Branko said. "Without the dancers."

"They make it jump, all right. They surely do."

The main cathedral sat at least ten thousand people. Seats rising up from the floor to at least four stories were arranged in seven pie-shaped wedges facing a wide curved stage, and the

99

ceiling soared above it all. The night obliged just then by washing the building in a yellow-green moonlight. The clouds parted as if by a divine hand and the moon beamed straight through the glass panes and Branko was reminded of movies from his childhood. The Archangels pounded away at their instruments. Everything sounded electronic. The trumpet reached a climax as the moon became brighter, more silvery. The bass came in heavily, with some help from an electric guitar and a keyboard instrument on narrow stilts that looked like a neon marimba-xylophone.

"What's the song?" Branko asked.

"It's called 'The Healer Comes.'"

Branko suppressed a smile. "Lots of energy."

"You a praying man, Sergeant?"

"Sometimes."

The trumpet player finished on a high-note after a flourish and ended the song with a nod of his head and a hip wriggle that was reminiscent of the late Elvis Presley.

"That Roy Prospero," the guard said. "What a musician."

Prospero was a skinny kid in his mid-twenties. He had stringy black hair that needed a trim and a shampoo, and he was wearing a black shirt with three buttons undone and a pair of white pants pegged at the bottom and flared out at the thighs, cavalry officer style. The bandleader glanced over at Branko and the guard but did not acknowledge their presence as he turned back for a musical huddle with his Archangels.

The guard pointed to a king-sized television apparatus to the left of the pulpit. "That's the Jumbatron. It throws God's word all the way to a GBN satellite. The satellite takes the word to Africa, Asia, the whole blessed world!"

"Terrific." Branko turned and headed out of the Great Cathedral. "What do they do in the summer, when the sun's out?"

"Automatic shades," the guard said, grinning at the marvels of technology. "They roll down like a greenhouse cover."

As they approached the outer door, an arched twin to the one leading into the cathedral, the linebacker left his chair and punched some buttons on another ten-button console. There was a clicking sound as the locks opened. The guard pressed another button and one side of the door swung open. In the parking lot, Branko saw a black-and-white from the Newport Beach station.

"Thanks for the tour."

"Anytime, Sergeant. Anytime. Got to stay in good with the local po-lice."

"What's GBN?" Branko asked.

The guard looked offended. "Gospel Broadcasting Network. It was founded by Pastor Clyde, in Lincoln, Nebraska."

Branko walked out into the night and heard the big door swing shut behind him. The air smelled freshly washed by the rain; blue-green lights on tall lampposts were reflected off puddles on the asphalt. Fog rolled up from the water. Half a dozen cars were parked in reserved slots next to the Tower. Each car had a bumper sticker that read PASTOR CLYDE IN '88. Branko kept walking. When he reached the patrol car, he turned to stare up at the Tower. He hadn't hit it off with Sister Winona Lee. He still had to interview Douglas Cade and the campaign manager, Wakefield. Maybe he could catch them in their offices this weekend.

He spent a couple of minutes checking signals with Officer Joe Romero in the black-and-white. Things were buzzing at the station. Officer Jamie Duncan had been assigned to guard the Williams girl, Delia Sue. "You seen that kid, Sarge?"

"Just a glimpse."

"My kid did her hair punker, I'd lock her out of the house."

"Disaffected, they call it."

"Yeah. I'd show her some of that, too."

Branko said good night to Romero and headed for his car.

At the top of the hill overlooking Promontory Chapel, he stopped the Volvo and got out. From where he stood he was almost level with the sixth floor of the Tower, where his interview with Mrs. Williams had taken place. He had a good view of the parking lot and the huge sloped roof of the glass cathedral. He counted seventeen cars in the parking lot down below, including the unit from the station. The lower parking lot was huge and could probably take two thousand cars. And the upper parking lot, where he now sat, could handle five thousand more.

There were more trees up here, some kind of coastal scrub, and over to the west, if you looked along the beach, there was a new line of eucalyptus, the favorite tree of the missionaries who had come to the area two centuries ago.

Branko fought back a sneeze as he climbed behind the wheel. His apartment was across the bay and he needed a shower and a change of clothes, so he headed out of the parking lot toward Jamboree. There were too many loose ends and blind alleys and everyone you talked to asked you your opinion because, down deep, they were dying to tell you theirs. Okay, what about some what-ifs on Mrs. Williams? What if she'd hired a shooter to whack her husband, scare him out of politics? What if they caught her paying off the shooter, thirty pieces of silver? What if she appeared in court wearing her floor-length dress with the round white collar and told the judge she'd hired the hit man for God.

What if?

He pulled into his parking garage next to the red Porsche, which belonged to Mr. Wonderful in 311. Branko lived across the courtyard from Mr. W., in 322. Sometimes they met in the Jacuzzi. Mr. Wonderful was in his mid-twenties, dark, with razor-cut hair and good shoulders and a Pepsodent smile that looked phony to Branko. Mr. Wonderful made Branko feel old.

The girls with their clean staccato clicks of high heels on the stone pavers of the courtyard on their way to 311 were snazzy, sharp, and foxy, and left a faint drift of perfume on the air. They stood straight and young and model-wispy while they rang Mr. Wonderful's buzzer. They went in. All was silence. Around midnight, they came out, started their cars, and left a bloom of silvery exhaust as they drove away.

Branko wished Mr. Wonderful would move his irresistible sex appeal to another complex.

The Porsche was sitting in its slot, gleaming snappily. There was a party going on two doors down, in 313. A light burned in 311, Mr. Wonderful's love nest. Branko unlocked his door and went inside. He'd run a load of dishes that morning and now the GE Super-Scrubber needed unloading. Save that for later. He plucked a Miller's out of the fridge and took it to the bathroom, where he stripped and showered. Images of Roscoe Smith and the wounded reverend and Sister Winona Lee Williams collided in his brain. A headache pulsed behind his right eye.

Wrapped in a terry-cloth robe, he sat in the living room in his bionic chair and rolled backward until his spine was parallel with the floor. "Ahhh!" he grunted.

The bionic chair was his favorite piece of furniture. It had no legs and was constructed in a soft L-shape that fit the curves of the human spine. There was a neck support that helped you relax and a matching ottoman that looked like a cross between a puffed-up peanut and a Walt Disney hippopotamus. When you sat in the chair your butt and legs were only six inches from the carpet. With a kick, you could roll the chair backward, so that the back of the chair rested on the floor. If you hung your legs over the front edge of the chair and closed your eyes and did your mantra, your muscles relaxed like magic.

Three minutes in the bionic chair made his headache better. He called the station and spoke to Tommy Osterhaus about Roscoe's condition and about his interview with Winona Lee Williams. Tommy said the chief's plane had been grounded in Sacramento.

"I'm bushed. I've got one more interview and then I'm heading for the corral."

"Task Force tomorrow," Tommy said. "You're on deck."

"Terrific."

"See you tomorrow."

"Yo."

Branko hung up and called the hospital. Roscoe Smith was resting but still on the critical list. Randy Whitson was sleeping. The reverend was on the phone, had been on the phone for an hour or more. The nurse thought it was long distance. He called Lissa Cody at the *Orange County Tribune*. She wasn't there, but she had left a message that she would meet him at Coco's Restaurant in Woodbridge at ten-thirty. Woodbridge was in peaceful Irvine, fifteen minutes inland. The time was 10:16 and he would be late. He left the television on while he went to the bedroom for clean clothes. "Miami Vice" was on. Watching it always made Branko smile. The hero, a movie-cop, needed a shave and a tailor who understood the proportions of the male body.

He could hear pop-pop movie shooting from the cop show as he rummaged in his dresser for clean socks. The bed was made, Branko style. It was a queen-sized bed and Branko always slept on the right, the side nearest the bathroom. When he got out of bed, he rolled over and flipped the covers up before climbing out. Thus, with the covers on one side straightened and approaching order, he could make his side more quickly. A tug here, a tug there, and the bed was made, Branko style. His ex-wife Karen had complained. His last real date, back in November, had made fun of his method. But when you lived alone, you developed a system. And that system kept you neatened up. And being neatened up could keep you from going crazy.

Maybe.

He pulled on clean trousers, a white shirt with flap pockets, fresh socks, and old tennis shoes. He strapped on his shoulder holster, checked the load in his .357, and shoved it in. He looked at himself in the mirror and tried a smile. He shook his head. Every day, he looked more like his dad, Jack Branko, back in Wisconsin. The same lines, the same weary look. It was time for another phone call to the folks. There was a photograph of his parents, Jack and Nicki, on the dresser across from the bed. They were smiling at the camera. He put on a khaki jacket, to cover the shoulder holster, and went out. He was about to turn off the set when Linda Calderon, her face glowing with excitement, came on with a Channel 3 update.

"Channel Three News has just learned of some startling new developments in the shooting this afternoon in Newport Beach, at the Balboa Fun Zone. Please tune in at eleven for a complete report."

Hot zing. The journalists were baiting the hook.

The party in 313 was still going strong, the pulse of the music heavy and jungle-potent on the night air. The light was off at Mr. Wonderful's, denoting whoopee in progress. Branko smelled a steak barbecuing. His stomach growled. Trees dripped pearly raindrops on him as he walked across the wet stones of the courtyard to his car.

The fog thickened as he came off Jamboree onto the San Diego Freeway. Headlights from southbound traffic probed the fog. Branko left the freeway at Culver. Coco's burned like a traveler's beacon in the middle of the planned development of Wood-bridge, near the man-made lake.

Lissa Cody was sitting at a table against the windows when Branko came through the door. She looked up without smiling and tilted her head in acknowledgment. No cheery wave from this lady. She was still wearing the khaki suit and the soft white blouse. There was a half full cup of coffee in front of her and a reporter's tablet off to the right. The page was also half full. Under the bandage on her cheek, at the edge, he saw the blue of a bad bruise.

She did not put down her ballpoint. "I was afraid you wouldn't get my message."

"I got it. Thanks." He slid in across from her. The seat of the booth had a rounded-out place, home of thousands of California bottoms, and for a moment there, watching Lissa Cody turn from greeting him to jotting a quick note, he wondered how it would have been to be a writer instead of a cop. "How's your face?"

She touched the bandage on her cheek. "It hurts. They gave me some pills for the pain and the bruising, but they made me drowsy. How's your wounded detective?"

Branko shook his head. "Roscoe was hit pretty bad. Took three slugs, one near the heart. Dangerous territory."

"The way you talk makes him seem like more than another officer."

"Roscoe's my buddy first. Partner second."

She put the ballpoint down. "Doesn't it make you furious?"

Branko nodded. His voice was tight with emotion. "I could kill all three of them on the spot."

"But you're a policeman and that's against the law."

"Right. But it doesn't stamp out the feelings."

The waitress came up and Branko ordered scrambled eggs and sausage, coffee, and whole wheat toast. For his headache, he ordered a beer. Lissa ordered eggs and toast, but no meat. The waitress walked away toward the kitchen.

"I didn't think I could eat," Lissa said, "after what's happened. But I'm hungry."

"Me, neither. I learned to eat in the Army. When there was food, you chucked it down."

"When was that?"

"Late sixties, early seventies. After the Army, I had a partner on the police force in L.A. who could see a stabbing or a gunshot death, write out his report, and eat a full meal topped off with two desserts. On my first few murder cases, even after the Army, I lost my lunch."

"But you got used to it."

He shook his head. "You never really get used to it. You just learn to eat anyway."

"When were you in Los Angeles?"

"A dozen years ago, when I first emigrated to California."

"How long have you been in Newport Beach?"

"This is my ninth year."

"Have you always been a policeman?"

"Is this for the record?"

Lissa Cody blushed. "Sorry. It's my inquisitive nature. I am shy around people, strangers especially, and I protect myself by asking questions."

"You weren't shy this afternoon, smacking the perp."

"Reflex." She sipped her coffee. "That's a funny word, isn't it? Perp."

"Cop talk."

The waitress came with his beer. "Sure you don't want something?" he asked Lissa.

"A glass of white wine would be nice."

"We have Chablis and Chardonnay," the waitress said.

Lissa ordered Chardonnay and the waitress walked off. Branko knew they were going to talk about the case, go over the details again, but he wanted to let it rest a minute. Lissa Cody was attractive, with a pretty face, a sensitive mouth, and a nice trim figure. He wondered if she was seeing someone. "I keep thinking we've met somewhere."

"At a party," Lissa said. "Two years ago, in October. The party was in Orange, at the home of a Chapman English professor. You were with a very attractive brunette."

"My ex."

"Oh? For how long?"

"Has she been my ex?"

"Yes."

Branko sipped his beer before answering. "Thirteen months."

"How have you been coping?"

"I don't miss the arguments. Karen's a good in-fighter."

Lissa smiled, showing even white teeth. "Sometimes a fight clears the air."

He indicated the ring on her wedding finger. "You married?"

She shook her head, but before she could answer, the waitress returned with their food and Lissa's wine. They waited while the waitress bustled around, rearranging plates and silverware and the salt and pepper. Branko asked for another beer. She set the ketchup bottle down with a thump. Branko dug into his food. The beer helped him relax, his headache receding, the edge of tension easing off. He was aware of Lissa Cody across from him, the click of silverware on Coco's china, her slender boned hands and wrists. She stopped eating for a sip of wine and looked him in the eye.

"I'm divorced, myself."

"Oh? How long?"

"It was final in December. I wear the ring as . . . protection."

"How are *you* coping?"

"In retrospect, I think it would have been better if we had fought. I'm surprised to find that I do like living alone. It's my mess if I make a mess. It's my time to do with as I please. I don't watch the clock, waiting for him. And I've started writing a book."

"What kind of book?"

"It's about politics."

"Local or national?"

"It's about killing and fatherhood and image and how it all mixes to form a candidate."

"Did you interview Reverend Williams?"

"Yes. And Congressman Sherwood. And poor Lonnie Chevron, the courageous Democrat from the Fiftieth District. I couldn't reach Senator O'Brien."

"What's Sherwood like?"

"Brittle."

"Brittle?"

"Yes. He's thin and bald, in his late fifties. He pastes this smile on his face while he talks, but if you look into his eyes you see no matching smile there. He won some medals in Korea, fighting the Communists, so he has combat going for him. He's a grandfather. In contrast, the pudgy reverend has no military service. He's a father, has a wife, two kids, one Mercedes, and a pleasant little hideaway in Palm Desert." Lissa sipped her wine. "That's what my theory's about."

Branko narrowed his eyes. "Hideaways?"

"No, Sergeant. Combat. War records. Reproducing the race and defending the boundaries of the clan-kingdom or the nation-state, whichever is larger. The politician as Father-Killer."

"Good title. I see it on the racks at the grocery stores already."

"It's an offshoot of the tribal-king theory, with some adjuncts from Jung and Joseph Campbell and Frazier. He did a book on vegetation myths. Do you read, Sergeant?"

Branko remembered the names from a college course in myth and literature at Madison more than twenty years ago. He decided not to push it. "Paperbacks."

Lissa plunged on. "In ancient kingdoms, the king could only be king if he had strength. There were two measures of strength. The first was defending the kingdom's boundaries against outsiders. The second was producing children—preferably sons—princes and little kinglets. If you read the Arthurian legends, it's mostly battles, jousts, killing dragons, slaying your brother knight because he wore the wrong suit of armor. Young Arthur became king because he had the strength to pull the sword from the stone."

"That's myth," Branko said. "Myth lost in mist."

"The reverend's running on the shirttails of the Christ myth. I've interviewed Christians who think Christ is coming next week. Do you know what the reverend's salary was last year?"

"A hundred grand."

"Two-fifty."

"A quarter of a million?"

"Yes. Not counting perks. His organization grossed over a hundred million dollars."

Branko drank some beer. "I'm in the wrong business."

"No. I don't think so."

"Huh?"

"You're in the right business."

"How do you know?"

Instead of answering, Lissa reached into her purse and pulled out a roll of film. "Josh took these this afternoon in the restaurant at the Inn. He's a girl-watcher, so the pictures won't be of the shooter, but I thought we might get some background stuff, faces, hairdos, telltale clues, that sort of thing."

Branko reached for the film. "I saw what was left of the camera at the crime scene. It was a mess."

"He loaded a fresh roll right before the shooting." Lissa closed her fingers over it. "Our deal was, Sergeant, that I get first crack at what you know. Rumor around the department, cop scuttlebutt, that sort of thing."

"Not to print."

"No. Not until you say to. Look, I'm a slow writer. I have to think about things. Most of the time, I don't have enough think-time. My stories feel . . . truncated. I'm a perfectionist and I hate that. This is a very hot story and I need the lead time. You can give me it." She opened her hand. The film sat there. "How about it?"

He wanted the film. "Okay." He stood up. "Let me call the station, see if there's someone there who can develop this stuff."

She nodded, and he walked through the restaurant to the phone. Tommy Osterhaus was on another line, but the dispatcher said the darkroom was closed and the technicians gone. Branko hung up and walked back to Lissa Cody with the news.

She reached for her purse and took out a ten. "No problem. I was a photographer in high school. There's a makeshift darkroom in my spare bedroom. If you'll follow me, Sergeant, I can have these developed by midnight."

Branko handed her six dollars, for his half of the check. Lissa put down twelve dollars, the tab including tip, and they walked out into the fog.

Lissa Cody lived across the lake from Coco's in a two-story Woodbridge condo overlooking the water. Southern California was crowded and Woodbridge Village had been laid out with green spaces and swimming pools and curved streets that gave the illusion of more space. The man-made lake added to the illusion. It was only deep enough for ducks and canoes, but the body of water took your mind off the fact that you were in a desert. From the living room window, Branko looked across the lake to the shopping center, lit up against the fog. Irvine license plates read "Just Another Day in Paradise."

The condo was cozy and feminine. The sofa was covered with a tasteful flowered print that matched the drapes. The rug was pale and soft. Lissa showed him the liquor stash and asked for a Scotch on the rocks while she used the bathroom. "Give me twenty minutes with the film." Then she walked upstairs, carrying her drink. On the kitchen table was a recent issue of *Ms.* magazine and a copy of Frazier's *Golden Bough* with a book mark in the middle. A bookshelf in the living room held works by women. Gloria Steinem. Nancy Friday. Sue Miller. Kate Millett. Adrienne Rich. Sylvia Plath. Two shelves held books on politics. One shelf was devoted to psychology and myth. Branko found no novels or fiction.

Lissa Cody was a heavyweight.

When he sat down with his Scotch, Branko realized how tired he was. His eyes closed and did not want to open again. The Scotch topped off the beer and he felt himself floating. Roscoe's situation was getting to him. He got up and called the hospital. Roscoe was asleep. He called the station and gave the dispatcher Lissa's number. The time was 11:07. The Channel 3 news was rolling, but so far there had been no news flash. Branko didn't expect much.

"You can look at these while they're drying," Lissa called down.

Branko turned up the volume on the television, just in case, and went upstairs.

110

The darkroom smelled of chemicals. There were two large sinks, with hoses running from the bathroom. More than a dozen prints dripped water from a makeshift clothesline.

Josh Breitman, the photographer, had focused on three women at the restaurant attached to the Inn of Cortez—a voluptuous brunette with sculpted shoulders; a skinny waitress with a twiggy figure; and a blond woman wearing a frilly summer dress with a medium neckline. The brunette had smiled into the camera like a movie actress. The waitress made faces. And the blond woman seemed to be avoiding the camera. One shot showed her turning away, neat profile, putting her face in shadow. A second photo showed her walking out of the restaurant, skirt swirling, seemingly in a hurry. She was slender, late twenties, early thirties. The photos were black-and-white. Except for the dress, which echoed a more distant time, she resembled Mrs. Jordan Maxwell.

"Josh was very interested in this one," Lissa said, "because of the style of her dress. She seemed to sense the presence of the camera. He followed her out, but she was gone."

"Did he name her?"

"Girl in Blue."

"Someone could have interviewed her. Maybe she saw something. I'll check."

"Keep me informed."

Lissa opened the bedroom door. The fresh air smelled wonderful. Branko yawned. It was 11:15. He led the way downstairs.

"How come you were down on Balboa, anyway?"

"We got a news tip that there would be some kind of procession on Balboa while the reverend was making a speech in the Fun Zone. I interviewed him twice, so I was interested."

"Was he news?"

"I wanted a connection between him and the Spyglass Hill Gang."

"Who's that?"

"Jordan Maxwell, Harrison Wakefield, a developer named Peter Grafton, a couple of others. The investors in Ministry Beach."

Branko nodded. "Where did the tip come from?"

"Through my editor. He thought it was from CASS."

"What do you know about CASS?"

Before she could answer, the television cut through their conversation. The weather man went away. Linda Calderon faced the camera, looking serious.

"Channel Three has come into possession of a videotape that allegedly provides exclusive coverage of the incident earlier this afternoon at the Fun Zone on Balboa Peninsula in Newport Beach. This tape has been received in our studio and we have reported it to the authorities. The tape has been reviewed, but not edited, by Channel Three."

Come on. Come on.

Lissa came in from the kitchen and sat on the arm of the sofa.

"What is it?"

"Film of this afternoon."

"Where from?"

"They didn't say."

Linda Calderon was on again.

"This is Balboa Island in Newport Beach, in the Fun Zone area, a favorite of young people and tourists. This afternoon, at three-oh-four, an attempt was made on the life of Reverend Terry Odell Williams, who is challenging incumbent James Sherwood for the seat in District Fifty in the Republican primary on Tuesday." Pause. "Is the film rolling?" the narrator asked. The screen went blank and suddenly there it was, Balboa on a sunny afternoon in May.

"All right. We're just going to roll this film for you and let you observe as the events transpire. An analysis will follow."

Branko leaned forward. The angle of the camera was from above the action, and Branko knew the tape had been shot from one of the rooms overlooking Cortez Alley. He had stood there this afternoon, looking down from that window. Had Shooter Three gotten this on tape? On the screen, people stood around watching Reverend Williams, who was dressed in his three-piece suit as the camera zoomed in. His face in close-up looked jowly. The teeth were magnificent. Officer Jamie Duncan slid by on the left side of the frame, a vision in pink shorts and a halter.

"Here the Sister comes," Lissa breathed. "With the magazines."

"Where were you?"

"Out of the frame. See the man on the motorcycle?"

Branko saw a big man wearing a white jacket sitting astride a purple bike. Would the camera zoom in on him?

"There," Lissa said. "That's the hit man. The dark-haired man easing along." His back was to the camera.

"The perp."

The camera moved and caught Sister Winona Lee squirting barbecue starter onto the stack of magazines from a red can. She touched a match to the pile and flames sprouted out of it. The camera zoomed in for a close-up of her face, which was filled with religious joy. As the camera zoomed out again, Branko saw Roscoe Smith looking to his left. There was no sign of the perp.

Lissa had appeared onscreen now, followed by her photographer. What happened next took only a few seconds. Lissa collided with the perp, who was holding a gun in his left hand. As Lissa fell, the camera swerved away from that action to the reverend, who was grabbing at his leg.

"Damn!" Lissa said.

The bodyguard was down. People were stampeding. Roscoe came into the picture now, his automatic presumably leveled at the perp, who was offscreen. Roscoe went down. Sweat trickled down Branko's forehead and neck.

Now the perp was running and shooting, running and shooting, his head down, his face in shadow. People in the alley stumbled over each other trying to avoid the line of fire. There was no sound as the film ended suddenly, in the middle of a frame.

Branko moved to the phone and dialed Tommy Osterhaus at the station.

Another voice came out of the television set while the phone buzzed, and then the screen showed the Channel 3 news team, the curved desk, the logo behind them on the wall, papers neatly stacked in front of the two anchors, Linda Calderon and Robert Spenser. This was definitely a scoop. Both anchors were trying to stay serious, but as they handled this one you knew they were thinking Emmy, Pulitzer, Emmy, Pulitzer. Fame is not objective.

Calderon was talking:

"What you have just seen on your screen is an actual videotaped recording of the Balboa incident. Reverend Williams was clearly recognizable, as was his wife, Sister Winona Lee. The assassin is described as a—"

The screen cut to a commercial as Tommy came on the telephone. "Francisco. I was about to call you."

"Did you see the tape?"

"I saw it. So did the lieutenant. He wants you in L.A."

"When?"

"ASAP. He's on the horn now to Channel Three. They're cutting a dupe of the tape for us."

Branko kneaded his forehead. The headache was back and there would be no sleep tonight. "Was that an order?"

"Afraid so. He told me to remind you to wear your shield and your weapon."

Branko rolled his shoulders, trying to ease the stiffness. "I was up in the shooting room at the Inn. See if Forensics has anything that shows the camera was there."

"Good idea. What's your reading on the film?"

"Amateur job. The thing played like a home movie. Mr. Bad Guy, the client, wanted us to see the reverend and his missus at their work. No close-ups of either perp. We're dealing with a real nut here, Thomas."

"Mr. Bad Guy. I like that."

On the screen, doting Mom and nervous Dad at a bathroom sink hovering over Junior, who didn't want to use fluoride on his teeth.

"Back it up," someone said from offscreen. "Can we back it up and start over?" The toothpaste commercial vanished before the parents were victorious and there were shots of the anchorpeople behind their curved desks. They had been joined by Hugh Danforth, the sports announcer, and by Dr. Reggie Rodgers, the Ph.D. meteorologist. The screen wiggled. The toothpaste commercial came back on, bright teeth and a dentist played by a Hollywood character actor explaining what this toothpaste did in the never-ending war against plaque.

"Where did Channel Three get the tape?" Branko asked.

"Some messenger service."

"I'll phone you when I get there. Anything breaks, buzz me on the radio."

"Good luck in that fog, Francisco."

Branko hated driving in fog. "Thanks. Keep an eye on Roscoe for me."

"Will do."

They hung up. Before Branko had finished briefing Lissa Cody, she put on her jacket, picked up her leather reporter's bag, and draped a tan raincoat over her arm. "I'm going with you."

Branko checked his watch. Eleven-thirty. "It's late, Cody. I may not get back until the wee hours."

Her chin jutted out with determination. "I'll drive up. You can drive back."

Branko grinned. It would be nice to lie back and let someone else take over, just for a minute. "Deal."

Lissa turned off a couple of lights. Branko stood in her open doorway, checking the fog. Then they walked together to his Volvo.

CHAPTER EIGHT

BENNY was with Doc Crazy for half an hour, getting the hook out and the gash bandaged. He hated that skater.

Doc Crazy had come to Benny's Travelodge on Sunset in a Red Star Cab. He was wearing a raincoat and green hospital pants and dirty white tennis shoes that made him look right at home in El-Ay City. His hair was long and he had the ripe red schnoz and the bloodshot eyes of a boozer. Once the doc was inside, he fussed around, eyes zapping the rooms, snuffling, muttering to himself like a bag lady in a trash barrel as he washed his hands in the bathroom. He came out wearing a white office coat that said WINSTED ADULT WORLD on the left front pocket and a strap around his head with an eyeglass magnifier attached.

Benny came close to passing out like a sissie schoolgirl when Doc Crazy dug into his neck for the hook.

Wobbling with a mixture of pain and relief, he paid the doc

three hundred dollars for the house call and took the pain pills with a shot of Kentucky bourbon. Then he phoned Michele, who was three rooms down. He told her to get gussied up. They were going to Cosmo's Cosmos to meet a man.

Michele was in a griping mood. She was watching the TV and wanted to stay in. "Why can't the man come here?"

"Because we always meet at the Cosmos, that's why."

"I've heard of Cosmo's. It's supposed to be full of criminals."

"Don't believe everything you hear, doll-face."

Benny was feeling better and better. The artist's composite on TV looked like his cousin Rafe back in Little Rock more than it did him. Where the hell did they get these police artists? The only one any good was in the movie *Bullitt*, with Steve McQueen.

McQueen was Benny's hero. He also liked Al Pacino in *Serpico* and Rick Nelson in *Rio Bravo* and Kurt Russell in *Escape From New York*. He liked them because they were short guys who could move and hit. John Wayne was not one of Benny's heroes. He never got tired of watching McQueen. In the room at the Travelodge Benny had a rented RCA VCR and a stack of Steve McQueen tapes. His favorites were *Bullitt* and *The Sand Pebbles*. It was time to buy a VCR and move to Malibu, where the movie stars lived. Benny had the bread, or would have in an hour. Saturday, he would hunt a place to rent.

Michele arrived wearing a nothing blue dress with a V-neck. Bangle earrings dangled from each ear. There was no slit in the dress, which went down below her knees. The hooker had turned into a church matron. Her heels dug into the motel carpet, and she was wearing a choker around her neck. Her bottle-blond hair was piled up on her head. Blue eyeshadow made her look like an owl.

"Where's the red dress? The one cut down to here and up to here?"

"I get tired of red, honey. Red, red, red."

"Then wear the silver."

"This is new, hon. Come on."

She was angling for a present, fishing for Benny to spring for a new wardrobe. He'd dump her on the street before it came to that. She owed him a piece for the hundred he'd given her in Newport Beach. Now that she'd driven the Caddy back to his home turf, he didn't need her anymore. "Whatever you paid, doll-face, you got stung."

Michele looked miffed. "It was a gift."

"Hey, hey."

They walked through the puddles out to the red Caddy, where Benny locked his weapons bag in the trunk. In it was a Colt .357 and a Llama Omni 9mm and an Astra A-80 9mm and an Ithaca Stakeout 37 20-gauge riot gun. The .22 from this afternoon had been retired for a while. Let that baby cool. There was a switch-blade in his boot.

He took the co-pilot's seat while Michele drove the Caddy to the Cosmos. For a broad, she wasn't a bad little driver. The pain in his neck had backed off some because of the pain pills, and he looked forward to making an entrance, Michele on his arm. Gray night fog curled through the sharp-bladed leaves of the palm trees, spinning sprinkly yellow halos around the neon. Summer was coming to California. Benny felt at home. Watch out, beach twinks. Shit, this was his town.

Cosmo's Cosmos was decorated on the outside like a bar in a movie about some zillionaire Arab oil sheik. The building was white with a gold dome on top. Shutters of fancy filigree covered the windows, reminding Benny of the outside walls of Dole Petroleum back in Little Rock. A red carpet led from the curb to the door. Michele's eyes got big as she handed over the keys to an L.A. fairy in a red monkey coat and white harem pants. Benny touched the spare set of keys in his pocket, next to the photo from the Fun Zone. Benny didn't like leaving his guns in the car, but house rules said no iron inside Cosmo's. He paid a hundred cover at the door and tipped King Kong fifty.

"Hey, King. Got a sweaty Mex coming for a meet. Hector Mendoza. Know him?"

"Fat Hector," the King said. "Lemme pat your ass down, Ben-ja-mino."

"Keep your paws offen my ass, King. Or them fairies in the parking lot will get ideas." Benny waited for the King to pat him down.

"I know that greaseball, Hector the Con-nec-tor."

"Send him to my table, okay?"

The King folded the fifty and grinned through teeth that seemed an inch long. "Hey, Ben-ja-mino, you the man."

They came into the Cosmos under blue lights winking down from the ceiling. The maiter dee said, "Good evening, M'sieu Ringo," and led them to a table near the stage, where a class band was playing. People watched Michele from their tables. The maiter dee said Kurt Russell would be in tonight. Benny beamed. Life was sweet if you had money and connections. Maybe he'd get old Kurt's autograph, teach the booger how to shoot.

While the maiter dee held a chair out for Michele, Benny waved at Solly Stein and Moses Rainer, sitting with two show-girls at a table across the room. They both waved back and Solly whispered to a blonde in silver. He'd done a job for Solly back in November, when he'd first hit town, two grand to pop a shyster at the dog track. When news about the Balboa hit got around the circuit, Benny's price would go up. Watch out world, Benny Rubidoux was on the move.

Michele ordered a gin and tonic. Benny ordered the usual. The waitress, a sexy number in shorts and a see-through blouse, nod-ded and said, "Bourbon and Coke, I got it."

"They know you, don't they?"

"Yeah."

Michele stared around, smiling into the dark. She leaned for-ward with a cigarette between her lips and Benny gave her a light. When he put the matches in his pocket, he felt the photo from the booth in the Fun Zone. He showed it to Michele.

"Who is it?"

"My Cousin Rafe. We were high school jocks together."

"He doesn't look much like a jock."

"Folks used to say we looked alike, me and Rafe."

Michele held the photo up against Benny's face and shook her head. "You ever think about growing a mustache, hon?"

Benny laughed. The disguise was a sweetie. He mentioned the blue dress again on the dance floor. They were dancing close so her perfume got all through his head. He felt Michele stiffen in his arms.

"Come on, hon. It's new and it's pretty. It's my best dress."

"No pizazz, doll-face. You got pizazz. The dress don't."

"I don't much care for that term, 'doll-face.'"

"Okay. Okay."

They did a couple more turns around the floor. Benny had to admit, he was one great dancer.

"You don't have to be jealous, hon."

Benny was watching the door for Hector, who should have been here by now. "Me? Jealous? Why should I be jealous?"

"Because he bought me this."

"Who bought you what?"

"The preacher. He bought this for me. Picked it out for me special, he said."

Benny was only half listening. "Then it was for some other broad, doll-face, and you got sloppy seconds. Preachers lie, like everybody else."

Michele broke away from him with an angry shove and hustled back to the table, hips working like two pigs in a gunnysack. Benny smiled and sauntered after her. Broads were always acting up. Michele blew her nose and stared down at the tablecloth.

Benny sighed. "Man oh man. Forget I said anything."

"It's a nice dress. It makes me feel very . . . feminine."

"How long you had it?"

"Since Wednesday."

"Wednesday?"

"Um."

"For your Dana Point nooner?"

Michele nodded. "It was okay. All he wanted was for me to put it on. A lot of johns do that. They bring something for you to wear. A lot of them like leather, which makes you all sweaty."

"I know all about leather, doll-face. You put on this dress and then you took it off and then what?"

Michele shook her head. "You know I don't like talking about it with other men."

"Jeez, now all of a sudden we're the bashful hooker." Benny put his hand on her leg under the table. She pulled her knees aside. "You put on the holy blue dress and what else?"

"Special underwear."

"Jesus. The dirty old man. Then what?"

"Blue shoes. Matching."

"You are something else, sweets. After that?"

"Nothing. Then I smoked a cigarette while the preacher, he—"
She stopped, looked over at the door.

Benny put his shoe on top of her foot, grabbed her wrist, and leaned close. "While he what—?"

Out of the corner of his eye, where Michele was looking, Benny saw fat Hector working his way through the tables. He was wearing a red silk shirt and a black leather jacket cut Mex-style and soft white bandido pants with no visible crease. He came in with a big smile, right behind his teeth and his chili belly. Benny let Michele go and slid the switchblade out of his boot and into his coat pocket. "Run powder your nose, doll-face."

She left the table as fat Hector came up looking greasy. In his right hand, he carried a red-and-white-striped paper sack with the picture of Colonel Sanders on it. Benny held out his hand and they shook.

"*Oye, amigo.*"

"Hello, Hector. What's in the sack? Tacos?"

"*Dinero.*"

"How come you lived here all your life and still talk Mex-ican?"

Hector nodded his chin at Benny. "How come you got the bandage of the red cross your neck, *amigo?*"

Benny stood up. "What's Spanish for chicken, *amigo?*"

"*El pollo. La gallena.*"

"Let's hit the men's room, *amigo.* Bring the poyo sack."

Benny followed Hector to the men's room. He was a squatty meatball of a Mex who stood maybe five-seven in his two-inch lifters. Benny had seen him once with his shirt off. Big soft arms, gut like a pregnant whale. Hector had a big head of hair, which he wore long in a Tijuana ducktail.

A fairy with punker hair was talking on the phone, his voice high-pitched and whiny. Hector pushed through the door marked Les Hommes and set the chicken sack down on the lav-atory while Benny checked the stalls. Three crappers, no one home. Flipping through the green, Benny knew right away he was being stiffed. Mr. No-Name, the mystery client, owed him fifteen big ones. What he had here was seven grand five hundred. He turned to Hector.

"What we got here, *amigo*, is half."

"The other is in *el coche, señor*."

"Shit. And where's that?"

"Outside, in the parking lot."

Benny pointed to the bandage on his neck. "See this, *amigo*? It hurts like somebody from down your way filled it with chili sauce. What it means is, I ain't in no mood tonight to fuck around with you. Mr. No-Name owes me fifteen. You bring in half. Who else is outside?"

"No one, *señor*."

Benny knew Hector worked with a slime bucket named Mace Williams. "Howsabout the Mace? You got him in the car for a backshooter?"

"No, *señor*." Hector was sweating, but that didn't mean much. He was a fat-ass Mex, always sweating.

Moving quick, Benny whipped out the switchblade, pressed the button, and shoved the knife tip into Hector's right nostril. His right hand pressed into the man's Adam's apple. "Me and you, *amigo*, we got us a chicken to pluck. This is as good a time as any."

"Me, I doan know what you—"

Benny shoved the blade deeper. Hector sniffled with fear as blood oozed out onto the shiny metal. "You and your Mr. No-Name fucked with my plan, Hector. There was a third shooter down there spraying hot lead around the hit zone. I could of been shot, you prick." He increased the pressure on Hector's throat. The Mex gagged, red-faced.

"What it is you—"

"I want the name and address of Mr. No-Name. Me and him will have us a cozy sit-down. And I want five more grand for my trouble down Orange County way."

Sweat ran down Hector's cheeks and onto his throat. The collar of the red shirt was dark with his reek. "*Amigo*, I don't think—"

The door opened and a man walked in. He was mid-fifties, bald, wearing a blue coat over an orange shirt open at the neck. One little strand of hair lay plastered down across his shiny dome. Benny held onto Hector's throat and waved the knife point at Baldy. "Inside the first stall, pal. Or you lose your nuts."

"Jesus H. Christ." Baldy didn't move. His lip trembled.

Benny kneed Hector in the balls, just to keep him tamed down. Hector doubled over with a *whoof* and Benny grabbed Baldy by the collar and rammed him head-first into the crapper. Then he tucked the chicken sack under his arm and grabbed a handful of thick Mex hair. It was blacker than the hairpiece from the hit zone. "Okay, *amigo*. Me and you are shimmying out of here to the parking lot. I got friends here at the Cosmos. Me and the bouncer are like that. Also, I didn't see one chili-belly *amigo* to help you if you squawk for help. We'll go to my car first. To my *coche*, you got that? We use the back door, which is around the corner from here. We pick up the money and find a phone and call Mr. No-Name and have ourselves a chicken pluck. Savvy?."

"*Si, señor.*"

Benny showed Hector the knife, palmed in his left hand. He shoved Hector through the men's room door, holding the knife close. The fag was still talking on the phone, probably to another fag. Michele was standing at the bar, watching the TV. Her back was to Benny as he turned Hector to the left behind a potted palm that had seen better days and headed for a red Exit sign. Good-bye, doll-face. A jig almost as big as King Kong came out of a door marked Manager. He was wearing a tux with a red bowtie. "Where you think you're going?"

"Police," Benny said. "Got me a fugitive."

The jig grinned. "Motherfuck, you lie." He reached for Benny in a pawing motion, his hand as big as a top sirloin steak.

Benny felt sweat pop out on his forehead as, in one smooth motion, he sliced at the jig's outstretched arm. The blade, razor-sharp, split the black flesh on the inside of the wrist. The jig got a surprised look on his face, clutched his wrist, and stumbled backward. The bigger they come, the harder they fall.

Benny shoved Hector toward the door. A sign read EMER-

GENCY EXIT ONLY. ALARM WILL SOUND WHEN THIS DOOR IS OPENED. Benny kicked the handle and a bell began clanging somewhere inside Cosmo's. The door opened and he shoved Hector through it. Outside, the fog lay thick on the bushes. Benny got Hector's arm in a hammerlock. The switchblade was against his ear as they stumbled around back to the lot. Cars everywhere, gleaming with moisture. No telling where the fags had parked the Caddy. "Where's your Chevy?"

Hector pointed to a line of cars. "There."

Footsteps came up behind them. "Benny! It's me. Michele!"

Goddamn. Just what he didn't need right now. "Go back inside, baby."

She grabbed Benny by the sleeve. In the light from the parking lot, her face and hair were swimming-pool green.

"What are you doing to him?" She meant Hector.

"Go away, doll-face. I'll see you later, okay?"

"Something!" she panted. "On the television news!"

"Not now, I said."

"It's your cousin, the one from Little Rock?"

Benny kept going. Still no sign of the red Caddy. "What cousin?"

"The one in the photo, with the mustache on his lip."

He spotted the Caddy, way the hell across the lot, wedged in by a Mercedes and a Lincoln Mark IV. The guns were there. And a set of cuffs for the Mex. He'd get his armament. Maybe Hector's Chevy was more accessible. The Mex was scared shitless, sweating like a shoat. Another minute and Benny would solve the mystery of Mr. No-Name. Should have done it before now.

"He shot the preacher."

"Who?"

Michele stared at Benny. "Your cousin. From high school."

"Rafe? Where?"

"Down south. In Newport Beach, at the Fun Place."

An electric charge zipped up Benny's spine. Hector was looking away from him, to his right. "What?"

"It was on television, the book burning and the preacher getting shot, people running every which way. I wouldn't of recognized him but for the picture you showed me."

"You got cookies in your attic, doll-face."

"No. There it was. Like a movie. The preacher had his arms raised up like he was calling to God almighty and a woman in a long dress squirting lighter fluid—" Michele stopped. "It wasn't your cousin. It was you."

Benny couldn't think straight. "Stifle it, okay!"

But Michele kept on, excited now. "You were there. This afternoon. You told me to drive the car back, only you were there, waiting for him, with a gun, because . . ."

They were twenty feet from the red Caddy and Benny knew he was going crazy, along with Michele the happy hooker. Benny kept Hector moving, but Michele had stopped back by the Mark IV. She was still talking to herself, trying to work it out. "You get any of that, *amigo*?"

"No, *señor*." Hector's teeth were chattering.

"Someone shot some film of the action."

"Me, I doan know noth—"

"Where's your vehicle?"

"*Allá.* There."

Benny saw it, a low-slung Chevrolet Impala parked at the end of a row. "Gimme the keys."

Hector pointed to his pocket. Benny reached in for the keys.

When they reached the Caddy, Benny forced Hector to his knees in a puddle of water. He fumbled for his spare keys and Hector chose that moment to make a try for him, grabbing Benny's thighs in a bear hug and heaving up like a wrestler on late-night TV. Benny whomped the Mex on the back of the neck with his fingers locked. The hold on his legs loosened, but Hector held on. Benny drove the switchblade into the leather jacket, three inches below the neck. There was a moment of nothing except neon lights with fog halos and then the Mex let go and sagged to the asphalt. Headlights came on two rows down. A car eased along. It looked like a Ford Fairlane, but the light was too bad to tell. He got the trunk open. Michele came up, still talking.

"It was you, down there. Wasn't it?"

"Get lost."

"You shot the preacher. Damn you, Benny!"

"Later, babe."

"The fuzz are all over, hunting for you. And where does that leave little Michele? Damn!"

He slung the shoulder rig over his right shoulder and stuffed the fake police ID in his hip pocket. He put the Llama 9mm in his belt while he held the .357 under Hector's nose. "Give me the name, *amigo*. The name and where I can reach him. Then we'll get that money from your *cochee*."

Hector shook his head. He was a tough bird, meaty, with seven layers of pork fat to stop the knife blade from getting too deep. Benny knew he was faking. He muttered something in Mexican and jammed the gun in Hector's nose.

"Stop it," Michele said, grabbing him. "Stop it this minute!"

Benny shoved her away and started going through Hector's pockets. He found a wallet and a Mex money-clip. In a shirt pocket was a business card with something written on the back. Tires squealed on wet asphalt. Bright lights lit up the red Caddy.

"Tell me, damn you!"

"*El Colonel*," Hector said. "He is called *El Colonel*."

Benny reached for the switchblade, but the handle wasn't there. Must have dropped out, or broken off. The lights swerved away. "You mean like an Army colonel?"

"I doan know." Hector coughed.

"Where does he hang out?"

"I doan know. *En las montan—*"

"Benny! Someone's coming! Hey!"

Ambush. Benny let the Mex go and rolled to the side. Bullets ripped through Hector's leather jacket, tracing a track up the side of the red Caddy. Automatic weapon, Benny thought. Burp gun or Uzi. Michele screamed. Benny duck-walked around the red Caddy. When he reached the front bumper, he saw the Ford parked two cars ahead. Someone was breathing behind him, sounding like Darth Vader. Benny crept around behind a BMW just as Darth showed himself. He was a big one, dark coat, the light bouncing off yellow glasses. Benny snapped off two shots at him. The .357 sounded like a cannon. Darth dropped out of sight. Benny kept low while he ran for the Chevy. Michele called from behind him. "Benny! Help!" Benny kept moving.

125

The chicken sack was tucked under his arm. A siren wailed somewhere out on La Cienega. He was unlocking the door of Hector's Chevy and almost home free when the headlights caught him. An engine revved and four headlights leaped forward. Half-blinded, Benny fired at the headlights. One went out in a sizzle of wet gray smoke. The other three kept coming.

Benny dove aside as the headlights plowed into the side of Hector's Chevy. The window on the driver's side was rolled up and he fired at it from seven feet away, shattering the glass. Voices called in the night. People streamed out the door of the Cosmos. The sirens were louder now, closer. He had dropped the chicken sack full of money.

Benny stood up. The .357 was out of ammo, so he pulled out the Llama and walked to the Ford.

A man was sitting behind the wheel, his face torn away by Benny's rounds. Benny knew from his shoulders and neck it was the Mace. A car honked and he heard the voice of King Kong coming from the front door. The Mace had been a pro football player and after that an actor who played a pretend cop with handcuffs at surprise birthday parties and after that a wheelman for two-bit bank robbers. He had a reputation for liking S&M and for fooling around with ten-year-old girls. Blood was oozing slowly down what was left of his cheek, losing itself in the dark collar of his shirt.

Benny spent a breathless minute hunting for the money sack around the wheels of the Ford. The sirens were closer now, moaning through the foggy night. Horns beeped in the parking lot as customers from the Cosmos tried to scoot before the fuzz came. The Ford was angled into Hector's Chevy, its nose gouged in maybe two feet. Neither vehicle was drivable. When he tried scrooching under to where he thought the sack was, he couldn't go far enough because the Chevy had been knocked off her struts and was only five inches off the ground.

He could not find the chicken sack. He spent a minute scrabbling around in the trunk of the Chevy. No seven grand there. He had eight hundred or so in his wallet. He had Hector's wallet and money-clip. Mr. No-Name, or *El Colonel*, owed him a bundle. His plan was to hole up until he could figure out how to get to *El Colonel*. Hector the Connector was dead, or close to it, but there *was* one old boy who knew where *El Colonel* was.

Mr. Inside Dope, the information supplier inside the preacher's cozy church.

Harsh lights swirled red and blue on the roof of the first police car as Benny cut around back, behind the Cosmos. It was tough running in his goddamn boots. On Melrose, he chose the first car stopped at the red traffic signal. It was a brown Mercedes, late-model, four-door. Benny jerked open the driver's door and came face to face with Baldy, from the crapper in the men's room. There was a woman with him, young stuff, with smooth white shoulders.

Pay dirt.

"What are you—?"

"Move over." Benny stuck the gun under Baldy's nose.

Baldy had trouble moving over because of the stick. He swore at Benny. Young Stuff swore too, a bitchy voice, surprising him. He showed her the piece and she shut up. Benny got behind the wheel.

"Where are you taking us?" Young Stuff asked.

"Shut your face." Benny drove at five miles below the speed limit to his Travelodge on Sunset. It was the only home he knew in the City of Angels. He needed time to think and plan and watch Cousin Rafe on TV.

Then *El Colonel* No-Name would pay.

TWO

CHAPEL PERILOUS

CHAPTER NINE

WHEN the surprise tape of the Balboa shooting flashed on the screen at Slattery's Saloon off the coast highway, Amity Pitcairn was sitting at the polished bar between a shy Marine with a short haircut and a loud-voiced brute of a salesman named Jack Gallagher, a life of the party type. Dull, dull, dull.

Gallagher had spent twenty years in the retail food industry but was now working in computers. Amity was not surprised by the Balboa tape or by Gallagher, a florid-faced man full to the gills with his own Irish blarney. "Yeah, selling electronic hardware is like selling a can of soup, darlin'. You got to get up early to do either one, or both, and that includes old Jack Gallagher. Us Capricorns, we know how to work, we do."

Slattery's Saloon was across the street from Fashion Island, an elaborate shopping mall in Newport Beach, where Amity had spent the evening shopping. She had a room at the Côte d'Azur, between the mall and Pacific Coast Highway. Slattery's was her fourth stop of the evening. The wood was brown and polished and the booths and curtains were green. The napkins were green. The waitresses wore green blouses and green skirts and black mesh hose. One waitress, a fox named Randi, had caught Amity's eye with a cute little wiggle of her tushie, but had left at ten-thirty with her boyfriend. Disappointment. You win some, you lose some. Amity had finished her job. Tomorrow she'd fly to France. Tonight she wanted action, a party, animal grunts and animal moans, flesh on flesh.

"How's about a refill, Kathleen Mavourneen?" Gallagher was a hefty man, thirty pounds overweight, with red hair that had thinned out on top to reveal a shiny bald spot. Jack Gallagher's technique for surviving in the world was to use his name, Jack Gallagher, yeah, that's me, a lot. Years of boozing had made his eyes perpetually shot with fine red streaks. He had ceased to be amusing in the first five seconds. "Mavourneen, you've got to be Irish. Let Jack Gallagher buy you the Irish moon."

Gallagher had beer breath. Amity hated that smell.

"You kill me, Gilligan." She beamed a bleak smile at Gallagher and felt the Marine shift on the stool beside her. The Marine had spoken only to order his first Bourbon and soda, which he was nursing as he watched the television screen. "Miami Vice" was over. The news was next. She could feel the Marine pulsing beside her, a hundred and ninety pounds of real red-white-and-blue All-American jarhead, with a line of muscle fiber running from his brain to his toes that spelled out Action, Halls of Montezuma, Take that Beach. He was sitting sixteen inches away on the next stool, working up the courage for his first tentative howdy. Amity was his figurative beachhead. The Marine was pretty, even with his ridiculous short haircut and the tight collar that cut a furrow into his neck. He had nice eyes and long eyelashes. Amity wished he had brought his sister. In a pinch, the Marine might do.

"Gallagher, Kathleen. Jack G. Gallagher. You are something else."

"Why, thank you, Mr. Gallagher!"

"Call me Jack, darlin'. Everyone does." Gallagher saw the television screen out of the corner of his eye. "Godalmighty, look at that!"

On the screen, Sister Winona Lee Williams was squirting lighter fluid onto the pile of magazines. The reverend, perplexed, traversed the space between himself and his wife. For videotaping the scene, Amity had used an RCA Camcorder 300 with a six-to-one zoom for close-ups. It was only her second try with the Camcorder, but the amateurish effect was what she had wanted. The Camcorder was in the ExpressMail drop at the Jamboree Post Office. It would cost Amity $32.50 to have it mailed to a similar drop in Chicago, where it would be held in the name of Rachel English. One of her survival rules for a job was leaving no hardware behind for the authorities to trace you to. She'd bought the Camcorder in Chicago for straight cash. It would go back to Chicago, through the pre-paid express drop. The post office had never failed her. It was one of the few things she loved about America.

"Hey," Gallagher said, staring at the screen. "I know that place. That's the Fun Zone, where the action went down. Would you believe my brother's kids were there today, having fun in the sun? Another round here, Mo. Okay. And one for the lady and my friend in uniform there. Judas Priest, what's the world coming to, Kathleen?"

Amity sipped her Scotch as the tape rolled on. The zoom on the reverend was shaky, but the one on his wife held nicely. The rabid religious expression on Sister Winona Lee's features—the tight line of the mouth, the strangely metallic eyes—would haunt the Liberal press for weeks. Amity was happy with the way she had kept the colonel's semi-pro shooter in the shadows. There he was, the colonel's scumbag bungler, at the edge of the frame, with his face turned away. She'd read his dossier. Rubidoux, Benjamin, born to lose, early.

Amity watched the tape through once, excused herself, and slid off the stool to head for the ladies' room. She spent a moment in front of the mirror, checking her appearance. She had changed from the blue dress of the afternoon into a forest-green jumpsuit with strategic zippers and military epaulets. Hunter's green, just right for Slattery's. The green jumpsuit came from Complice, a stylish European import shop in Fashion Island. Her salesgirl had been a naughty brunette with ripe lips named Karin. Amity had asked Karin out, but the little bitch had been busy. Tied up, probably for the evening.

Now, standing at the mirror, Amity touched up her lipstick and ran a comb through her hair. When she replaced the lipstick in her handbag she saw her passport and the Air France ticket to Nice. Her flight left tomorrow at noon, from Los Angeles International. She would turn in the rented Buick at LAX. There was a stopover in Washington, D.C., and then on to another lovely summer at her villa on the Riviera. The beach below her villa was a treasure. Amity would be glad when she left California. The last time she'd been here, two years ago, was during a rainy March. The job had taken a week and she'd caught a terrible cold waiting for just the right moment.

She left the ladies' room and walked to the pay telephone, where she dialed the number of Cólonel Bobby Devane. The name "Bobby" was a nice touch, packed with heavy irony. She called him "colonel," which suited him right down to his tight military ass. He was the archetypal soldier, medals and spit shine and a mind that saw only one campaign, and then another, and then one more, looping out to the horizon. To Devane, winning was important, but fighting was everything. Life was a struggle. Let the contest go to the best fighters. No one knew how many people—soldiers and support personnel and tourists and innocent civilians—Devane had killed or ordered killed. Some estimates at Harbinger Inc., a clandestine think tank in Palo Alto that kept records on non-governmental (e.g. mercenary) military actions, went as high as ten thousand dead. The numbers were highest in Africa, 6,721 dead or accounted for.

He was a real killer.

She'd met Devane in London, three years ago, but she'd heard about him through the underworld grapevine and through Angelina, her professional mentor. Devane was infamous, a real devil who specialized in genocide instead of homicide. He had the narrow eyes of the professional soldier, and walked with a slight limp, the residue of an old wound. He even came wired with a twinkly smile and a deceptive good-old-boy vocabulary. There were stories floating around about what a trader Devane was.

The Balboa job had been her fourth for Devane, and she was technically curious about the eventual outcome. Like many artists, Amity didn't care for the bald obviousness of politics. Asking pigs for votes was too gross for her. She didn't care whether the reverend won the primary on Tuesday or soared off on a winding silver staircase to meet his maker. Amity was a technician, a professional, subtle and classy. She knew this was a test for Devane. If his plan got the reverend through the primary, Devane would try the same tactic again, in some other state, probably on a senator. And probably with Amity on board.

There was money to be made in political hits.

134

The line was busy. Amity hung up and tapped her fingernails on the ledge beneath the phone. Slattery's was sparsely populated. The foxy little waitress had gone. The two attractive women left in the place were with suits. Company-wise, this was turning out to be a zero evening. Orange County was a turnoff. In Europe, she had her network. If she ventured beyond the network, she'd find someone pleasant right on the fringes, with lines into another network. She yearned for Europe. Orange County was the Philistine Midwest plopped down on the edge of America.

She tried Devane a second time. Still busy. The tape had been delivered to Channel 3 by a messenger service in the San Fernando Valley. Once it flashed on the screen, Amity's job was capped off. All she needed now was the pickup site for her fifteen thousand. She shivered and hugged herself, a delayed reaction from the afternoon's work on Balboa. When she finished a job, she had a need for contact, for rubbing her naked body up against another naked body, something as smooth and cool as a statue, with a fierce inner heat that surprised and delighted. Flesh was one of Amity's few weaknesses. Angelina had warned her about it. "You're cold, dear. That's why you're so good at this work. Stay cold and you'll live to be a hundred."

She walked back to the bar, where she flirted with the Marine. His name was Jed Masters and he was from Montana. Amity introduced herself as Rachel English. Jack Gallagher excused himself and walked unsteadily to the men's room.

"Reminds me of my old man," the Marine said, indicating Gallagher.

Amity ran a fingernail along the Marine's wrist, along the line of his wristwatch, and then underneath, where the flesh was as soft as a girl's. His Adam's apple bobbled as he gulped and tried a smile. If she had to settle for a man, it might as well be a jarhead with pretty eyelashes and tricky hidden softnesses.

"Are you a captain, or what?"

"Corporal, ma'am."

"Corporal, would you be interested in following me to my hotel? The fog spooks me and I'm just a little afraid."

The Marine's eyes widened and his face got beet red. The

135

beachhead was storming him. "Would I fol—?" He gulped, hunting for words. "Yes, ma'am." He almost saluted.

Amity patted his hand. The poor eager thing. "You just wait right here." She slid off the stool and walked back to the pay phone and dialed Devane again. She was in luck. This time he answered. Her watch said 11:38.

"This is Crap Shoot. Sign on."

"This is Backup," Amity said. "Is the line clear?"

"Clear as an Eyetalian tenor on Easter Sunday. Where you holed up, kiddo?"

"At the Côte d'Azur."

"Where is that?"

"On PCH, near Fashion Island."

"You did a sweet job out there today, Backup. Your money's at the Marriott, under the name Rachel English."

"Thank you, Colonel. I'll be in touch."

She was about to hang up when Devane broke in. "Wait up a minute. I got another job for you."

"Sorry, Colonel. It's vacation time. I'm off for the summer."

"Pays twenty grand."

"Sorry. I need a rest."

"Thirty."

She did need some cash to put in a new veranda. But she'd been working steadily since January, and her nerves were frazzled by all the detail. Besides, she hadn't worked in three summers. Teachers took time off. So did Amity. "I can recommend someone. He could be here by noon tomorrow."

"I got a time problem," Devane said. "And this one needs some tracking."

"Oh?"

"Yeah. You saw the Scumbag file?"

"Yes."

"That old boy needs to be taken out."

"It could have been accomplished earlier."

"I thought of that. Would of took the spotlight off old Lard-Ass. Tell you the truth, my troops blew it in L.A."

"Do you have a location?"

"Gone to ground. Somewhere in L.A."

"L.A.'s a big place, Colonel."

"Forty grand."

"My choice of a hit zone?"

"Your choice of hit zone, ammo, whatever."

It was a buyer's market, and Amity loved getting the best of a horse trader like Devane. "All right. Here's my price. Fifty thousand in Swiss francs, plus two of those uncut Russian stones you showed me yesterday. From the little black bag."

Devane chuckled his wintry chuckle. "Christ on a crutch, kiddo!"

There was a long pause while Amity listened to Devane breathing. The Marine was sitting at the bar, one foot on the floor, like a sprinter in his starting blocks. The dear boy. She could feel him vibrating at her all the way across the room. Wait till she went to work on his little wonder wand.

"Okay," Devane said. "Fifty in Swiss currency. Two Siberian rocks. I got a man in LAPD, code name of Phoenix. He'll target old Scumbag. You can stay briefed by calling him. You got a car phone?"

She'd have to steal something else, leave the Buick in a parking lot. "I will have. Where was the target last seen?"

"Joint called Cosmo's Cosmos, in Los Angeles. Know it?"

"Only by the sewage stench. One other thing."

"You already got me quartered and dried. What is it?"

"I get half up front. This is not my style and since I'm doing you a favor, I'll give it until Sunday at six. After that, I'll abort the mission."

"You are tough. I could bring in someone else."

"That's your choice, Colonel."

Devane wheezed at the other end of the line. "Okay. Damn. You got a deal. Hardware?"

"I need a rifle—I like the AR-Fifteen—and some explosives. Small stuff, with three electronic detonators. And a LAW."

"You got it. And keep me posted."

A woman had just entered Slattery's, alone. She was tall and brunette, with heavy black hair and the mahogany skin of a Chicana. She was wearing a black dress and a red jacket that stopped at her perky ass and sharp heels that gave an extra curve to her calves. Jack Gallagher came out of the men's room, his face pale. The brunette surveyed the room, scanning the drinkers one by one, until her gaze came to rest on Amity. Amity's luck was turning.

"This is Backup; out." Amity replaced the phone and stared at the brunette. The Marine was forgotten. The brunette smiled and Amity smiled back, then turned and sashayed into the ladies' room, hips swaying in the green jumpsuit. She was in front of the mirror when the door opened and the brunette stepped inside. She was in her late twenties, a couple of years younger than Amity, and slightly overweight, four pounds, five, just enough for ballast in bed. Her lips were full and sensual, with a pouty look. Her dark eyes held the knowledge of centuries.

"Slow night," the brunette said.

"Not any more." Amity's look was arch.

"Wanta party?" the brunette asked.

Reaching into her purse, Amity brought out a hundred. The brunette, a shrewd observer of human need, shook her head and held up two fingers. Amity brought out another hundred. The brunette tucked the money into her purse. "You want a threesome?"

"Three's a crowd."

"I came by taxi. You have wheels?"

"Yes."

"Do we go out together?"

Amity thought of the Marine. "Yes."

The brunette smiled. "I'm Maricella."

"Rachel English," Amity said.

"You from around here?" Maricella asked.

"Just passing through."

"That's a honey of an outfit. The green does your eyes real great."

"It's imported," Amity said.

They shook hands and walked out together, past the Marine and a glowering Jack Gallagher, into the fog of Slattery's parking lot.

The bedside phone rang in the reverend's room at Seaport General. He reached out for it. On the television screen above his bed Channel 3 was running another replay of the Fun Zone videotape. The reverend's excitement kept growing with every replay, each time the screen showed a close-up of his face. Seeing himself on television was erotic. Commentators talked about the look of terrible knowing fear in his eyes just before the assassin had tried to kill him. Terrible knowing fear—he liked that. The analyses went on and on as professional journalists groped for words to explain what had happened on Balboa earlier in the afternoon. The reverend liked watching them search for those words. It drove the pain away.

"Hello?"

"Reverend Williams, this is the nurse's station. We would not have disturbed you at this hour, but we have your son on the line."

"Terry? Terry Junior?"

"Yes. He's calling from the Bay Area."

Thank God. "Put him on. Put him on."

There was a crackling sound as buttons were depressed. Then he heard Terry Junior's voice. "Dad? Are you there?"

"Terry. Where are you, son?"

"Berkeley, Dad. At the house. I just heard. The police were here, waiting for me, and I guess I should have listened to the radio but I was working on a French tape for finals and . . . Dad, I just saw the tape. The tape of the shooting. Jeez, Dad. That was something pretty awful!"

Where else had the tape reached besides the Bay Area? Had it gone East already, to New York? The time was wrong; it was three in the morning in New York City and no one would be awake to see it. Had it made it as far as Chicago? Houston? Miami? Would this gunshot make him famous?

"Dad, are you there?"

"Yes, Terry." The bit about studying was a white lie. Terry Junior had been busy committing fornication with his girlfriend, Anne Granger, of that the reverend was almost positive. Like father, like son. Anne Granger was dark and intense, with the nature-girl type of beauty so common to young women in Northern California. She wore little makeup and her wild frizzy hair always needed attention. Anne Granger was not half as pretty as Helen of Troy, which was a pity, but she did possess a certain bestial quality that the reverend sometimes found unnerving. "Are you all right? Are you safe?"

"Just fine, Dad. They've got the frat house covered. They'll keep an officer on me all the time, in class, everything. I feel like a celebrity. Crazy, huh?" There was a pause. "Dad?"

"Yes, son. What is it?"

"I'm driving down, Dad. They can't keep me here like some kind of prisoner. I'm coming home."

The reverend felt his heart swell. His son wanted to be with him in his hour of need. "You don't have to do that, son."

"I want to, Dad. I feel I should. After seeing what happened on television, I—"

Ah, the power of the media. "What about finals, Terry?"

"I've asked Annie to talk to my profs. They're okay. They'll understand, especially when they see what happened. I can take incompletes and work off the stuff this summer."

"What about Europe?"

"Annie says it's okay about Europe."

"I've always liked that girl," the reverend said.

"Yeah. I wish Mom felt the same."

"Your mother will come around, son. She'll come around."

There was a long silence while the reverend thought about his wife's eyes.

Then his son spoke: "I should be there by the morning, Dad. I'll come right to the hospital."

"It's a long drive, Terry. Is your mind made up?"

"Yeah. I'm coming, Dad. I should be there around five or six."

"Fine. Fine. I'll tell the police."

"Don't tell Mom, okay? Let me tell her."

"Of course. Of course."

"This is a terrible thing," Terry Junior said. "Have they got any idea who did it?"

"No," the reverend said. "But I do. A very good idea."

"You do?"

"Yes."

"Who?"

"I'll tell you when you arrive, son. Drive carefully."

"Okay, Dad. See you soon."

140

The connection was broken and the reverend hung up the phone. He would be glad to see his son. He needed someone to help him through the labyrinthine ways that would follow. There was a poem he had memorized in high school, "The Hound of Heaven," by Francis Thompson. "Flee him, down the nights and down the days. . . ." the reverend whispered. "Flee him down the labyrinthine ways. . . ."

He stared at the television screen. A policeman in a leather jacket was being interviewed about a shooting somewhere in Los Angeles. Cameras were on the scene and their lights reflected off puddles on the tarmac. The reverend was only vaguely interested in what was transpiring in Los Angeles, so he worked the buttons on his remote channel selector until he found a news program that was doing yet another recap of the Fun Zone incident. He liked the ring of that name. Incident at the Fun Zone was even better. He could work that into his statement for the press. As he watched, he jotted notes. Fun at the Fun Zone. Incident on Balboa. Fame. Hum de dum.

Should he implicate his opponent Sherwood in the first sentence? Or should he wait until the climax and let the suspense build? He picked up the phone and asked for a long distance operator, and then he called Harrison Wakefield at his home in Big Canyon. He had to talk to someone about the implications of his wound. As he waited for Harrison to answer, God appeared before the reverend's eyes. He wore a long white robe and he spoke with a soft Southern accent and called the reverend Sergeant Chub, just like Daddy always used to.

On the San Diego Freeway heading north to Los Angeles, Branko relaxed in the passenger seat of the Volvo while Lissa Cody drove. Traffic on the freeway was medium and there were enough heavy trucks barreling through to split the heavy fog. Lissa was a good driver. She kept her speed steady and seldom used the brake.

"You're a good driver, Cody."

"Thanks. I took lessons in defensive driving. For a feature story."

"That explains it. You don't use the brake much."

"My dad taught me about that. He said, 'Melissa, honey, only bad drivers ride the goldang brake.' And I never forgot."

"Where is he now?"

"He died last year. He'd been laid off from the factory eight months. He tried starting his own plumbing business, but times were too tough."

"Where did he live?"

"Peoria. I grew up there. Blue-collar daughter of a blue-collar family."

"I grew up just north of you. In Beloit, Wisconsin."

She looked at him out of the corner of her eye. "You've lost it, Branko."

"Lost what?"

"Your Midwestern innocence."

"Thanks. What has replaced it?"

"California guile."

Branko laughed. "You ever get back there?"

"I went for the funeral. It was in the middle of March and snowing. My nose almost froze off. I remember the year I graduated from high school it snowed on May fifteenth."

"I remember it snowed in Wisconsin once on the thirtieth of May."

The radio crackled, interrupting them. Branko answered.

"Sergeant Branko?" a voice said.

"This is Branko."

"Officer Ramirez here, from the Signal Hill Station. We've got a patch through from Sergeant Osterhaus in Newport Beach."

"Go ahead."

There was the hollow sound of a switch being thrown and then Tommy's voice came on. "Francisco. Where are you?"

"We just passed Signal Hill. Is this a recall, I hope?"

"No luck. You need to head up to Cosmo's Cosmos. It's on La Cienega near Melrose. A shooting just went down and LAPD thinks our perp was involved."

Branko sat forward. He knew the area. "Did they get him?"

"He got away. There's an all-points out. Now that he's invaded L.A. turf, interest is up."

"Were they tipped?"

"Anonymous tip, around eleven. By the time they arrived at Cosmo's, there were two stiffs on the ground and two hurt. They bagged some neat customers, some in their robes and Korean flip-flops."

"Any description of our perp?"

"Bandage on the neck. Could shoot like John Wayne. One witness says he was a runner."

"Black hair?"

"Blond. No mustache."

A partial M.O. was better than nothing. "No leads on the anonymous tip?"

"Nothing so far. The officer who called us says he knows you. An old friend named Carruthers."

"Dink Carruthers. He taught me about being a homicide cop."

"Carruthers is on the scene," Tommy said. "I called Channel Three and asked them to deliver the tape to you at Cosmo's."

"Where's the lieutenant?"

"Took off for home. Lucky thing you were en route, Francisco."

"Yeah. When are you taking off?"

"I'll stay here until I hear from you. This might be our break."

"Any word on Roscoe?"

"Nothing new. Ten-four, Sergeant."

They came into Los Angeles from the south, feeling the dark of the city close around them like a distant memory of Hell. Fog slithered along the streets. Branko gave Lissa directions.

"You know your way around."

"I used to call this home."

"Did you frequent this place, what's it called, Cosmo's?"

"It wasn't built yet. But I remember the area."

The city seemed dirtier now, meaner. Branko wondered how Dink Carruthers was doing after his divorce. How many marriages was that for the Dink? Two? Three?

The Volvo was stopped by a police barrier two blocks away from Cosmo's. Branko flashed his shield and they let the Volvo through. Up ahead the street in front of the crime scene was filled with official cars. Red roof lights swam through the dark, turning the white Spanish-style buildings a rosy pink. There was a television truck with the Channel 3 logo near the scene.

Branko parked fifty feet behind the nearest police unit. While he was locking his car, an officer in a yellow rain suit asked what he was doing there. Branko flashed his shield again. The inquiring officer was a big man, six-four, with a long jaw to match his long nose. He was carrying a five-cell flashlight. He stared at Lissa, who was clipping on her press pass, then swung his eyes back to Branko.

"All right, Sergeant. You know the routine. But do me a favor and stay out from underfoot, okay?"

"Is Dink Carruthers around?"

"The lieutenant was in the parking lot. You know him?"

"Yeah. We go way back."

The officer moved off, and Branko and Lissa headed for Cosmo's. Lissa brought out a mini tape recorder and spoke quietly into it. "Testing, testing, Cody on the scene at Cosmo's Cosmos, a Los Angeles night club in the La Cienega area." She put the recorder back into her purse.

An ambulance passed, siren growling. A cameraman was shooting footage from the roof of the Channel 3 truck. In front of him, policemen moved across the ornate doorway. Beside the entrance, a huge draping bougainvillea was in flower. A red carpet stretched from the entry to the edge of the parking lot.

Two tow trucks worked under the lights, trying to pry the nose of a late-model Ford out of the side door of a dark Chevrolet. Officers were clustered around a red Cadillac, parked thirty feet away from the two trucks.

They found Linda Calderon at the edge of the parking lot, interviewing a thick-bodied man that could only have been Branko's old pal, Dink Carruthers. The Dink looked older. He was Branko's age, forty-three, but he looked at least fifty and he was carrying some extra weight under the snappy leather sports coat. His round face glowed pale green under the lights from the parking lot. A wristwatch flashed as he gestured to Linda Calderon. He was wearing dress boots, the kind that zip up the sides

144

and retail for three hundred. As Branko and Lissa walked up, Linda Calderon terminated the interview and the camera pivoted away from him.

"Hey, Dink," Branko called.

The Dink swung around. "Is that my old buddy from night patrol?"

Branko stepped forward, grinning. "How's it hanging?"

"Goddamn." He pumped Branko's hand. "Frankie the Serb. You're here pretty quick."

"I was already on the way. Thanks for the message." Branko turned to Lissa. "Dink Carruthers, meet Lissa Cody."

The Dink's eyes lit up as he shook hands with Lissa. "Pleased to meet you, ma'am. Everything I say is off the record, okay?"

"Of course."

The Dink grabbed Branko's arm and gave it a squeeze. "You look fit, Frankie. Goddamn if you don't. Still hitting the tennis ball, I bet."

"When I can. What went down here, anyway?"

The Dink let out a long sigh. "I should exercise." He patted his belly and then pulled out his notebook and flipped it open.

"We got two dead and two wounded. Forensics will tell us who shot who tomorrow or the next day, but right here is the way it fell for me, for now. Corpse number one is Hector Mendoza, a citizen with no visible means of support. Hector-baby was carrying eight bills on his person, plus change. His weapon was a Winchester pump, twelve-gauge, the cut-down version, only it was on the seat of his vehicle, an 'eighty-seven Chevy Nova, and not in his hot little hands. Hector hails from the barrio, in central L.A. His nickname was 'the Connector,' and street scuttlebutt has it Hector was the official agent and go-between for clients wishing to hire your Chicago traveling roofers. For this service, he took ten percent, payable by the client. Hector was in the service, in Veetnam, along with you and some other fine horseflesh.

"Corpse number two is L. Mason Tompkins, a.k.a. the Mace. Mason-baby served time in Oregon state for sexual offenses and had a known appetite for young stuff. Pardon my French, Miss Cody, but some of the girls were ten or eleven. He's been brought in on three different occasions for sexually assaulting a minor. He did time in Oregon and spent three years upstate for armed robbery. The Mace's only visible means of support was Hector Mendoza.

"Wounded one was Alonzo J. Frenetti, a punk from Las Vegas who used to wrestle for television. Alonzo was bigger than the Mace. He was shot from about twenty feet with a medium-bore slug, probably a three-fifty-seven. The way we got it, Alonzo went for his target with an Uzi and took a blast from the three-fifty-seven.

"Wounded two is one Michele Nygren, a hooker down from Portland trying to escape the damp of the Pacific Northwest. Michele has one bullet in her shoulder and a head concussion from when she was slammed against the side of a car. Witnesses say she was with the perp inside Cosmo's. The maitre d' called him M'sieu Ringo. The bouncer at the door knew him as Benny Ringo. We're running both names through our database of known assailants."

"Was he left-handed?" Branko asked.

The Dink shook his head. "Nothing on that, sorry."

"What went down?"

The Dink sighed. "Well, as far as we can figure, the Mace was waiting in his Taurus when the perp came out with Hector. Alonzo was in the shadows, only he didn't move fast enough, so by the time he got into the action the perp was into the trunk of that red Caddy over there, pulling together his arsenal. In the Caddy we found three boxes of ammo for a three-fifty-seven, two for a nine millimeter. There was an Astra A-Eighty, which retails on the street for six bills, and an Ithaca Stakeout Thirty-seven."

"Twelve-gauge?"

"Twenty."

"Jesus."

"Anyway, the Mace rammed his Ford into Hector's Chevy. Neither vehicle will run at present. The red Caddy is registered to a B. R. Rubidoux, with an address in Santa Monica that we are tracing at present. In the purse of Ms. Nygren we found a receipt from Overnite X-Press. The receipt was a carbon, one of those

146

press-hard-you-are-making-four-copies deals. It got wet, so the writing's gone. In a twenty-four-hour period, Overnite X-Press sends seven-thousand-plus packages from the L.A. area." The Dink closed his notebook. "You folks want to tour the inside of this cathouse?"

"Sure."

As they headed for the front entrance, Branko asked a couple of questions. "You guys get a tip, or what?"

"Yeah. Call came in to the switchboard, male voice, said the hitter from Orange County was hanging out at Cosmo's."

"What time was that?"

"Just after eleven. I can check the log on that."

"Could he have seen the news and recognized the perp?"

"My guess is somebody saw him at the bar." The Dink nodded at the officer on the door, then stepped aside so Lissa could enter Cosmo's.

They followed Lissa in. "Have you seen the tape?"

"Our property guys have the original. There's a dupe for you boys down in Newport. Standard four-buck cassette. No identifying marks or scars."

"Can your techies find out what kind of camera was used?"

"Hell, I don't know. This ain't the movies." The Dink looked at his watch. "Man, am I bushed. Had a date tonight and she's probably run off with an airline pilot to Timbuktu."

"Nice watch, Dink."

The Dink shot his wrist out of his cuff. The watch was a handsome Rolex, bright and pulsing and expensive. "An aunt died, back in Minnesota. Left me some dough. I took a trip to Hong Kong. Picked this baby up for two hundred on the street." He showed the watch to Branko with a broad wink. "Fools everybody."

Cosmo's was all mirrors and deep-blue furniture. The carpet was deep-blue. The mirrored shelf behind the bar sparkled with colored glass. Lissa wandered toward the bar.

"Date means you're no longer a married man."

"Yeah." The Dink sighed. "Lainie kicked me out. Was that before you went south or after?"

"I didn't know Lainie."

"Shit, I didn't either. She was a showgirl, Vegas, Hollywood, finest legs I ever saw on a woman. Met her on the rebound from Dianne, at one of these goddamn hot-tub retreats near Lake Arrowhead. She had a teenage kid named Megan. Cute and insufferable, as my old man used to say. I forget, Frankie. Did you know Dianne?"

"I heard you speak fondly of her legs."

"Speaking of legs, the ones on Brenda Starr there are quite a set."

"We just met."

The Dink slapped Branko on the shoulder. "And life, old buddy, is short."

Branko walked with Carruthers across the blue carpet and through a door with a sign that said RICK'S ROULETTE.

"Inside scenario. Our man comes in with Michele. They have a drink, dance. Someone remembers them arguing. Place is full of hoods and their floozies, so you can't expect total recall here. One witness saw the perp take Hector-baby into the men's room. They come out and head for the emergency exit. An employee tries to stop them and gets his arm slashed open. There's a gun check at the door or the employee would have been wasted."

Across the room, Lissa was sitting at the bar, talking to a blond man in a reporter's trench coat.

"Why don't you guys close this joint down?"

"Vice was working on it. I'm still in homicide."

The Dink led the way into the casino, where a forensics specialist was poking through some broken glass, placing bits into a white envelope. Two plainclothes dicks stood at a second door smoking. Branko recognized the older one, a man named Burt Held. Held gave no sign he recognized Branko.

The casino contained three roulette wheels, a dice table, and three baize-covered tables for assorted other games. There were colored gambling chips everywhere. Branko picked up a pink one. The face of the chip read "$100 at Rick's, Los Angeles CA, under the Swaying Palms." Branko dropped the chip on the table.

Dink Carruthers pointed to the door where the detectives stood smoking. "Steam, massage, Jacuzzi. Cosmo's supplies towels, robes, hot water, you name it."

"What's the tab?"

"Two bills for the total treatment. Plus a bill at the door. Word on the street says it's not expensive, since they want you to relax and lose your shirt in the casino."

Three hundred was expensive for Branko. Exorbitant.

They wheeled three massage tables to the emergency door, where a forensics man in a worn gray suit was dusting the brass handle. Dink Carruthers asked him, "When can we get a make on those prints, Joby?"

"Eight o'clock, Lieutenant."

"Is that A.M. or P.M.?"

The forensics man smiled and went back to dusting.

Branko would have liked to stop and ask some questions, but he knew it would be out of line. This wasn't his turf. He would have to wait for evidence from the LAPD. It was lucky that the Dink was on the case. That way, the evidence might reach Newport Beach in time to be of some help.

At the front entrance, an officer handed Branko a package with his name on it. Inside was a VHS videocassette. The label on the cassette said BALBOA, NEWPORT BEACH.

"The receipt on the original was from a service called Mercury Courier. It's an outfit in the Valley, eight-one-eight area code, logo that reads faster than a speeding bullet. We've got a unit out there, trying to round up the manager, but it was probably a blind drop."

"Any description of the delivery guy?"

"A male Caucasian, early thirties. Wore dark slacks, a white shirt, and a bowtie. No one saw his vehicle."

"Neat job, Dink."

"Yeah. I'd love to meet the mastermind who thinks this shit up."

They walked outside and were joined by Lissa Cody.

"Any dirty old spent shell casings?" Branko asked.

"With Forensics."

"How soon can I get a report?"

"We should have a report down to you by mid-morning. How's that?"

"Terrific."

Branko shook hands and promised to stay in touch. He took

one last look at the shot-up Cadillac. It was this year's model and probably retailed for twenty grand. His watch said 1:22, which reminded him how tired he was. Lissa matched his stride as they headed for the Volvo. He kept remembering the Dink's comment about her legs. The fog was thicker now, sliding along the street.

"What was that poem, about fog and cat's feet?"

"Sandburg wrote one. So did T.S. Eliot."

"Yeah, I liked that Sandburg. Had a teacher in high school who rubbed my nose in poetry. Great lady."

"What was her name?"

"Westheimer. Had eyes that could see right into your soul."

Branko unlocked the car and they climbed in. He started it up and set the wipers on intermittent. Then he headed toward the freeway, making only one stop at Ship's, a twenty-four-hour restaurant, to fill his thermos with coffee.

Lissa indicated the thermos. "You are a planner, Frank Branko."

"I've been called worse."

The Volvo slid south toward Orange County through patches of fog. Lissa sat on her side of the car, feet curled beneath her, sipping coffee. They were in Orange County, with signs ticking off Costa Mesa, Corona del Mar, Newport Beach, Irvine, when Lissa brought up Dink Carruthers.

"How long have you known the lieutenant?"

"Years. He taught me about being a homicide cop."

"The one who could munch hotdogs at a murder scene?"

"Did I say hotdogs?"

"Poetic license." Lissa shifted on her seat. "Is he heading up the Cosmos investigation?"

Branko caught the tone in her voice and looked over. "He's either the number-one man or the number-two, why?"

Lissa waited before answering. "That man I spoke to at the bar inside was from the L.A. *Times.* He had one piece of information your friend Carruthers didn't have."

Branko felt the hair tingle on the back of his neck. "Like what?"

"Money."

"How much?"

"Seven thousand inside the Chevrolet. Another seven thousand in a Colonel Sanders fried chicken sack underneath the Chevrolet."

"Fourteen grand," Branko said.

"The reporter said it might have been more. Fourteen was an estimate."

"What is this, Cody, a story about police corruption?"

"Horrible thought, isn't it? Your brother officers on the take?"

Branko thought of the leather jacket, the Rolex watch—an imitation, said the Dink—the fancy thin-soled boots, trips to Hong Kong, the weary eyes. Fourteen grand, split up among the boys. It wouldn't be the first time.

Something was eating his old buddy.

"You're barking up the wrong political tree, Cody. I've known him a dozen years. He wouldn't do it."

"There was no reason for the *Times* man to make it up."

"Well, he's wrong about the Dink."

"How long has it been since you saw him?"

"Six years. Seven."

"This is my exit," Lissa said. "Peaceful Irvine."

Branko switched on the right-hand turn signal and eased over into the right lane, preparing for the exit. The dashboard clock read 2:48. He had a Task Force meeting at eight and he should get in to the station early and organize his notes. The Volvo hummed off the freeway. He stopped at the signal on Culver and then made a left turn when it changed to green, heading over the foggy freeway toward Lissa Cody's place on the lake in Woodbridge Village.

Lissa Cody brushed his shoulder as she slipped out of the car. "See you on the firing line, Branko."

He watched her hurry up to the door of her condo, a slim figure under the blurred gray-blue streetlight on the corner. Then he backed out of her driveway and headed for his place in Newport Beach.

Was Dink Carruthers on the take? Or was Lissa Cody's liberal imagination working overtime?

CHAPTER TEN

S ATURDAY morning Susannah was up early. A look out the window revealed a beachcliff world laced with filmy fog. She could see the cul-de-sac outside her window and a piece of the road that wound up Spyglass Hill but not the houses and the ocean beyond. The streetlights burned with an eerie gray glow.

She drank her ritual glass of grapefruit juice and dressed in shorts and jogging bra and a sleeveless white pullover that left four inches of bare tummy showing above the waistband of her shorts. It was chilly in the big house. Carrying her running shoes and ankle socks, she walked barefoot along the carpeted hallway and down the stairs. At the bottom, Susannah used the stairs to do five minutes of slow stretches, left heel on the fourth stair, right foot on the floor, both legs straight, feeling the muscles in her back and legs slowly release as she relaxed into the stretch. She bent sideways and grabbed her bare toes and pulled ever so slowly. When she felt her muscles loosening, she touched her head to her left knee. After ten repetitions, she reversed positions, right heel on the stair, left foot on the floor, left leg straight, bending, bending ever so slowly, listening to the muscles in her body.

Working out was Susannah's way of fighting time, of holding back the clock. . . .

She'd been plain until the age of twelve, just another flat-faced tomboy and a joyous natural athlete without training. She'd been a fierce ice skater and a terrific right fielder. She'd scraped her knees on the soccer field, just like the guys.

Then, almost overnight, her breasts had budded and her legs had gotten longer and the same boys she'd played baseball with in the long high-ceilinged Chicago summers were staring at her with sideways smirks. They talked behind her back, she knew that, she didn't know what they said. The comradeship was gone. Childhood was over. And Suzie Novak was lost in confusion.

In September of that year, an uncle from Sheboygan who smelled of cigar smoke and cheap wine had put his hand up her skirt and told her how pretty she was. Uncle Gabe. She could still remember the roughness of his touch, the primitive crudeness of his blunt fingers on her smooth skin, the creepy feeling of being used. Being touched by Uncle Gabe had made her queasy, nauseous, dizzy. She'd wanted to tell someone, but her father was dead and her mother was either always working or out on a date. Uncle Gabe was her mother's older brother. There was no one to tell. So she locked her door at night and steered clear of Uncle Gabe whenever he made a grab for her. When you were rich and something happened, you sucked your thumb and had breakdowns and saw the shrink. When you were poor, you got on with your life. Uncle Gabe went back to Sheboygan. She got on with her life.

The smirks from the boys increased in intensity that fall. Suzie turned to books. She ran alone. She ice-skated with girls. But the days of team sports were over. Rich kids played tennis, but Suzie thought tennis was for the birds. Then, when she was thirteen, a boy named Rudy Kravitz gave her a Baby Ruth bar wrapped in pretty silver paper and a note that said *I love you, Suzie. Signed, Rudy.* Rudy Kravitz was two years older, a heavy-shouldered football player of fifteen whose father owned a dry-cleaning establishment on Chicago's South Side. Trembling, she let Rudy kiss her. It didn't hurt. She saw stars. He wanted to do other things, unmentionable things. She could feel his desire pulsing, hot and out of control. His tongue felt funny in her ear.

In high school, a girlfriend named Molly Basinger taught her how to wear lipstick and choose just the right clothes to turn the heads of the boys. It wasn't long after meeting Molly Basinger that she realized being pretty set you apart from other people. When you were pretty, people stared at you and talked about you and called you stuck-up even when you were poor and just trying to get on with your life. When you were pretty, people wanted something from you, especially the boys. There was no name for it, no word you could use to describe it, to pin it down. But it was there, the wanting. She thought of it from their side as being hungry. From her side, it made her feel like a meal about to be wolfed down, eaten, devoured with a wink and a sly smirk. They had a sly word for it—*personality*—that thing that made you special and popular even though you had no money for milk to go with your lunch that you brought from home in a brown paper sack. And that's what saved Suzie Novak—feeling special, having personality, possessing it. She knew she had it when she walked into a room packed with sweaty kids. She'd wear the right lipstick and a dress that swirled around her legs. There'd be a silence as she came in, a hush, a vacuum waiting to be filled. She could feel them out there, wanting it, the whole crowd of them like a great wide mouth, yawning open, and that gave her a kind of power.

The boys wanted her and she wanted attention. Through the rest of high school, Suzie Novak's dates gave her presents. They brought her flowers and candy and perfume and wool mufflers to keep out the Chicago cold. They took her to movies and dances and one boy took her on a sleigh ride on New Year's Eve and it was magical. A boy with thick glasses gave her books. Dickens and *Jane Eyre* and *Moby-Dick* and three Penguin Shakespeare's. She devoured them all, got lost, escaped momentarily from the hunger. She read *True Romance* and *True Confessions*. The boys kissed her and put their hands on her and begged her to undress, unzip, unsnap her brassiere, lift her skirt, open her legs, let me touch there, or there. She refused. She kept herself pretty. She kept herself aloof and pure. No hanky-panky in somebody's back seat. No hand between her thighs. She was saving herself for her husband.

At Christmas of her seventeenth year, Suzie met a guy named Vincent Maggio, a slick-haired narrow-faced Italian whose parents had made money in the restaurant business. The Maggios lived in ritzy and exclusive Kenilworth, on the North Shore, in a huge house with Greek columns in front and a butler and a cook and a black wrought-iron fence to keep out undesirables and a covered tennis court. Vincent's sister Maria was an aspiring player. When she wasn't on the court, Vincent and Suzie would bat the ball around, just for fun. Vincent was clumsy in a funny, big-footed way, but Suzie was a natural. She already knew how to hit a baseball with a narrow wooden bat, so connecting with the same size ball with a tennis racket was duck soup. She could also throw, which taught her wrist how to rotate. Consequently, the borrowed racket felt like an extension of herself as she danced across the pale orange clay of the Maggio court at Kenilworth. To Suzie, the smell of the clay represented untold wealth, so much money you could never spend it.

God, she'd been hungry.

One day that spring when she was batting the ball around, Suzie attracted the eye of Maria's coach, an old pro named Horace Herzog, who rallied with her for a couple of minutes and told her she reminded him of a fledgling Alice Marble. Horace was a sad-eyed man with tanned arms who moved around the court in white pants and a soft cotton shirt and tennis shoes. He had played on a thing called "the circuit," and had played Don Budge and Wilmer Allison and other names she'd never heard of. His strokes were clean and efficient, and Suzie loved his volley and overhead smash. So crisp, so effortless. She found a book by Alice Marble in the school library. The women in the old photographs wore white skirts and starched blouses and funny little sun hats, and they played on grass, in a place called Forest Hills. To Suzie, it was a world of distant magic—Germantown, Longwood, Newport. The grass was cool, green, wet. Suddenly, she yearned to go East to school.

Suzie had a job as a go-fer at Marshall Field's. She took on six more hours a week at seventy-five cents an hour. She paid Horace Herzog five dollars a week—half price—to teach her the game. He told her she was starting late but she could make up for that with work. Maria Maggio gave Suzie some of her old tennis dresses, but Suzie, ever the tomboy, preferred shorts and a T-shirt.

The shorts won her a lot of admiring looks and even some whistles, but Horace never looked at her legs, never stared at her. He only talked about footwork, balance, getting to the ball without having to take a taxi, tennis, playing percentages, winning.

Suzie was still seventeen when she won her first tournament, beating a girl named Beth Anne Gingrich from the Rock River Country Club in Rockford. The tournament was an Eighteen and Under in Lake Forest, a place full of snotty rich kids and pretty tennis moms. She had never been so happy. A week later, Vincent Maggio sailed for Europe, leaving his souped-up Ford with Suzie. "Don't wreck my heap, babe."

Suzie took a job in a tennis camp on a lake in Wisconsin. Vincent wrote her postcards from Rome, Venice, Florence, Siena, Capri. Vincent was a college boy from Notre Dame, four years older than Suzie. He'd been around. She knew he had experience in the love department, but when he wanted into her pants she made him wait, just like the others. Nothing doing. She was saving herself for her husband.

The summer Vincent was away, Suzie moped around. Her tennis game went to pieces. She lost herself in teaching the game to rich kids with big mouths, braces on their teeth, and no talent. Horace watched her with sad eyes. She imagined Vincent with his arms around Monica Vitti and Sophia Loren. Italian girls smoldered with sex appeal. Everyone knew that. Suzie felt the competition all the miles across the Atlantic. Now *she* had a hunger.

When Vincent came home, Suzie wept tears of relief and let him make sweaty, groaning love to her in his bedroom overlooking Lake Michigan. A photo of his grandfather stared down at the lovers from its place on the wall. Vincent was an expert lover and an Italian stallion with meaty brown thighs and hair on his chest. Suzie was a scared Chicago virgin with long tanned legs and an overbite and a mouth that was too wide. In her underwear, Suzie froze, covering herself with crossed arms. Vincent laughed, played, kissed her belly, tongued her navel, thawed her out. She thought he was a magician, making her feel so warm, so loved, so with it, jeez, like nothing she'd ever felt before. There wasn't much bleeding. The pain everyone talked about was hardly there. She thought it was love, forever. She heard wedding bells. Vincent knew better. He went back to Notre Dame, to his fraternity games. When he didn't telephone, Suzie went wacko. When she got clingy and phoned him, Vincent dumped her.

156

Pain shot through her like a knife, but Suzie Novak had made a discovery. Love was not a percentage game.

Her senior year, she went into mourning. She started wearing black and brown and dingy gray. She would not wear lipstick or makeup. She cut her hair short and threw her earrings into a drawer. She got jobs baby-sitting, which paid more than wrapping gifts at a department store in the Loop. She kept up her tennis lessons at an indoor court in Evanston. All winter, she rode the elevated to Evanston and worked out on the breezy indoor court while her breath exhaled gray and sad as she tried to blot out Vincent Maggio. She drove herself with a cool, controlled frenzy and lost herself in the game. She won an indoor tournament and got a scholarship offer to Northern Illinois in De Kalb but nothing from the hotsy-totsy schools back East. Suzie was disappointed. She wanted to go East to school and study literature and political science. She wanted to play on the cool green courts of Longwood and Germantown. Radcliffe, Vassar, Smith—the names whispered to her, mocked her because she was an outsider.

Instead, she played with men who asked her out on dates. Across the net, she would detect man-smell, see the hunger in their eyes. She would say no. "Gotta study," she would say. "Gotta work." Tennis was her way of forgetting, her way of evening the odds against life.

In her first tournament of the summer—the Michigan Invitational in East Lansing—Suzie lost in the finals to a girl three years younger who had been playing since she was six. She knew then what Horace Herzog had meant by starting late. "Forget it, Suzie," Horace said. "She was born with a golden racket between her teeth. Keep working. You'll make it."

But the girls who started early had already made it, and Suzie was too old for the big-time. The greats—Billie Jean and Helen Wills Moody and Althea Gibson—had started early. Chrissie Evert had reached the quarters at Forest Hills when she was sixteen. Suzie was seventeen.

At De Kalb, Suzie kept to herself and wrote papers and dreamed of going East. That's where the rich kids went. The guys went to Yale and Harvard and Dartmouth. The girls went to Smith and Barnard. The term load at Northern Illinois was five courses, so she took seven, an overload. She wanted the truth, wanted to even the odds against life. She devoured English literature, psychology, history, art, marketing, accounting, communications, drama, speech, art history, physical education. There was no women's tennis team, so she faced off with the men on Saturdays, playing the game Horace had taught her—craft, guile, percentages—and beat them. She made all As and earned the respect of her teachers. They couldn't believe that a pretty girl with piercing blue eyes and a sexy smile could study so hard. She took a job in a local bookstore, where they gave her an employee discount on books. She attracted all kinds of men, hulking college jocks who asked her for dates, businessmen who had the hunger, teachers. She went to movies with them, dances, frat parties, but said hands off when it came time for necking and she began to smell the man-smell. No hanky-panky in the backseats of cars. Love was a stiletto, not a percentage game.

Suzie was a sophomore when she learned about Freud and Jung and subliminal seduction and selling products in the marketplace with fantasy sex. This was it. This was the truth. This was an explanation of how to turn the hunger inside out. She read books on consumer behavior. She researched the tactics and techniques of advertising. She wrote papers on tricks used by advertisers. She research articles by a man from Vienna named Ernest Dichter, who had watched male car buyers in auto showrooms running their hands over curved car bodies and made the connection—automobile as sex object—that boosted car sales in the forties. She wondered if Dr. Dichter had done any research about man-smell.

In December of her sophomore year, her favorite professor, Dr. Jerry Morgan, took her to dinner in Chicago and confessed he was in love with her. His eyes were lit up and he stammered a little as he said he wanted to go upstairs and, well, um, you know. Dr. Morgan was an associate professor of psychology, thirty years old, single, and semi-attractive. He wore glasses, but that didn't bother Suzie because they made him look smart. Over dessert, Suzie looked behind the glasses into his eyes and saw the image of Vincent Maggio. She saw the primitive male-hunger that knew only itself. Seeing it in Dr. Morgan's eyes surprised her. He was a serious young man who wore tweeds and smoked a pipe and played handball on Saturday with the baseball coach. Love, she reminded herself, was a stiletto.

"Well, all right."

She had been thinking about this moment for a long time. Years. How to stack the percentages in favor of love.

Dr. Morgan rented a room, and she went upstairs with him in the elevator. She stood close, her head on his shoulder, tendrils of blond hair twining down his tweed coat, smelling the man-smell. In the room, she let him kiss her while she loosened his tie, unbuttoned his shirt, worked his belt loose, slid his zipper down. He smelled of cologne and pipe tobacco and something professorial. The odds were on her side. He was hungry. Life was a restaurant where she controlled the menu. Could she also set prices?

When he was undressed, Suzie looked at him, his penis quivering at attention, his legs a ghostly Midwestern white in the light from the bedside table, and told him it would cost fifty dollars. His answering grin, a twisted grimace filled with pain, immediately made her understand she had not charged enough.

"You little bitch!"

"I'm a poor college girl, Professor. And I want to go East to school." Her voice sounded older, more mature, tinged with a heavy feminine irony, a knowing sound she had only heard in her mind before that moment. That irony, Suzie knew, was a thousand years old. Two thousand. Three. Older than time. His face was pale with hate. She pulled off her sweater, a brown mohair. She knew what she was doing. He was a boy, not a man. To the boy-professor, she was a fantasy from a world that existed in his arrested imagination. She was a photo in a magazine, a picture on a flickering screen. In one of her research papers for Dr. Morgan, she had pointed out that the desired female sex object was a mother-symbol, curves and promises and the hope of a vanished womb-safety. In the margin next to that paragraph, Dr. Morgan had placed a triple exclamation mark, acknowledging a super insight. The paper had earned her an A-plus.

"They're right." His foot caught in his trousers as he tried to get his pants back on. "About your being a campus whore."

The name was meant to hurt, all a part of the war, the driving man-hunger, but she wasn't listening. If Dr. Morgan would pay fifty dollars, there were probably men out there who would pay more. Suzie was from Chicago, the home of *Playboy* magazine, and she remembered a centerfold that showed a woman undressing—right foot on a chair, left foot on the floor, blouse half undone, skirt hiked up, hair hanging down in a seductive curtain and hiding her face as she unsnapped her garter belt—and as Dr. Morgan berated her she assumed that pose.

It was market research. Testing. Testing. She was a fantasy, a symbol, an image packed with power. He paid the money and she gave him what he wanted. She was nineteen and a sophomore in college when she founded Nightingale Enterprises.

She was a Chicago girl who had grown up with the image of the Palmer House, so that's where she did business. The john paid for the room. She charged three hundred a night, six hundred for the weekend. She had a sixth sense about men that told her when there was trouble brewing. One warning and she was out of there, out of the room and down the hall to the elevator. No explanations. No money changing hands. If she didn't have control, Suzie Novak walked.

In her junior year, Suzie met Robert Devane. She knew he was some kind of soldier on leave. The suit hanging in the closet looked like a uniform. He was neat and clean, with strange blue eyes and lots of money. He tipped her a hundred when she undressed for him the first time on Friday night, saying he admired talent. He tipped her another hundred on Saturday and two hundred more on Sunday when he drove her to the bus station in his rented car. He carried a small bottle of olive oil, which he called grease from Greece. He used the olive oil to take Suzie from behind. . . .

Susannah was thinking of that first weekend with Devane in the Palmer House in wintry Chicago as she left the house on Spyglass Hill and walked out into the wet foggy morning. She shivered at first, feeling the damp on her bare arms and legs. She started slowly, hearing her Nike runners tapping the asphalt of the curved road, but by the time she reached Sandcastle she was running smoothly and perspiration soaked her sleeveless white top.

Sandcastle ran into Marguerite, which ran southwest to Pacific Coast Highway. Once she reached the coast highway, Susannah boosted her speed. There were few cars out this early, and the streetlights were still on, because of the fog. She turned right on Center Drive and headed up to Fashion Island. A maintenance man wearing a blue uniform waved as she ran past and she waved back. She circled Fashion Island. There was more new construction underway. Newport Beach was filling up. You'd think a buyer would surface for her house.

She finished her circuit and headed back toward Spyglass Hill. It was an hour over the hill to Devania and an hour back. She had shopping to do. Then, later on, she would hold the last party for poor Reverend Williams.

She was looking forward to only two things in the coming week. Tomorrow, she had her regular Sunday match against the club's assistant pro, Miguelito. She planned to murder him. And then on Tuesday she would collect her thousand dollars from Roberto when the reverend lost to Congressman James Sherwood in the primary. She would serve Roberto a plate of crow.

As she thought of her wager with him, Susannah shivered. She dreaded her trip to Devania.

In the dream, the reverend drove his yellow VW, following behind Susannah Maxwell in her gray BMW. The yellow VW was his college car and he was twenty again, his body tough and hard and tanned from lifeguarding.

The license plate of Susannah's BMW was neon-blue, neon-pink, blinking off and on, like a heart beating. When it was off, he couldn't read the letters. When it was on, the letters spelled out Helen of Troy. The reverend was wearing a white wedding suit and the VW was headed south on Pacific Coast Highway toward the Pirate's Cove Motel.

There it went again. Blinking on. Helen. Of. Troy. And then off.

The BMW pulled into a parking place around the corner from

the motel office. A tall blond woman stepped out, displaying her exquisite legs, and walked to the door of room 113. The blue dress shimmered in the heat and the high heels made her ankles look pretty. The reverend licked his lips as he watched her. Then he parked the VW three cars away and followed her.

His hand was on the doorknob when the door opened and his wife stood there, gray hair and fierce gray eyes and a mouth twisted with scorn. "There!" Winona Lee grabbed him by the throat and pulled him inside. A blond woman dressed in blue was sitting on the bed, smoking a cigarette and rocking one leg over the other. She was not Susannah after all. "Jezebel! Whore of Babylon!" Winona Lee hissed.

The woman in blue kept on smoking while Winona Lee danced around the reverend, cursing. The woman stared through the smoke at a small boy of twelve who stood on a stage in a saloon in Hollywood under lights filled with a thousand romantic dust motes while he sang "O Danny Boy" to a hushed house of drunks and philanderers like Daddy.

"Jezebel!" Winona Lee hissed again.

And Daddy raised the pistol and blew his brains out. . . .

The Angel of Death hovered above the reverend, a shadowy figure mired in the smell of Juicy Fruit gum. Mama had chewed Juicy Fruit—for her voice, she said. Daddy had sucked Sen-Sen, to clear his palate, he said.

"Are you all right? Are you all right?"

"The pain," he grunted. "The pain." He could not breathe.

She gave him a shot, and in moments he felt the pain recede and he could breathe again. Relief bloomed inside him like a great flower. He was awake. He was in a hospital. The motel of his weekday noontime adulterations was behind him, somewhere along a loop in the great skein of biblical time. He'd been dreaming. His mouth tasted of filth and grime. Helen of Troy had sailed off into the sunset. He'd given the prostitute two hundred dollars and let her keep the blue dress. The wound in his leg burned with all the fires of hell.

"Your son is here."

"Terry Junior? Where?"

"Outside. He's just arrived. The poor thing drove all night. Do you feel like seeing him?"

"Of course. Of course. Send him in."

The nurse went away and the reverend inched his way up in bed against the pillows. He wondered what day it was and then realized it was Saturday morning. He'd been shot yesterday afternoon. Had the news reached New York yet? He flicked on the television as the door opened and Terry Junior came in. His son was wearing baggy gray trousers, tight at the ankle, a pink shirt, and a dark jacket with shoulder pads. His eyes looked concerned as he neared the bed. His handshake possessed the strength of youth. There was no replay of the Balboa tape on television. Perhaps none of this had happened.

"Dad, are you okay?"

The reverend studied his son's eyes. Thank God, they did not resemble Winona Lee's. "It hurts, but the medication helps. You look pooped, son."

"I got in after six. Mom was here. She filled me in on stuff." Terry Junior pulled up a chair next to the bed.

"Where did your mother go?"

"To the church, I think. She said she'd be back later."

The reverend listened while Terry Junior explained once more why he hadn't learned earlier about the shooting.

"We were studying, Dad, really burning the books. Annie has this new tape and we played it over and over and—"

"How is Annie?"

"Great, Dad. Just great. She wanted to drive down with me, but she's got a big whinger of a final on Monday. She'll be down Wednesday, if all goes well."

"You should think of your own schooling."

"It will keep, Dad. It will keep."

"Do something for me, son."

"Sure, Dad."

"Help me brush my teeth. My mouth feels as if a garbage truck spent the night there."

"Brush your teeth?"

"Yes. Help me to the bathroom. I've been in this bed too long. It feels like a grave."

"Gosh, Dad. Don't say that."

"The nurses must not know."

His son put strong hands on him. With his son's help, he could move mountains. "Sure, Dad."

One leg, and then the other leg, and the pain hovering about three feet away, and then the lifting up and the slow testing of space, a motion made twenty-four hours ago with zero pain now claiming one hundred percent of his concentration as the burning began in the upper thigh near the wound and he bit his lip to keep from crying out because what he was really doing was taking a test walk to prove to himself he could get up under his own power before Winona Lee arrived with her accusing finger to tell him she knew about the weekday adulterous assignations with Helen of Troy and all the whores of Babylon.

It was nine when Susannah left the house. She was wearing a yellow skirt that buttoned up the front, a white blouse, and white shoes with medium heels. Under the skirt, her legs were bare, the way Roberto liked them. She wore bikini underpants but no brassiere.

She drove south on the coast highway through Laguna Beach and South Laguna to Dana Point. There she turned north on Del Obispo, passing through San Juan Capistrano. She crossed the San Diego Freeway on the Ortega Highway, and put on a tape of Chopin. The road twisted and turned as if climbed, and there were still wisps of fog clinging to the bushes at the side. As she entered the Cleveland National Forest, the road wound into a wooded area near a creek. Then, as it climbed once more, she left the trees behind. She topped the pass as the sun was breaking through. Below her, to the left, was Lake Elsinore.

The BMW purred smoothly as she down-shifted and started her descent into the valley. The road twisted past houses leaning out from the hills on stilts. Signs warned truckers to use lower gears. The sun was baking hot as she left the mountain behind. The tape reversed for the second time and she pressed the eject button and put in a Mozart tape. *Eine Kleine Nachtmusik*. It had been one of Jordan's favorites.

Susannah made a right on Grand, near the military academy, and drove southeast. She hadn't gone three miles before a road sign welcomed her to Sierra Monte, population 521. WELCOME TO SIERRA MONTE, the sign read, A SLICE OUT OF THE OLD WEST.

Sierra Monte had a main street, a hardware store, a bank, three motels, five cocktail lounges, a corner café, a feed store, a Western clothing store, a Texaco station, and a courthouse that looked like a picture postcard. In the courthouse parking lot, Susannah counted seven black-and-white units from the sheriff's department. Two men without shirts were hosing them down. She knew they worked for Roberto. She glared at the Bank of Sierra Monte as she drove past. It was the bank that held the mortgage on her house.

She stopped at the phone booth at the Arco station and phoned Devane. He answered on the first ring. "This is Crap Shoot, go ahead."

She smiled every time she heard that. It was so boylike, the silly codes. "Roberto, it's me."

"What's your ETA, kid?"

"Twenty minutes, Roberto."

"Alarms are off, kid. You got a twenty-minute window. If you get delayed, give me another call."

It was the same routine every time. "Yes, Roberto."

She got back behind the wheel and drove out of Sierra Monte. The lake was behind her now as she turned right, heading up a road into the hills. Pepper trees lined the road and sunlight filtered through the pale green leaves. After a mile, the asphalt turned to gravel and a sign reminded her that county maintenance ended there. The road was still damp from last night's rain. Up ahead, Susannah saw the gate and the signs that said No Trespassing. A six-foot storm fence stretched out on both sides of the gate, the boundary of Devania. She reached into the glove compartment for the electronic door opener Roberto had given her. One touch and the gate swung open and she drove through.

The road wound up through a ravine. A deer crossed the white gravel ahead of her, heading for some bushes and making Susannah smile at its little white tail. A mile from the main compound, she turned off the road and parked behind a large rock outcropping. There was shade there, from the rocks. She left the windows cracked an inch, got out, and locked the car. Jordan's leather carryall was in the trunk. She tested the beam of the flashlight. Still bright. Steadying herself on the fender of the

165

BMW, she changed into high-topped boots and put her high heels into the carryall. Then she pulled a light cotton sweater over her white blouse. The tunnel was always dusty and she liked to arrive looking like a photo from Roberto's favorite magazine.

She brushed a strand of hair away from her forehead, threw the carryall over her shoulder, and headed for the tunnel.

Sitting at the curved console in the War Room, Devane watched Suze on the screen. It gave him a view of her car—today she was driving the little BMW—and a good look at her legs as she changed her footwear.

The phone rang just as Suze left the screen, heading for the tunnel, her leather satchel over her shoulder.

"This is Crap Shoot, go ahead."

"Bobby, it's Bat Shit Two." Jimmy Jack Jessup, calling from Washington, D.C.

"Well, J. J., where's my cash?" Devane, who never trusted anyone, pressed the record button on the cassette player attached to the phone.

There was a pause at the other end. "There's been a delay, Bobby. The bank transfer was held up in Zurich."

Devane kicked back in his swivel chair and put his feet on the desk. "You're letting your old CIA buddies ace you at the trough."

"I'll be there, as scheduled, but it'll be Monday instead of Sunday. Where's the merchandise?"

"Stacked at the depot, waiting on the bureaucrats to finish jacking each other off."

J. J. sighed. "It's not easy at my end, Bobby."

"Shit." Devane was studying a map of the world that showed the proportion of whites to non-whites. Color codes detailed population growth in three-year jumps between 1975 and 1988. Each year, the number of non-whites ballooned while the number of whites grew smaller, which was a good reason to keep on killing wogs and gooks, Devane told himself. By Monday, he hoped Amity Pitcairn would have the Rubidoux deal wrapped up. "I heard you Banana Knife boys moved your office, over to Alexandria."

"How the hell did you hear that?" J. J. spluttered.

"Intelligence," Devane said. "Ever hear of it?"

"The Pentagon paper pushers want another accounting. We can handle it."

"You better, or them guns will head east instead of south."

"Damn you, Bobby. We had a deal."

"Buzz me when you hit town. I'll send a staff car to ride your ass in."

"I hate that tunnel, Bobby."

The line went dead.

Devane finished his coffee and pulled up the computerized inventory ledger on the arms shipment. The money, $9 million in U. S. currency, had been due Friday in the Bank of Sierra Monte. The shipment old J. J. was so worried about was in Devane's warehouse, ready to be loaded onto flatcars and transported along the narrow gauge railway through the Santa Ana mountains to a truck depot on the ocean side. The shipment consisted of small artillery, 500 bazookas, 750 machine guns, and 1,000 M-16s left over from a forgotten war in Asia. Devane had thrown in some cases of hand grenades and a few land mines. The shipment had cost Devane $3 million. He was selling it to Jimmy Jack Jessup's Pentagon Strike Group Four for a profit of $6 million before he paid off the Cadre.

With that money, he could keep Devania running for another couple of years. Devane hated digging into his capital or his gemstone cache for the Cadre. He knew the shipment would head south, down Nicaragua way, where it would go to waste, rust out. That was not his worry. Guns had zero morality. If he'd been five years younger, he'd have gone down there and showed the contradictory *contras* how to win a two-bit banana war.

They wanted guns, they came to him, even when they worked in the fat-cat Pentagon with cowboy names like Black Bag and Banana Knife. Let the wogs knock off the gooks and the gooks knock off the wogs and Devane would take the high ground with a few white men and make money off both sides. For the taxpayers who footed the bills and sat around with their thumbs up their asses, he felt only contempt.

James J. Jessup was a bird-colonel from Virginia attached to a general who was attached to a military adviser who was in bed with the president, Charley Donnelly. Newspaper reporters called J. J.'s people "black-baggers" and sniffed around trying to find evidence of a "black budget." They hadn't even come close.

J. J. was Devane's black budget man in the Pentagon. Back in Vietnam, Jimmy Jack had been Special Forces, Intelligence. Now he was Pentagon, Special Ops. He wore size thirteen boots and he had been overweight even in the jungle.

The problem with J. J.'s current outfit was the budget crunch—just a lousy couple billion, which had to be divided between CIA covert and Pentagon Special Ops. Devane had worked with Special Ops before. The pricks never paid on time and they could screw up any timetable. There were too many officers and not enough grunts. This particular deal had made him laugh—shipping guns to Nicaragua under the code-name "Operation Banana Knife." In his mind, the *contras* were just wogs who spoke a special brand of Mexican. They had no leadership. Their military objectives were microscopic. Better to stand 'em against a wall, tie on the blindfolds, and go bang-bang.

Old J. J. was a true bureaucrat. His first thought was protecting his own ass. His second thought was keeping the bureaucracy going. His third thought, if he ever got there, was his assignment.

Well, when the Tuesday primary was over, Devane would set up a meeting with Reverend Lard-Ass and get the lines straightened out in Washington. The money was there, floating around. All you had to do was scoop it up and truck it to a bank. Too bad old Jordy Maxwell wasn't around to see how his plan finished up. Devane had already owned a couple of kings. He was looking forward to owning his own congressman. It would be like training a dog to heel, fetch, bark on cue, and generate appropriations for armchair soldiers like J. J. Jessup.

Devane hit the button that sent the inventory back into computer storage and walked to the kitchen, where he pulled out a bottle of Plymouth gin. He put the gin in a bucket, packed ice around it, grabbed two limes and a cutting board, and then carried the whole set-up to the Rumpus Room. On the way, he eyeballed the quad through his security peephole. Members of the Cadre were policing the area where he still wanted his polo field. He double-checked the bolt on the front door, then tested a couple of window shutters, sliding them closed on their tracks until only firing slits remained. He'd paid plenty for those shutters. They made him feel secure.

The house was modeled on a hacienda he'd seen down in Mexico that was owned by a rancher-politico named Don Juan de Cordoba who was one of Devane's conduits for military hardware to bidders from the Third World.

The Rumpus Room was L-shaped. The bed was king-sized and its head was pushed up against an inside wall. A large walk-in closet separated the Rumpus Room from the library. He stepped to the rear of the closet and unbolted the door that led to his escape tunnel. This was Devane's secret back door. A tunnel had helped him escape Dien Bien Phu, back in 1954, when ten thousand of his buddies from the Foreign Legion had been captured by the goddamn Viet Cong. He'd spent six months in the jungle, hiding out. That tunnel had saved his ass. This one was an old mine shaft, left over from a ninety-day piss-ant gold rush in the Elsinore area back around the turn of the century. The vein had played out. The tunnel had stayed.

The tunnel was the main reason he'd built Devania where he had. Since he'd met up with Suze Novak again, it had come in handy. Devane didn't allow women to visit Devania. If his Cadre wanted pussy, they applied for a leave and got a stamped pass from the duty sergeant and headed out for the whorehouses of civilization. If they ever got smart and rich, which wasn't likely, they could build their own haciendas with their own compounds and warehouses and helicopter pads. You had to earn your way to the point where you could play rumpus games with fancy ladies like Suze Maxwell, especially if you wanted to win. Devane had at least two secret visitors a week. For a quarter of a century, he had operated on a need-to-know basis. There was no need for his troops to know about the tunnel, and that included smart-asses like Willie Hazzard.

In the closet, Devane listened but could not hear footsteps yet. He set the gin on the bedside table.

Today, the troops were busy at the warehouse, taking inventory on J. J.'s black-budget arms shipment. His first assignment for Suze, once she came over to his side, was to courier some cash into his Zurich bank. Today, he would discuss it with her.

For their morning rumpus, Devane was wearing fresh combat fatigues, starched and pressed, with a knife-edge crease in the trousers. He took a minute to buff his boots and check his reflection in the mirror. Then he plumped up three pillows on the bed and lay down to wait for her. He flicked on the television. There was a morning news roundup with two minutes on the Fun Zone shooting—no leads yet, but a slick stop-action rerun of the tape showing the main events—and three minutes on the Cosmo's Cosmos shooting last night in Los Angeles. The tape had been a dynamite idea, and Operation Lard-Ass had worked out good. But he admitted to himself he'd made a mistake with Sergeant Mendoza.

An all-points bulletin was out for a Robert Ringo, last seen leaving the parking lot of Cosmo's on foot. The same old composite flashed on the screen. If you have seen this man, do not take action. Inform the authorities and stay out of the way. Devane pushed the off button and the image faded to blackness.

Suze was due any minute now. While he waited, Devane made notes on a scratch pad. Finish loading Banana Knife shipment. Connect Phoenix in LAPD to Amity P. Finish Benny Scumbag. Meet with J. J., get money first. Tie off the Tuesday primary. Contact Reverend Lard-Ass, training begins. Finish deal with Suze's house. Meet the diamond cutter in Los Angeles, see if he knows his ass. Fly down to Honduras, for the gun deal with Hernan Gorgonio.

He heard the tunnel door opening inside the closet and then there were footsteps and a pause. Clothes rustled and he figured she was changing shoes. He was right. She pushed open the closet door and stood there leaning against it, smiling her sultry hooker's smile. The leather satchel was over her shoulder. The high heels made her legs look even better. And three buttons on her blouse were undone. Sweet.

"Did you bolt the door?"

Suze nodded, then dug into him before he could pour the gin.

"Are they here?"

"Is who here?"

"The killers. If they're here, perhaps I could see them."

"What killers?"

"The ones you hired, Roberto. To do the shooting on Balboa." She walked to a window and stared out at the loading operation. "I'd love to be introduced."

Devane left the bed to pour her a drink. "What the hell gave you that idea?"

"It's your style, Roberto. 'Leave the tactics to me,' you said. And then you said, 'latest hit single.' I know what a hit is."

Devane handed her the gin, then sat down on the bed. He had known she'd figure it out. But not quite so fast.

Suze sat down in the easy chair and crossed her legs, making damn sure the skirt hiked up to show him some sweet meat on her inside thigh. She was his weakness and he was willing to admit it. Damn the bitch. He sat on the bed, smiling a thin smile. Suze smoothed the skirt along her thighs, just to remind him about the goodies lurking there. "I understand, Roberto. You want to import Nairobi politics into Orange County."

"You could always turn a phrase, Suze."

"What on earth were you thinking of? Winning our little bet?"

Devane lay back, one hand behind his head. "Washington," he said.

"Washington?"

"Yeah. You and me in a fancy-ass house in Georgetown."

There was a long silence. Then she said, "Together?"

Devane nodded. "Yeah."

"You'd leave here? Leave the hacienda?"

"Yup."

She shook her head and re-crossed her legs. "I don't believe you."

"Wait until Tuesday when the votes are counted."

"The reverend could have been killed."

Devane shook his head. "No. Wasn't in the plan."

"That bodyguard, Mac White. He was Jordan's friend."

"He was a soldier. Had to get it sometime. Died a soldier's death, in combat. Did himself proud."

Suze stared at him for a moment, then looked away. Sweat

171

appeared on her upper lip, a good sign. She brushed at the space in front of her eyes with her left hand. He liked her revved up, smoky.

"You had it all planned, didn't you? When you got me drunk and made that bet?"

"Timing is all."

She got up and walked over and stood staring at him. "Roberto, this is not darkest Africa or some banana republic. You can't gun people down to get what you want."

Enough talk. He reached for the bitch, but she backed away. Her eyes were cold as she snatched her purse and started for the closet. Devane was off the bed in one easy motion. He caught her in the closet, just as she was unbolting the door, and swung her around.

"Damn you, Roberto!"

Her wrists were warm and he was always surprised at how strong she was. It was one reason he liked her—the sheer physical strength unleashed in a woman who looked like Suze. She tried to knee him in the crotch, and he turned his hip to block her. She pulled him off-balance, throwing him against a wall. Clothes on hangers broke his momentum. Suze jacked the bolt back and swung the door open. Before he could grab her, she was out of the closet and down the steps into the tunnel. He followed her down, caught her by the hair. Any other woman would have screamed, but not Suze Maxwell. Instead of pulling away and tightening his hold on her hair, she came at him, kicking and hot. There wasn't much light down there from the closet, but he could have sworn she was smiling like a goddamn Amazon. He grabbed her blouse and heard it tear. She bumped him with a shoulder, driving him off-balance. He slapped her ass a good one with the flat of his hand. She made a grab for his privates. He chopped her hand away and drove a fist toward her stomach. She dodged and his fist caught her on the edge of the pelvic bone, making her whimper. They were both breathing hard now, panting. Devane was sweating, fucking up his fresh fatigues. He felt her fingernails claw at his face. He nailed her in the upper torso with his elbow, throwing her off-balance, then got an arm behind her in a hammerlock.

When she felt the advantage shift to him, Suze stopped fighting. She was quite a faker.

"I hate you!"

He hunched her up the steps and into the closet, the smell of her perfume strong in his nostrils. In the light now, he saw that her blouse was indeed torn. Her right shoulder gleamed in the light. The nipple on her right tit was as sharp as a fresh-poured bullet.

She made one more try for his privates as he half shoved, half carried her to the bedroom. He blocked the kick and kneed her in the thigh.

"You're bruising me, you bastard."

Devane didn't answer. The time for words was over. She was here. He was here. He held her face down on the big bed, one knee on the small of her back. The yellow skirt was hiked halfway up her thighs. Her hair was mussed. He let his knee up, grabbed the blouse, and pulled. There was a tearing sound. She cursed him. He flipped her over like a fish in a frying pan. Her body looked better today than it had fifteen years ago. Suze lived outside the bounds of time. Other people got old, but Suze Novak Maxwell possessed the secret of eternal youth. She was a witch. Which was one more reason he wanted her. She cursed him again and tried to roll away. He grabbed the blouse and tore it off her. Her tits swung free. Being bare-ass excited her. He grabbed her hair. That always stopped her. He pulled her over to the bedside table, opened a drawer, and got out the olive oil. She tried to knock it out of his hand, but he pulled away, grinning.

"Roll over, Suze."

"Go to hell."

He never knew when she would give in. Sometimes she gave in easy. Sometimes she made him work. He was boiling now. Sweat gleamed on her back, throat, ribcage. It took him a couple of minutes to wrestle her back onto her belly. He pulled the skirt off and shucked her out of the panties and jackknifed her up, elbows and face on the pillow, her fine golden ass hiked into the air. Grinning, Devane unzipped. When he took her from the rear, she was still wearing the high-heeled shoes and he was wearing his combat fatigues.

He was finished with her in ninety seconds. The action was hot, sharp, tangy, victorious.

Breathing easily, Devane left her on her belly on the bed and zipped up. She lay there, not saying anything, watching him with a flat-eyed look. It was always the same. The female fought and then gave in. He knew she'd be back. He walked to the library, where he kept a leather-bound copy of *On War* by Karl von Clausewitz. He opened the book. Inside, the pages had been hollowed out to make a square hiding place. In the hiding place was a soft black sack. He put the sack in his pocket and moved to the big desk, where he unlocked a drawer and took out a brown folder tied with red string. On the folder were the words SPYGLASS CIRCLE, MAXWELL. Carrying the folder, he returned to the Rumpus Room. Suze was on the bed, sipping gin, the sheet over her legs.

"Roberto, that olive oil smelled rancid."

He tossed the sack onto the bed. She picked it up and looked at him.

"Open it."

She set her gin down and tugged at the leather drawstring, then poured herself a handful of uncut stones. "Diamonds?"

"Yep. Latest goods from Siberia."

"What are they worth?"

"This sack, just over eleven million."

"Why show them to me?"

"Choose one, kiddo. It's yours."

Without hesitating, she chose a medium-sized rock from among the hundred or so stones. "This one."

"Something to remember me by."

"Roberto, you are unforgettable. Always have been."

"I planned it that way, Suze."

"What about the rest?" She pointed to the diamonds.

"Meeting a cutter next week. See if he knows his ass. You want to come along?"

"What day?"

"Wednesday. Maybe Thursday."

She shook her head. "I'm busy."

Devane tossed the folder on the bed and poured himself a

glass of red wine. He studied the color against the light from the windows. She sat cross-legged on the bed, flipping through the pages of the folder. "These are loan papers."

"Like I said. My bank bought your paper."

A shiver ran over her. "You're in a hurry."

"Yep."

"Now what?"

"Now we renegotiate the loan."

"Who is we?"

"You, me, and Byron. Of course, if you don't want to re-negotiate, we could foreclose."

"You wouldn't dare!"

"Try me." He was finished with her for now. If she didn't leave pretty quick, he'd throw her out. "How about that visit to the cutter?"

"You bastard. Of course I'll go."

He raised his glass and smiled. "Here's to us, Suze. To us, to the democratic process, and to Washington."

She raised her glass and drank, but said nothing.

It didn't matter. He had Suze between a rock and a hard place. He could squeeze her anytime.

Chapter Eleven

BRANKO woke at six-fifteen on Saturday morning, sneez-ing, with a pounding headache and a memory of a dream. He and Roscoe Smith had been roaring hell-bent in a po-lice vehicle across a wasted plain, chasing a purple motorcycle. Branko was wearing a khaki uniform. Roscoe was dressed in a tuxedo with a red cummerbund. The Honda had faded behind a low rise and vanished into a puff of green smoke. Roscoe had climbed out to check for tire marks when the ground crumbled away beneath him and he slid into a crevasse. He was hanging onto a scruffy low-growing weed when Branko reached him, his hand out. There was no footing, nothing to hold them up except air. Branko grabbed his partner's wrist in a fireman's grip and hauled. As he pulled up, Roscoe smiled and let go.

"See you, Pancho," he whispered.

Sick to his stomach, his eyes hot with tears, Branko watched Roscoe until he was out of sight in the dark crevasse.

Branko rolled out of bed and took two aspirin. He put water on to boil and stood under the shower for five minutes. The image of Roscoe falling lingered. Wearing his battered blue terry-cloth robe, Branko made instant coffee and tried to picture himself waking up next to Lissa Cody. That would help drive the dream out of his mind. Miss Cody was the kind of girl who wore a nightie to bed, full-length. Or soft cotton pajamas. Branko slept in boxer shorts and a T-shirt, remnants of his days in the Army.

Humming some Mozart, he rinsed out his thermos and turned it upside down to dry. Lissa Cody had nice ankles and slim wrists and a good mind. He wanted to see her again. It was a good feeling. He hadn't been interested in a woman since before Christmas.

The coffee helped. So did the music. Back in the bedroom, he flipped the switch on his bedside radio and heard something that sounded like Beethoven waking up after a long winter. He kept the radio tuned to KFAC, one of three classical music stations from Los Angeles. In the bathroom, staring at his weary eyes in the mirror, he lathered and shaved, using the shaving brush and mug given to him by his grandfather when he'd graduated from high school. The bristles on the brush were worn down to within an inch of the handle. It was time for a new brush, but Branko liked the one he had.

He dressed in the tan trousers and white shirt from yesterday. He had four pairs of trousers at the cleaners, along with half a dozen shirts. He hadn't done laundry last weekend, and there would be no time for it this weekend. He found one pair of clean Jockey underwear and a pair of clean brown socks. There was a hole starting beneath the ball of the foot on the right sock. He strapped on the shoulder rig, shrugging until he got the straps just right. He didn't like wearing a gun, especially in the summer. Homicide work was mostly luck plus legwork plus hunches, along with a lattice-design of what-ifs. He hadn't used his gun on a case in five years and he felt dumb wearing one. Before he left the apartment, he called the hospital. Roscoe was sleeping and still listed as critical.

The fog hung thick and gray as Branko headed up Jamboree to Pacific Coast Highway. The streetlights were still on and he kept the Volvo just under twenty miles an hour. Traffic was light on the coast highway, and the signal glowed through a soft red nimbus of mist. He drove past Le Club and Spanky's Saloon. At Newport Boulevard he turned right and headed up the hill toward Seaport General. He parked in the lot. There was no officer on the entrance from the parking lot. A sleepy-faced deputy stood at the information desk, sipping coffee and talking to the woman on duty. Branko flashed his shield and went up to Intensive Care on six.

The sixth floor hummed softly with the buzz of electronic machinery. From one room came a steady beeping sound. Branko stood at the door to Roscoe's room, looking in. His partner was lying in bed, head turned away from the door, not moving. Above the bed, a signal blipped slowly across Roscoe's green computer screen. Branko felt sick to his stomach. His partner was a good cop and a good friend. He'd been sandbagged yesterday by events and a madman, and now he was here in bed, the only sign of life a flashing blip on a screen.

Branko sat by the bedside for ten minutes, remembering some of the good times with Roscoe Smith. The Beach House Case. The Newport Strangler. The Blue-Movie Killer. Roscoe was organized, like Tommy Osterhaus. He assembled facts and came to logical conclusions based on the evidence. Branko didn't get anywhere being organized. When he was on a case, his mind did crazy leaps, zigging and zagging from one illogical place to another. Sometimes it helped him if he wrote junk poetry with crazy rhymes. Sometimes he got closer to a case on the tennis court, or on a run, or while he was working out with weights in the police gym. Roscoe hardly ever exercised, but he was a crack shot who spent at least three hours a week on the pistol range. Branko's shooting, like his tennis game, depended on his mood

177

and what day it was. If he was on, the bullets drove home to the bulls-eye. If he was off, blah. Roscoe was a sharp dresser, with an awesome collection of suits and shoes and neckties, and he and Branko had had lots of arguments about the proper attire for a working cop.

In the bed, Roscoe moaned, shifted slightly beneath the blue quilt, and then was still again. Branko leaned close, listening to his friend's breathing, but it told him nothing. Before he left, he scribbled a note on a page from his notebook. *Roscoe—we're closing in on the perp. Get well, buddy.* He sighed it "Pancho" and left it folded on the bedside table.

He made one more stop at the nurse's station. Roscoe remained on the critical list. The nurse said he was doing as well as could be expected. Her face was neutral but her eyes looked sad. Seaport General was full of sick people and the smell of death. Was the nurse's sadness for Roscoe? he wondered.

After leaving the hospital, Branko drove out along Balboa Boulevard to the crime scene. There was no roadblock at the corner of Seventeenth and Balboa, and when he reached Cortez Alley, he saw a police truck and two men in coveralls putting away the last of the sawhorses from the crime-scene barrier.

If the sun came out, he told himself, the merchants would be happy.

He spent twenty minutes doing a walk-through of the action. A café was open a block east of the alley, but the rest of the shops were closed. He pinpointed the main players and events on his diagram—Shooter One, Bodyguard, Reverend, Photographer, Roscoe, book burning, escape route, Shooter Two, bike, Shooter Three, Officer Duncan, window, camera—and was amazed at how well-planned it had been. The weather was chilly this close to the water, and his stomach rumbled. As he headed for the café and coffee, a florist's truck pulled up in back of the flower shop and the blond woman from yesterday got out. On Balboa, life continued.

In the café, Branko had the waitress fill his thermos with coffee. He bought a dozen Danish for the troops. And then he headed for the station.

Branko's morning was a frustrating maze of dead ends. He spent an hour briefing Phil D'Agostino, the chief, who was irritable because he'd waited all night in the airport at Sacramento for the fog to lift. Chief D'Agostino was in his fifties and needed his sleep. He wore baggy coats with professorial elbow patches and reminded Branko of his grandfather from Zagreb.

The task force meeting had to be postponed three times. They were still waiting on the computerized Rubidoux dossier to come down from Dink Carruthers in LAPD. Branko tried five times, without success, to get the Dink on the horn.

At ten, Branko was called over with the chief to the office of Mayor Hackman in City Hall. The mayor was a chubby man who cracked bad jokes with a vacuous smile. He had the round face but not the deep tan of Reverend Williams. At ten-thirty, the mayor's secretary opened the door to reveal eight hungry reporters, four photographers, and two television cameras. The mayor killed twenty minutes assuring the citizens of Newport Beach that the Fun Zone investigation was proceeding apace and that the assailants were on the verge of being captured, if, mind you, they were still in the area. He urged the citizens to be on the alert as they went about their business, and that nothing like this would ever happen again in their fair city. Then the mayor stepped aside to allow questions for the chief, who stepped aside to let the reporters go at Branko.

The reporters knew Branko as a straight shooter. Flashbulbs popped.

"Frank, what progress are you making?"

"We've got a lead on the killers."

"Can you tell us what kind of lead?"

"Sorry. They're still at large. I don't want to jeopardize the case."

"What's the connection between the shooting in Los Angeles and the Fun Zone incident?"

"It's in your mind."

"The mayor says an incident like yesterday's can't happen again. What do you think?"

Branko cut his eyes toward the mayor, who had his politician's smile pasted on. "Our officers are out in force to prevent it."

"What's that supposed to mean?"

"We've tightened security on Reverend Williams and his family. We've got every officer we can spare working on the case."

"Does the police department see a political connection, Frank?"

"No comment."

"With the primary coming up on Tuesday, how can you not see it?"

"Sorry. I've got to get back to work."

The mayor shook Branko's hand for the cameras, but his eyes were hard. Branko got the message, which was, Shit rolls downhill. As he and the chief walked out, they were intercepted by Lieutenant Robin Hood Archer, who was wearing a snappy blue three-piece power suit. The Archer was pissed that he hadn't been invited to the mayor's powwow.

"The FBI has arrived," he announced, puffing. "Agents Friedkin and Moore. They're in my office."

"Bring them to my office, Bob," the chief said.

The Archer eyed the television cameras. "What went down at Hizzonor's?"

"Quickie press conference. Frank here handled it."

"Phil, I thought I was executive liaison."

"You are, Bob. You are. Now how about those Feds."

The Archer's face was pained. "I want to be kept in the information loop, Phil."

"Frank will see to it, won't you, Frank?"

"Yes, sir."

"Don't stonewall me, Sergeant." The lieutenant's eyebrows raised up menacingly. "I'm warning you."

"Sir?"

"You heard me." The Archer turned on his heel and walked off.

The chief shook his head. "Let me know when that dossier shows up from LAPD, Frank."

"Will do."

Branko was on the phone to the hospital when the FBI men paid him a visit. There was no change in Roscoe's condition.

180

Agent Friedkin was short and chunky. Agent Moore resembled a recruiting poster for the Navy, square jaw, tidy little mustache, sharp gray suit and all. Where did these guys get the money? Branko wondered. He brought them up to speed on the Fun Zone shootings. Moore, the recruiting poster, had a voice like Ronald Colman, the movie actor who had discovered the secret of eternal life in an old movie called *Lost Horizon*. He was pushing Branko on the Cosmo's connection when the phone rang. It was Dink Carruthers, from LAPD. There had been a delay on the Ringo dossier, now called the Rubidoux dossier, but it would be on the wire no later than noon. With the FBI men at his desk, Branko said as little to the Dink as possible. In the back of his mind was the item Lissa had mentioned, about Dink and the sack of money. Branko said thanks and hung up.

Agent Moore, a real yo-yo, leaned across the desk. "Sergeant, we want to brief your task force people on terrorism."

"How long will it take?"

Agent Moore checked his watch, a Rolex. "If we can get started chop-chop, we should finish the prelims by six. Tomorrow, we'll need a half day."

Branko shook his head. "My people need to hit the street, ask questions."

"Pounding the pavement won't net terrorists, Sergeant. What we're dealing with here is something national, maybe even international. We've cleared with your exec on this."

Branko leaned forward until his face was six inches away from Agent Moore's. The guy had yellow eyes. "A murder went down in my city. We have leads to follow up. We have people to protect. It's my job to find the killer, whether it's a perp acting on his own or a Mafia hit or the Red Army in California. Theory won't get it, pal."

Agent Moore's smile was filled with smug superiority. "Don't bury your head in the sand, Sergeant. Your lieutenant was high on our suggestion. Very high."

It was three minutes to noon and time for the task force to assemble. "I can give you half an hour, max."

"Impossible," Agent Moore said. "There's too much to cover."

"Jack here is an expert, Sergeant," said Agent Friedkin. "He's lectured governments, kings, corporations. You wouldn't believe the stuff he knows."

Branko stood. "Half an hour, gentlemen."

The officers on the task force were sitting around a table in front of a white board covered with lists. Ted Forney was there, his face puffy under his beach tan. Next to Forney was Don Taylor, from Traffic. Then Joe Romero, who was on the security team for Mrs. Winona Lee Williams. Next to Joe was Jamie Duncan, wearing her uniform. Jamie had spent the night at the Williams home on Singapore Circle, acting as security for the daughter. Her eyes were bloodshot and she kept yawning during the session.

Freddy Lyle sat behind Jamie, staring at the back of Jamie's blond head with a satisfied smile. This morning, Freddy was wearing a "Miami Vice" jacket, dove gray with punk-rock shoulder pads, and baggy white pants pegged at the ankle. Next to Freddy were the two uniformed officers who had been on the scene yesterday at the Fun Zone, Frederich and Gardino. The officers were tired. Lieutenant Archer entered the room just as Branko introduced Agent Moore, the terrorist expert. The lieutenant took a seat next to Jamie Duncan, whispered in her ear, grinned like an idiot, then crossed his arms and pretended to listen to the terrorist briefing.

It turned out to be a capsule history of the major terrorist organizations—Red Army Brigade, Baader Meinhof, the PLO, an outfit with Libyan connections named Dakiri—with no visible connection to anything that had happened yesterday. Agent Moore paraded at the front of the room, talking, gesturing, emitting hot air and old data. Frederich yawned. Gardino could barely keep his eyes open. Jamie Duncan's face, usually so animated, was tight with fatigue. Branko left the room twice. The first time he went to the men's room to pee. The second time he stopped in to the chief's office to beg. "Chief, would you get these G-men off my back. The guy's been talking nonstop for an hour."

The chief smiled. "Bob Archer thinks it's valuable stuff."

"It's overcooked, Chief. Anybody who can read or watch the news knows it already."

182

The phone rang and the chief answered. "I'll try to think of something, Frank."

Branko went back to the briefing room, where he suffered through twenty more minutes. He knew FBI guys had to have law school. Two years, three. Maybe that's where they learned how to bullshit.

Agent Moore finished at last. The lieutenant said a few words, rah-rah-cheerleader stuff, go-team, top priority, let's hit the boards, yuk-yuk, and then invited Agents Friedkin and Moore out to lunch. Probably take them to the Ritz, Branko told himself.

It was one-thirty and no one from the task force was on the street yet. Branko gave the troops a five-minute pit stop. When they filed back in, they were edgy and in no mood for sitting around. Tommy wrote on the white board with a black marker while Branko read off the names of the suspects. At the top was Congressman Sherwood. Next to Sherwood was his right-hand man, Timmy Vick. Then three others in the Sherwood organization—Rose, Dalrymple, and Whittington. After each name, Tommy printed the name of an officer who would do the interview. Branko was to interview Sherwood. Tommy went on listing names. Lonnie Chevron, the Democrat, and his supporters from Laguna Beach, Gladys Bromberg and Wanda Zahn. Bromberg was a feminist. Zahn was a known atheist who had picketed the reverend's church over on Back Bay.

Branko turned to the group: "Bromberg, according to what we know, is the one who convinced Lonnie to run. As it looks now, he'll be the Democratic candidate."

Don Taylor spoke up. "Would Lonnie rather run against Sherwood or Williams?"

"Good point, Don."

Tommy Osterhaus grinned. Today he was wearing a blue shirt and a light tweed jacket and gray pants. "That brings up the Wounding Shot theory."

"Is that connected to the Libyan Dakiri Theory?" Ted Forney asked.

Tommy looked around at the task force. "This is Frank's idea, so he'd better have the floor."

Tommy sat down, yielding the floor to Branko. Branko felt tired. Would this lead anywhere, or would he wind up like Agent Moore, the FBI yo-yo, talking through his ears? He shoved his hands in his pockets and tried to look relaxed and competent. He took a deep breath.

"I know you're hungry for lunch. The lieutenant asked us to join him at the Ritz."

Laughter, a few grins.

"Okay, this might not fly. I share. You shoot it down. Witnesses—Jamie included—agree that Shooter One was a real pro. He could have taken out half a dozen more people, mostly civilians, on his way to the boat. He was close enough to the reverend to waste him, but instead he shot him in the leg. So what does that mean?"

Branko turned to the white board and printed the words WOUNDING SHOT in large black letters. He circled the two words and drew lines out from the circle. At the end of each line he wrote a name.

"Winona Lee Williams," he said, printing in block letters. "Jasper Gilroy. He's the assistant pastor. Then we've got the church elders, Caxton, Wakefield, and that crowd." Branko continued to print as he talked. "Then on the political side we've got this guy Wakefield again and a man named Cade and several smaller people, Garrett, Welch, Bracker, Obtfeldt, and—" He paused to look at Tommy Osterhaus, who checked his notes.

"Lowe," Tommy said.

Branko wrote Lowe down under the political cluster.

"Okay. Let's say, for one motive or another, someone wanted to send the reverend a message. His wife doesn't want him in politics, so she hires a hitter. Check. Jasper Gilroy is mad at the reverend, so he hires one. Check. Wakefield and Cade, over on the political side, think this will generate some positive PR, so they hire one. Check. Check." Branko went through his list, adding what-ifs. When he was finished, he handed the black marker to Ted Forney. "It's a theory, team. Let's pick it apart."

The officers wrangled for thirty minutes and suddenly there was energy in the room as Branko's theory engaged their minds. On the board, names filtered into two loosely cohesive groups.

The Kill group wanted the reverend dead. The Wound Only group wanted to warn him or to generate publicity. Jamie Duncan took the marker and moved Jasper Gilroy over to the Kill group. Other officers took their turn with red and blue markers, moving names, adding their insights and what-ifs. Through it all, Tommy Osterhaus took notes. At the end of the half hour, the room was crackling with electricity and Branko knew they were really interested in the case. He checked assignments for interviews for the afternoon. Tommy continued to write everything down in his meticulous hand.

Branko stood at the white board, sweating. "Okay, get some lunch and then hit the street for those interviews. Tommy coordinates the scoop. I handle the assignments. We need action on this thing. And keep a sharp eye out for the Libyan PLO."

The officers laughed.

They were starting to file out the door when Molly Brazelton came in holding a folder containing a computer printout. "This just came in over the modem from LAPD." She handed the folder to Branko. It was the yellow sheet on Robert Ringo/Rubidoux, the owner of the red Cadillac from Cosmo's Cosmos.

"Hold up, guys. Sorry, Jamie. This is important."

The officers moaned and filed back in. Branko summarized the report. "His name is Robert Ringo, a.k.a. Rubidoux, twenty-nine, from Little Rock, Arkansas. Some of his aliases are Benjy Robinson, Robbie Benjamin, Benson Roberts, Benson Ridgon, Robin Roberts, Floyd Lovejoy, Benjamin Robertson. He graduated from high school in Little Rock and went on to a junior college where—get this—he studied police science. He excelled at small arms and won two trophies for the school in national competition."

"Goddamn," Don Taylor said.

"Good work, Jamie," Freddy Lyle said.

"What are the priors, Frank?" Tommy Osterhaus asked.

Branko flipped to the next page. "Our boy was picked up and booked in Houston on a DUI and charged with carrying a concealed weapon, but the judge let him off. That's Texas for you. He served thirty days in Odessa for interfering with an officer in the line of duty. He served three months of a six months' tour in Yuma, Arizona, for breaking and entering. No weapon found. Got off on good behavior."

Branko skipped down to the bottom of the page. "Here's something. He was picked up by the Anaheim PD last December. Several weapons were found in his car."

"What's the make of the car, Frank?" Tommy asked.

"Cadillac Eldorado," Branko said. "Red. California plates. I saw that car last night, in Cosmo's parking lot. In Anaheim, the judge set bail at fifty thousand. Our boy was back on the streets in two hours."

"Connections," Tommy said.

"Does Anaheim still want him?"

Branko nodded. "The warrant is outstanding." He closed the file. No murder arrests, not yet. "Robbie-boy might be on the road to Little Rock, but let's keep our eyes peeled anyway."

"Can we do another composite, Frank?" Jamie asked. "I might do better the second time around."

"That would be terrific."

"I'll check with Little Rock," Tommy said.

"I'll huddle with the artist," Jamie said.

"I'd like a piece of that huddle, doll," Freddie Lyle said.

"Ease off, Hot Lips."

Freddie Lyle laughed.

The task force filed out. Branko stayed behind to check signals with Tommy, then returned to his desk, where he tried the number of Candy Woodmere, the clerk from the Inn of Cortez. The phone was buzzing at the other end when the chief walked up to Branko's desk. He sat down heavily. Branko hung up.

"How are your troops, Frank?"

"Tired. But ready for the last charge," Branko said.

"Security on the family?"

"Tight. The son is sticking with the father. That makes it easier on us."

The chief took a moment to study the composite drawing of Shooter One. "When can we get a mug shot?"

"It's coming down from LAPD."

"Anything on Shooter Three?"

"Nothing, Chief."

The chief ran his hand through his thick gray hair. "What does your cop's instinct tell you? Were they hired by the same nut? Or by different nuts?"

"The same, is my guess."

"Who have you got for suspects?"

Branko read him the two lists.

The chief looked at his sergeant. "You really think Mrs. Williams could hire someone to whack her husband?"

"Have you seen her eyes?"

The chief shook his head. "No leaks, okay?"

"Okay."

The chief peered at Branko. "You look terrible, Frank. You looked tireder than I feel. Circles under the eyes, lines in the face. Ever since that wife of yours left, you've looked like the ghost of Frank Branko."

"Yes, sir."

The chief stood up with a grunt. "When this is over, Frank, take some time off. That's an order."

"Yes, sir."

"You're a good cop, Frank. You use your mind. You stretch yourself. But you aren't Superman. And I don't want you sleeping at the switch when the train rolls in."

"Yes, Chief."

The chief put his hands on the small of his back and arched his pelvis forward. "Where do you think Bob Archer took those FBI guys for lunch?"

"The Ritz. Or the Cote d'Azur."

"I tell Bob to watch the budget. So what does he do? He pulls the SWAT team off crowd control so he can spend two hundred bucks wining the Feds." The chief walked off shaking his head.

Branko drank the last of the coffee from his thermos while he put in a call to Lissa Cody. He wanted to invite her for a quick lunch while he gazed into her green eyes, but she wasn't at the *Tribune*. Her home phone didn't answer, either. He left the station and drove down to the Newport Pier, where he had a fish sandwich and a beer at the Oyster Bar. Outside the window he could see the dory fishermen hawking the catch of the day.

Could you make enough as a fisherman to get your Rod Laver tennis shoes resoled? he wondered.

He made the mistake of ordering a second beer. When he left the table, he was woozy and tired, so he went back in for a cup of coffee. The waitress, Tanya, was a cute brunette with glasses, a ponytail, and a shapely bottom under tight white shorts. When she smiled, Tanya reminded him of Annette Berg, his first love.

"Want a refill?" Tanya stood there, young, healthy, and bursting with life, holding the coffeepot.

"Thanks. You ever study mythology, Tanya?"

"You mean like dragons and dungeons?" She finished pouring.

"More like Halcyone and Eryx," he said.

"Gosh," Tanya said. "No. I guess not."

She moved away, trim legs twinkling with their fresh coat of tan. Branko felt old. He finished his coffee and walked to the telephone near the rest rooms. He flipped his notebook open to the page containing his afternoon list of Must Do's. The name of James Sherwood was at the top. Branko sighed and dialed Sherwood's election headquarters, identified himself, and told the voice he had police business with the congressman. The voice on the other end sputtered, busy, busy, election near, can't see any—

Branko cut him off. "This is in connection with a murder investigation. My name is Branko, Sergeant Branko. I'm with Newport Beach Homicide. I'll be there in fifteen minutes."

Branko hung up and walked to his Volvo. He unlocked the door and climbed in behind the wheel. The Volvo started right away with a sweet reliable purr. The car payment—a hundred and twenty-five dollars—was due at the credit union on the fifth of the month. Payday was the first. He was behind two months on his dues at Le Club. He owed money to Roscoe and Tommy and Teddy Forney and two other police officers, as well as his Uncle Joseph, back in Milwaukee. Don't think about it, he told himself. Maybe he could pick up a quick hundred playing Mrs. Maxwell. He'd have to beat her first. And she had played Forest Hills and Wimbledon. Branko had always wanted to see Wimbledon. That took money. Everything took money. It was a sun-roof day, but the Volvo had no sun roof, so he turned on the radio. The KQZ news said the reverend had climbed three percentage points in the latest polls, but election watchers still predicted a landslide win by the incumbent, James B. Sherwood.

So much for police what-ifs and the Wounding Shot theory.

Branko pushed in a Mozart tape. On the ride over to Sherwood election headquarters at the fashionable Cote d'Azur Hotel, he allowed his mind to be soothed by the strains of *The Marriage of Figaro*.

Thank God for old Mozart.

Saturday morning the reverend's temperature rose a degree. By noon he was sweating with expectation. He had no appetite, which was strange for him, but he could feel his energies pulsing and every time he closed his eyes he saw visions from the Bible. He saw Christ on the Cross. He saw Moses cleaving the Red Sea. He saw David and Goliath, Samson and Delilah. He saw Bathsheba and Lot's wife and Susanna bathing while the Elders stared at her. This spelling of Susanna had no *h*.

There was a poem about Susanna, one his daddy used to quote. He remembered phrases from the poem—*green evenings, green going, red-eyed elders*—but not whole stanzas. His memory roamed. The plan simmered in his brain. He could taste fame.

The reverend phoned his son, Terry Junior, and told him to be at the hospital at four-thirty. "Bring my blue suit from Brooks Brothers and some underwear and that new blue tie and don't let your mother know. This is a surprise." The funeral services for Mac White were set for five-thirty and the reverend wanted to make an entrance. He would need time to get dressed.

The police objected. The officer in charge, a man named Forney, said it would be impossible to guarantee the reverend's safety. But the reverend knew the killer was gone. God had appeared that afternoon and told him so. The reverend was sweating. He had to utilize this opportunity. "I'll take responsibility, Officer. My friend is being buried today. I must appear."

His son arrived, and he made it to the bathroom without

189

fainting. Because of his wound, he could not shower, but his son helped him with a sponge bath.

When he was dressed and seated in the wheelchair he felt better. He was suddenly thirsty. He wanted a whisky, a double, with a beer chaser. There would be liquor at Susannah Maxwell's, Susannah with an *h*. He did not feel crazy. For the first time since he'd been a lifeguard, he knew what he was doing.

"You okay, Dad?"

The wheelchair was in the elevator, aimed at the heart of destiny. "Yes, Terry. Thank you."

He rode in his son's VW Rabbit, with the wheelchair folded in the rear. A police car followed thirty feet behind. They arrived at Promontory Chapel at five-twenty. The reverend instructed his son to park in the private spot marked Reserved, next to Douglas Cade's Mercedes, which was the only vehicle in a long line without a PASTOR CLYDE IN '88 sticker. The pain was a dull fullness in his leg as he lifted himself from the passenger seat to the wheelchair. For a moment, he thought he might pass out. His hands felt weak on the arms of the chair. "Wheel me in, Terry."

He was recognized immediately inside the church. People came up to shake his hand, pat him on the back, touch him. The laying on of hands in reverse.

"Good to see you, Reverend."

"Reverend Williams, thank God you're back."

"We saw it all on television. We were shocked."

"I came to see my friend buried," he said. "I came to speak some words for Mackenzie White."

He thanked them. His face felt frozen, like a patch of tundra. He swung his smile back and forth across the faces, washing them, washing them all, like a lifeguard playing a healing spotlight across the drowning waves. Terry Junior pushed the wheelchair down the hallway leading to the main cathedral. More people came up to him until he was surrounded. "Hey, it's Reverend Williams! He's right here! Hey!"

"I came here to see Mac White buried."

A laying on of hands.

The sound of music pulsed through the great arched doors. The doors had been Jordan Maxwell's idea, copied from a medieval church in France. Terry Junior wheeled him through. On the dais, under the giant camera cranes, was Jasper Gilroy, his face wet with perspiration. Jasper had gained weight, which made the reverend feel smug. Most of the ministers he knew had an eating problem. It came from being born poor, grabbing for victuals whenever they were available. There was no sign of Winona Lee. The coffin containing the body of Mac White sat on the front edge of the dais. The lid was open. Behind Jasper Gilroy, the Archangels played "Rock of Ages." The Archangels had been Jasper's idea. As usual, they were stridently off-key.

Hands reached out to the reverend as he made his way down the aisle toward the dais. Jasper Gilroy looked up and saw him and almost stumbled coming down the short flight of stairs. He pumped the reverend's hand. "Thank God! Thank God!"

"I'll want to say a few words, Jasper."

"Of course. Of course." Jasper mopped his face with a handkerchief. "Should you be out of bed? What will Sister Winona Lee say?"

"Terry," the reverend said, "push me up that ramp."

They were almost up the ramp when Winona Lee appeared in the small door that led to the private corridor. She was wearing a dark blue dress with the inevitable white starched collar. The hem of the dress brushed the floor. The white collar was cinched tight around her narrow throat. As she approached the dais, her eyes flashed at him. She mounted the stairs, holding her skirt up primly, like a woman from another age, another world.

Winona Lee kissed his cheek, pressing cold lips to his face. "Husband, this is totally unexpected."

"Mac White was my friend. I owe him this much."

"You look fatigued, husband. Exhausted. Why did they allow you to leave?" She turned to her son. "You should not have brought him here."

"But, Mama, I—"

She cut Terry Junior off and gestured at Jasper to begin. Jasper stepped to the microphone and asked people to be seated. His voice quavered. The reverend rolled forward, until the wheelchair nudged the podium. "Give me the microphone."

Jasper handed it over. The reverend was sweating now, feeling faint. A camera crane moved into position and he thought of all the fire-and-brimstone services he had pitched from this podium. A song rose in his mind and he recognized the tune as "Just As I Am." He had saved thousands to those rhythms. If he could get elected to Congress, he could save California. If he could get elected senator. Or president . . .

Inside his head, words careened against images—a cross, a mountain, a fountain, a place of rocks and death, a vulture swooping at his naked eyes, Helen of Troy in blue, the motel bed where he had wept tears of guilt over the molten bodies of prostitutes from Harbor Avenue near Disneyland. He spoke into the microphone, hoping the words would come to him from the Lord. His voice trembled. A large ugly bird sat on his shoulder, but when he raised a hand to brush it away, he saw that the bird was Winona Lee. Her eyes were blank stone.

"My friends, thank you for coming today. We are here to mourn the death of a good man. His name was Mackenzie White and he had taken on the job of guarding my life. Up until yesterday, it did not seem all that dangerous. It was just routine. Then, yesterday afternoon, just after three o'clock, Mackenzie White was gunned down, murdered in cold blood. The murderer—or I should say murderers, plural—are still at large."

The reverend paused to let that sink in before going on. He took a deep breath and felt the power of the podium, the Tower rising up from the sea of humanity. People were sheep. Without the podium, they were lost, like sheep wandering in the wilderness. "You Christians out there know why Mac White was killed. He was killed because he tried to save my life. That was his job. That was what he was paid for. But when he saw there was danger, he thought first of me and only second of himself. Mac was a trained soldier. He knew how to survive in battle. But yesterday he lost his life protecting me. And I am here today to mourn him, and to carry on the fight. There must be a reason for his death. God took him from us. God has a reason."

There were murmurs and the rustling in the dark that told the reverend he had them going. He wanted desperately to clear his throat. He wanted a whisky. Drinking ran in the Williams family. His daddy had drunk. His son drank. He drank.

"As you know, I am running for political office in the Fiftieth Congressional District of the state of California. Yesterday, when Mac White was killed, I was making a speech about freedom and democracy and protecting our children from filth and the smut of pornography. I was making a speech about sins that stain the soul, about sins that dirty the mind. And in the middle of that speech, Mac White was cut down.

"Fellow Christians, there is no doubt in my mind that the shooting yesterday was politically motivated. And while the police search for the killers, I say they are here among us."

There was more rustling. They were awake out there.

"Yes, they are here in Orange County—the killers and those who hired them. They are near, like wolves circling in the darkness, and I say to you they must be stopped. Their purpose yesterday was to put the fear of God into me. But I know God better than they do. They wanted me out of this race. They wanted me to die. Instead, they killed Mac White, and that is where they made their mistake, because I am alive, and I am well, and I am staying in this race—for God Almighty!"

He lifted his right hand in a clenched fist and shook it at the camera. He hoped it was enough. He wanted a drink and he wanted to ask for money. They were ready to pay tonight. Blood always brought the dollars out. Death scared the be-Jesus out of them. They were sinners and they knew it. Tithe and double tithe and triple tithe.

Out in front of him, fanned in a great semicircle under the ceiling of the great cathedral, the faithful clapped and cried Amen, Amen, send the reverend to Washington. The semicircular seating arrangement had been Jordan Maxwell's idea. The design had come from a line in the Paradise section of Dante's *Divine Comedy*, where the poet spies Beatrice among the angels, who sit in seats arranged like petals from a flower. The reverend had read Dante in English. Jordan Maxwell had read Dante in Italian and he had told the reverend that Susannah was his Beatrice. The design had worked. It did seem holy and angelic.

Now he held up his arms for silence and then said a prayer for Mac White. When the prayer was finished, he handed the micro-

193

phone to Jasper Gilroy, who announced that Sister Winona Lee had been called by the Lord to perform a healing on her husband.

The reverend rolled back to where his wife was seated. Her hands were folded in her lap. Her eyes were cold, like Arctic ice. "This was madness, coming here."

"It is God's will." But he wasn't sure. Not really.

He could feel her eyes boring into him, probing. Behind him, the Archangels broke into a rock rendition of the healing music, "Just As I Am." Two church employees wearing business suits wheeled the healing platform into place.

"What's this?"

"I shall do a healing."

Her breath was a cold wind on his neck. "Now?"

"You are here. God is here." Winona Lee put a hand on his shoulder. "You must lie down, husband. It is time."

He felt suffocation close around his face, like a mask without holes for his mouth and nose. "Terry," he said to his son. "Get me back to the hospital."

Terry Junior started toward him, but Winona Lee held out her hand palm forward, causing him to stop. Terry Junior looked from his mother to his father, eyes shifting nervously, not wanting to take sides. The reverend could not wait. He was weak, and his wife sensed his weakness. Winona Lee was a silent warrior. Her suspicious intuition held great power. Using the last of his strength, the reverend turned the wheelchair and headed for the ramp leading down off the dais. The sudden tilt of the chair as it started down threw him off-balance and he felt the chair lean sideways and then strong arms from below were holding him and he saw a policeman in uniform on his right and a stout Christian fellow with a smiling face and he knew God was talking to him once more.

God was a genius. When He did not allow you to fall, it meant something.

"Parking lot," he whispered. "Hospital . . ."

His exit was accompanied by clapping and a host of rhythmic amens. If the polls had been open, he'd have beaten Sherwood, hands down. Would they remember until Tuesday? he wondered.

Before they reached the door, Terry Junior caught up with the wheelchair and took over. "Sorry, Dad. I got flummoxed, I guess."

"It happens," the reverend said.

It was easier getting into the car this time. He was learning to maneuver his body in the wheelchair and he even stood on the bad leg, putting some weight on it, for a moment, testing the pain. When they were headed out of the parking lot, the reverend made another decision.

"Turn up there."

"Where?"

"San Miguel."

"That's not the way to the hospital."

"No," the reverend said. "It's not."

For the first time in her life, Susannah had something she could use on Roberto Devane. But she didn't know how to use it. She couldn't go to the police with what she knew. Devane had hired killers to attack the reverend. A policeman had died. Susannah could prove nothing.

It was after two when she arrived home from her wrestling match at Devania. Sex like that always made her restless and left her aroused and unsatisfied. She stripped off her skirt and torn blouse and put on fresh workout clothes—blue shorts and a jogging bra and a pale blue pullover. She spent an hour in the workout room on the Total Gym. When she had a good sweat going, she left the house and jogged down the hill to the beach, where she ran on the sand for an hour.

A plan took shape in her mind as a gull swooped down for a bite of garbage. The attack on the reverend had been coordinated. Roberto had needed someone inside to feed information to the killers. Someone inside the reverend's organization. Who was it? Harrison Wakefield? Douglas Cade? Some faceless bookkeeper? One of those frenetic rank-and-filers in CASS?

She was back at the house by four-thirty. The upstairs ice-maker was working, a happy symbol of order restored. She took a long hot shower and then did her hair and dressed for the party, picking out a navy-blue dress with a plunging back, one that did not allow for a brassiere. She chose dark hose and navy-blue shoes with naughty high heels to go with it.

The guests arrived at five, chattering about the shooting and how lucky it was the reverend had been spared. There was extra help tonight and she would make sure they were paid by Douglas Cade. She was guarding her money like poor Silas Marner these days.

Harrison Wakefield arrived at six, looking like Sidney Greenstreet in his Palm Beach suit. He had gained weight. Three minutes of careful questions told Susannah she'd been right—Wakefield was too dumb to provide useful information to any set of killers anywhere except in a B movie.

Douglas Cade arrived at six-fifteen apologizing for his tardiness, and Susannah excused herself and took Cade into the library, where she opened up the safe. The house that he leased on Lido Island did not feel secure, he had explained, and the safe at Spyglass Hill was a Fichet-Bauche Diplomat, made in Switzerland and installed for Jordan Maxwell by specialists from Geneva.

She opened the safe, then retreated to the other side of the room while Douglas sat on the sofa and pawed through his baubles. As an accountant and sometime economist, Douglas Cade had an unusually paranoid mistrust of banks and governments, which he swore were in collusion against the welfare of thrifty citizens everywhere. His solution to the problem was to deposit tidy caches of jewels and negotiable coins in various spots around the world. Susannah's eyeballed estimate of his holdings in her safe ran to a couple of million. If you put it all together, Douglas was probably worth something like twenty million—about one-sixth of what Roberto Devane was worth—and she had toyed with the fantasy of pushing Douglas in front of a car and taking his money for herself.

Too obvious. She didn't work that way.

Now she mixed Douglas a drink—he liked a very light Scotch and water, no ice—and began probing.

"What are your plans, Douglas?"

He looked up from examining his treasure. "If he loses, you mean?"

"You don't seriously think he'll win?"

Cade smiled patronizingly. He was a fussy little man with small hands, a robotic smile that seemed painted on, and a monkish bald spot at the back of his head. He wore his hair combed straight across, right to left. His suits were tailored by a man in London. His shoes were handmade of the finest leather by a shoemaker in Florence. In his relations with other people, Douglas Cade kept a discrete distance. He allowed only a few people—Susannah among them—to call him "Douglas." With most people, he preferred "Mr. Cade." He formalized first names, making them longer if possible. Names like Mike and Bob and Pete became Michael and Robert and Peter. It was very East Coast.

"He's up five points in the polls."

"That's not enough to catch Sherwood."

"With elections, one must wait until the votes are counted."

"If he wins, you'll stay on then?"

"We've had discussions, Harrison and myself. Contingencies, et cetera."

Cagey Douglas Cade. Susannah had been in his office only once, with her late husband. Cade had used an egg timer to keep his phone calls to three minutes. It was silver and it made a soft bonging sound when the three minutes were up. When he made an appointment, Cade brought out a slim leather-bound notebook and wrote down the time and place and who the appointment was with in a neat, meticulous hand.

On the ring finger of his left hand Cade wore a wedding band of hammered gold. Every third weekend he left town to fly back to see his family in Newton, Massachusetts. The story was his wife was a Philadelphia girl who had visited Paris a dozen times but had never ventured west of the Mississippi. The story was his wife loathed California. His children were in school in upstate New York. The boy was named Gerald. The girl was named Katherine, after Cade's wife's mother.

Susannah didn't believe Cade's story. The family photo on his desk, she believed, was a fake. She had no idea who he really was. She found him slightly mysterious, in a dull sort of way. He knew numbers and computers and spreadsheets. Since he had joined the team to elect the reverend to Congress, there had been tighter controls on spending. Susannah kept trying to place his accent. East Coast, upper crust, that moneyed sound. Cade was like a character out of Somerset Maugham or *The Great Gatsby*.

When he wasn't out of town visiting his fictional family in Massachusetts, Cade spent the weekends working on the books in his office in the Tower at Promontory Chapel. The fact that he kept his survival cache here in Susanna's house forced him to be cordial. He was Douglas. She was Susannah. He made contact by phone at least once a week and made a point of giving her three minutes of elementary economics and his metallic smile whenever they were together at a function. Use of the Maxwell safe had been an arrangement Cade had made with Jordan, shortly before his death.

Susannah stood up, walked to the bookshelf, and plucked out a leather-bound edition of Adam Smith, the eighteenth-century economist. She handed it to Cade. "Jordan wanted you to have this."

He took the book lovingly in his hands. "I couldn't. This is priceless."

"You must."

Cade opened the book and read the inscription. Susannah sat down beside him on the sofa, three feet away, and crossed her legs. Her skirt rode up and she left it there long enough to make sure she had his attention. A slow flush crept over Cade's face as he watched her out of the corner of his eye. Susannah detested voyeurs.

"Well," Cade said. "Thank you."

"Not at all."

Susannah freshened his drink from the cut-glass decanter. It was the last of the whisky. "Did Jordan ever mention a man named Devane to you?"

There was a long empty moment, as if the air had been sucked out of the room. Cade shook his head and stood up nervously to replace the strong box in the safe. "Who?"

"Devane. His first name was Robert. He had a military career and was supposed to have been a soldier of fortune."

198

Cade had his back to Susannah. "Sorry. I never heard of him."

Susannah shifted ground. "You met Jordan back East, didn't you?"

"Yes. At the Round Table Club. But I'd known about him for some time. He was a famous entrepreneur."

"Jordan told me this man Devane introduced you."

Cade looked at Susannah with wide eyes. His face had turned pale. "Whaat?"

Susannah re-crossed her legs. Perhaps she should have worn sheer stockings, to enhance her tan. "Jordan said that you two were introduced by this Colonel Devane."

"Impossible. Should I relock for you?"

"Yes."

Cade closed the safe. There was a satisfying click. He did two spins of the dial and stood up. "When did Jordan tell you this?"

"The day he died."

"Extraordinary. Why would he do that?"

"He owed this colonel some money. He'd hoped to pay it back. He said you knew the colonel and could intercede for me."

"And that's when he told you about this man, what's his name, Devane?"

"Yes."

Cade stood in front of Susannah. She reached out a hand toward him and he moved back a step. "I'm afraid I must be—"

"Douglas?" Susannah reached farther.

"What?"

"I need your help."

"What sort of . . . help?"

"I need you to intercede."

"How?" His voice was choked.

"This man. This Devane. He wants my house."

"I can't help you."

"But you know him, Douglas. You know him!" She grabbed his hand. It was ice cold and tiny and fastidious. The palm was as smooth as glass. Her warmth shocked him, the poor man. All his life, he had protected himself. He had stacked numbers between himself and the world, a sort of buffer. He had saved and counted and re-counted and saved. But there was no buffer against Susannah. She did not want to stand up and tower over him. "Douglas. I'm begging you."

"No." His eyes were wide and his breath came in short little gasps, like the little engine that could. "And even if I did, I—"

Through the door there came the sound of applause and rebel yells. Susannah held him with her gaze for a long moment, probing him with her eyes but keeping her face sad and sympathetic. Let him sleep on it, she told herself. Perhaps he would come around later. She had his number at home and at work. She had his number, period. She thought about maneuvering him into bed but feared he might have a cardiac arrest. She gave his icy paw a squeeze and let go. Instead of sitting back against the cushions, she stayed on the edge of the sofa, so that her dress draped open for the little voyeur.

Douglas Cade said, "I'm so sorry," and moved toward the door.

There was a knock. Cade opened the door. Julio was standing there and the noise was louder.

"What is it, Julio?"

"Mistah Williams, he come."

"What?"

Julio's face was round, like a tropic moon. "Mistah Williams."

Susannah stood up. "Here?"

"Come in chair. With rollerballs."

Susannah looked beyond Cade and Julio and saw the reverend in a wheelchair, heading toward the library from the den. He was being pushed by his son, Terry Junior, a chunky college boy with muscles and a face full of smooth suntan. Like his father, Terry Junior was a trifle overweight. There was a uniformed police officer two steps behind the reverend surveying Susannah's guests with a suspicious eye. Susannah stepped out. Julio was grinning. Cade's face was still red with embarrassment. There was another police officer stationed at the main door.

The reverend smiled when he saw Susannah. So did his son. They had the same neon teeth, the same blond hair, the same needy look. Like father, like son.

"Susannah, my dear lady."

"Reverend Williams, should you be out of bed?"

"I never felt better."

His hand was hot when they shook, feverish. His eyes seemed crazed and his face was covered with sweat. Monty Hawthorne, the Western actor, appeared in the door of the den to let out a rebel yell and motioned to Susannah.

"Oh, Susannah doll, you should see the rev on television."

"What?"

The reverend smiled up at her. "I went to the chapel, to say a few words for poor old Mac."

Cade brushed past them on his way to the den.

Applause filled the house as Monty Hawthorne began to sing "Stand Up, Stand Up for Jesus." The guests joined in, the sound swelling. Her house, it occured to her, was full of born-again drunks. Susannah took a quick look at the television; the reverend was sitting in his wheelchair beside the pulpit of his church on the Back Bay, talking earnestly into the camera. Then she understood—he had left his hospital bed to deliver a eulogy for Mac White. Uncanny timing. Perhaps she had misjudged Reverend Williams after all.

She felt him roll up behind her. "Susannah?" Terry Junior was talking to Frieda Entwhistle, a divorcée who had an itch for young men.

She turned. "Yes?"

"Could I trouble you for a drink?"

"Of course." She looked around for Julio, who was nowhere to be found.

The reverend was wheeling himself toward the library. Susannah left the sound of the television behind and followed. He asked for a whisky and Susannah poured from the cut-glass decanter. Only one drink left, and three-quarters of a case in the liquor storage. Eyes bright with fever, the reverend drained half the glass. "My God, you are so beautiful!"

"Are you sure you feel all right?"

He held out his hand and after a moment she took it. "Susannah, I am going to win on Tuesday! I can feel it here." He pointed to his heart. "The Lord appeared to me in a vision and told me I would win! The primary's what's tough in this county.

Your husband—God rest his soul—knew that oh so very well. Once you're through the primary, the voters will swarm to you on that Tuesday in November. Have you been to Washington, Susannah?"

"A couple of times."

"I've only visited in pictures. And in my dreams." He drained the rest of the whisky in one gulp. "Come with me, Susannah. Come to Washington!"

This was certainly shaping up as her day for invitations, deals. Crazy Saturday. "What would Winona Lee say?"

At the mention of his wife's name, the reverend threw his head back and laughed.

The laugh was mad.

CHAPTER TWELVE

A T midnight on Saturday, Frank Branko took a much-needed catnap on the battered sofa in the lounge at the Newport Beach station. The material covering the sofa, a neutral gray, smelled stale. There were coffee stains on the arms and a rip in the middle cushion. The sofa needed a good cleaning.

He woke at half-past two feeling weary and got back to his reports. His mouth was fuzzy with coffee. His eyes burned. The leads in the case were drying up as he sat there working through the sentences on the departmental typewriter. For three years now, he had been promising himself he'd learn to use the computer, but he'd never found the opportunity. The rookies joining the force knew how. Roscoe Smith had even offered to coach him in the finer arts of word-processing. It was time to learn. Or perhaps he had computerphobia, fear of computers. Roscoe had chided him with grade-school kids who were computer whizzes. Branko still typed with his two index fingers, like a burnt-out sportswriter.

He finished the reports on Sherwood and his two underlings, signed them and put them in a manila folder, and wrote the chief's name on the outside of the folder. He thought about coffee, a beer, coffee, Lissa Cody. Coffee and beer sounded stale. Lissa Cody sounded good. She had left a message but no number. He called Seaport General. Roscoe Smith was resting, the nurse said. He called Marcie Deegan, Roscoe's girlfriend, and left another message.

On top of his message stack was a pink message from Lissa Cody that said she had stopped by the station mid-afternoon Saturday. She would be in Los Angeles on a story and would get in touch on Sunday. Branko read it again.

The phone rang. It was Officer Ted Forney, calling from home, checking in. He had just come off duty at Seaport General. He provided a rundown on the reverend's nocturnal adventures outside the hospital.

"How long was he in the Maxwell place?" Branko asked.

"You mean we," Forney said. "I was in there with him, me and Romero, for an hour."

"Did you sit down and eat with the quality?"

"It was my first asparagus sandwich, yumma-yumma."

"Asparagus?"

"Swear to God. Thin little two-bit white bread slices, no crust, thin layer of butter—it had to be real butter—and then some mashed-up green shit some Hollywood babe told me was asparagus. The place was jumping with showbiz types, Monty Hawthorne, Liz Randel, all of them coughing up dough for the campaign. Liz Randel had on tight pants and a see-through black shirt. I ate seven and each one made me hungrier. Maybe that's how she stays wicked."

"Who? Liz Randel?"

"Nah. The unsinkable Mrs. Maxwell."

"In a see-through shirt?"

"Mrs. Maxwell wore blue, sexy and expensive. A thousand bucks for the dress, ten grand easy for the jewelry. She steered the reverend around in the chair, took him into the library for some one-on-one. I wolfed down asparagus sandwiches and champagne. The bubbly up there, Frankelovich, is the absolute best."

"How long were they in the library?"

"Ten minutes. The Williams kid was snuggling up to a Newport Beach quiff in a red dress. His daddy comes out, looking like he'd seen God and heard an angel chorus. Me and the kid pack him and the chair into the Rabbit. We zip him back to the hospital. You know what I think, Frankie?"

"It's late and I don't dare ask."

"I think she jacked him off. It's the only way to account for a look like that. Like he'd heard the angels sing."

"Jesus, Teddy."

"Okay. Okay. Then maybe she—"

Branko cut him off. "Is your wife at home, Teddy?"

"Boston," Forney said. "Visiting her folks."

"Take a cold shower."

"You're a chilly bastard, Frankie. No heart. Ice water in your veins."

"See you tomorrow."

"Try some bubbly yourself, pal. Relax."

They hung up and Branko walked to the conference room, where he spent an hour making lists, sweating, playing what-if.

What if Shooter One hadn't known about Shooter Three?

What if Shooter Three was hired by Client A and Shooter One was hired by Client B?

What if you reversed that?

What if Client A lived in Newport Beach?

Who would want to whack the reverend?

Sherwood?

Mrs. W.?

Jasper-baby?

Delia Sue?

Terry Junior and his Oedipus complex?

The invisible Mr. Cade?

Branko's brain buzzed from too much caffeine. His stomach grumbled. There was no sense of breakthrough, no overriding pattern to any of it. With each homicide case he had worked on before, he had been able to find a key that opened a door. Sometimes he found the door first. Sometimes he found the key.

With the Fun Zone case, he hadn't found either. There was no door, no key.

He wrestled with the what-ifs another ten minutes and then went out for coffee. He sat in a booth in Denny's on Pacific Coast Highway, filling yellow legal-sized pages with cluster diagrams. His coffee grew cold. The refill did not tempt him. He paid his check and walked out to the Volvo.

When he got back to the station, Chief D'Agostino met him at the door. The chief looked rumpled in a tweed coat and a shirt with no tie. "Hospital just called. It's Roscoe."

"What's wrong?"

"They took him back to surgery."

"Why?"

"Something popped."

"Where?"

"They didn't say."

Branko left his car at the station and rode with the chief to Seaport General. The smell of death hit Branko as they entered the hospital and headed for the waiting area outside the operating room. The time was three-fifteen. Branko paced the floor while the chief sat in a chair. The chair was made out of curved plastic, pink, with little metal struts for legs, and just barely strong enough to support him.

Marcie Deegan came in at three-thirty, still wearing her flight attendant's uniform. Marcie was an attractive woman in her early thirties, divorced, with a teenaged daughter. She had a college degree from the City University of New York and had worked in advertising. Her skin was coffee-colored, lighter than Roscoe's, and she wore her jet-black hair short. She ran toward Branko, her eyes wide, and threw herself into his arms. "Oh, Frank. Where is he?"

"In the operating room, Marcie."

"We had engine trouble in Kansas City. I just got home a while ago and there was your message. I called the station and they—"

"He'll be okay, Marcie. He's tough."

The chief was on his feet, waiting to be introduced. Branko made the introductions. The chief shook Marcie's hand and muttered how sorry he was and that Roscoe was a good man, the

205

best. Marcie sat down, knees close together. The chief walked off to get her some coffee. She was wiping her eyes with a white handkerchief when the door opened. A tired-looking doctor in a green surgical suit was standing there, staring at them.

"Smith family?"

"Here," Branko said.

The doctor came toward them and sat in a chair. He looked at Branko and then at Marcie Deegan. The chief came through the door with Marcie's coffee just as the doctor said, "I'm sorry. We lost him."

"What?" Marcie's voice was a stifled scream.

Branko was hit by a wave of dizziness. He gulped back the lump in his throat.

The doctor shifted gears, looking at the chief. "It was the central wound that gave us trouble. A vessel ruptured, started spilling blood into the chest cavity. There was a shard of metal lodged near the spine, about three inches below the atlas major. We had to be careful. One slip and he'd have been—"

The doctor stopped. Marcie Deegan was crying now, elbows propped on her knees, face buried in her hands as her shoulders shook with grief. Branko felt tears welling in his eyes. "Damn!" he said. "Goddamn!" He wanted to grab the doctor and shake the bastard until his teeth rattled. Instead, he felt the hand of the chief on his shoulder.

"Thank you, Doctor," the chief said.

"I'm sorry. We did all we . . ." There was a squeak of plastic as the doctor pushed up out of his chair and walked away.

So. It was over for Roscoe. No advanced degree. No teaching job. No escape from the police force. Not in this lifetime. Marcie kept on crying and blowing her nose. She excused herself and ran crookedly to the ladies' room. Branko pulled out his handkerchief and blew his nose.

"Sonofabitch," the chief said.

Branko said nothing. His feet felt frozen. His eyes and throat burned. His brain felt sluggish, muddy. He wanted revenge.

An orderly led them to a room on the sixth floor where Roscoe lay, the color drained from his face. His eyes were closed. Sheets covered the wounds that had allowed the life to seep from his body. Branko and the chief stood near the door while Marcie sat in a chair near the bed and whispered last words. Branko's mind was on the funeral. Roscoe had asked to be cremated, his ashes spread on the sea off Catalina. Branko had promised. But this was not the time to talk about it.

They left Roscoe on his bed and walked slowly out of Seaport General. Fog hung heavily in the parking lot. Branko drove Marcie's car, a late-model Camaro, while the chief followed. Marcie lived in a recently built condo in Costa Mesa. The two policemen made sure she got in safely and then drove back to the station. The chief pulled up beside Branko's Volvo, and both men got out. When they were halfway to the entrance, the chief stopped Branko.

"Get some rest, Frank."

"Not now."

Branko felt the chief's hand grip his arm. "These things hit hard, Frank. Roscoe was your buddy. It hits deep, where you can't see it. Go home. Mix yourself a drink. You're off-duty today. I mean tomorrow. What the hell day is it, anyway?"

"It's Sunday, Chief. And I'd rather go on working. I want those bastards."

"Orders are orders, Sergeant. And your orders are to ease off. Back away for a day. Your task force is out there. Tommy can handle the scoop as it comes in."

"Chief, I—"

"That's an order, Frank. Give me a call at the station around noon. If something pops, you can come in."

"Chief?"

"Go home, Frank. Call up a girlfriend. Take a swim. Play some tennis. Roscoe's gone, and I'm as sorry as you are."

Branko nodded and turned back to his Volvo. He was tired, very tired. He knew he wouldn't sleep. There would be no rest until the perps were either dead or in custody. Right now, he wanted them all dead.

The chief lifted a hand as Branko drove away into the fog.

It was after five in the morning by the time he reached his apartment. One beer made him drowsy, but when he climbed wearily into bed, sleep would not come. He got out of bed and walked to the bathroom, remembering some sleeping pills left behind by his wife. Branko hated sleeping pills. They made his mouth as dry as cotton. A ten-minute search failed to turn up the bottle of blue pills, so he drank another beer. He watched television but his mind would not focus on the horror movies. He felt drugged by the death of Roscoe Smith. Life was its own horror show.

He thought of phoning Lissa Cody, asking her to bail him out. Hi, this is Frank Branko and I know it's early but I need—

No. Forget it. The lady will think you're crazy.

He was about to drink a third beer when he decided to go for a slow jog. Sweating it out, the rhythm of body movement, might help. He put on running shorts and an olive-drab T-shirt, but could not find his Brooks runners. He was poking through his closet when he remembered they were in his locker at Le Club. The last time he'd gone for a run in his Rod Laver tennis sneaks, his back had hurt for two days. He drank half a cup of instant coffee instead, standing in his stocking feet staring out his kitchen window at Back Bay. Promontory Chapel was out there, perched on the shore, but was not visible from where he was standing. He found his car keys and his wallet and headed out for Le Club. It was almost seven. Roscoe Smith had been dead just over three hours.

Sunday-morning joggers were already out as he headed up Jamboree to Pacific Coast Highway. A line of bikers wearing helmets and black shorts and shiny striped jackets pedaled southwest, toward Laguna. The fog was lifting as he made a left turn on PCH and used his plastic key card to get through the gate at Le Club. There were three cars in the lot—a Pontiac Trans Am, a yellow Porsche, and a chic BMW, gray flannel. He didn't see Miguel Ortega's blue RX-7 and that tapped his memory bank— Miguel's weekly match with Mrs. Maxwell was on Sunday. But he didn't see Mrs. Maxwell's maroon Jaguar, so he assumed the match had been cancelled.

Two men he didn't know were playing on Court Four. The player at the near end was heavyset, with thick legs and a twenty-pound stomach. His opponent was short and wiry. The heavy man was the hitter, the short man the retriever—a classic contest of opposing styles.

As he went into the locker room Branko heard the sound of a ball machine ratcheting as it slung balls automatically across the net, and then the answering *plock* of a ball being struck by a racket. It was too early for an attendant to be on duty. Branko unlocked his locker and got his shoes out.

Outside, the ball machine was still going, so he walked along the corridor between the courts until he came to Court Fourteen. He looked through the fence and saw Mrs. Maxwell hitting ground strokes. She had the machine set so that it was driving her from corner to corner, a forehand, then a backhand, then a forehand. The machine, a squat blue robot, sat on the opposite side of the net, rotating on a turret as it fired balls in automatic sequence. In each corner, flanking the ball machine, Mrs. Maxwell had set up targets, bright orange traffic triangles about fourteen inches high. When she scored a hit, the metal triangle made a soft bonging sound. Branko watched her hit six balls before the machine ran out and stopped with a soft chug. Five direct hits, Branko thought, and the sixth ball was only a whisker off target.

For her morning workout, she was wearing silver warm-up pants and a white sleeveless sweater over a pale yellow tennis shirt. The shirt was soaked with sweat, but she was breathing easily. She must have felt Branko watching because she turned to face him.

"Hello." Her voice sounded friendly, inviting, not what he'd expected.

Branko spoke without going for the gate. "Didn't mean to interrupt." He turned away and had taken a few steps when the gate opened.

"Sergeant?"

Branko turned. She was leaning against the gate. "Yes, ma'am."

"Miguelito didn't show. I was hoping you'd hit a few with me."

Branko shook his head. "Sorry. Some other time." He gave her a brief wave, turned, and started walking again. He heard quick footsteps behind him and turned back to see Mrs. Maxwell coming. Then she was beside him, her face showing concern.

"What is it?"

"Nothing. Go back to your machine."

She put a hand on his arm. Her fingers were warm. "Please. There's something."

Branko shrugged. "A buddy of mine just died."

"Oh. I'm sorry." But her hand stayed on his arm. "Would you . . . would you like to talk about it?"

Branko shook his head. "No. It wouldn't . . ." Then he stopped. She was offering to listen. He let out a long sigh. "Sure. You have the time?"

"Of course. Where would you like to go?"

They sat on a bench at courtside while Branko talked about Roscoe Smith. She was a good listener, concerned, interested, with just the right touch for prompting him whenever he stopped. She sat with a towel wrapped around her throat, long legs stretched out. Branko gripped the bench with both hands, as tense as a swimmer ready to hit the water. In his telling, he got all the way back to those early days on the Newport Beach force, beach patrol in summer, traffic duty, his decision to switch to homicide, Roscoe the Egghead with the sociology degree. He talked about cooking steaks and drinking beer at Muldoon's because Roscoe's birthday was St. Patrick's Day. "Roscoe was a crack pistol shot, great with computers. He'd learned word-processing and accounting spreadsheets and two database programs, while I'm still typing with two fingers."

"He sounds like a marvelous person."

"He was."

"I wish I'd known him."

"You're too late, lady."

Mrs. Maxwell was quiet. Branko stared at the green windscreens. From another court came the sound of a foursome warming up for their Sunday doubles match.

"How are you feeling?" she asked.

"I should have been there."

"Where?"

"The Fun Zone. It was my day off. I could have worked security for the reverend. But I had a match with the Spider. I owe him two hundred bucks and I wanted to work some of it off." His eyes were watering again.

"How could you know?"

"I didn't. But if I'd been there, Roscoe would be alive."

"And you might be dead."

He looked at her, the regal Mrs. Maxwell. Why was she being so nice? "Better me than Roscoe."

She did not admonish him to look at the flowers and the trees and the sky, even though it was the perfect moment for a lecture on the beauties of existence. Instead, she stood up, her long legs unwinding nicely in her skin-tight silver warm-ups. The sun had not yet broken out from behind its shield of fog and the day was still gray. She stood over him, hands on hips.

"When my husband died, I thought I'd die, too," she said.

"When was that?"

"December. Two weeks before Christmas. We'd been married a dozen years. I depended on him for everything—companionship, wit, insight, guidance—and when he died I just sat and stared at the wall. I spoke in monosyllables and stopped seeing people. And then one day I made a discovery."

"What was it?"

"You'll think it's silly."

"Try me."

"Sweat," she said.

"Big discovery."

"I knew you'd say that. I discovered my body was full of poisons. When I started sweating I came alive again. Slowly. Painfully. I sweated out the pain and sadness."

Branko nodded. "Spare me the health-food lecture, okay? I tried macrobiotics."

She surprised him by putting her face close to his. He caught a whiff of perfume that sparked his senses. Her face in close-up showed two tiny worry lines at the corners of her mouth, a lacework of tiny crow's feet. Otherwise, her skin was flawless. "I had a doctor who could diagnose by his sense of smell."

"What's the diagnosis, Dr. Maxwell?"

She straightened up, but not before she'd taken in a good noseful of Branko. The sudden intimacy of it startled him, made him grin.

"Poisons, Sergeant. You need to sweat."

"I was about to run when you sidetracked me in here for therapy."

"I have the court until nine. We could just rally."

He thought about it. Roscoe was still there. He wouldn't mind.

"Okay."

Mrs. Maxwell picked up balls while Branko jogged to his Volvo for his tennis gear.

They hit for a while. Branko's timing was off and he was feeling the combined effects of beer and coffee and no sleep and Roscoe's death. Across the net, Mrs. Maxwell moved like a ballet dancer, stroking the ball with control and confidence, pivoting, getting down to the ball, following through nice and high. There was no waste in her game, her strokes compact, efficient, deadly. At the end of fifteen minutes, Branko was sweating and panting.

"What about an easy set?"

"I don't think so."

"Numbers are fun. They take your mind off life."

How come she was so smart? "Okay. One set."

Mrs. Maxwell gave him the serve, and they started. She made no unforced errors. At the end of three games, Branko was trailing love—3 and he'd won only one point out of thirteen. He was thinking about Roscoe Smith sitting at the departmental computer, crunching numbers.

Mrs. Maxwell won the set easily, 6—1.

"Another?"

Branko felt the slight edge of competition. At least he should be able to get her out of the warm-ups. "Sure."

She was ahead 3—0 when he found his timing. He started booming in his serves and charging the net, Branko-fashion. His volleys were crisp and deep, and he began to push her back on her heels. At 3—all she removed the silver pants. At 5—all she removed the sleeveless tennis sweater, revealing a cutoff top that showed four inches of tanned belly. When they changed courts at 6—5, with Branko ahead, he saw that her face and throat were covered with sweat. He felt like a wet washcloth.

Working the ball with spin and control, Mrs. Maxwell brought him to 6—all. They were neck-and-neck in the tie breaker, 7—all, 8—all. Branko's game was on; he was able to push death aside for the moment. Roscoe's death was a metaphor, a harbinger. He might be next. On the tennis court that morning with Mrs. Maxwell, he set death on a shelf. The sun came out. He slammed a cannonball serve past the outstretched racket of Mrs. Maxwell. On his next serve, he charged the net. She placed a dink at his feet. He half-volleyed. She took his ball in the air and drove it down the line. Branko was there for a peel-the-orange volley that angled sharply crosscourt to her forehand. She was there, gasping out a little shriek, sliding the ball across the net with sidespin, displaying that maddening control.

Branko wanted to win now.

He dove for the shot, seeing a melon of a ball on his strings as he hit a drive volley crosscourt. She tried for it, but his shot was too good. Branko felt terrific. He felt alive. She patted the strings of her racket in simulated applause. People were waiting for the court. It was 8:50; no time for a third set.

They shook hands at the net and Branko wondered what she would do if he put his nose close to her and took a whiff.

"Sweat," he said.

"I hoped you'd say that."

"For a beautiful woman, you have some real good ideas."

She smiled, accepting his compliment. "If you aren't busy, why don't I buy you breakfast."

He was turned on now. She was sending. He was receiving. If he could keep the banter up with Mrs. Maxwell, he could keep death on the shelf all day. "You're on."

The sun was higher now as he followed her BMW into the ritzy heart of Newport Beach, toward Spyglass Hill. She drove fast, fifteen miles over the limit.

She led him up the hill on a winding road in the California sunlight. The Maxwell place was the last of three houses—call them mansions—in a cul-de-sac on the very top of fabled Spyglass Hill. The street was called Spyglass Circle, and curved in a half-moon shape. The three mansions sat together, in isolated splendor, on the north side of the street. On the south side, across the curved street, was a priceless view and a sheer drop to the next level, and smaller houses, worth only two million. No clutter up here. The fog was clearing. Soon, you'd be able to see forever.

The BMW stopped in front of a gate leading to a curved driveway. There was no number. The house was huge and white, like a tourist hotel in Mexico. Branko could see an electric motor mounted on the gate. He drummed his fingers on the steering wheel while he waited for her to open up. He hummed Mozart. What kind of music did Mrs. Maxwell like? he wondered. What would she serve for breakfast? Was this her usual Sunday routine? Had she banged Miguel Ortega, the assistant pro? Ease off, Pancho. The beautiful lady wants to buy you breakfast and that's it. She feels sorry for you because your partner died in the line of duty and that's it. The gate opened and he followed her through. She parked the BMW in front of a five-car garage—just the right number of cars for life on Spyglass Hill, he told himself—and he thought of the maroon Jaguar. Probably drives a different car for each day of the week.

She climbed out, displaying her excellent legs. "I'm starved." She brushed a strand of blond hair from her face.

"Me, too."

"It's the cook's day off. We'll have to have potluck."

"Can you cook?"

She smiled at him and let out a short laugh.

Score one.

They went in through the front door. The house was two stories, with a thrusting three-story entryway that allowed light to stream onto the white tile. The place felt Mediterranean-ritzy. On the outside wall, narrow windows reached up to a beveled skylight. The floor of the entryway glowed. Beyond the entry Branko saw a large living room that looked like a photo setting out of *Architectural Digest* or *Town and Country*. Off to the right were the double doors of what he assumed was a library.

It was a big mother of a house. King of the Hill. Make that queen. He estimated a dozen rooms, maybe more. From where he stood, you couldn't see the kitchen or the laundry room.

214

"Would you like a shower, Sergeant?"

Maybe she'd smell him again, eyes closed, nose searching. "Great."

She led the way up the curving stairs and then along a carpeted hallway to a workout room that was larger than Branko's apartment. In one corner was a Jacuzzi at rest, the steam rising. Exercise equipment ranged along the walls, one of everything—Nautilus, Super Bike, Nordic Cross-Country Skier, Total Gym. He recognized several pieces from the Sharper Image catalogue. The Nautilus would have cost him four months' pay.

"Jesus," he said.

"Please." She pointed toward the shower room. "There are robes inside, freshly laundered. I'll see to food." And then she turned around and left him alone.

Before undressing for her own shower, Susannah pressed the intercom that connected her bedroom with Julio's room at the back of the house. There was no answer. It was Julio's day off, but she wanted to make sure he was out.

In her bedroom, Susannah slowly stripped off her sweaty clothes. Now that she had the policeman here, she asked herself, what was the next step? He was a forceful tennis player, aggressive, with a daredevil quality that provided him energy. She had played her best, but it hadn't been good enough. She'd fought the policeman with every shot, every trick, every change of style in her repertoire. He'd won by attacking, by overpowering her. He'd won because he was a man, with more muscle mass. Susannah resented that. More muscle mass translated into an imbalance in the universe. As she unlaced her shoes, she wondered what he'd be like as a lover. Single-minded? Overpowering? Tireless jock? Daredevil?

She kicked off her shoes and sat down to remove her ankle socks. Then she unzipped her shorts and stepped out of them. As she stared at herself in the mirror, she felt a tingle of anticipation, a little shiver running up her spine, a telltale heat between her thighs. She was turned on. How nice. She did not turn on easily.

She hooked her thumbs into the waistband of her underpants

and pushed them down, taking her time. She wondered if the sergeant was married. There was no wedding ring, but with men that didn't mean much. Men could fake anything—except being men. She was naked now from the waist down. She raised the yellow shirt over her head, tossed it aside, then unsnapped her brassiere. Her breasts swung free. Hands on hips, she took a long appraising look at her image in the mirror.

Critical analysis time.

The package still looked good.

Staying in shape was tougher for a woman, because of that extra layer of fat that lay hidden just beneath the skin. The extra layer was terrific when you were a little girl—it contributed to that smooth look, soft little you, the archetypal girl—but a couple of extra pizzas in your teen years and the extra layer turned into cells gone mad. The result was fat city. Susannah had stayed thin playing tennis. Now she worked out. The result— arms too lean, shoulders too bony, collarbones that jutted out almost comically. Her stomach, however, was flat, the hips sleek. Her thighs were nicely muscled, matching her athlete's calves. The face was long, the mouth too wide. Her eyes never looked bright enough, even with drops from the ophthalmologist. She had always wanted eyes like Gretchen Nordyke, the rich girl from Wisconsin with the soft serve and the maddening lobs.

Susannah walked into her closet for a robe. There were seven to choose from. Five were floor-length, two were short, the hems reaching just to her tanned cheeks. She chose a floor-length sunny yellow terry cloth. When it was on and snugly belted, she changed her mind and put on a sheer, pale purple shorty. As she belted it, her nipples hardened. She stepped into some matching wedgies and posed for a moment in front of the mirror. The robe barely covered her. The wedgies made her legs look even longer.

The policeman's friend had died in the Fun Zone shootings. Roberto had engineered the killings. Cade knew Roberto, but she didn't know how well. Roberto wanted to get at her through her house, this debt-ridden piece of real estate with the awesome view. Roberto had always been sociopathic, but he had never turned on her before with such speed, such venom. He was extremely efficient, she'd give him that. He could own her house within the week. His nasty little man could foreclose. As Jordan always said, it's the banks who have the money, and that's why we come begging.

The bits of information lodged in her mind were like apples and oranges—they refused to add up. She needed a catalyst, a linchpin, a mental food processor. If you put apples and oranges into a food processor and pressed the On button, out came orange-apple juice—a pleasing blend if you added gin. A policeman was a walking license to kill, a lethal weapon in a uniform. She opened the robe, bent her right knee in a stylized pose, smiled her best smile, and wondered how good a shot the policeman was.

She tightened the sash and turned away from the mirror. As she entered the workout room, she thought again of the diamonds from Siberia. Roberto used trinkets as pretty lures to bring her back. If the policeman executed Roberto, how could she get the diamonds away from Devania?

Susannah walked across the grass-tex carpet of the workout room. The door to the bathroom was half open and she could hear the shower drumming. As she entered the bathroom, she felt the steam and broke into a sweat. Susannah loved to sweat. Sweating meant you could drink more gin. The sergeant was humming. It sounded like Mozart, but that wasn't possible. She could see him dimly through the glass door of the shower, tanned legs and torso, the white midsection. He would have white ankles and feet, a tennis tan.

She opened the door and stood there waiting. The sergeant was under the shower head, eyes closed. His body was lean, hard, masculine. What kind of policeman was he? Burglary? Narcotics? Homicide? Had he ever killed anyone?

The sergeant opened his eyes. As she had thought, his feet and ankles were bone-white.

Susannah stood there, posing, letting him look. "Was that Mozart?"

"Yeah. From *Figaro*."

"You have a good ear." She unbelted the sash and shrugged out of the robe. It fell at her feet.

"You like Mozart?"

She stepped out of the purple wedges. "Love Mozart." She felt the spray on her face as she entered the shower. It was an oversized stall, with nozzles on opposite ends. Both nozzles were equipped with massage shower heads. She turned on the second nozzle and adjusted the temperature. Then she gripped the sergeant's bare shoulders, digging in her fingernails, and stepped close. Her eyes were almost level with his. She liked that. Her bare thighs pressing against him felt his readiness, making her smile. She put her face up for a kiss, seeing his eyes grow wide, then narrow with decision. Their mouths met and she opened her mouth to seek his probing tongue.

She had known two other policemen. A homicide detective in Chicago, who had protected Nightingale Enterprises against silly vice sweeps, and a narcotics detective in New York, a gruff burly Italian named DeTorio who had cousins in the organization and always wore cologne. She wondered where the sergeant was from. The Midwest, she guessed. Not a native Californian. They kissed for a while beneath the spray of water. The massage shower head pounded her skin deliciously.

She opened her eyes to stare at the sergeant. Her hand moved to guide his entrance as she lifted one leg and braced her buttocks and lower back against the wall of the shower stall. His eyes widened as he slid in, admiring her slick readiness.

"Jesus!" he grunted.

"Hurry!" she said, writhing. "Give me your mouth!"

She bit him on the lip as he came. She bit him hard enough to break the skin and make his lip bleed, and then she felt her own orgasm start and she came crashing through her own sexual barriers, there, in the hot steaming shower stall in the house that was still only barely hers on Spyglass Hill.

CHAPTER THIRTEEN

I N the dream, Branko was in his khaki police uniform, but barefoot and bareheaded. An empty holster slapped against his ribcage as he ran after his partner, Roscoe Smith, who was riding a white horse toward a blue-green horizon. The empty holster was on his right side, where the wound was. The leather stung Branko's scar tissue. Signs along the road read, THIS WAY TO THE FUN ZONE and TURN RIGHT TO DIE. Roscoe was wearing a white shroud and carried a sword raised above his head, like a knight in armor or one of the four horsemen of the apocalypse. Branko called for Roscoe to wait up, and at the same time he realized his partner was bleeding. Blood soaked the shroud. "Wait up!" Branko called. Roscoe did not look back, and acted as if he had not heard the call. Branko stubbed his toe on a rock and fell to the dirt. He reached out his hand as Roscoe rode over the hill. . . .

Branko snapped his eyes open. He was covered with sweat and his feet were tangled in the bedclothes. He smelled coffee, perfume, the sea—the smells of reality. The dream faded. Thank God. He was alive. Death was back on the shelf.

Branko rolled over and looked around. He was in a big bedroom with blue carpeting and white furniture and mirrors on the closet doors. Across the room was the door to the bathroom. Two empty wine bottles sat on the bedside table. A third bottle, half full, sat on a table against the windows. The wine was a Chardonnay. Mrs. Maxwell was nowhere to be seen. He thought of Roscoe, dead in a hospital bed, and Marcie Deegan, crying.

The drapes were open and bright Sunday sunlight streamed through the windows. The clock on the bedside table said 12:02. Time to call the station.

He rolled out of bed with a groan and stumbled to the windows, shielding his eyes with one hand. The windows looked north and west across the low California coastal hills, up the coast and toward the city of Newport Beach. This was high ground, expensive, ritzy-rich. No worries here, up above the world.

Branko searched for the mechanism that closed the curtains. His hand touched a control box with four buttons. He pressed two of the buttons and the drapes—soft white stuff, filmy as a dream—slid shut with a slick whisper.

Better.

With the light dimmed, he sat on the edge of the bed and stared at the phone console. It had six lines, with colored buttons for each one. On the right-hand side were fifty smaller buttons coded for automatic dialing. Names were penciled in beside the buttons. There was a small speaker box so you could chat from across the room and a built-in gizmo that answered when the maid wasn't home. The damn thing looked like it could fly you to Mars.

Branko punched line one and dialed the station. Officer Molly Brazelton picked up on the third ring and patched him through to Chief D'Agostino. Branko did not want to move. If he stayed here, death could not clutch at him.

"Frank? Did you get some shut-eye?"

"Affirmative, Chief."

There was a pause. "Nothing cooking here. Everyone's feeling down about Roscoe. No word from LAPD on the perp. Tommy's coordinating interview material from your task force but won't give me a reading until he's got it all. I do not smell victory there. We've got another head session with the FBI. This time they've called in Treasury, some big hotdogs coming in on a night flight, all the way from D.C. The meet's scheduled for nine A.M. Monday. You can bone up tonight, relieve Tommy. He's an old fart, like me. He needs his lucky eight. You check in at six."

A friend dies. Life goes on. Night work had clobbered Branko's marriage, had made his wife leave home. He sighed. "You sure, Chief?"

"I'm sure. I want you in between me and Bob Archer. Leave a number with the desk, in case we need your body before that."

Branko signed off, then gave Molly Brazelton Mrs. Maxwell's number and hung up the phone. The name beside the tenth button in the left column was D. Cade. Could that be his boy?

Branko sat for a long moment staring at Cade's name before padding in his bare feet to the bathroom. He relieved himself with a long piss, then splashed his face with water. When he came out, wearing a towel around his hips, Mrs. Maxwell was just entering the room pushing a room-service table on wheels. She was wearing a blue workshirt with long tails down to the tops of her golden thighs. The shirt had a couple of its buttons undone and it was clear she wasn't wearing a brassiere. The smell of coffee filled the room. Yum.

She wheeled the cart across the carpet to a table beside the window. "Sergeant, you were heroic." She leaned over and the tail of the shirt hiked up, revealing an evenly tanned bottom. Her voice had a smoldering, dusky sound. In bed, she was hell on wheels—sexy, confident, female, yielding. What game was she playing now?

"Thanks."

"Likewise."

"You made me forget. For a while."

She nodded, looked at him briefly, then finished setting the table and sat down, crossing her legs. "There's a robe in the closet. The brown should fit."

Branko found a brown terry-cloth robe hanging on a hook just inside the door. It was a man's, expensive, one-size-fits-all. When he returned to the table, Mrs. Maxwell was biting into a Danish. Sitting there, she looked very good, young, almost dewy. What was her secret for holding back the clock?

"Whose robe is this?"

She kept on chewing as she poured his coffee. "A guest robe." He sat down.

She stared at him. "Jealousy is unbecoming in a sergeant, Sergeant."

He was angry at himself. He had no claims on Mrs. Maxwell. He dropped two sugar cubes into his coffee and changed subjects. "Haven't seen sugar cubes since Europe."

"Oh. When were you there?"

"Early seventies. On my way back from Vietnam. My buddy

and I stopped off in Paris and toured the wine country. We knew a French guy there, from Saigon. He showed us around."

"Some sport with the local ladies, I trust?"

"Some."

"Now *I'm* jealous, Sergeant."

Branko laughed, and they touched coffee cups. "Touché."

He lifted the warmer lid and found scrambled eggs, American bacon, and Canadian bacon, just in case you didn't like American. Under another warmer lid was a plate of breakfast rolls. On the side were little jars of orange marmalade and black-currant jelly and tupelo honey. The butter was on a jazzy cut-glass butter dish that belonged down the road, at the Ritz Carlton Hotel. An ice bucket held four Coronas. The two that were open had lime slices wedged into their throats.

"You should hire out, brunch at the Maxwell House."

"Help pay for the mortgage, right?"

Branko looked around. People like Mrs. Maxwell had money to burn. With her, mortgage was only a word. Six sips of coffee got him ready for a roll. A roll readied him for eggs and bacon. He drank a Corona with the eggs. Across the table, Mrs. Maxwell was eating with gusto, bright white teeth gleaming against her tan. A lady of appetites.

"They say around the club you played Forest Hills."

"Um." She nodded. "The last year of grass. And then two years on that awful gray clay."

"How far did you get?"

"I made the semis on grass, the quarters on clay."

"I'm impressed."

"A little girl of sixteen put me out in the semis. I was in college at Columbia. Her father was a coach in San Diego. She'd been playing since she was three. She lost in the finals."

"What did you study at Columbia?"

"Literature and political science."

"You wanted to teach?"

She spread butter on a roll. "No. I liked to read and I've always been interested—now it's amusement, really—in the political process. I wanted to work in politics, for someone who really cared."

"Did you find someone?"

"No."

"Is that where you met your husband? Politics?"

"No. We met at UCLA, when I was a graduate student. Jordan gave a talk on international marketing. I was in the audience. He had this really bold grasp of how things worked globally. Afterward, I asked questions and he gave me his business card and I gave him my phone number. He called me the next time he was in town. He was quite a bit older, but I'd fallen in love. We lived together for a while and then we got married."

She was quiet for a moment, squeezing a lime into a glass and filling the glass with Corona. Branko was on his second beer and feeling no pain. This was the way to shut the world out, he told himself. Use your lifestyle as a buttress to lean against the walls of the world when they pressed in, when they threatened to choke you, suffocate you.

"I heard it was his idea to get the reverend into politics."

She nodded. "Jordan brought a few people together. The reverend had been impressive on the city council, and Jordan wanted someone to run against Sherwood."

"He didn't like Sherwood's politics?"

"No. Jordan cared nothing for politics. Sherwood didn't understand economics, the way the marketplace worked. Jordan was an oil man, so he had a feel for spot markets and currency exchanges. He wanted someone in Congress to fight the marketing fight."

"Could you elaborate?"

"Of course. Jordan felt the trade deficit could be solved with solid marketing. The Japanese sell us their cars because they've done their market research. Jordan was from Oklahoma and he used the Subaru as an example of how the Japanese won the Rockies with four-wheel drive."

"Could the reverend handle that?"

She shrugged. "Jordan thought so."

"Smart guy, your husband."

"I miss him."

"You planning on getting married again?"

She smiled and hoisted her glass. "Sergeant, is that a proposal?"

Branko's face got red. "Just asking."

"I take it you're already taken."

"I was married ten years. My wife split and went back to New York. She's into literature, words. Editing."

"A noble task, words. Do you miss her?"

Lissa Cody had asked the same thing. "I don't miss the fights."

"A good fight can clear the air."

"Maybe for you. It just makes me madder."

"How mad, Sergeant?"

He didn't answer because his temper was deeply buried, coiled inside him like some kind of dragon from prehistory. She reached out to put her hand on top of his.

"Have you ever killed anyone?"

His throat was tight. They were back to death as a topic. "Yes."

"May I ask where?"

"In Vietnam. And in Los Angeles. I was a cop there."

"I can tell you don't want to talk about it. Please excuse my probing. It was . . . indiscreet." Mrs. Maxwell shifted in her chair to recross her legs and the front of the blue shirt opened slightly, revealing the inside curves of her breasts. During their lovemaking, if that's what it had been, he had explored those curves with his tongue and lips. Now, sitting in the chair with the light playing tricks, her moves seemed natural and contrived at the same time. She was onstage. Branko sat in the audience watching a gifted actress perform. What was the price of the ticket to this performance? he wondered.

Suddenly, he wanted her again. The blond hair and the slanted blue eyes made her look feline, like a pussycat. She smiled at him. He had the feeling she could read his mind.

"What sort of name is Branko?"

"Yugoslav. One story says it's Serb. The other says it's Croatian. The family argued about it a lot."

"Your accent. It's sort of Middle West."

"I grew up in Wisconsin, little town called Beloit."

"Beloit? I used to play tennis at your country club."

"What year?"

"Early seventies. 'Seventy-one. 'Seventy-two."

"I was slugging it out with Charley in the jungle." Branko paused. "Then you're from Chicago?"

"Yes."

"Where?"

"South Side. Near the university."

"Do you ever go back?"

"No. My mother died, two years ago. My dad died when I was a little tyke. It's ghetto territory now."

"What was your maiden name?"

She hesitated. "Novak."

"Czech?"

She nodded with her mouth half full. "Um. My grandparents arrived here, according to the family legend, in 1910. They came from Prague, spent a year in New York and then ventured West, to Chicago. One grandfather worked on the railroads. The other was a bookkeeper." She ate a last bite of Canadian bacon and raised her glass. "To the Midwest and all its phobias."

They clinked glasses. Branko was aware of his pulsing desire.

"Was your father a policeman?"

"No. My grandfather was." Branko was about to tell her about his grandfather Stefano, but he stopped. "Do you know Douglas Cade?"

"Why do you ask?"

"Saw his name on your supersonic phone."

"I know Douglas."

"I need to interview him. About the shootings."

"When?"

"Soon."

Mrs. Maxwell stood up and walked to the phone. She pressed an automatic dial button and waited for an answer with her legs twined at the ankles, like a little girl posing for a Brownie camera. Branko could feel their time together ending. He felt regret, waking up from this Technicolor dream.

"Douglas? Susannah Maxwell here."

Old pals.

They exchanged society pleasantries and then Mrs. Maxwell mentioned Branko's desire for an interview. She listened, nodding, then turned to Branko. "How is four o'clock?"

"Great. Where?"

"At his office. In Promontory Chapel. The Tower, they call it."

Branko had already been there. The Spartan room with the family photo and the computer. "Great. Tell him I'll be there."

"Thank you, Douglas. Four o'clock will be fine." She hung up and looked at Branko. "Douglas is a workaholic. He usually works on the weekends, anyway."

"I appreciate it."

"No problem. One does what one can to keep society's wheels turning." She picked up the bedside clock.

Branko stretched his legs out in front of him.

"Don't move." Mrs. Maxwell left the room.

Branko walked into the bathroom, where he found a drawer full of new toothbrushes in plastic wrappers. It was a British brand and he smiled as he tore off the plastic. Nothing but the best for Mrs. Maxwell. He was rinsing his mouth when she appeared in the doorway carrying a bottle of champagne but no glasses. She stood there, not speaking, working the champagne cork. The movement of her fingers was vigorous and there was a zany smile on her face. The bottle dripped with beaded moisture.

"Watch out, Sergeant!"

He dodged as the cork blew and caught it in his left hand. She spewed him with champagne. As he charged, she laughed. She shook the champagne bottle, holding her thumb over the top like a little kid in a Coke fight. Her eyes were lit up, a deep, sparkly blue. Branko made a grab for the champagne bottle, but she dodged away and ran out of the bathroom. The chase was prehistoric; they could have been back in the primeval jungle. Branko laughed as his robe came unbelted. Desire blossomed into lust. This was one entertaining lady.

They made love on the floor with the sunlight coming through the windows. She was tender, playful, crazy, intense, dangerously female. She whimpered and moaned and bit his

226

shoulder and cinched her long legs around his waist. He had a flashing image of centaurs galloping across mythical pastures of long green grass, and he admired her physical strength, the sheer force of her torso and legs. When they were finished, she drank champagne from the bottle, then passed the bottle to him. Her face seemed open and vulnerable, perhaps a little sad. She was still wearing the workshirt. The brown robe was on the floor in a heap.

He wanted to know more about the mysterious Mrs. Maxwell, but she kept asking the better questions and he kept answering them. He told her about Karen and his childhood and the Wisconsin winters and being a high-school jock. He told her about the photo album in his grandparent's house and about the pictures of his grandfather as a young cop in Zagreb. She ran cool fingers across the scar on his right side beneath the arm and he told her about being wounded in Vietnam. He told her a little bit about the Fun Zone shooting and a lot about Roscoe Smith. Where had she learned to listen? he wondered.

"You're very good at this."

She smiled. "At what?"

"Asking questions. Looking interested in the answers."

"I don't just *look* interested, Sergeant. I *am* interested."

Branko grinned. "You're a great actress. That's what."

She traced his lips with one fingernail. "And you are a very perceptive man." She reached down and he felt her hand. "And a very alive one."

"Why me?"

Instead of answering with words, she leaned down to flick him with her tongue.

"You're a beautiful woman. Money. Class. Style. Five cars."

"Only three," she said. "And one's on the blink. So's my upstairs ice-maker."

"Tough life, without an ice-maker."

She nipped him with her teeth, hint of danger.

"You invite me up here. You could invite the president or the king of Sweden or a gold medalist from the Olympics. What do you want with a cop?"

She smiled at him as if she were a willing slave from his fantasy harem. What a laugh. This lady was nobody's slave. After a long moment filled with pleasure, she let him go and sat up to strip off the shirt. The motion made her breasts swing, her bronzed shoulders gleaming in the sunlight. Then she lay on top of him, stomach to stomach, until he was ready for her again. It did not take long.

"You want to know why you're here? Is that it? You want to know why it's you and not the king of Sweden?"

He didn't really care. Her flesh blotted out the world with its ripe, smoldering heat.

"The king of Sweden," he said slowly, "was an accomplished tennis player. I used to read about him when I was a high school jock. Used a wooden stick strung with troll's whiskers."

He felt her chuckle. Her lips were on his throat when she said: "You're here, Sergeant, because I want you to kill someone for me."

He broke rhythm, making her smile, and she clutched him with expert muscles, drawing him deeper. "Okay. No problem. Who?"

"Douglas Cade," she said. "In your interview. At four o'clock."

She raised her face and he saw her golden smile, and he laughed.

What an actress.

At twelve-thirty Sunday, Benny Rubidoux left the motel on Sunset to pick up the Beard in Manhattan Beach. The motel room was paid up for four days, cash, and he was going stir-crazy from watching TV and laughing at the fuzz. He had a headache from too much booze and a belly-ache from pizza.

Benny hung a Do Not Disturb sign on the doorknob. Baldy and the bimbo with the smart mouth were tied up and sleeping like babies. Benny'd fed them four sleeping pills apiece in a paper cup of lukewarm Orange Slice. If they croaked in there, so what.

By mid-afternoon on Sunday, Benny had the situation scoped out. The Beard rode shotgun, blowing his big nose with Kleenex. He still had his head cold, but he had shaved the beard. Without the hair, his face looked fat, middle-aged, pale as a fish belly. Call him No Beard? They were heading south, toward Newport Beach and an old boy in a white suit who could lead them to Colonel No-Name. The constant hawking and sneezing and blowing made Benny wish he'd left the Beard back in Manhattan Beach.

Benny's neck hurt.

And he had other problems. The goddamn Camaro drove like a Sherman tank. The twink who owned her—the glove compartment was filled with lipsticks, fake pink fingernails, spare pantyhose, and three bottles of polish remover—didn't know squat about keeping her running. The engine kept missing and she needed an alignment, bad. Benny's cash, including eighty from Baldy's wallet and thirteen singles from Smart Mouth, was down to four hundred dollars and change. The money was in a Mexican clip, next to the fake police shield, in his hip pocket.

The Beard twisted the knob on the radio, trying to get some news. "We should of kept the Mercedes, Charlie." He was still calling Benny "Charlie Tuna."

"Too hot, man."

The Beard took time out to blow his nose, then went back to fiddling with the radio dial. "Whyn't you steal a car had a search deal on the stereo?"

"I was in a hurry. Why don't you quit bitching?"

"I'm worried about finding this old dude, what's his name?"

"Wakefield. You watched him all week, you still can't remember his name?"

"Shit. Never could remember anyone who was old. They just seem to turn white and fade out, like my grandpap. No balls."

Benny cut his eyes at the Beard. "Wakefield rode in the limo with the preacher. He manages the campaign. I saw him on the TV. Wears white suits."

"And you think he's the inside guy?"

"Yeah. That's what I think."

"And this guy Wakefield, he knew Hector the Connector?"

"Yeah." Benny was getting irritated. "And he knows the colonel."

The Beard sat back with a smug look. "Told you he was military."

"How much jack you got on you?"

The Beard pulled out a wad of bills. Slowly, he counted them. "Seven hundred. You?"

"Couple hundred."

"All that dough, whoo."

"Colonel No-Name owes me, man."

"Owes *us*, you mean. On this job, I get half."

Benny did not answer as he left the San Diego Freeway for Newport. The beach traffic was thick, like summer. It took them more than half an hour to crawl down to Pacific Coast Highway. Benny stopped at a 7-Eleven to check Wakefield's address in the phone book. Shit, that old white-suited dude had to live somewhere around here, all the fancy iron, all the rich cats. Might stop and knock off a house or two, just for running-around money. He spent four dollars in quarters calling all the Wakefields in the book. Several numbers did not answer. Two gave him busy signals, so he kept trying. He was proud of his technique. He'd ask for Mr. Wakefield. When the man came to the phone, he'd ask if this was the Mr. Wakefield connected to the campaign, and if so, Benny wanted to make a donation. In thirty-four minutes, all he'd turned up was Sorry, no connection. Be just like the old creep to have an unlisted number. He was holding the phone, about to clink in another quarter, when the Beard walked up and put a meaty hand on his shoulder.

"What?"

"Guess what I just saw."

"Madonna and Cyndi Lauper."

"Nah. That white church limo."

Benny touched his neck. "Where?"

The Beard pointed at a long white stretch limo heading southeast on the coast highway. Benny hung up and they headed for the car.

"Find the old geezer?"

"Not if he's in the limo."

"What if he ain't?"

"He is."

"What'd you say on the phone?"

"Told them I was a Christian and wanted to contribute money to the campaign."

The Beard laughed and honked a wad of greasy snot into a tissue.

The traffic was Sunday gridlock. Benny sweated as he eye-balled the limo, four cars ahead, in the left lane. He clicked on his left blinker and eased over. When the limo turned left on Jamboree, Benny was only three cars behind.

He kept a three-car buffer between the Camaro and the limo as they zipped up Jamboree toward Promontory Chapel. He'd learned about buffers in junior college, studying police science. This was the way the Feds did surveillance—buffers, switch tails. At Promontory Chapel, cars were two lanes deep in the upper parking lot, waiting for a chance to squeeze in down below. Benny parked up top. A cop directing traffic waved the white limo through and on down the ramp. Benny checked his Llama 9mm, then opened the door of the Camaro and stepped to the edge of the cliff and looked down. The limo had stopped at the main entrance and who was getting out but Mr. White Suit, old Wakefield himself.

Benny walked back to the Camaro to report.

"What makes you think you can go in there, Charlie?"

Benny pointed to his eyes. "No shades, man. No hair piece. No face hair. All they got is a picture of Cousin Rafe wearing Kevlar. They don't know me, man."

The Beard folded his arms. "Think I'll stick here, man."

Benny showed him the fake police shield. "Yellow is the color of chickens. Green is the color of chickenshit."

"Let's hit his house, man. Steal his rich ass blind."

"Your cut is down to thirty percent," Benny said.

The Beard folded his fat arms and stared out the window. As Benny walked off, he heard another sneeze. Just as well leaving him there, he told himself. Alone, he could be in and out in ten.

As Benny trudged down the road with the Christians, it felt like Sunday school in Little Rock. He spotted three pretty girls. One of them, a brunette, winked at him. Benny winked back. The women were wearing dresses with high heels and several of the men wore business suits. Benny checked the watch he'd taken off Baldy, back at the motel on Sunset. It was 4:12 as he trudged with the afternoon crowd through the wide double doors. Churches were spooky. He smelled sweat and perfume. Jesus rock music whomped from inside. A cop was standing to one side, talking to a woman in a yellow dress. There were security guards in three-piece suits but they weren't carrying. It was cool in there, with a hallway off to the right and a great big corridor in front that led to the main cathedral. Benny had been inside, for a look-see, last week. He stepped up close to a security guard and flashed his fake police shield. "You work here?"

"Sure do."

"I'd like to have a word with Mr. Wakefield."

"Do you have an appointment?"

"Tell him Detective Briggs. LAPD. I drove a long way to speak to him. It's urgent."

The security guard picked up a phone and punched three buttons. He explained the situation, then hung up. "Detective? You can go up. Sixth floor. I'll walk you to the elevator. It only works with a key."

"I do admire tight security," Benny said.

Music pumped at them from the cathedral. Benny did not recognize the tune. They started up the hallway, toward the elevator. Benny's brain buzzed, the way it always did when he was into action. Things went just terrific until they were twenty feet from the Tower elevator. The voice came from behind him: "Sir! Excuse me! Sir!"

The security guard turned, then touched Benny's arm. "I think she means you, Detective."

Out of the corner of his eye Benny saw a lady cop walking toward him, wearing a khaki uniform and packing a piece. She looked familiar, a tight body, blond hair piled up on her head, and then he knew. It was the skater.

"Would you hold up just a minute—"

There was a *bong* and a red light lit up and the door opened and out stepped a punker, sixteen, maybe seventeen, with a chimney sweep's black eye and purple hair. Miss Purple Hair was wearing a Madonna costume—white leggings, a short black skirt, and a bright red top. She had a sexy mouth and looked like she was about ready to suck her thumb.

"Sir?"

"Detective?" The security guard was staring at Benny with narrowed eyes, unsure of what he should do. "That officer wants to speak to you."

Benny grabbed the guard's arm and slung him against Purple Hair, who went *wooof* against the wall. Benny shoved the guard inside and grabbed Purple Hair around the neck with his right arm.

"Delia!" the skater yelled. "Get down!"

Benny jerked out the Llama and fired, taking the skater in the shoulder just as she pulled her piece. The sound of the Llama echoed down the corridor. Purple Hair was twisting and screaming. The guard made a try for Benny from behind and Benny clubbed him back with a vicious swipe of the muzzle. Blood spurted from the guard's nose as he crashed into the metal wall.

The skater fired at Benny, the slug clawing a chunk of marble out of the wall above his head. He dragged Purple Hair inside and punched the button for three. Nothing happened. The skater fired two more rounds, mainly for effect. As long as he had Purple Hair, no fuzz would shoot to kill. He was sweating now, jabbing buttons, hearing voices outside in the hall. The only way out was up.

"What's wrong with the goddamn elevator?"

"A key!" Purple Hair wailed. "You need a key!"

Benny swung around to look at the guard, who was slumped against the wall, eyes closed. "Sonofabitch!" He holstered the Llama and threw Purple Hair to the floor. She squealed and he heard the skater call out for him to throw out his piece and surrender. He flipped the guard over on his belly and found the key on a gold ring attached to his belt inside the suit coat. Sweat burned his eyes as he jammed the key into the lock. A man shouted outside, some dude with a bullhorn. Then the doors closed, shutting out the world.

Purple Hair sat up, staring at him. Her lip was bleeding as she

233

wiped her face with the back of one hand. "What do you want with me?"

It was hostage time in Promontory Chapel and girls counted more than boys. Benny grinned at her and thought she answered with a cute little shiver. If he had time, he'd treat Purple Hair to some of the old Benny Rubidoux Arkansas Tonic.

Benny pressed the button for three and then changed his mind and pressed six. He needed breathing space. His hands and face were sweaty. There was something cold in his chest, like a cake of ice. As the elevator rose, he heard a bell go off.

"What's that?"

"An alarm," Purple Hair said.

He grabbed her arm and pulled her close.

"Now it's me and you, twink."

CHAPTER FOURTEEN

B RANKO was sitting in Douglas Cade's office finishing up a dry and uneventful interview when the red button blinked on Cade's phone. Branko's chair was hard and uncomfortable. Cade's desk was Spartan and bare, like Cade himself.

Cade spoke with a dry, mechanical voice, the tips of his fingers pressed together to form a tent. He'd held the same position for twenty minutes. He was wearing a business suit, a gray three-piece made of summer-weight wool. His shoes had a high polish. His conservative tie was neatly knotted. Branko would have bet five dollars that Cade was wearing ankle-garters, like Mr. Waterbury, the president of the Beloit State Bank back in Wisconsin.

In contrast, Branko had on his clothes from yesterday—tan slacks, white sports shirt with double pockets, and Brooks runners. His jacket was in the car. So was his shoulder holster and the .357. He was technically off-duty until six. Other officers were on duty downstairs. He'd seen no reason for wearing the gun into the church for this interview.

All through the interview, Cade had been neatly and precisely evasive. While he smiled and wore the face of cooperation, he hadn't come across with much hard information.

Yes, he'd joined the campaign last autumn, at the behest of Jordan Maxwell, he'd told Branko. He'd known Maxwell for a dozen years. They had mutual business friends, mostly back East. It was no secret that the campaign finances had been in slight disarray when he took the helm. That, of course, was his métier, his currency, if you will, in the vast world marketplace. He knew how to turn red into black. He was, of course, not at liberty to divulge specific financial information at this time, but he had done his best to control the cash flow and handle the accounts receivable. Politicians in general had no sense of how to conserve money. Nor did preachers. He thought of it (thin smile then) as Cade's Corollary: the higher the office, the huger the deficit. A New York publisher had approached him about writing a book on the subject, and he was toying with the idea. Yes, the shooting of the reverend had been a travesty. No, he had no earthly idea who would conceive of such a thing. He declined to predict the outcome of Tuesday's primary. Branko noticed that Cade kept his distance from the reverend by referring to him as Reverend Williams. He was a staunch conservative.

Cade was hiding something, of that Branko was sure. He could feel it hovering over the tidy desk that stood between him and the effeminate, prissy little man who made precise tents by pressing his fingers tip-to-tip. Cade was hiding something and there was no way to sweat it out of him. Especially on Sunday. Branko sighed and was about to close his notebook. He was due at the station at six. He just had time to zip by his apartment for a change of clothes. Thinking of the station made him think about Roscoe Smith, Marcie, funeral arrangements, ashes on the sea.

Now the red light was blinking on the phone and Cade excused himself to answer it. Branko shifted, trying to get comfortable in the metal chair, and hid a yawn behind the back of his hand. Images from his adventures on Spyglass Hill made him smile—Mrs. Maxwell in a man's workshirt, the champagne squirting, her face as she listened to him talking, sunlight on tanned flesh. The lady understood therapy. He had felt like a crocodile from the dawn of time, sinking down in warm wet mud. The chief was right. He could use some more of this R&R. Mexico, maybe, baking in the sun. Cozumel. Oaxaca. Puerto Vallarta.

"I'll be right down." Cade hung the phone up with a sharp little bang and stood up, his beady gray eyes on alert. "There's something—something going on downstairs. I'm afraid, Sergeant Branko, that our interview has been temporarily interrupted."

Branko nodded. He was through anyway. "No problem. Thanks for your time."

"Not at all. One should cooperate with the authorities."

Cade straightened his tie as he bent down to flip a control on the console. "This is Mr. Cade. Can you give me a report?" There was a crackling sound on the other end and Branko heard voices from a long way off. "Blast!" Cade let out a controlled snort and led the way out of the office.

The hallway was quiet. As they passed the office marked REV-EREND WILLIAMS, the door opened and a college boy popped his head out. The kid, who was dressed in loose-fitting pants with narrow cuffs and a baggy rock-star jacket, somehow looked familiar to Branko. He wore his blond hair in a mod crew cut.

"What's up, Doug?"

"I'm sure I have no idea."

Behind the kid Branko saw the reverend and a heavy man in a white suit. The reverend was sitting in his wheelchair and the heavy man stood at the windows, staring out. One look and Branko realized the kid was Terry Williams Junior.

Branko and Cade kept walking. As they approached the elevator, Cade pulled a key ring out of his pocket and inserted a key in the lock to call the elevator. The floor indicator showed the elevator was on one. Cade tapped his foot impatiently as he eyed it. "I keep telling these people, machines need service. In the modern world, maintenance is all."

Down below, Branko heard a dull sound, like a muffled explosion. He looked out the window at the parking lot full of cars. Cade twisted the key in the lock once more. A few beads of sweat popped onto his forehead and his eyes narrowed to tight slits.

"I cannot imagine what on earth is —"

An alarm bell cut him off. Biting his lip, Cade turned to Branko. His eyes showed fear. "The alarm. The alarm. Damn this elevator." Cade removed his key and stared at it before trying it again. The elevator had left the first floor and was rising toward the second.

The stairs were at the other end of the corridor. "Meet you downstairs, Mr. Cade." Branko trotted toward the stairs. As he passed the reverend's office, the door opened and the reverend's kid looked out. "What's up, anyway?"

The alarm was still ringing. Branko didn't answer. As he reached the stairs and started down he thought of his Magnum locked in the trunk of the Volvo, which was parked outside in the lower parking lot.

In the elevator, Benny felt his chest constrict. He coughed, but that didn't help. He'd get out of this one, but he didn't know how. Not yet. His throat was tight and his head ached. Purple Hair stared at him from her position on the floor. The door opened on two. *Bong.* An usher with a white name badge started to get on but Benny stepped forward and put his hand in the usher's face and the muzzle of the Llama on his throat and shoved. "Up yours, sucker!" The usher fell backward, windmilling his arms, and Benny stepped back inside.

The doors closed. Purple Hair had moved over closer to the wall and was whimpering like she was about to die. Benny told her to shut up. The guard was out. They passed three, four, five. The alarm kept ringing, banging his ears, wham, wham. The sound rolled around inside his head, around and around. Goddamn that skater. He was edgy, ready to kill. He had a twink hostage. He'd demand money, a ton of it, and a car to take him to Mexico. Yeah, a list of demands, the way they did it in the movies.

The door opened on six and the first person Benny saw was a

dude in a gray business suit with his elevator key stuck in the lock.

"Delia Sue," Business Suit said, blinking, "it's about time."

Benny hit the emergency lock, keeping the doors open, and waved the Llama at him. "On the floor, hotdog. On the *floor*, belly down, hands behind your fucking ears!"

Business Suit went down to one knee, and Benny pushed him with his foot to help him the rest of the way. He toppled over like a bundle of dried twigs. Benny sat on his back, the gun at his neck. "Who else is on this floor?"

"No one." His voice was muffled, shaky. "Just Reverend Williams and—"

The preacher. "Where?"

"Down there. Three doors down."

Okay, Purple Hair and the guard and Business Suit. Now the preacher, his old pal from the Fun Zone. Four hostages, maybe four stiffs, nothing to sweat. "Anyone else?"

"Yes. His son. Terry Junior. He's—"

At that moment the door down the hall opened and the reverend came out, riding in a wheelchair. Behind him was the fat man, Wakefield, and a kid with fancy-ass college-boy clothes. Right off the streets of Westwood, shit. He leveled the piece at the reverend. "Just keep on coming, Reverend. Keep coming slow and easy."

"You!" the reverend said. "You filth! What are you doing here?"

Benny grinned as he swung the muzzle over the reverend's head to cover Joe College. "No funny stuff, sissy-pants. Who else is on this floor?"

Joe College looked at Business Suit. "No one."

Business Suit spoke. "There was . . . a policeman."

Benny felt a shiver crawl up his spine. "A cop?"

"Yes. He went down the stairs."

"Shit. Where?"

Business Suit pointed. "The end of the hall."

"How long ago?"

"A minute. No more."

He had to work fast before the cop came back. He shoved his

hostages into the office, then kept them covered while Purple Hair roped their wrists with telephone cord. All the while, the reverend kept talking to Benny, talking about God and salvation and eternal damnation. "Now is your chance, my son. Give up this life of sin. Give it up now."

"Easy, preacher. Don't rile my nerves."

The reverend's hands were tied in front of him so he couldn't reach his wheels. Business Suit's left hand was tied to Joe College's right. The guard groaned when Purple Hair tied him up. The reverend was no use, so Benny left him alone while he took his work crew down the corridor. Grunting and moaning, they built a barricade against the door marked STAIRS, using chairs and a desk from the nearest office. The fat man acted like he was about to die.

Not just yet, pal.

It reminded Benny of that old movie, *Bridge on the River Something.* "Good show, troops." Then he herded them back to where the reverend sat with his hands tied.

Branko could not open the door to the ground floor, so he started back up to two. When he got there, the door was open. The elevator was still on six and he had no key. His beeper went off, so he tried the doors along the corridor until he found one that was open. The sign on the door said INFORMATION BANK. Inside, there were eight desks, separated by metal walls about five feet high. Each desk had its own computer terminal. Three of the desks were tidy. The other five were cluttered. He sat at a cluttered desk and called the station. After five rings, Molly Brazelton answered.

"Police, Officer Brazelton."

"Molly, it's Frank Branko."

"Oh, Frank. Where are you?"

"At Promontory Chapel. What's up?"

"Promontory Chapel? Did you see the shooting?"

Branko felt a cold chill pass over him. The muffled explosion he'd heard had been a gunshot. He tried to keep his voice calm. "Fill me in."

"Jamie Duncan's hit. Jamie says it's the perp from Balboa."

"Here?"

"Yes. He's taken two hostages up to the sixth floor. The elevator's jammed. Lieutenant Plotvik just left with his SWAT personnel. Lieutenant Archer is en route."

"Where's the chief?"

"We're trying to raise him."

Branko's knuckles were white on the telephone. "What's Plotvik's ETA?"

"Seven minutes. Maybe ten."

"See if you can raise him on the radio. Tell him I'm inside and not to blast away, okay?"

"All right, Frank. What are you going to do?"

"I'm going back upstairs. Maybe I can take the perp from behind."

"Be careful."

But Branko had already hung up and was out the door, heading for the stairs.

Amity Pitcairn had just left Huntington Beach and was heading south for Newport Beach and the Fashion Island shopping mall when the car phone buzzed. She was driving a stolen PacBell service truck and wore the orange-and-white uniform of a PacBell repair technician. Her time was up. She'd looked for the target for two days, as agreed. Tomorrow, she'd be on that plane for Nice and the French Riviera. She answered. It was Officer Invisible, code name Phoenix, Devane's mole inside the LAPD. His voice was a monotone.

"Agent Blue?"

"Yes."

"Your target has surfaced. He may be found in the Tower of Promontory Chapel in Newport Beach, on the sixth floor. The street address is 1 Back Bay Drive. Your target is armed, one handgun, perhaps two. He has at least three hostages in custody. An officer is down. That is all. Your instructions are to terminate with prejudice."

Before she could reply or ask questions, the connection was broken.

Amity eased the PacBell truck up over the speed limit. When

she came to a traffic light, she pulled out her AAA maps of Newport Beach and located Back Bay Drive, a curved street that roughly followed the shoreline. Jamboree was the quickest way there. After a mile she turned left on Jamboree, leaving the coast highway behind. Going up the hill, she saw two police cruisers turn right onto Jamboree. Amity smiled because she knew where they were headed. Their roof lights were turning, flashing red and blue in the afternoon sunlight. Amity followed them at a distance as they parted traffic for her, all the way to Promontory Chapel.

Inside the reverend's office, Douglas Cade was trying to figure out a way to save his own life. The killer's eyes were crazed and, for the moment, he seemed interested in Harrison Wakefield.

"You. Fat Man." The killer waved the pistol at Harrison. "Outside."

"Why me?"

"Because, Mr. Inside Dope, you and me got a chicken to pluck."

Harrison struggled to his feet. It was difficult to move with his arms pinioned behind his back. The killer marched him out, leaving the door open about five inches. Cade heard a sickening sound of metal on bone. "Okay, Fat Man, where can I find the colonel?"

Now Cade had an advantage over the others—he knew Colonel Devane. The killer wanted the colonel. Perhaps a trade was in order, some form of barter. Cade had passed along information to Colonel Devane, schedules and timetables, that would have allowed for the shooting on Friday. That was his job. He was a numbers man.

Cade was a freelance accountant who knew how to keep his mouth shut. He had spent seventeen years in New York, tidying up the books for Angelo Sattui, an Italian businessman. "These Feds, they get us on the income tax. With you on my team, Dougie, we'll beat that rap." Angelo Sattui had beat the income-tax rap, but they'd convicted him on a murder charge. After the trial, Cade had taken his talents overseas, first to a German arms manufacturer, and after that to Riyadh, where he had tidied up the books for an Arab oil emir.

He had met Colonel Devane while working for the German. Devane was a mercenary at the time, fighting obscure little wars in Third World countries, and he was always calling in the middle of the night to place an order for delivery in some remote spot in Africa or Central America. One thing about the colonel, he always paid his bills, which set him apart from the average soldier of fortune. And he, in turn, appreciated having Cade on site to expedite important shipments. As the colonel had said, "It's tough titty having your guns arrive after the war's over, and these wars last maybe a week. That's why I need you on board, Doug."

When the colonel returned home to America to build Devania, he kept in touch with Cade. Just last October, he'd hired him to keep a steady hand on the spending for the campaign of Reverend Williams. His second assignment was to salvage what he could of the Ministry Beach fiasco. Only Cade knew that the colonel had poured half a million dollars into the reverend's campaign.

Cade had been raised a Catholic, and he found Protestantism simple-minded and childish. He had understood that the colonel wanted his own man in the Congress. That was nothing new. The Sattuis had their congressman. But the reverend was a buffoon, full of hot air and simplistic ideas about the universe and the marketplace. Anyone else would have been a better choice.

Three months ago, the colonel had requested information from Cade about parades and gatherings. He had obliged. He had not known the specifics of the Friday shooting. As the colonel had said, he had no need to know.

Cade had visited Devania, several times. He knew about the tunnel. Perhaps he could use his knowledge to save his own life. He struggled to his feet and walked to the door.

"You, out there. Let him alone."

The killer was standing over Harrison Wakefield, who was slumped over on the floor. "Hey, it's the suit."

Cade eased the door open with his foot and stood in the doorway. His knees were trembling. "In my safe, down the hall, there is two hundred thousand dollars in cash."

The killer laughed. "Hot zing. I don't need no cash. What I need is a fucking Sherman tank to take me to fucking Mexico."

"With two hundred thousand you could buy a tank."

"Douglas?" the reverend called. "What's going on?"

Cade ignored him. "It's been collected . . . for the campaign. It's in small bills, tens and twenties, a fifty here and there. Once you get out of here, you could—"

The killer was interested. "Show me."

"Down the hall. In my office."

"Can't spend it up here."

Cade stepped into the hall. The telephone wire hurt his wrists terribly. He needed a place where he could negotiate. "You'll get away. They'll have to allow it. Take her with you."

The killer stared at him through strangely yellow eyes. "You try any tricks, Suit, and your ass is grass."

Cade nodded. "I understand. No tricks."

Cade waited at the door while the killer tested the bonds on the others. He was aware of the reverend's eyes, which tried to burn a hole through him, so he stood with his right shoulder turned toward the reverend, not looking at him.

"Douglas?"

Cade did not answer as he led the way down the hall to his office.

Branko wasted a couple of minutes in the stairwell at the door to six, trying to get through. First he used his shoulder, then he tried wedging himself between the stairwell and the door and pushing with his feet. The door wouldn't budge.

He went back down the stairs to five. The offices were locked. He was hoping to find a heating duct to crawl through, so he took off his left shoe, held it in his left hand, and smashed the glass of an office near the center of the Tower. He was sweating as he put his shoe back on. When he reached through to unlock the door, he felt a sharp jab of pain and knew he had cut himself. He jerked his left hand back. Blood oozed from two fingers and a cut on his palm. His stomach felt queasy.

It took him a minute to locate some clean towels in an executive washroom. He found scissors in a desk drawer and made a clumsy bandage. Blood soaked through the towel in no time. Branko hated the sight of blood.

He was about to give up his idea of surprising the perp when he remembered seeing a fire escape outside a window near the stairs. He trotted toward that end of the corridor. A sign on the window read, IN THE EVENT OF EMERGENCY, BREAK GLASS AND PULL LEVER. WARNING: AN ALARM WILL SOUND WHEN WINDOW OPENS.

Down below, the SWAT wagon had arrived. He could see Plotvik giving directions. The lieutenant was wearing his customary yellow shooting glasses and carried a red police bullhorn. A siren wailed with a low moan and officers cleared a path for the vehicle of Lieutenant Archer. The vehicle rolled to a stop and the Archer stepped out, dressed in white boating slacks and a blue captain's blazer. He conferred with Plotvik and then took the bullhorn from him.

"Now hear this. This is Lieutenant Robert M. Archer of the Newport Beach police station and I am ordering you to give yourself up. We know you have hostages."

There was no answer. The Archer repeated his order. Branko used the phone in the office to call the station. Molly Brazelton answered.

"Frank Branko, Molly. Did you get through to Stan?"

"I'm still trying, Frank. Where are you?"

"I'm on the fifth floor. There's a fire escape I may be able to use to get up to six. The lieutenant just arrived to take charge. I have to open a window that sets off an alarm. And I don't want to get my butt shot off doing it."

"I'll try him again, Frank."

"We don't have much time, Molly. The perp could start wasting hostages any minute."

"Affirmative, Frank. I understand."

Branko gave Molly the number he was calling from, then hung up. While he waited for the phone to ring, he checked the situation down below. Deputies were emerging from a black-and-white sheriff's department vehicle. One deputy carried a rifle that gleamed in the afternoon sun. Another black-and-white was easing down the hill. People streamed out of the main entrance to the chapel and uniformed officers directed them behind yellow police barriers. Evacuation was important. If the perp had a rifle, the whole area would be in danger. The parking lot seethed with cars. Branko checked his watch. Forty-five seconds since he had talked to Molly.

The phone rang and Branko answered. It was Stan Plotvik. "Frank, where are you?"

"On the fifth floor. I want to try using the fire escape to get up to six. Can you hold off firing?"

"Yes. Are you armed?"

"Yes."

"Go with Allah, Frank."

He hung up. If he got to six, he'd be on the outside. That meant he needed something small and heavy to break a window with when he got there. The exterior glass was thicker than the stuff inside. His running shoe wouldn't work. He came back and hefted the telephone receiver. It would do. He unplugged the receiver.

Back at the fire escape, he broke the glass and pulled the lever, causing the alarm to go off. He was just climbing onto the windowsill when rifle fire started up from down below. Cursing, Branko squatted behind the sill. A bullet whined through the open window and slammed against the wall of the corridor. Someone—the perp, probably—returned fire from somewhere above him. There were two more shots and then Plotvik's voice on the bullhorn:

"Cease fire, deputy! That's an order! Cease fire immediately!"

The firing stopped.

Branko looped the cord from the receiver over his shoulder, to keep his hands free, and climbed onto the fire escape. He told himself not to look down. Vertigo City. He kept his eyes straight ahead as he climbed. There was a breeze, and he was aware of many pairs of eyes on him as he moved higher. Left foot, right foot, steady there, six more steps to go, left and then a right and then a left and don't think about vertigo.

Sweat covered him as he reached the window on the sixth floor. The pane was thick, and it took three hard blows to smash through. The alarm was still ringing, so when he flipped the lever to open the window, nothing happened. He had a tense moment as he stood on the edge of the fire escape and swung the window outward. He held his breath. The wind made a sighing sound and for a moment he thought he was falling. Then he caught himself and swung his weight over and got one leg on the windowsill and could breathe again.

As he swung himself inside, he happened to glance across to the upper parking lot. He saw a PacBell service truck. A repairman was hanging, using his belt, from a utility pole directly across from the Tower. PacBell never slept.

Douglas Cade was turning the tumblers on his office safe when the gunfire started. Immediately and without hesitation, the killer broke the glass of the window and returned the fire.

"Take that, you fuckers!" he cried.

Cade's knees turned to water and he sank to the floor gratefully.

At the window, the killer kept up a furious fire, emptying his weapon, and then squatted down on his haunches to reload. From a pocket of his suit coat—a cheap, ratty garment that looked as if it had come from a fire sale—he produced a long cylindrical device packed with cartridges. Cade watched as the killer flipped one device out and the other in, all in one smooth motion. A new alarm rang steadily, pounding in Cade's ears.

The firing from below stopped. The killer stared at him. "Okay, hotdog. Get on with it."

Cade's hands trembled as he turned back to the safe. He had to start all over, thirty-five right, fifteen left, the numbers fading in and out of his memory. If he got out of this one alive, he vowed to depart the Southern California scene and disappear forever into the sanctuary of Switzerland. Thinking of Switzerland made him think of the cache of money and small coins and precious gems he had stored in Susannah's safe at the house on Spyglass Hill. Before he left, he would contact Susannah and get his property.

"Hurry it up, Suit."

The alarm was playing havoc with Cade's concentration, but the tumblers finally fell into place and there was that always satisfying sound, even on cheap mechanisms, of the releasing *click*. Cade opened the door. The money was there, as promised, neatly arranged in small bills. He handed the money over to the killer, who looked at it briefly before stuffing it into Cade's attaché case, a handmade job from Florence. Then he leveled his gun at Cade.

"How'd you like to be the first one to go, hotdog?"

"I know the colonel," Cade whispered.

The killer grinned, insanely, but the grin kept shifting into an ugly grimace. "You're Mr. Inside Dope?"

Cade nodded. "Yes."

"You?"

"Yes."

The killer shoved the muzzle of his gun beneath Cade's nose. It was as cold as ice. "You don't mean Colonel No-Name?"

Cade didn't want to move. The gun muzzle felt as if it were protruding up his nasal passages and into his brain. The pain was terrible. "Y-y-y-es."

"You know where he's at?"

"Y-yes."

"What's his name?"

Cade shook his head. "Devane. Colonel Devane. The name wouldn't mean anything to you. He's very . . . secretive."

"Sonofabitch. You know where he hangs out?"

Cade nodded, but said nothing.

"Well, I'll be a sonofabitch."

The killer moved toward him in a blur. There was a sharp stabbing pain in Cade's nose and he thought for a moment that the killer had pulled the trigger and splattered his accountant's brains to the far corners of the room. His shoulder slammed against the wall and he heard himself screaming—something he hadn't done since he was a child back in Newton, Massachusetts—and he realized dimly through the pain that the killer had raped his nostril with the wicked tip of his weapon.

He clawed at his nose, trying to stop the pain. Blood rushed onto his white shirt. The sight of his own blood made him realize his own mortality. He would die at any moment. He grabbed his pocket handkerchief to stanch the flow. The killer, from two feet away, grabbed his tie and jerked him forward.

"Where is he? Where can I find this Devane guy?"

"Near here."

"Where? How far?"

Cade pointed east. "He has a place. Across the mountains. Near Lake Elsinore."

"Motherfuck." Light suffused the killer's face.

Cade said nothing.

"Selling the colonel to save your ass?"

"Yes."

"Hot damn, pal. You got one cheap ass." The killer laughed. He rubbed the muzzle of the gun against his left cheek, and then prodded him out into the corridor.

The minute the killer left the reverend's office with Doug Cade, Terry Junior scrooched over to his sister and tried to untie her hands. The knots were pulled tight. When he couldn't loosen the wire around her wrists, she tried to help him.

"How's it going?" the reverend asked.

"It's awful tight, Daddy. It hurts."

The reverend was seething with anger. What was Douglas Cade up to, giving away money? What had happened to Harrison Wakefield? What did the assassin want? When would this nightmare end? His children were beautiful, stalwart, resilient. His heart overflowed with love.

There was firing from down below, and then return fire, five or six shots in quick succession, from the Tower. Presumably, the killer was having a fine time trying to hurt more innocents.

Anger blinded the reverend for a moment, and then he spied the intercom on his desk. He inched the wheelchair forward with his feet and leaned his upper body down across the top of the desk. He could barely reach the buttons that turned on the intercom. He had the idea that he might be able to talk to someone who was listening in. It wasn't much of an idea, but when you're in dire straits, he thought, hope springs eternal.

He managed to depress a button or two—he wasn't sure which ones or where they went to—and was wetting his lips in preparation for calling out when he heard voices. He recognized Cade's voice. And he recognized the voice of the killer. For a moment, he didn't know what they were talking about. Then he heard money mentioned and the name of someone called a colonel. Douglas Cade's voice was a whisper. The reverend could barely hear him. He didn't catch any other name, but he did hear the killer refer to Cade as "Mister Inside Dope," whatever that meant.

"Got it!" Delia Sue said triumphantly.

Across the room, his son held up his freed hands.

"Shhh!" the reverend said, and bent his head to listen. But there were only whispers from Cade and the killer.

Terry Junior was now working on Delia Sue's bonds. The killer still had the gun. "Be still, Terry! Delia Sue!" The reverend could hear scuffling sounds. It was clear that Cade and the killer had a relationship, a connection that superceded what was going on here, in this time and place.

What was it? How could Douglas Cade be previously acquainted with a paid killer?

From where she was hanging on the power pole, Amity Pitcairn had a clear view of the Tower. She estimated seventy yards for the shot, but her position was too visible. She clambered back down the pole and unhooked her safety belt. Opening the rear doors of the PacBell truck, she removed the explosives she had received from Colonel Devane. The truck was parked near the edge of the cliff, in a no-parking zone. Clouds were gathering over the Pacific, promising rain, but for now the sun was still a bright orange and the whole scene below was in view.

People streamed in hurried hordes from the chapel, a huge monstrosity of metal and stone and glass that could have been created only in the twentieth century. Carrying the explosives and keeping herself below the roof line, Amity scurried to an unattended police car that was parked seven rows away, near the top of the ramp. Half a dozen people were watching the scene below, their backs to Amity as she placed explosives underneath the gas tank and made sure the detonating device was connected.

Fifteen feet away was a second police car, diversion number two. She placed a second explosive charge under the left rear wheel and then returned to the PacBell truck. Her favorite church was at Chartres in Normandy, southwest of Paris. She opened the Samsonite gun case and brought out a sniper's rifle, an AR-15, nicely crafted. She snapped the stock onto the barrel assembly and shoved home the locking pin. Before she attached the scope, she used it to survey the Tower, where the target was. There on the cliff at the edge of the upper parking lot, Amity was almost on a level with the top of the Tower, and the scope was powerful enough to bring it into range. From here, a kill would be easy.

Amity Pitcairn smiled.

She wondered idly who would be on the Riviera this year. There was Annette, the sweet young redhead from the Sixth Arrondissement in Paris. There was Jacky, the dancer from the Folies Bergère. There was Greta, from Berlin, but Greta was a little too butch for Amity's taste. And there was Clothilde, dear faithful Clothilde.

Through the scope, Amity saw movement at a window. Quickly, she attached the scope and sighted down the barrel of her converted AR-15. The window was near the fire escape and for a moment she thought it was her target trying for a mad escape down the side of the building. Then she saw it was a brown-haired man wearing tan slacks, a white pullover, and tennis shoes. His left hand was bandaged. In his right hand was something yellow. Definitely not her target. Amity followed him through the scope as he climbed the steps of the fire escape. He stopped at the sixth floor and slammed the yellow object against the window, breaking it at a corner. Then he carefully pulled the glass away from the frame, creating a space to reach through. He swung the window out and vanished inside the building.

Too bad, Amity thought. And too easy. If the man with the bandaged hand had been her target, it would all be over by now and she would be on her way to Fashion Island, to switch vehicles.

Crouched in the rear of the PacBell truck, Amity Pitcairn put down the AR-15 and hefted the LAW bazooka to her right shoulder. She lined up the crosshairs on the window where the man had disappeared. This was diversion three. Then she settled down to wait.

Branko was in a small office on the sixth floor that faced southwest, so there was plenty of light from the big orange sun. He squatted for a moment, gulping air while he looked around for a weapon. He was still holding the yellow phone, but now he needed something longer, with more authority. The alarm still clanged. If the perp came in now, he'd be finished.

A sturdy wooden cross hung on the wall above the desk. It was a light tan color, four feet long, with a crosspiece of about eighteen inches. It took him a few moments of sweaty tugging to free it from the brackets that held it to the wall, the plaster crumbling as he strained. Finally, the cross came free. Feeling like a crusader in a kid's comic book, he tried a couple of practice swipes with it. It was heavier than it looked, with a nice heft. If he got room to swing, he could do some damage.

It was 4:38 as he crossed to the door and opened it. He was just in time to see Mr. Douglas Cade turn left into an office farther down the hall, near the elevator. Branko thought it was the reverend's office. A figure in a rumpled white suit lay huddled on the floor outside the office. Behind Cade, holding a gun and carrying a leather executive satchel, was a blond man in a cheap brown suit.

The reverend's mind raced with possibilities. Why had Cade come to work for the campaign? He'd said he wanted to get away from the snow back East. Who was this colonel person? Who did Cade work for, Sherwood and the opposition? Cade kept to himself. Perhaps he'd been hired by Sherwood and company to keep an eye on him? Yet Jordan Maxwell had recommended Cade. He was good with books and numbers. He had saved the campaign lots of money. The moment he'd arrived, things had gone smoother in the financial area, which was not the reverend's strong suit. Winona Lee resented Cade. The reverend usually defended him.

There was no more talk from the intercom. That meant Cade

and the killer would be returning. The reverend wanted his hands loose.

"Any luck?" he asked Terry Junior.

"Almost done, Dad."

"Better ease off, son. They're coming."

Terry Junior made one last twist and Delia Sue's hands were free.

"Lie down," the reverend said. "Both of you. As if you were still tied."

Doug Cade came in first, holding a handkerchief to his nose. Blood had spattered his shirt and was drying on his impeccable summer suit. His hands were no longer tied. The killer, carrying Cade's expensive briefcase, came in right behind him. The phone rang on the reverend's desk.

"Answer it, Suit." The killer shoved Cade toward the phone.

Cade picked up the phone and listened for a moment. "Yes," he said. "Here he is." And he handed the phone to the killer.

"Who's this?" the killer asked. "Hey, Lieutenant, get me the chief of police up here, or the mayor. No one's really hurt yet. A few bruises and shit, but nothing serious. Here's the deal. I got me five hot hostages—make that six—up here and I'm gonna waste one in about five minutes if I don't get what I want. Shut up and listen. First, I want transport out of here. I bring the girl, little Purple Hair, and I'll have my piece between her sweet virgin thighs. One move from you heroes and she's wasted. Second, I want a plane, a very big plane, standing by at your two-bit airport. Purple Hair stays with me while we fly to Mexico. Third, I want a million bucks in small bills—no, make that a million-five—loaded onto the plane. I've got a dude here who knows money. He'll do the count for me. You got an hour. Make that a half hour. The next sound you hear from this here church will be little-girl screams and the sound of angel wings flapping."

The killer slammed the phone down and stood with his legs spread wide, staring around at his hostages.

The reverend looked at Cade. "Douglas?"

"Hmmm?" Above the bloody handkerchief, Cade's eyes showed fear.

"Who's this colonel?"

Cade stared at the reverend. "What?"

"I heard you two talking. What does 'inside dope' mean?"

"Shit," the killer said.

"Tell me, Douglas."

"It doesn't matter. Not now."

"Douglas?"

The killer leveled the muzzle of his pistol at the reverend. "I should of wasted you Friday, pal."

"You slime," the reverend said. "You filth. You —"

Rage flashed in the killers eyes, rage and triumph and indecision. His face contorted and sweat dripped off his nose. The reverend knew it was time to die. All his dreams—gone.

Terry Junior rose to his feet in a lunging motion. As the killer fired, Terry Junior slammed into him from the side. They were about the same size, young men, vigorous. The force of Terry's onslaught threw the shot off and the slug went past the reverend's ear. He felt the heat of its passing. The two combatants vanished from his view, scuffling down behind the desk. Douglas Cade took the opportunity to scurry toward the door. There was nothing the reverend could do to stop him.

Delia Sue joined the melee on the floor.

"Delia. Watch out!"

As Cade went through the door, he collided with someone and was thrown back into the room. The reverend saw that it was Sergeant Branko, the policeman from the hospital. The sergeant was wielding a large wooden cross. One hand was bandaged.

"Wait!" Cade grabbed the cross. "You don't —"

There was a muffled gunshot from behind the desk. The sergeant broke free of Cade and took two steps, swinging the cross like a baseball bat. At the same time, the killer pushed himself up from the floor, turning from Terry Junior to face the policeman. The pistol was in his left hand, held low, aimed at the sergeant. As it went off, the cross connected with the killer's left side, smacking the pistol and knocking it out of his grasp. The shot went wild. The killer launched himself at the sergeant, who swung the cross again in a terrible arc. The second blow caught the killer on the side of the head and he went down. The sergeant stood over him, still holding the cross.

"Kill him!" the reverend breathed. "Finish him off!"

The sergeant turned and stared at the reverend. "Is the phone working?"

"Kill him! Kill them both!"

Before he did anything else, Branko wrapped the killer's wrists with telephone cord. Then he pressed two fingers to the throat of Terry Junior and nodded. "He's okay. Needs medical attention." The sergeant knelt beside Cade to take his pulse. "Shock," he said. "Didn't know who it was. Hit him pretty hard." Douglas Cade's face was pale and he was breathing shallowly. The reverend did not want Cade to die before he answered some questions.

The phone rang again and the sergeant answered. "Branko," he said. "Who is this?"

Delia Sue was in front of her father, untying his hands. Suspicions boiled in his mind. Was Douglas Cade in league with someone who had hired the killer who had slain Mac White? Why?

First, the reverend would see to his son. Then there would be revenge to seek.

Vengeance is mine, sayeth the Lord.

CHAPTER FIFTEEN

IT took a full three minutes for Plotvik's SWAT guys to clump up the stairs, eyes wide with anticipated action, caps on backward, rifles held at port arms. Those three minutes told Branko he'd been right. His head ached and his left hand throbbed mercilessly and if he closed his eyes he still saw the ground below the fire escape, the upturned eyes of the crowd, himself toppling over, falling.

It took seven more minutes for the paramedics to hustle upstairs with their stretchers and IVs. The elevator door was jammed shut—no one knew why—so while they waited for a repair technician they took Terry Junior down six flights of stairs on a stretcher. Mr. Wakefield was too heavy to carry downstairs, so they set up an IV unit in the corridor and made a call to Seaport General.

The paramedics gave Cade a shot for the pain in his nose. One paramedic thought it was broken. His partner disagreed. Cade's eyelids kept fluttering. The reverend looked calm in his wheelchair while a paramedic checked his blood pressure and vital signs. Delia Sue, standing at her father's side, brushed the hair away from her right eye while she stared around at the activity. Her mouth seemed cast in a bright, edged smile.

Lieutenant Robert Archer stalked around the office in his white deck shoes and natty white sailing slacks and blue blazer. The blazer was the double-breasted kind, with snappy brass buttons. The Archer was enjoying himself, giving orders, trying to assume control of the situation, maybe bag some gold stars for his own personnel file. The perp was lying on a collapsible stretcher near the windows, his wrists handcuffed to the chrome struts. From where the Archer was standing, he did not resemble in any way the composite drawn by the artist from the Balboa descriptions on Friday. A paramedic dabbed at his face with a cotton swab. The wooden cross lay on the desk, broken in two pieces. It would make terrific headlines:

COP SLAMS KILLER WITH OLD RUGGED CROSS
FREES HOSTAGES AT NEWPORT CATHEDRAL

By the time a paramedic got around to bandaging Branko's hand, twenty minutes had passed.

"You need stitches, Sergeant."

"Okay. I'll hit the hospital, first thing."

"This is a mess up here, isn't it?"

Branko nodded. The paramedic was a hefty guy in his thirties, with dark hair, dark eyebrows, and a bald spot at the back of his head that he tried to hide by brushing the longer hairs over, pasting them down. He gave Branko a pain pill. Branko was eager to get to the hospital to check on Jamie Duncan.

Now the Tower crawled with cops. Ted Forney was across the room with his clipboard and tape recorder, talking to Delia Sue. Her face gleamed with excitement, eyes dancing, hands gesturing whenever she made a point. Delia Sue was her father's child, the obvious heir apparent to a man who had made his way in the flashy media world. Branko edged her way and caught part of the recap:

". . . and then Mr. Cade—Mama won't let us kids call him Douglas—and then Mr. Cade took him, the killer I mean, into his office and he opened the safe—at least I *think* he opened the safe, because when he came back there was that briefcase just filled with money—only by that time I had untied my brother's hands and he had almost untied mine, only Daddy told us to stay put in that voice he uses when he means business and then the policeman came in here holding the cross, only I didn't know he was a policeman, not then, and he, the killer, tried to shoot Daddy but wasn't able to because my brother stopped him, and that's how . . ."

Branko moved closer to Tommy Osterhaus, who was standing over the perp, his notebook open, asking questions. The perp stared up at the ceiling. There was a bandage covering his ear down to his neck. His neck was having a bad week.

"So it won't hurt to give us your name, son. I read you your rights. Even in the service they give their name, rank, serial number."

"Nothing doing," the perp said. "I get a lawyer in here before I say fucking word one."

"Easy, son. I know you're hurting."

"Up yours, fuzz."

Tommy cut his eyes at Branko. "Rubidoux's not talking."

"I told you, fuzz, my name ain't Rubidoux."

Branko nodded as he studied the perp. The guy had flat eyes. He was five-ten, weight maybe a hundred and sixty, and he spoke with a redneck accent, leaning on the *r*'s, and drawing out the vowels. The reverend had already identified the perp as the hitter from the Fun Zone on Friday, and Branko was sure the records would filter through the great bureaucratic information maze and identify him legally as Rubidoux/Rigdon/Roberts. They'd need ballistics to tie him to the Fun Zone shooting. Jamie's testimony would help. LAPD would want the perp for the work he'd done Friday night at Cosmo's. This hostage caper would get him thirty years-to-life. Except for the eyes, flat and stone-cold, he looked like your average beach yo-yo, late twenties, hot car, fat ego. His face had a California tan. When he talked, he kept his teeth clenched to enhance his beach smile. The sweat had dried on his blond hair, matting it down. Hostage-taking was sweaty work.

"Where's the mustache, Rubidoux?" Branko asked.

The perp stared at the ceiling, then cut his eyes over to Branko. "My goddamn neck hurts. When do I get out of here?"

"They're repairing the elevator."

"That piece of shit."

Branko looked at Tommy and gave him a tired policeman's shrug.

Stan Plotvik was standing at the desk at parade rest, boots spread wide, talking on the telephone. He was nodding, yes, yes, absolutely. He set the phone down, his eyes caught Branko's, and he raised his fist in a thumbs-up signal. Victory is ours.

"Listen up, people," Plotvik called. "The Tower lift is hereby operational and we are to begin loading on the casualties. There is space for only one stretcher a haul. Mr. Wakefield makes the initial trip, followed by Mr. Cade here. Then the reverend and this little lady." Plotvik tossed a smile at Delia Sue, then glared at the perp, smiling his thin-lipped smile. "You're last, buddy-boy."

The perp looked away. He was out of it.

Chief D'Agostino arrived as they were wheeling Cade out. He was wearing a summer sports coat of light brown, a white shirt, tan slacks, and a soft yellow tie. His wide face was red. With him were the two FBI agents, Moore and Friedkin, who stood together, talking quietly. The chief came into the room, nodded at Archer, and walked over to talk to Branko. His eyes took in the bandage. "You all right, Frank?"

"Yes, sir."

"Stitches?"

"Not yet."

The chief indicated the stretcher where the perp lay. "Is that our man?"

"Yes, sir. He fits the description of Shooter One. We're pretty sure it's Rubidoux, from Los Angeles via Little Rock. If he was at Cosmo's, LAPD will want him too."

"I'll handle that, Frank." The chief smiled and slapped Branko's shoulder. The blow made Branko wince. The chief stared around, one hand in his pocket, jiggling change. His eyes gleamed. "Those Feds are green with envy, Frank. Nice work. How's the reverend?"

"Heroic, and holding steady."

"We've never met. Introduce me?"

"Sure."

Branko led the chief over to shake hands with Reverend Williams. They bathed each other with their smiles, two hefty guys who had survived in a world of headlines and television screens. Branko tuned out. The Archer was in a huddle with the FBI agents, probably planning their next lunch.

When the chief was finished, he shook hands again with the reverend and came back to Branko.

"Nice fellow. Hope he wins this primary."

Branko said nothing.

"One down. Two to go."

"We still don't have Mr. Big, the client."

"Did we sweat Rubidoux about that?"

"Tommy asked him some questions. No luck."

"I want that buyer, Frank. This is fast work. A hit on Friday, an arrest on Sunday. We're writing the book on anti-terrorism." The chief looked past Branko at the Archer and his FBI agents and grinned. "Well, a chapter anyway."

"Yes, sir."

"They say you took him out with a cross. That right?"

"Yes, sir."

"Where was your piece?"

"In the trunk of my car."

"You were off-duty, right? Just happened onto the scene?"

258

"Yes, sir."

The chief's eyes blinked and his gaze wavered. He was thinking. "Appropriate, Frank. Damned appropriate. The Old Rugged Cross, hey! I love this PR mileage! Great for the department!"

"Yes, sir."

Tommy Osterhaus came up to brief the chief.

"Just a minute, Tommy." The chief turned to Branko. "That hand needs stitches, Sergeant. Get your butt over to the hospital ER, on the double."

"Yes, sir."

The chief licked his lips. "Okay, Tommy. Let's have a talk with our Balboa perp. Who the hell does he think he is, anyway, blasting away in our fair city, screwing up the Fun Zone. Hell, my kids grew up down there, on the water, in the sun. . . ."

The chief walked with Tommy toward the perp on the stretcher. A paramedic wheeled the reverend out. Branko nodded to the FBI agents and followed the wheelchair to the elevator, where Delia Sue was waiting with a sheriff's deputy. In the elevator, going down, the reverend held onto his daughter's hands but said nothing as he stared straight ahead.

When the doors opened on one, Branko saw a forensics team at work. There were splashes of blood on the white marble tile and he thought again of Jamie Duncan, wounded and lying in the hospital. The reverend was wheeled out. Branko and Delia Sue followed. Sister Winona Lee Williams appeared in the corridor, a ghostly figure in royal purple. Her face was as hard as stone.

"Oh, Delia Sue. My dear, my darling baby!"

Sister Winona Lee hugged her daughter fiercely but only gave her husband a perfunctory brush on his shoulder. Branko kept moving, past the Williams family. Behind him he heard Delia Sue start up her recap, using the same words she had used upstairs and speaking with the same cutesy-teen cadence. Tomorrow, she'd be on national TV. Her beach pals would love it.

Outside, dark clouds wheeled over the Pacific and the sun hung like a dim orange ball, only half visible against the quickly gathering darkness. Crazy weather. Branko looked up toward the promontory and saw sunlight reflecting off the side of the Pac-Bell truck. There was no sign of the technician.

The lower parking lot was crammed with vehicles from the police and sheriff's departments. The SWAT van was parked at an angle to provide a traffic buffer between the onlookers and the ambulances. Branko estimated the crowd at fifteen hundred, with more coming down the driveway from the upper lot. Two officers stood midway down the ramp, turning people back, but it was a job that required more personnel. He'd need a bulldozer to clear a path for the Volvo.

As Branko watched, a Seaport General ambulance backed up to take the stretcher holding Douglas Cade. Cade's eyes opened and he saw Branko and then they closed again. His face was pale, but he'd live. A sheet covered his snappy gray suit.

Branko's left hand was throbbing now, and his face felt gritty, making him aware of how much he had perspired. He spotted Lissa Cody, wearing a pale-green jacket and white slacks, waving from behind the yellow crowd-control ribbons. A camera swung from one shoulder. He waved back and walked toward her. When he was close enough he reached out and took her hand. Smiling, Lissa ducked under the police barrier. She stared at him a moment, holding him at arm's length, and then she came close and gave him a fierce hug.

"Damn you, Frank Branko! Here we only just met and . . ." She didn't finish.

"Does that mean you care?"

"Yes. Damn you!" He felt her shiver. "Are you all right?"

He showed her his bandaged left hand. "I need stitches. Taxi me to the hospital and I'll fill you in."

"One condition, Branko."

"What's that?"

"Dinner on me. Drinks. A shower." She squeezed his arm and lowered her voice. "Candlelight. Soft music. The works." Lissa's smile was warm, a sweet welcome for the hero of the hour.

Branko put his right arm around Lissa's waist and pulled her close. He was aware of the eyes of the crowd, people staring at him, probing, assessing. He was aware of the unspoken jeers and the questions and the snide thoughts and he didn't know how the reverend lived so much of his life in the spotlight. Why would anyone in his right mind choose to become a public figure?

Thirty feet away, in the shadow of the arched doorway leading into Promontory Chapel, the reverend had pushed himself out of the wheelchair to a standing position so he could argue with his wife. Sister Winona Lee stood stiffly in her purple dress, her back ramrod straight, her iron-gray hair looking darker, more shadowy, in the late-afternoon sunlight as she waved a flat green-and-white envelope at her husband. Their daughter, Delia Sue, stood near her father, holding his hand.

"Family tussle," Lissa said. "Just the thing to spark an election."

"Let's get to the hospital."

"Where's your car?"

"Hidden in the mob. Where's yours?"

"Up top."

Branko grinned a silly grin and Lissa grinned back. He was alive. One shooter was in custody. Two to go. They passed under the police barrier and started working their way through the crowd.

"Hey!" A man wearing a blue tank top grabbed Branko's arm. His face was ugly with excitement and he smelled of stale sweat. "You're the guy on the fire escape, right?" And then, without waiting for a reply. "What went down in there?"

"Police business. Let us through, please." Branko showed the man his bandaged hand as they pushed past.

"Hey, come on, pal."

Farther along, a reporter with a press badge tried to speak to Lissa, but she shook her head and the man turned back to the ambulance scene. They came to the Volvo, and Branko unlocked the trunk to get his .357 in its shoulder holster. He handed the gun to Lissa, who put it in her reporter's bag, and then he picked up two speed-loaders and put them in also.

"Expecting a war?"

"Better late than never," he said. "From now on, I'm sleeping with this."

261

"Very Freudian, Branko," Lissa said archly, and bumped him with her hip.

"Very pre-Freud, Cody."

She smiled, showing white even teeth in an honest face. "Timing is all, Branko."

The Volvo was blocked from the road leading out by at least a dozen vehicles. "I need stitches and a shot of something that dulls the mind."

"I know just the remedy."

They threaded their way through the crowd. The sky was darker now and a breeze had come up.

"Hey!" someone shouted behind them. "Maybe this is him!"

"The killer!" A woman cried. "They're bringing down the killer."

"Dirty creep!"

"Evil devil!"

Branko and Lissa turned for a moment and saw the perp being wheeled toward the white Seaport General ambulance. In front of the stretcher walked Stan Plotvik, wearing his yellow shooting glasses. Behind the stretcher was the Archer and the two FBI agents. The chief and Tommy Osterhaus were twenty feet behind, heads together as the chief read something from Tommy's notebook.

"Is that really him?" a young girl asked. "Is that really the killer?"

Branko shook his head and kept on walking.

The way out of the lower parking lot followed a four-lane asphalt driveway that curved gently as it rose toward the top. Traffic markers allowed the closing of a lane, so that three lines of cars could move up at once, with only one going down.

"Did you ever see so many Pastor Clyde stickers?"

"I barely heard of him until this week."

"You live in another world, Branko."

They stopped halfway up so Lissa could take several photos of the scene below. Spectators jammed the way out. Suddenly, there was an explosion on the top floor of the Tower of Prayer. Flames mixed with smoke billowed out of a window. Someone down below shouted, "Fire!"

262

"Oh, my God!" Lissa grabbed his arm.

Out of the corner of his eye, Branko noticed that the rear door of the PacBell truck was open.

As they hurried up the ramp, the parking lot shook with an explosion. A woman screamed. Fire spurted from beneath a Newport Beach police car. Branko felt the hair raise on the back of his neck. Shooter Three was close. Shooter Three had killed Roscoe.

"Frank!" Lissa's eyes were wide.

"Where's your car?"

"Over there. About halfway from the entrance."

"Let's go."

They ran up the ramp, shoving people aside.

Down below, there was pandemonium. Paramedics had gathered around the perp's stretcher. Branko saw Tommy Osterhaus point up the hill, at the PacBell truck. Plotvik was deploying his SWAT guys. The Archer and the two FBI boys had taken up positions behind the SWAT wagon, guns out, ready to fire.

As Branko and Lissa reached level ground a second police vehicle burst into flames, and the PacBell truck, driving at normal parking lot speed, wheeled toward the exit. Branko felt the rush of flames as he ran past the burning police unit, with Lissa five steps behind. They reached her yellow Honda as the PacBell truck pulled out of the lot. People were streaming up the driveway now, calling to each other. Men shouted hoarsely. Women cried for their children.

The first vehicle exploded, a large orange ball of flame followed by huge clouds of smoke. Lissa unlocked the Honda and got behind the wheel. She was a good driver, Branko reminded himself. Let her roll it. He climbed inside. Lissa's hand shook so badly that she couldn't get the key into the ignition. Her breath came harsh and quick.

"Now what?"

"Follow the PacBell truck!" Branko inserted the key, turned it. The car started.

"Why? I didn't see anything?"

He turned to her, knowing his eyes were crazy. "It's our only shot, Cody. Go!"

She shoved the Honda into gear and burned rubber leaving the parking lot. The PacBell truck was nowhere in sight. Branko found himself wishing for a two-way police radio.

"Right." He jerked a thumb in that direction.

"Why?"

"Just go, goddammit! Hang a right!"

The tires squealed as Lissa bounced them out of the parking lot and onto Bayview Drive.

Driving toward Fashion Island in the stolen PacBell truck, Amity Pitcairn kept checking the rearview mirror. Her rented Buick was seven minutes away, in a shadowy corner of the parking lot near Robinson's. She'd change clothes in the truck, where there was room to stand. Then she'd transfer the suitcase holding the weapons to the Buick, spend a few moments at Complice before the center closed, then drive to her motel. The PacBell uniform would go with her, to be dumped in a trash bin. She was looking forward to a hot bath and a night on the town. The old urge was on her like a banshee. She needed to feel warm flesh, the pulse of life.

The LAW bazooka had worked nicely. The explosives had blown up the two police vehicles capable of pursuit. The ramp had been jammed.

The road behind her was clear. Amity relaxed and kept driving. She was on Jamboree, heading for the Pacific. Today marked her thirty-eighth kill. A fire engine passed her going the other way. A fire in that church was a blow struck for sanity.

Twisted Sisters blared from the stereo as Amity braked for the stoplight at Santa Barbara. The police station was to her left, Fashion Island only two blocks beyond. A second fire engine turned the corner. Today's hit would earn her more money than she'd made her entire first year in the business. She thought of herself as an exterminator of vermin, a trained technician who kept the earth cleansed of pests. She was Diana the Huntress. She made war on members of the male race, most of whom deserved to die. She had never taken a job with a female as the target.

The light gave her a green arrow to the left and just before

Amity eased the stolen truck onto Santa Barbara she spotted a yellow car in the rearview, coming fast. She thought nothing of it as she turned. Her mind was shifting backward, into the past, to her first kill. . . .

His name was Ron Carr and he was a tight-assed, thick-lipped Missouri football hero, eighteen, with a sexual track record among the high school girls that made Amity want to vomit. She was only fourteen, a freshman in high school, when Ron Carr stole her virginity. In his senior year, Ron Carr had been captain of the football team. In addition, the team had voted him Most Valuable Player. He was thick and boringly masculine, with satiric brown eyes and a snotty way of staring at her legs when she went upstairs wearing shorts. She was blond and delicate, a piano player who liked to read and dream. Ron was buddies with her brother, Jimmy. Her father was out of town a lot, on business. Her mother, a socialite, spent her days doing good works, having lunch, playing bridge. Their house was a five-bedroom two-story colonial in Webster Groves, a fashionable suburb of St. Louis. A couple of weeks after her first piano recital, Ron Carr trapped her in her bedroom on a sunny Wednesday. Music lovers had said she'd go far with her piano, but Ron Carr changed all that.

Graduation had made him restless. College was looming on the horizon, and he boasted about becoming a BMOC, joining a fraternity, dating sorority girls. He was strong and he used foul language. His breath smelled of beer and cigarettes. And that Wednesday, he knocked on the door and said he'd come to see her brother. She did not invite him in. He came in anyway. She stopped practicing on the piano and went upstairs to get away from him. She heard the fridge door open, knew that Ron Carr was helping himself to a beer. She heard him come up, his footsteps heavy on the stairs. He stood in the doorway to her room, sipping beer, grinning his muscle-bound grin as he stared at her bare legs. She was wearing white shorts and a pink blouse, trying to read. Her long blond hair was pulled back in a ponytail. Ron Carr's rude stare made her feel creepy. Several of her girlfriends had crushes on him, but not Amity. She steered clear of boys.

When Ron Carr pinned her on the bed, the smell of his B.O. made her gag. He forced her legs apart and tore her blouse. He called her Miss Personality and breathed on her. Foul words streamed from his mouth. As long as she lived, she would hate the sickening smell of beer.

"Hey, Miss Personality."

"Get away. Jimmy won't like it."

Ron Carr put a hand on her bare leg, hurting her. His grip was strong. "What Jimmy-pal don't know won't hurt him. Shit, he's got the itch for you himself. What a set. How come you keep 'em hidden, Miss P.?"

She fought him, but he was too strong. He ripped her brassiere and pulled her hair. He bruised her legs when he had trouble getting her shorts off. She remembered being surprised that athletes smoked. She closed her eyes against the pain. He seemed quite experienced, knew just what to do. She called him names. Pig. Filth. Nothing stopped his advance. If she ever had the chance, she would destroy Ron Carr.

The rape took only moments in real time. Remembered later, it seemed like an eternity. It was a foul nightmare, with her teeth clenched in a silent scream.

Ron Carr grunted with pleasure and rolled away from her. Then he zipped up and left, grinning.

She locked herself in the bathroom. Her body ached. Her spirit was dirtied forever. The bleeding stopped after a while, but the black memory would not go away. She kept the truth hidden away, deep inside, through that week, that summer, on into her sophomore year and the rest of high school. But revenge burned in her soul. She would not date, would not fall in love. She learned to detest men.

She had her first lesbian experience when she was seventeen, with a gym teacher named Naomi Gervaise.

Her chance for revenge came about by accident. She was twenty-four, living in New York, trying to make ends meet by playing piano for society parties. Her music degree was worthless, but she was pretty and vivacious and men still wanted to spill their seed into her. The world was a disgusting place. It was Christmas and she had a job playing background music—oldies from the fifties—for a party at the Park Avenue home of Mrs. Standish H. Collingwood. At the party, she met Angelina Scarlatti.

Angelina was tall, beautiful, sensual, intelligent. She wore gorgeous clothes with designer labels from Raquel and Complice. Her Lincoln was driven by a chauffeur named Vince. Angelina loved Brahms, Bach, Beethoven, Vivaldi, Verdi, Puccini. She had a box at the opera. She traveled often to Europe and smoked sexy Egyptian cigarettes using an ivory holder. She was in her early forties when Amity met her and craved companionship. Amity craved money. They had dinner—Gulf shrimp and a subtle French pâté and a lovely avocado salad—and became instant, passionate lovers. With Angelina, she discovered a safe harbor. It was a meeting made in heaven. Amity was broke and lonely. Angelina was rich and lonely. Both women scorned men, preferred the company of women. Amity moved in. The view from the penthouse looked out across Central Park. She had her own room but she spent the nights in Angelina's bed. Her first night, they snacked on broiled salmon and drank a Pouilly-Fuissé and she told Angelina about Ron Carr.

"A real bastard," Angelina said. "But typical, nonetheless."

Two weeks later, when Angelina was sure of her, she let her in on the big secret. "I do jobs for people. I wanted you to know. You'll find out sooner or later."

"What kind of jobs?"

"I terminate."

"Is that like exterminate?"

"Sometimes."

"Who do you terminate? Or exterminate?"

"Targets."

Amity indicated the penthouse. "I thought you'd inherited all this. Money from home."

Angelina smiled. "My clients prefer to call it eliminating. But it's killing, pure and simple. It's taking a human life, and I find it better to look at it *sans* euphemism."

"Why do you do it?"

"Because," Angelina said, "I'm very good. And because it pays very well. There's so much less stress. It's not like nine-to-five. It's a noble profession."

Angelina took a deep drag of her cigarette. They were lying in bed in her bedroom, Amity sipping some very good cognac, loving the life she'd stumbled into. She was surprised she hadn't reacted more strongly to Angelina's revelation. The idea was . . . intriguing.

"You make it sound so . . . I don't know."

"Cold?"

"Yes. So emotionless. And you're so full of emotion. Yet when you told me, your voice changed."

"I am more than one person, Amity. So are you. Women all have that little girl inside, the scared child, the child lost in the shadow of her parents. Then there's the mother, the sister, the daughter. We all have a Mother Destroyer inside, just dying to be let out."

"I read something about that, in college. Didn't she have teeth in her . . ." She smiled, remembering.

"Vagina dentata." Angelina looked at her. "When I take a job, I make certain that the target is a man. I make certain he needs killing. A lot of them need it, of course. It's like a social service."

"Who pays you?"

"Clients."

"Why are you telling me?"

Angelina paused while she stubbed out her cigarette in the ashtray and removed the spent butt from her ivory holder. "It's what you want, isn't it, for that bastard who raped you? You want to kill him."

Amity hugged herself. "No. I don't want that."

But she did. And it didn't take her long to admit it. Once she did, learning the killing techniques took some time. Angelina taught her everything—researching the target, disguises, protective coloration, setting up a safe house, tools of the trade. Angelina taught her to shoot, to defend herself, to blend into a crowd, to escape without leaving a trace. "It's easier for a woman. Police are mostly men. Convicted murderers are mostly men. When a murder is committed, the police don't hunt for women. They start a 'manhunt,' purely on percentages. Few police can imagine a 'womanhunt.' It doesn't sound right, doesn't ring true. Historically, women have killed with poison, perhaps a knife, seldom a gun. There's the occasional ax murderess, but you and I, dear, stand at the forefront of history."

When she was finally ready for the hit, they found Ron Carr. He was in a dirt-grind job, teaching physical education at a high school in Lawrence, Kansas. "Forget you knew him when and think of him as The Target. Stay cool. Try to channel your emotions into precise technique."

"All right." But to Amity, Ron Carr was still the rapist who had destroyed her teen years. She hated him.

The rapist was married. His wife was an ex-cheerleader who had lost her figure. She drank too much, smoked too much, and wore dark glasses to hide her bruises. Angelina's research revealed she'd been hospitalized last year, the result of beatings. She had declined to sign a complaint against her husband.

Her husband was living it up, carrying on a secret affair with an unsuspecting junior in high school. The lovers met in a ratty motel on route 59, on the road to Oskaloosa. The girl was a busty brunette with thin white legs. Amity learned that Ron Carr had impregnated two other students—a girl who waitressed at a local bar and a freshman from the university—in the past three years. Once a bastard, always a bastard. When the rapist drank, he lost control. Physically, he was still beefy, meaty, sly. The women she interviewed found him attractive. Animal charm, she wrote. Inexplicably there, until death.

Terminating the target would be like ridding the world of a bad smell.

She was afraid she would fall apart when she killed the rapist, just come apart like a hooked rug unraveling. She lined him up in the cross hairs of the telescopic sight—she loved the way it brought the target in so close, so true—and caressed the trigger the way Angelina had taught her and down he went. It was a cold March day with the wind blowing from the north at fifteen miles an hour, and she'd allowed for the wind, corrected her sighting. She was afraid she'd vomit on the upholstery of the rental car, but she didn't. There was a tightness in her head, near her temples. And that was all.

A week later, Angelina admitted the truth. "I knew you could do it when I saw you play. Your fingers on those keys were so precise, so correct. They weren't connected to anything but the music. They could have played without you. That's when I knew."

Angelina was a mind-reader. And she had explained what was wrong with her music. No heart.

They did some jobs together. The money rolled in. They entertained sad-eyed men with big stomachs—underworld types, Angelina called them, men of the dark. The money rolled in. She did her first job alone, a pornographer in Chicago who made movies of little children. He was skimming money from the sad-eyed men. A loving caress of the trigger and the target was gone. She was pleased with her own shooting, her own creative protective coloration. Angelina was pleased. The money rolled in. She was good at it, a real pro. Against Angelina's advice, she stopped being so fussy about who got eliminated. If the price was right, she took the job. The money rolled in. She felt smart, exultant, in control. For the first time in her life, she had power over the male sex. Bang, you're dead. She loved it.

Then just last year, Angelina had retired and moved to Italy, to a villa she owned outside Florence. Amity had taken over the business. In October, at Claridge's in London, she had met Colonel Robert Emory Devane, a grizzled blue-eyed paranoid white supremacist whose elitist politics and theories of government were somewhere to the right of Genghis Khan. Devane's theories of racial pollution were rigorous and unyielding. He had a terrible fear of tainted blood, of a world full of gooks, as he called them, spics and niggers and the whole colored tide. He thought of himself as the last white man, the ultimate Caucasian. "Shit, gal. Look at the map. Half the Soviet nation's colored. Otherwise they'd of whipped our ass before now." He despised homosexuality. "Greek soldiers cornholing each other, shit-fire, that's the way to chigger-bite an army from the inside out." He paid lip service to marriage and family life. "Every white man should marry a white woman and produce four white kids, minimum. What's killing this country is that horseshit about zero-population growth." He made her understand that he would hire her despite her sexual preferences. "I got me a natural detestation for queers and lesbos, honey, but if you can shoot like they say, I can overlook who you screw, man, woman, or jungle beast."

"Thank you, Colonel. That's very broad-minded."

He eyed her with frank admiration. "Damn waste, honey. Girl like you, complexion like a rose in bloom. A pure damn waste."

"Colonel, I take that as a compliment."

"You got hair like corn silk."

The colonel was a dirty old man.

He tested her technique on a job in Brussels. Fifteen thousand in Swiss francs and German marks for eradicating a rich Belgian. It was her seventh job in Europe. Colonel Devane paid her the money, plus a bonus, and invited her to visit him in Southern California in late May. "I like your style, honey. You're pretty as a picture and colder than a witch's tit."

The California job—backing up a showboat semi-pro from Los Angeles who was putting a bullet into the leg of an evangelical preacher who wanted to run for Congress—sounded simple. She was to aid the semi-pro's escape, record the action on videotape, and have the tape delivered to a television station. Then it was off to France and the Riviera.

But the colonel's plan backfired. He'd planned to have the semi-pro interdicted in Los Angeles, where the big television stations could plug into a nationwide network. But his triggermen hadn't done the job. For a price, she had neatened things up.

She pulled into the parking lot and turned right, rolled past Bullock's and Robinson's, and parked in a shaded spot near the entrance to Atrium Court. The rented Buick sat where she had parked it Saturday morning. There was no sign of pursuit. She set the handbrake and turned off the engine. The radio died. A drop of rain plopped on the windshield.

As she stepped to the back of the van to change clothes, she totted up her cash savings. She had $357,000 in Swiss francs in

271

her Zurich bank and another $132,000 in three banks in the U.S.—Wells Fargo, Chase Manhattan, and Interstate—because eighty percent of her contracts were here. She had $34,000 in cash and American Express traveler's checks, which she kept in a moneybelt around her waist. She wore the moneybelt everywhere except the bathtub. In her purse, she had another $36,000, which included the money she'd made in the Fun Zone and the advance on today's job. The diamond was tucked away in amongst the bills in her purse.

As she stepped out of the PacBell van, she saw that the sky was dark with the impending storm. She was wearing the pretty blue frock from Friday. It had frilly sleeves and a modest neckline and it reminded her of a recital dress worn by a young maiden long ago as she sat at the keys of the grand piano for a showcase performance at the tender and vulnerable age of fourteen. Where had that young maiden wandered to?

She had fifteen minutes before the shopping center closed. It would take them several hours to find the PacBell van. She checked to make sure the Beretta in her purse was loaded and then walked through the doors of Atrium Court carrying her umbrella, her mind on the leather jumpsuit in the window of Complice, the European import shop. Atrium Court reminded her of a marketplace in Europe—*les fruits, les viands*. As she took the escalator up, she thought of Karin, the foxy little brunette who would get a commission for selling the jumpsuit and then be appropriately grateful. Sundays were notoriously slow. Perhaps Karin would be free this evening.

Amity Pitcairn smiled.

As they entered the Fashion Island parking lot, Branko saw no sign of the PacBell truck. A stiff wind was blowing from the ocean and shoppers exiting the double glass doors looked up in surprise at the rain. "Cruise around."

"This is a goose chase," Lissa said, turning a corner toward Atrium Court.

Stray raindrops spattered the windshield. Lissa turned on the wipers and drove slowly down the rows of angled-in cars. Branko was about ready to head for another lot when he saw the van's white top sticking above the roofs of the cars.

"There, Cody. Stop about three cars away."

He pulled out the .357 and checked to make sure it was loaded. Lissa made two turns that brought the Honda within fifty feet of the PacBell van, which was parked between a Buick and a new Volvo 760 Turbo. Branko opened the door, his left hand throbbing, and got out.

Raindrops pelted him as he moved toward the van. There was no one behind the wheel, no one in the passenger's seat. He tried the rear doors. Locked. A woman with two children stared at the gun in his hand as she hurried to her own car. He reholstered the .357.

A car honked behind Lissa's Honda and she wheeled into an empty space. Branko moved back to the window on the driver's side. His temples throbbed with that old helpless feeling as Lissa rolled down the window.

"Nothing," he said.

"What now?"

"I'm going inside."

"I'm coming with you."

"No. You stay here. Watch the truck."

"Blah." Lissa opened the door and stepped out.

"Your hair will get wet."

Lissa locked her car and moved ahead of Branko, toward the doors of Atrium Court. A security guard with a deep beach suntan stood at the doors. He was armed and listening to a walkie-talkie. He smiled at Lissa's wet hair.

"We close in seven minutes, folks."

Branko flashed his shield. "See a guy in a PacBell uniform?"

"Nope."

"Thanks."

Branko moved through the colorful shelves of Atrium Court at a jog. Foodstuffs were everywhere. Lissa stayed with him. "How do you hope to recognize him?"

"I don't know."

"A goose chase."

Branko took the escalator steps two at a time. They reached the main ground level, where shoppers with umbrellas were hurrying through the rain, and he stood at the wide glass doors and scanned the seating area, deserted now except for a man in a raincoat feeding a dog from his hand. Outside he could see a bookstore and a candy store and the fountain in front of Brooks Brothers. Beside him, Lissa was breathing hard and her red hair was plastered to her scalp. The helpless feeling had not gone away. Thinking of Roscoe Smith dead, Branko pushed through the glass doors.

The rain was falling harder now and the temperature had dropped. Across the way, shoppers clung to the walls under the ten-foot overhang. At the doorway of a shop he saw a blond in pale blue. She looked familiar, but he couldn't place her. The shop was called Complice. The clothes in the display windows looked imported and expensive. She was standing in the doorway talking to a brunette wearing a tight leather skirt and a white sleeveless blouse, so that Branko could only see her profile. In her hand was a compact umbrella, black, with a handle that disappeared.

Lissa was watching her too. "That woman, the blonde in the doorway of Complice. Do you recognize her?"

"No."

"She was at the Inn of Cortez on Friday." Lissa spoke in a tight, excited whisper. "She's the one Josh photographed. He called her Blonde in Blue."

Branko's spine tingled. "Small world."

Lissa prodded him in the ribs with her finger. "Let's talk to her."

"Now?"

"She might remember something. Maybe she saw the phone man."

"Long shot, Cody."

"It's a goose chase, anyway."

Lissa brushed past Branko and started across the mall calling, "Excuse me! Miss!"

The woman in blue turned and saw Lissa coming, and then her eyes swung to Branko and registered a moment of recognition, and without hesitating she stepped back into the store.

"Miss? Would you —"

Lissa entered the store and Branko followed, just to get out of the rain. He was sure it was a dead end.

In the domain of Complice, Lissa stood talking to a brunette sales girl, the sexy number in the leather skirt. A woman standing in front of a mirror admired herself in a tiered light purple evening dress while she tried on a gold lamé evening coat with a price tag that had to be out of sight. There was no sign of the blonde in blue.

"Branko! This way!" Lissa hurried past the dressing rooms through rooms filled with racks of clothes and smelling of fabric dye. Branko followed her to a rear entrance. "She ran away, Branko! Doesn't that feel suspicious?"

"Probably got a date."

He was following Lissa because there was nothing else to do. His throbbing hand reminded reminded him it was time for the hospital. "Or maybe she hates reporters."

Lissa pushed through the door and stepped into the rain. "Oh, miss! Yoo-hoo!"

They were in a narrow walkway, deserted except for the rain and the sight of the woman in blue running. She turned a corner and was gone. Lissa ran after her, stumbled, almost fell. Branko caught up to her as she was taking off her shoes. "She ran. That means she knows something!"

"Cody, you'd make some cop."

At the end of the walkway they turned left. The woman in blue had opened her umbrella and was walking away from the glass doors of Robinson's after a salesperson had refused to let her in. Shoppers straggled by, heading for their cars. It was five o'clock on a Sunday, time for a cocktail, some dinner, some *Masterpiece Theatre*. The umbrella hid her face, but her ankles were neat and trim and the blue dress was a giveaway.

"Miss?" Lissa called, waving. "I'm from the *Tribune* and I'd—"

It happened fast. The umbrella dropped to the sidewalk and the woman in blue was standing in the shooter's two-handed stance, feet spread wide, something dark and ominous-looking in her hand. Branko grabbed Lissa and pulled her down. He heard a silent *splftt* and knew it was a silencer and in that moment he also knew she was Shooter Three.

This one was for Roscoe.

"She's the—" Lissa began.

"Find a phone," he said. "Call for backup."

The woman in blue darted away. Branko hurried after her, his gun in his right hand. The rain slanted against his face and shoulders, and he tried to form a picture in his mind of the layout of Fashion Island. Visibility was bad. If it got dark enough, she might be able to slip away in the shadows. Lightning jabbed down out of the sky and he saw a figure moving in the sudden flash of light. Two teenagers passed, wheeling along on skateboards. The figure vanished behind a line of potted palms, then reappeared against the pale stucco buildings, heading toward Atrium Court.

The PacBell van was parked down there.

"Stop! Police!"

She ran into the pale circle of light marking the court's entrance. At that moment, a man and woman came through the double glass doors. The man was wearing a golfing jacket and the woman a tennis skirt and pink sweater. She had good legs, trim, muscled, California legs. The doors swung shut behind them as the woman in blue reached them. Branko was twenty yards away when he assumed a kneeling position and took aim and the couple walked right into his line of fire. "Get down!" he shouted.

The man in the golfing jacket grabbed the woman's arm and pulled her to the side. Branko saw the security guard, a figure in black, holding the door closed, shaking his head, and that's when the woman in blue shot him. Branko heard the sound of thick glass shattering. Behind the shattered door, more civilians were knotted in a cluster. Branko could not fire, so he was up and running again, his feet splashing through the puddles.

The woman in blue had vanished. Branko elbowed a man aside. Just inside the entrance, the security guard lay in a puddle of his own blood. A shriek came from the direction of the escalator. Branko reached the top in time to see the woman in blue forcing her way down with a small automatic in her hand.

Except it was the up escalator and she wanted to go down. A mistake.

Civilians were scattering like chickens from a fox. A limp figure in red lay twisted on the metal stairs rising up toward

Branko. A sunburned teenager carrying a skateboard was about to climb on when he spotted the woman in blue, and then Branko at the top of the moving steps, and he ducked out of sight. The limp figure in red reached the top of the stairs and hung there, his inert body bumping against the rising steps of the escalator. The woman in blue was at the bottom and turning to shoot when Branko fired.

In the enclosed area, the .357 boomed like a howitzer. Down below, his target staggered, twisted, tried to take aim, and went down.

Silence followed the single explosion. Branko was breathing hard. He hated shooting people. It left a taint on the spirit like black shoe polish on clean silk. A child wailed somewhere below. An unseen bass voice called out, "Jennie?" Branko stood there, trembling. The woman in blue did not move. Her gun, a small silver automatic, lay two feet from her right hand. She was a delicate-featured blonde, trim figure, neat ankles, excellent reflexes. A security guard in a black uniform with his pistol out approached slowly and knelt down to put two fingers on her neck. He looked up at Branko and made a circle of his thumb and forefinger.

The limp figure in red was a senior citizen who needed medical attention. Blood oozed from a hole in his jacket. With each bumping step, his eyes fluttered. With an effort, Branko moved him off the escalator. A woman from a fancy bedding store brought the senior citizen a pillow and a blanket. Life goes on.

Lissa Cody came up beside Branko and took his hand. She told him backup was on the way. Then she led Branko around the corner to the down escalator. Her Honda was outside, in the rain. The hospital was waiting. Branko had avenged Roscoe Smith. He didn't want to wait for the backup and the shooting team. He wanted to go somewhere and hide.

THREE

VOX POPULI, VOX DEI

CHAPTER SIXTEEN

AT Seaport General, the reverend sat with Delia Sue and Winona Lee in the chilly waiting room outside the Operating Room, waiting for the doctors to finish surgery on his wounded son. Delia Sue had changed her bloodstained blouse. Her face needed scrubbing and that sad purple hair looked terrible. He made a vow not to badger her. Not tonight. His daughter had been heroic and he loved her for it.

The reverend was edgy, with pulses of that spasmodic energy he felt going before the cameras to deliver a heated sermon to the multitude of wanderers in the wasteland. His shirt collar was soaked with sweat. His hands kept clenching the arms of his wheelchair and he was having trouble getting through to God. Several times, he pushed himself up out of the chair and found he could walk, though with a severe limp. The waiting room smelled of antiseptic and human sweat and strong, industrial-strength floor cleaner. When Nurse Greenfield happened by, he took her aside and asked her to find him a cane. When she brought the cane, he asked her to check on Douglas Cade.

"I think he's been released, Reverend. Let me find out."

The reverend was torn: on the one hand, he wanted to leave the hospital and confront Cade about this colonel person; on the other hand, he couldn't leave until he had news about Terry Junior. He must see his son's face.

There was a police guard on the door, to keep out the press and the host of assassins and all unauthorized visitors. He knew the press would be swarming below, in the lobby area, in a lather for news. Beside him, Delia Sue was slumped in her chair. Winona Lee was in the ladies' room, but she had managed to leave her heavy, guilt-producing presence in the seat next to Delia Sue, almost like the Holy Ghost. Nurse Greenfield came back with news about Cade. "Mr. Cade was released a quarter of an hour ago."

The reverend's hands tightened on the cold chrome of the wheelchair. "Thank you, nurse."

Nurse Greenfield walked away and Winona Lee came back in, carrying the shiny cardboard envelope with the green-and-white insignia of Overnite X-Press. "Husband," she said. "We must confer."

The reverend stared at her. "Now?"

"Now. At once." Winona Lee brandished the envelope as if it were a weapon.

He used the cane and followed his wife to a room filled with hospital linens and detergent in heavy blue drums. As he came through the door, Winona Lee whirled on him, her hands like silver daggers in the pale yellow light. Before he knew what was happening the envelope was open and she was thrusting photos at him, color Polaroids that showed a man committing naked adultery with a woman with a tanned body and bleach-blond hair. The woman was Helen of Troy. The man looked like Odell Macaulay Williams, the reverend's dead father.

He looked through the Polaroids twice, searching for her face. He remembered her body, not his. Some other Helen had tried the same game, a year ago. The reverend had paid out $200,000 to keep her quiet. Cameras became more sophisticated every day. His voice trembled. "Where did you get them?"

"They were delivered by a messenger service."

"When?"

"Today. On God's holy Sabbath. Husband, you are a fool!"

He bowed his head as the tears began to flow. He knew what she wanted. The dream was over. When he turned to go, Winona Lee pursued him into the corridor like a Harpy, clutching the photographs. "Withdraw!"

He didn't think she would use the photos against him. "All right."

"Make the announcement tonight. The press is downstairs."

"I need time . . . to write something."

"No. Do it now!"

282

"Tomorrow, Winona Lee." His voice sounded firmer than he felt.

"Tomorrow," she said, "we must discuss your return to the church."

"Yes." It was difficult to walk now, but he wanted to get away from her. "All right."

But Winona Lee was on a holy warpath. She waggled the Polaroids in his face. "How long, husband? How long has this adultery transpired?"

He had no answer. Helen of Troy was gone. The dream was over. As he turned away from his wife and walked back to the waiting room, all he could think about was the small boy of twelve singing in a lounge in a Hollywood of long ago on the edge of movieland with Daddy's fingers on the keys and Helen of Troy sitting alone at the table with a cigarette and her legs crossed and one shoe dangling from a stockinged toe. Yes, singing his heart out.

"Husband!"

The reverend walked on.

A few minutes after nine, Sergeant Branko stopped by to see how things were going. His trousers were wrinkled from the rain, his left hand was heavily bandaged, and his eyes were tired. As the sergeant sat down, Winona Lee shifted her position in her chair, turning at a forty-five-degree angle, putting her back to the policeman. The sergeant told the reverend that the officer who had been wounded by the gunman was now in the recovery room.

"She was the one guarding my family?"

"Yes."

"We owe her a heavy debt."

"That was her job, Reverend. How are things shaping up with your boy?"

"We should have news any minute now."

"Would you care to pray with us, Sergeant?" Winona Lee asked.

"Sure. I'd like that."

The four of them boxed their heads while Winona Lee offered

283

up a labored prayer. The reverend clenched his eyes shut but could not for the life of him make contact with God. He saw Helen of Troy, nude, on the bed in the sordid motel. He saw Douglas Cade's dishonest face, his rodent-like eyes. He heard Cade's precise little voice on the Tower intercom and saw a close-up of Cade's fingers turning the dial that rolled the tumblers that opened the safe where the money was. He wondered how much the sergeant knew about Douglas Cade.

The sergeant excused himself and left.

A nurse came into the waiting room and spoke to Winona Lee, who then left the room without a word. In her tight white collar and dark dress she looked for all the world like a sister from a Catholic nunnery. Except Winona Lee would never have been a nun. She would have gone from the real world straight to the position of mother superior. And from there on to become a cardinal and then the first woman pope. It was an irony that Winona Lee hated Catholics and Catholicism.

Winona Lee walked out, her back stiff, chin up, nose and head tilted back in ultimate disdain. The reverend shook his head. He was writing his withdrawal speech in his head. Dear Friends, it began, it behooves me to announce, with deep regret, that I. . . .

Would anyone care?

Just before ten, Dr. Grimes came through the swinging doors leading to the operating room. He was wearing blood-spattered surgery scrubs and his eyes looked hollow. He sat down wearily and removed his pea-green surgical cap. His thinning reddish hair was tousled and beads of sweat dotted his forehead. "He's okay," Grimes said. "It took us forever to find the slug, but your son's going to be okay." He ran his hand across his hair. "The slug was lodged near a rib. Hitting the rib mashed the lead up pretty bad, so once we found the slug we couldn't be sure we had the whole thing. Hunting for the rest took time. It was pretty hairy in there. I tell you, Reverend, it was a good time to be a praying man."

"When can we see my son?"

"Couple of hours, anyway. He's gone down to Recovery now. Time for you both to get a nap."

Dr. Grimes shook hands and left the room. He'd been gone

ten minutes when Nurse Greenfield appeared. She no longer looked like the Angel of Death.

"Reverend, your wife's on television, making a statement. You'd better come watch."

He followed Nurse Greenfield to the nurse's station, where three nurses and an orderly were standing in front of a television. Winona Lee's face and haughty eyes filled the screen. A nurse with frizzy red hair stared at the reverend. Winona Lee was speaking:

". . . .and now that my husband has seen fit to leave politics and return to the pulpit, he has asked me to urge his supporters to cast their votes for Congressman Sherwood. Thank you. My husband will make a formal announcement tomorrow. That is all."

The reverend shook his head. The man of words had no words.

He was sitting in the waiting room, holding Delia Sue's hand, when the doors opened and Winona Lee marched back in, accompanied by Congressman James B. Sherwood, the reverend's stalwart opposition in the Republican primary. Jimmy Sherwood was wearing an expensive corduroy jacket and tan slacks with a sharp crease. The man was fifty-nine. His face looked skeletal.

Winona Lee's eyes fixed on her husband's face. "Did you hear?"

"Yes."

"It was for the best."

The reverend said nothing.

"Well, Reverend," Sherwood said.

"Well, Congressman."

The air was close in the room. The reverend remembered times like this on the beach at Malibu, when the clouds would build out over the Pacific and the wind would stop and the whole world would be enclosed in a plastic cocoon where all you could hear would be your own breathing and the rhythmic thud of your heart. Back in Malibu, he'd been closer to God.

"My congratulations on coming out of this the way you did," Sherwood said.

"Thank you, Congressman."

285

Sherwood rubbed his hands. They looked soft, from too much desk work, from handling too many pieces of paper. The reverend looked at his own hands. They, too, looked soft. The preacher and the politician. Sherwood cleared his throat. His eyes were bright with the light from a thousand remembered television cameras. The reverend knew that look. He had seen it in his mirror.

"Did you know I almost became a minister?"

The reverend shook his head. "No. Did you know that I almost became a candidate for Congress?"

Sherwood chuckled like a winner. "I admire you. You were a tough adversary."

The reverend avoided his wife's eyes. "It's over."

"I'd like to have you join me in fighting this little pinko from Laguna. Together, we can run his tail right back to Moscow."

"That would be . . . interesting."

"You gave me a good run, Reverend." Sherwood patted him on the shoulder. "When, ah, do you expect to make your statement?"

"I'm writing it now."

"Good, well, I've got to get back." Sherwood started out.

"Get back out there, right?"

"Yes. No rest for the weary."

"Or for the wicked."

The congressman from the Fiftieth District pushed through the door and was gone. The reverend was alone with his family.

So it was over.

He sat numbly in the wheelchair, staring at the wall, allowing his memories to roll. How had he arrived at this place? What was he doing here, anyway? His daddy was always talking about tending to the inner man and paying the piper. Was it time to pay the piper?

He needed a drink. Needing a drink made him think of Daddy at the kitchen table in the house in Glendora, dressed in his white suit and white shoes with the tiny little holes punched in the toes, the straw boater tilted back on his head, the big pistol on the table next to the bottle of Scotch. He and Terry would sing Army songs, "Over There" and "The Caissons Go Rolling Along," and "My Bonnie Lies Over the Ocean," which Daddy liked because of the harmony.

The reverend left the waiting room and went to the men's room and stared at his face in the mirror. As a young man, he had taken after Daddy in his looks, but in temperament he took after Mama. He had Daddy's handsome face and fine sensitive hands and thick blond hair. He had Mama's memory and the ability to get somewhere on time. Mama was tall and stately. Some people said she looked like the Queen of England. Mama had iron-gray hair and a beautiful singing voice. Folks who heard Mama sing said she could have made it all the way to the New York City opera if she'd only had her chance. She did a lovely Aida and a voluptuous Delilah from *Samson* by G. F. Handel and a glorious Amina from *La Somnambula* by Bellini. He was seventeen before an English teacher told him *Amina* was the Latin word for soul, *anima*, only spelled backward. That made him want to study Latin.

His favorite time was when Mama got dressed up in a kimono made of a white sash and a pale-blue silk nightie and sang the departure song from *Madame Butterfly*. Mama was a soprano and he was a tenor and sometimes they would sing the duet together. Mama would sing Butterfly and he would sing Pinkerton, the American sailor who left his Japanese lady behind while he sailed off to more adventures. Anyone listening to them singing got a lump in their throat for sure.

Daddy was a Southern boy from a family that had owned slaves before the Civil War. His favorite poet was Rudyard Kipling—"'Now in India's sunny clime, where I used to spend me time . . .'"—and he could talk like an English aristocrat. He would quote Latin ("*Arma virumque cano*," which meant "I sing of arms and of the man") and in the same breath talk redneck ("Them as got, gits, and don't yew fergit"). And he was always talking about paying the piper.

Daddy cried when Martha Sue died. Martha Sue was his baby-sister. He hardly remembered her. But he remembered Helen of Troy.

"Is your name really Helen of Troy?"

"Sure it is, honey. Sure it is."

"You are very pretty, Helen."

"Thanks, honey. I wish other people felt like you."

When they got home from the bar, Daddy always made him

strip. Daddy would sit at the table in the rented house in Glendora and he would stand in the center of the kitchen and take off his trousers and his shirt and his shoes. One by one, he would hand his clothes to Daddy, who would rifle through them searching for money. Daddy was a Ballantine's drinker. He also liked French brandy and fine California burgundy and Old Milwaukee beer and Polish schnapps and Russian vodka and Mexican tequila and a drink from the islands called a "Cuba Libre."

"Here's an all-man truth, Sergeant. It costs money to live, a pile of the green stuff just to subsist and survive. You'll find out someday, mark my words, you'll find out just how much. It costs money to eat and drink and be merry. Christ, yes, merry, merry quite contrary. And where the be-jesus is that garden? So I'm the big dog and you're the little dog and when you get money from those puling drunks who think they're my friends it's divvy-up time. Do you understand, Sergeant? Do you read me, loud and clear? Divvy-up time, loud and clear!"

"Yes, Daddy."

"Yes, General Pershing."

"Yes, General Pershing."

Daddy got paid on Saturdays, so on Sundays he drank until he got the crazies. His eyes were dark brown, almost black, and when he got the crazies they narrowed down to two slits and made his son think of the black slots in the walls of an old-time fortress from the days of Robin Hood, one of the reverend's secret heroes when he was a boy.

"Daddy?"

"Yes, Sergeant?"

"Why are your eyes like that?"

"Like what, Sergeant?"

"Like the slits in the evil King's castle."

"Embrasures, Sergeant. Those are called *les embrasures des flèches.*"

"Yes, Daddy."

"Yes, General Pershing."

"Yes, General Pershing."

"Repeat after me, *les embrasures des flèches.*"

"Embray— I can't."

288

"French is the language of love, Sergeant."

"Yes, General Pershing."

"Too bad you're too young to drink, Sergeant. Women are chewing me alive and I need a drinking buddy. Women are chewing at my soul—your mama, her mama, even Helen of Troy—chewing at my soul. I married her for her teeth, you know, and now she's chewing away at my ever-withering soul."

"Yes, General."

According to Mama, Daddy didn't have a soul.

The reverend loved his daddy and he especially loved singing in the bars and getting paid for it. With a quarter for a song, a fellow could save some money for a movie or a comic book. He would wait in the shadows with a glass of milk or Coke or sometimes a glass of Meldon's Sarsaparilla on the table in front of him while he ran his fingers over the names of the drunken lovers carved in the dark wood in the bar on the edge of Hollywood and would wonder if God would ever allow him to play the piano as good as his daddy.

And then his moment would come.

"Rabble, allow me to introduce my only son, Terrence Odell Williams. He was named for one of my ancestors, Colonel T. Odell Williams, who fought on the Confederate side in that mythic and distant War between the States. Any man, or woman, for that matter, who doubts me, can view assorted lithographs of the general staff of General J. E. B. Stuart. I tell you, the Williamses had class back then. Oh, yes, class and big houses with Greek columns and Greek porticoes. . . ."

And he would be poised to sing.

And then Daddy would forget where he was. ". . . and, uh, where was I? Oh, yes, Terrence. The gods on Mount Olympus gave him the voice of an angel. Terrence, my boy, come up here and give the folks a treat with that golden throat. The gods have been good to you. It's time, my son, to placate Olympus."

Helen of Troy would squeeze his hand and he would leave the safety of his table and walk into the circle of light with Daddy, and Daddy would ripple the piano keys and give him his opening chord, and right then he would utter a prayer to Mama's god, the one who lived in the Bethlehem Baptist Church on Fourth

Street, to help him through, oh please. Sometimes God heard him and gave a sign. Sometimes God was busy and there would be no sign, only a silence and a funny feeling in his tummy. But he knew how to gut up for a song.

He would walk away from the safety of the dark and stand in the weak spotlight near Daddy's piano, with the smell of whisky and the smoke drifting through the light. Daddy would give him a chord and an admonition. "Gut up, Sergeant!" And he would begin to sing, allowing his voice to do the work, and if he listened he could hear a voice singing, rich and high and flawlessly perfect, the voice of a true boy soprano piping up into the darkness of Dublin O'Rourke's while out there beyond the circle of light there was only silence and the occasional snore. He would hear the voice following the piano and the song would come to an end, and the notes would hang in the air and then the money would rain on him from the dark. . . .

Now, standing in the men's room at Seaport General in Newport Beach, California, the reverend remembered the five dollars from beautiful Helen of Troy and how he'd hid the money in his underpants. He remembered folding it up in a special way, creasing and creasing and folding the corners in on themselves like he'd watched the paper boys in Glendora do when they delivered the morning paper in the early dawn, before the sun was up, so that the folded square would fly through the gray morning dark onto the porches. He folded it that way and tucked it into his underpants. He remembered being afraid Daddy would look there, too, would force him to pull down his pants right there in the kitchen, with Mama and Grandma out of the house shopping. He remembered Daddy going into the crazies at the kitchen table and his narrow eyes like slots. *Les embrasures des flèches.* He remembered the bright ceiling light and the cold floor, which Mama kept clean enough to eat off of. And he remembered praying to God to let him keep the five dollars.

God had been there that time.

His daddy hadn't found the five. And he still remembered the terror. And the excitement of getting away with it.

Like father, like son.

He was dozing when Nurse Greenfield came to push him upstairs to a room on the same floor where he had lain with his wound from the assassin's bullet. A policeman in uniform was sitting in a chair outside the door. The reverend went inside. Terry Junior looked green. An IV trailed from his arm. In the bed, he was no longer the image of the tanned and handsome lifeguard from Malibu, the young reverend, born again from the father's loins.

"Hello, Dad."

"Hello, son."

"Tired, Dad. Very tired."

"Yes."

He watched Terry Junior's eyes close. He was still sitting there when Winona Lee came in. She stared at her husband and then at her son. She pulled up a chair and sat at the bedside, fingers clasped white-knuckled in prayer, her eyes closed. Without a word to his wife, the reverend wheeled himself out of the room.

In the waiting room, he shook Delia Sue awake. Together, they rode the elevator down to the lobby. It was almost midnight and the lobby was deserted except for two members of the press corps who asked him if he was still in the race.

"A statement will be issued soon," he said. "Very soon."

CHAPTER SEVENTEEN

B RANKO drove with Tommy Osterhaus from Seaport General to the station. He needed a shower, a shave, and some sack time, and more than anything he wanted to go home and lock the door and deal with what he'd done. He hated killing people. The fact that the dead person was a woman made it worse. That was one reason he was in Homicide—to catch the killers, to stop the killing. When he killed, he felt sick to his stomach. He dreaded going over it with the shooting team, the questions, the explanations: the subject was here, at the spot marked X, and I was here, at the spot marked Y, and before I shot I made certain that I had identified myself as a . . .

Tommy parked the unmarked unit in the lot, and the two men walked in together. The rain had stopped and fog was curling in, licking its way east from the edge of the shore. Branko shivered.

As they came inside, they passed Delgado from Traffic. With him was a big white-faced man wearing a dirty T-shirt. Tommy was busy telling Branko a story about the Archer, so he didn't notice the big man. Branko took several steps, stopped, and followed Delgado and his prisoner downstairs to the fingerprint area. The offender was huge, weight around two-eighty, height at least six-three. His belly filled out the white T-shirt and his gray trousers bagged around his ass. The man's head was bald on top and his jaws were pale, as if he'd worn a beard, keeping off the sun, and then given himself a shave.

"Hey, Delgado. What have we got here?"

"Stolen car report, Sarge, Corvette reported missing from Manhattan Beach. Picked him up on Lido Island. We think he was casing a two-story down there, preparing for the old Lido ripoff."

Branko picked up the rap sheet. The man's name was Walter Pickett. His address was in Venice. Something hummed in Branko's mind. "Kind of out of your territory, Walter. How come?"

The big man shrugged. "The car's a loaner. From a friend. I'd like to see my attorney now."

Branko scratched his head. Too much had happened. His mind raced and he knew he was missing something, a detail. Tommy stood in the doorway.

"Come on, Francisco. Let's get going on these reports. I'm a grandfather and I need my rest."

Branko spoke to the arresting officer. "Who you working with, Delgado?"

"Feinman. He's down at the scene on Lido, hunting for a weapon."

"What weapon?"

"Feinman thinks he saw the guy toss some heat into the bushes."

"Be lucky to find anything in this fog. How long's he been down there?"

"Half an hour."

Branko looked at the big man, who stood stolidly silent. He walked out into the corridor. It was a long shot. He spoke to Tommy. "Let's run Walter up to Seaport."

"Who's Walter?"

"The big guy. In there."

"Why?"

"Because I want Jamie Duncan and Randy Whitson to take a look at him."

Insight dawned in Tommy's eyes. "You think he's Shooter Two?"

Branko nodded.

Tommy slapped his thigh and grinned. "Damn!"

Officer Jamie Duncan was asleep when they arrived at Seaport General with Walter Pickett. She'd been out of surgery for two hours and needed her rest. Officer Randy Whitson was also asleep. His nurse, a snake-hipped brunette named Swindon, objected to having her patient disturbed. Tommy soft-soaped her, and Branko watched him work. Let somebody else carry the load.

"All right. Three minutes with my patient. And then you're out of there if I have to call in the Marines."

The officers went in with their prisoner. For the moment, the big man seemed docile, with his hands cuffed behind his back. Officer Delgado, riding shotgun, had some leg irons in case the prisoner got tricky.

Randy Whitson blinked a couple of times coming out of sleep. Branko explained why they were there. Whitson stared up at the big man. "I don't know, Sarge. The guy had a beard. He's the same size generally, but . . ."

Branko wanted the case over with. His voice shook. "Take your time, Randy."

"He was pretty far away. Wore a white jacket like a fairy tennis player." He cut his eyes toward Branko. "Sorry, Sarge. And he rode that chopper like a real pro. Can he come closer, under the light here."

They edged the big man closer to Randy Whitson's bed. Sweat streamed down off his bald head and onto his face.

"Did he say anything, Randy?"

"I don't remember, Sarge. Yeah. Wait a minute. I think he said Come on."

"Say it," Branko nudged the big man in the back.

"Say what?"

"Say, 'come on'."

"Okay. Come on."

"It was louder, like a shout."

"Louder," Branko said.

"I'd like my attorney now," the big man said.

"After you say it."

"*Come onnn!*" The sound was like a roar.

"Shit," Officer Whitson said, smiling. "I think we caught us a shooter." He leaned toward the big man. "You dirty sonofabitch."

The attorney was named Brock Danforth, from the office of the public defender. Attorney Danforth did not like being called out of bed late at night on Sunday. His business card had an address in Corona del Mar.

They used Interrogation Room One. Attorney Danforth sat on one side of the table with his client. Tommy and Branko sat on the other side. Officer Delgado sat at the end, watching the big man, who was still handcuffed. The walls were an institutional beige and there was a worn green carpet on the floor, thin as grass-tex. The room smelled of sweat and fear. Identification had not come through yet on the big man.

Branko started. "So, Walter, tell us about Benjamin Rubidoux."

"Don't know him."

"Where were you on Friday?"

"Which Friday is that?"

"Last Friday, Walter. Two days ago."

"Venice. On the beach. Taking some sun."

"Who with?"

"A lady."

"Did you shave the beard before hitting the beach? Or after?"

"Huh?"

"Ever hear of Reverend Terry Odell Williams?"

"Nope."

"He's running for political office down here and he got shot Friday on Balboa."

"Sorry to hear that. Some of my best friends are preachers."

"What made you decide to hit a house down here?"

The big man shook his head. "I was just cruising the area, captain. Wasn't gonna hit no house."

Branko changed his tone and his strategy. "Were you in the service, Walter?"

"Yes, sir. I served my country and did it proud." The big man sat up straighter in his chair.

"Where did you serve?"

His voice steadied. "Southeast Asia, sir."

"What unit?"

"Ninth Cavalry, sir."

"Did they teach you to shoot?"

"Weapons were part of the training, sir."

"Did Rubidoux order you to reinforce his assault on Balboa Island on Friday?"

The big man opened his mouth to speak, but the attorney broke in. "Don't answer that."

"Hey, Counselor," Branko said.

The attorney looked at his watch, an expensive gold number. It was Sunday night, but he was wearing his working clothes, a three-piece suit. His tie clasp was gold. He probably shopped the same stores as Robin Hood Archer, Branko told himself.

There was a knock on the door. Molly Brazelton stuck her head in and motioned to Branko. He turned the Q&A session over to Tommy and stepped outside.

"It's Mrs. Williams," Molly said. "She just made a statement on television that said the reverend was withdrawing from the race."

"Are you sure?"

"Yes. I only caught the tail end."

"Crap." There went his theory of the Wounding Shot.

Molly walked away. Branko stretched and yawned. He was about to go back inside when Officer Roy Feinman walked up holding a plastic evidence bag. Inside the bag was a huge revolver with a six-inch barrel. Feinman grinned as he handed it over. "Pay dirt."

Branko took it. "Where'd you find it?"

"In the bushes on Lido Island, near where we picked up Goliath in there. I tried not to mess up the prints."

"Good work."

"How's it going in there?"

"Sweet as candy. See if the ID section has anything on him yet."

"Will do."

The weapon looked like a Colt .44. If the slugs matched those taken out of Randy Whitson, the big man was a goner. Back inside the room, Branko held the piece behind his back, where the big man could not see it. "What rank were you in the service, Walter?"

"I already told you. An E-Four."

"And what was your job?"

"Supply."

"Did you see combat?"

"Yes, sir. I was attached to an airborne unit for a while."

Branko brought the piece out so the big man could see it. His mouth curled and his eyes blinked involuntarily.

"This belong to you, Walter?"

"Where did you get this?" the attorney asked.

Branko ignored him. "Walter, when we run this iron through ballistics, we'll nail you to the floor for your part in the Friday shooting. It had your prints on it."

The big man licked his lips. His stink filled the room. He stared at Tommy, the gun, Branko. Then he leaned over and whispered to his attorney.

"I'd like to confer with my client in private, gentlemen."

The three policemen went outside. Officer Delgado excused himself for a trip to the men's room. Branko sighed and stared down at the big-muzzled .44 revolver.

"How soon can ballistics do a job on that?"

"Tomorrow, if we rush it."

"He's ready to spill, Francisco. I can feel it."

"I hope he confesses before I keel over with fatigue."

"Being a peace officer is hell."

Officer Roy Feinman hurried over with a file folder. The name on the folder was PICKETT, WALTER J. Tommy opened the folder. There was a FAX copy of the big man's face, wearing a scraggly beard. "It's our guy, Francisco. Listen to this. Walter J. Pickett, forty-one years of age. He graduated from high school in Troy, New York, then spent six years in the Army. They put him in ordnance and supply. He made sergeant first class and received a dishonorable discharge when the Army CID found him and six other sergeants diverting supplies to half of Southeast Asia. He's served time in New York and Pennsylvania. He ran with the Hell's Angels for a while and was booked in Oakland with three of his biker pals for armed robbery. The case never came to court because the complainant moved out of town and would not testify."

"Good driver for the Honda."

The door opened and Attorney Danforth stepped out. His client wanted to make a deal, full disclosure for a lesser plea. Branko's pulse raced. A break, at last. "He was down there, wasn't he?"

"I am preparing a statement," said Attorney Danforth.

They roped in an assistant D.A. to make a deal on *People* vs. *Pickett*. Danforth read his statement in a scratchy voice. In it, the big man admitted to being hired as wheelman—in this case, bike pilot—by one Benny Rubidoux at the flat fee of three thousand dollars. He did not admit firing a weapon. In return for divulging information, the charges against him would consist solely of felony car theft.

Branko didn't like it, but he wanted information. "Who hired Rubidoux?"

"A Mex name of Mendoza."

"Who hired Mendoza?"

"How the fuck should I know?"

"Come on, Sergeant. You were a soldier. You know how to keep your ear to the ground."

The big man sighed. "Okay. I told him it was a military guy."

"Who?"

"Benny called him Mr. No-Name, but I said, no, it was General No-Name. Then come to find out the guy was a colonel."

"Colonel who?"

"Colonel No-Name, I guess. That's why we motored back down here, so Benny could find out."

"Find out how?"

The big man looked at his attorney, who nodded. "The Mex had inside dope, from the rev's campaign. He'd pass it on to Benny, so Benny figured it had to come from somewhere inside."

"Who was it, Walter?"

"Benny went into the church to see the fat guy, Hatfield, something like that."

"Wakefield?" Tommy asked.

"Yeah. Wakefield. Old guy. Wore white suits."

Branko looked at Tommy and nodded. They left Walter J. Pickett alone with his attorney. As they were walking out, Molly Brazelton handed Tommy a file folder with a name ENGLISH, RACHEL on it.

"Shooter Three," Tommy said.

"Bring it along."

They got into Tommy's car and drove back to Seaport General. On the way, Branko told Tommy that the reverend was withdrawing from the primary.

"There goes your theory."

"Yeah."

At the hospital, Harrison Wakefield was sleeping. He could not be disturbed.

The two policemen sat in the hospital lobby, drinking coffee, piecing together what they had, hoping a lead would surface on the client, Colonel Big Time. Tommy opened the file on Shooter Three, which he summarized. Branko listened with his head resting on the wall, eyes closed.

"Okay. Shooter Three profile. Here we have a Rachel English, a.k.a. Jessica Kane, a.k.a. Rebekka Truesdale. Three passports, one for each identity. No criminal record on any of the three names. The moneybelt contained thirty-four grand in cash and Amex traveler's checks. The purse contained thirty-six grand, along with an uncut diamond that we'll have appraised tomorrow. There was a checkbook from the Banque National de Paris. The name on the checks was Rachel English. Three weapons. An AR-Fifteen, laser scope. A LAW bazooka. And a Beretta nine-millimeter. Some little arsenal. She had a ticket for France, leaving from LAX on a noon flight tomorrow. The Buick was rented here, at John Wayne International on Thursday, one of those executive check-in deals where you phone in and they leave the keys in a drop. No one saw her arrive. No one would see her leave. No labels in the clothes—they'd all been cut out—except for what she'd just bought at Complice. That's a very expensive store, by the way. The concierge at the Inn of Cortez doesn't remember her. And the clerk, Candy Woodmere, is still out of town."

"What's your hunch on Wakefield as the inside guy?"

Tommy shook his head. "I'm a detail guy. The hunches, Francisco, I leave to you."

Branko's brain felt numb. They had the three shooters, but Colonel Big Time sat out there in the dark, waiting.

"Drive me to my car, Saint Thomas. I've got to get some sleep."

"Likewise."

The Volvo sat in the lower parking lot of Promontory Chapel, its roof dappled with moisture from the fog. A sheriff's deputy in a yellow rain jacket passed them through. A fire engine was parked near the main entrance. A second deputy told them the top two floors of the Tower had been gutted before fire fighters had contained the blaze. In the fog, the Tower loomed darkly above them. The vehicles that had exploded earlier in the afternoon had been hauled away. Branko said good night to Tommy and unlocked his car and got behind the wheel and started it up. He drove home slowly. The red Porsche was not in its parking space.

Inside the apartment, Branko opened a Miller's and put in a call to Lissa Cody. There was no answer at her apartment in

Irvine, but there was a message at the *Tribune* offices: *"Branko. Meet me at Seven Singapore Circle, Newport Beach—Have news of Spyglass Hill Gang. Signed, L."*

"When did she leave?"

The voice on the other end was irritable. "Sorry. I have no earthly idea. That's all there was."

"Thanks."

Branko hung up and sat in his bionic chair, willing his body to relax. The beer helped. So did lying down on the floor with his feet dangling from the lip of the chair. He wanted to meet Lissa Cody, but he didn't want to go outside his house again tonight. When you got outside your house, bad shit rained down on you.

On the television screen, Linda Calderon was working hard for her Emmy with an update on events in Orange County. She was pointing to a floor diagram of the sixth floor of the Tower of Prayer, and pronounced Branko's name Bronco, with a Spanish inflection, like the wild horse. At the end, she reported that the reverend was retiring from the race. He would issue a statement tomorrow.

Lissa was waiting.

Branko finished the beer. The shooting team had his .357. His only other handgun was a .38 Police Special, which he kept in a bedroom drawer. He was certain it needed cleaning. He stuffed the weapon into his shoulder holster, then dropped two speed-loaders into his jacket pockets and headed out.

Seven Singapore Circle was the home of Reverend Williams.

Maybe he would get lucky and have another stimulating face-off with Sister Winona Lee.

In the police car on the way home, the reverend was wondering how far he could maneuver without the wheelchair. Delia Sue was half asleep beside him, her body as warm as a smooth round rock on the beach at Malibu. The car turned a corner onto Singapore Circle and slipped toward home. Where was Daddy's pistol?

The car pulled up into the Williams driveway and the reverend swung his right leg out. Some trouble there. The pain leaped at him, charging up his spine when he eased his left leg out. He bit his lip and broke out into a sweat. There were pain pills in the house. He forced a weary smile and thanked the policeman, who answered in a sleepy voice.

"You're welcome, sir. Glad it's over."

The car eased off, and they were left alone in the foggy night.

"Gosh, Daddy," Delia Sue said as they moved up the walk. "I'm pooped."

"Open the door, honey." He braced himself on the hospital cane and handed her the key.

"Will there be policemen around all the time now?"

He looked back at the empty street. "Not anymore."

"I liked Jamie a lot. She was funny, always making jokes. And she didn't bug me about my hair. I'll miss her."

"You can visit Officer Duncan in the hospital."

"Hey, Dad, that's rad."

The door opened with a click and they went in. He didn't know how much time he had before Winona Lee arrived home. In her present mood, she might easily choose to keep a vigil at Terry Junior's bedside all night. Delia Sue said good night and went to her room. Using his cane, the reverend went into his study for his secret bottle of Ballantine's Scotch, locked in a drawer down below two fat file folders.

Daddy's pistol was on the top shelf of the study closet, behind some textbooks the reverend had used in seminary. He sat at his desk, sipping the whisky, trying to write his withdrawal statement. Dear friends and fellow Christians . . .

The pistol lay on the table. Mama had asked him to throw it away after Daddy had used it to commit suicide. The pistol was a reminder, a memory of those kitchen-table times with Daddy. He dialed Douglas Cade's number, but the line was busy.

The reverend picked up the gun and stared at it. It was a revolver. He broke it open the way Daddy had taught him. Six cartridges, loaded no telling how long ago. He brought the pistol together again with a satisfying snap and picked up the phone.

Sitting at his desk with the pistol and the Ballantine's, the reverend made two calls. The first was to the Red Star Cab Company, for a taxi. The second was to the Newport Beach police station. When the police dispatcher answered, he requested that security be restored at his house. "My daughter heard a prowler," he said. "And Mrs. Williams and I would be grateful for your help, at least until the Tuesday primary is over."

The dispatcher, a man with a nasal voice, did not sound concerned. After all, the shooting was over and the perpetrators were in custody. "A unit is on the way, Reverend."

"Thank you."

He left the study and walked heavily to the bathroom for the pain pills. He returned to the living room, feeling the pain grow dim, and strategized as he waited for the cab. In his mind, he was Robin Hood the Bold, charging the evil Sheriff of Nottingham. The cane was his longbow. The pistol was his band of Merry Men. He found Delia Sue's red rucksack hanging on a hook in the front closet. He placed the pistol inside and zipped it closed.

When the taxi arrived, he limped down the curved walk, the rucksack over his shoulder, the fog swirling against his legs. He needed a shower and a change of clothes. His face had a day's growth of stubble. His mind was on revenge. He had forgotten to brush his teeth.

A police car came around the corner and headed toward his home. He entered the cab with only minimal pain, settled back against the seat cushions, and gave the address of Douglas Cade, a cottage on a beach-front street on Lido Island. Cade was a slippery fellow. The reverend hoped he wasn't too late.

The cab was on the Lido overpass before the cab driver pointed out they were being followed. The reverend gripped his pistol. "Drive on, my man. Drive on."

When he arrived home from Seaport General, Douglas Cade mixed himself a stiff Scotch and phoned Susannah Maxwell on her private line. It was half past ten and Cade's hands were like ice.

The phone rang at least eight times before she answered. "Hello?"

Cade was sweating now. "Susannah? It's Douglas Cade."

"Douglas. Are you all right? I heard some terrible things on the radio."

"I'll be fine. Listen, Susannah. The reason I'm calling, it's about that package I left in your safekeeping."

"Yes?"

"I'd like to pick it up tonight."

There was a pause. He could almost hear her thinking. "What time, Douglas?"

"Things here have—" He stopped, trying to find the right words. "I've decided to leave town. I've resigned from the campaign. Before I go, I thought I'd retrieve that package."

"Of course, Douglas. Tonight? Tomorrow?"

He checked his watch, but the crystal face had been smashed in the altercation with Rubidoux at Promontory Chapel. It was a Rolex, worth $48,000, and he'd bought it on the black market in Hong Kong for $4,300. The clock on his desk said 9:33. "Around midnight, Susannah, if that's all right." He would pick up his cache and leave town, drive to Los Angeles, put up for the night at an airport hotel. He would fly East tomorrow, after his nerves had settled a bit. It was out of character for Douglas Cade. He usually planned ahead.

"The fog's very thick, Douglas. Can't this wait until tomorrow?"

Her questions irritated him. He was not an admirer of the sensual Mrs. Maxwell. Women like her only made life more troublesome. "If I can get there earlier, I'll call."

"Very well, Douglas. Just honk when you arrive and Julio will let you in."

He finished the first drink and started packing, but he was still feeling jumpy. The Scotch was Chivas Regal, a present from Colonel Devane, and he thought of Devane now as he poured the second one thirty percent stiffer. Ah, that was more like it. But when he had finished number two, he still felt the edge of fear, so he upped the Chivas in number three by twenty-five percent. He thought he heard a car door outside. He was not aware he was moving more slowly, so he was surprised when the doorbell rang and he noticed that it was midnight. He thought of phoning Susannah, to tell her he would be late.

The door opened to reveal Reverend Williams, leaning on a cane. His face looked haggard and a lock of blond hair hung down across one eye. His tie was unknotted and his shirt was soiled with sweat. Cade wanted to close the door, but the reverend brought his hand up. In it was a black pistol. The reverend's eyes were mad.

"There's a spy out here, Douglas."

"What?"

The reverend motioned with the pistol, and Cade stepped outside, into the fog. A woman lay slumped against the railing of his porch. When he touched her, she moaned.

"She followed me," the reverend said. "She's a reporter."

"What?"

"Get her inside, Douglas."

Cade was not a strong man. He grasped the limp woman under her arms and pulled her inside. "You hit her."

The reverend smiled and shoved him, and Cade took a couple of steps backward. The woman slipped out of his grasp. He was aware of her red hair, of the room spinning wildly. He heard the door close and saw the pistol in the reverend's hand come around in a blur and then he felt the pain, white hot and screaming, and then he was on the floor staring up. The pain tore through him. There was water on his face and his shirt was wet. The reverend loomed above him. The woman lay on the floor, still not moving.

"All right, Douglas. It's time for twenty questions."

"What?"

He felt the tip of the cane against his throat. "Who is this Colonel What's-his-name? Where can I find him?"

The pain came again and he almost blacked out.

"Hurry, Douglas. My boy is lying in that hospital and I've got a bullet in my leg that burns like holy Hades and you know who paid that stinking little killer and you're going to tell me."

Cade tried to hold out. He was afraid of the reverend, but he was even more afraid of Colonel Devane. The reverend kept hammering at him with his voice, prodding him with the cane, slapping him around. He only held out for a few minutes before telling everything he knew about Colonel Robert E. Devane.

The reverend forced him to pick up the reporter and carry her to the garage. His head was spinning.

"You are the driver, Douglas."

"Where are we going?"

"Lake Elsinore. To visit Colonel Devane."

"In this fog?"

"Yes. In this fog."

Cade started his leased Mercedes. The redhead was lying in the back seat. The fog curled thickly against the headlights. Cade was exhausted. They tried to get over the mountain to Lake Elsinore, but they had to turn back and check in at a cheap motel in San Juan Capistrano. Cade could not sleep with his hands and feet tied. He hated violence and was afraid. He had never felt such pain.

There was no sign of Lissa Cody or her yellow Honda when Branko arrived at 7 Singapore Circle. The reverend lived in a big Mexican-style house with a tile roof, stucco exterior, nice row of palm trees, and pavers leading up to the door. A police unit was parked in the driveway. When Branko rang the bell, the door was answered by Officer Joe Romero.

Romero had not seen Lissa Cody. Mrs. Williams had come in about a half hour ago. The daughter was sleeping. There was no sign of the reverend. Romero had seen a Red Star cab leaving the house as he drove up.

Branko used the phone in the study to call Red Star Taxi. Yes, they had made a pickup on Singapore Circle at two minutes after midnight. The destination had been an address on Lido Island. Branko got the address and headed out the door.

Lissa had said it earlier. This was a goose chase.

The fog forced him to keep his speed down to fifteen miles an hour. As he neared the beach, he had to stop twice until the fog swirled away enough for him to continue. The trip from Singapore Circle to Lido Island, normally a ten-minute drive, took twenty-five minutes. He could not see cars approaching until they were twenty feet away. He was poking along, hunting for the address on Lido Island, when he saw the yellow Honda angled into the curb in front of a small brick cottage.

Branko parked and got out. His nerves were on edge. He pulled the .38 out of the shoulder holster as he approached the house. A light was burning in the living room. The light seemed to come from below the windows. He looked in through a window. A lamp was overturned on the floor. A chair lay on its side. Books and papers were strewn about the room.

The door was locked. There were signs of a scuffle, so Branko went back to the Volvo and called for backup and a search warrant. Then he broke a window and climbed in. He found blood spots on the carpet and could smell vomit. On the floor near the sofa was a NOW badge.

Now the bastards had Lissa.

He found a Heineken in the fridge and opened it, then stood in the living room, drinking the beer, trying to piece together what had happened. Lissa had followed the reverend, but why had he come here? Cade was the money man of the campaign. Maybe he knew something. He remembered that Mrs. Maxwell knew Cade, had his phone number handy.

Branko pulled the door open and jogged back to his Volvo. The beer was half gone. It was against the law to drink and drive, but Branko didn't care. The fog seemed even heavier as he started back for the mainland. He passed two police units, roof lights turning, as he drove slowly up the street toward the Lido overpass.

The bastards had kidnapped Lissa Cody.

Now Branko was really mad.

The drive over to Mrs. Maxwell's took thirty-seven minutes. When he pulled up in front of the big house on Spyglass Hill, the front door opened and a short guy in a white coat came out to open the gate. Branko liked that kind of service. He stepped out of the car and headed for the gate.

"Hey. You not Mistah Cade." The speaker had a wide face and a suspicious look in his eye.

Branko showed him his shield. "Police. Here to see Mrs. Maxwell."

The gate started to close, but Branko pushed it open. "Police," he repeated.

The man shook his head. "Not Mistah Cade." Then he led the way inside.

In the artificial light, the big foyer seemed empty and forlorn.

"You wait." The houseman pointed to double doors leading to the library. "Missy come soon."

Branko walked across the marble floor to the library. The carpet was thick and there were books everywhere. Double French doors led outside, to a patio. Bookshelves lined the walls and there was a mezzanine about fourteen feet above ground level. Book lovers could reach the mezzanine by means of a circular wooden staircase. Nice room, Branko remarked silently.

He was examining the handiwork on the staircase when Mrs. Maxwell came in wearing a flowing floor-length house dress, pale yellow, with long sleeves and a plunging neckline. The yellow material was expensive and sexy. She wore no brassiere and was barefoot.

"Well, Sergeant!" Her voice had changed from that of the sultry sex queen of the afternoon. "Did you forget something?"

"Your houseman called me Mr. Cade."

Mrs. Maxwell walked to the wet bar and poured herself a short brandy. "Drink?"

"No, thanks. Were you expecting Cade?"

"Is this police business?"

"Yes. I think he and the reverend have kidnapped a friend."

Mrs. Maxwell sat down and crossed her legs. Her face in this light did not appear ageless. Her magic was gone. "Are you serious?"

"Yes. I was hoping they'd brought her here."

"Here? What on earth for?"

Branko indicated the room, and the house beyond. "Good place to hide someone. Big. Isolated. Lots of rooms."

"Well, feel free to search."

He walked toward her now, feeling his anger build. She knew more than she was telling. He stood over her, sweating.

"Tell me about Cade."

She sipped her brandy. "What would you like to know?"

"Where did he come from? How long has he been here? How well did you know him?"

"Haven't we been over this, Sergeant?"

"Tell me again."

"Very well. He came from somewhere back East. He's married, with two children. I have not met his wife. My husband knew him in business. I'm not sure how. Douglas was brought in to control campaign spending. My husband was ill, and couldn't keep up with his work. In a month, the reverend spent something like seven hundred and fifty thousand dollars on promoting himself. Douglas arrived last fall, October, early November. I know him only casually."

"How come your phone bank upstairs has his number?"

"Jordan put it there. I haven't changed it."

"Why was Cade coming here tonight?"

"He keeps something in my safe."

"What?"

She shrugged. "A small package. I wouldn't know."

"Open the safe."

She stared at him a moment, then set the brandy snifter down. She left the chair in a fluid motion of long limbs and soft yellow gown and turned to kneel and pull aside a slide panel in a built-in cabinet near the wet bar. As she squatted down to turn the dial of the safe, the yellow material pulled tight, outlining her trim bottom and thighs. She looked female, erotic, primitive. Branko heard clicks of the dial. The safe opened. She reached in and came up with a small metal box. "Douglas has the only key."

"Get me a paperclip."

Mrs. Maxwell found a paperclip in the desk and handed it to him. Branko bent the end of the paperclip, then inserted it into the lock. Two turns and the box was open.

"My, my," Mrs. Maxwell said. "Such police work."

The box contained over a hundred gold coins, several gemstones, and bank notes in three currencies—Swiss francs, German marks, and Japanese yen. Branko knew nothing about stones. Mrs. Maxwell identified diamonds and rubies and emeralds and a large opal.

"Cade was coming here to pick up his stash?"

"I suppose."

"That means he was leaving town."

"If you say so."

"How much would you say is here?"

"I could guess. A quarter of a million."

Branko whistled. Mrs. Maxwell poured herself more brandy. When she sat in the chair this time and crossed her legs, the house dress came open. Branko looked at her legs. She stared back at him, challenge ripe in her eyes. "Is there something else, Sergeant?"

He replaced the money and jewels in the metal box and left it on the desk. "How well do you know the colonel?"

There was a pause before she answered. "Which colonel might that be?" Her voice was thick with suppressed emotion.

"The colonel who hired three shooters to mess up the reverend. The colonel who murdered my friend."

She shook her head and covered her legs. "I'm afraid I don't know what you're talking about, Sergeant."

Branko slapped the brandy glass out of her hand. She tried to stand, but he shoved her back down. The flesh beneath the yellow gown was soft, pliable. "You asked me to kill Cade. Why?"

"It was a joke. You're a policeman. You wouldn't understand. I should have know that."

He squeezed her arms. "You know the colonel, goddammit. I can see it in your eyes."

"Let me go."

The door opened and the houseman stepped in. When he saw Branko wrestling with his mistress, he ran forward. Branko leveled his .38 at him. The houseman stopped. "Tell your boy to go to bed."

Her voice was rough. "Go on, Julio. Go to bed."

"Call policia," he said.

"No. It's all right. Go to bed now."

The houseman walked out and Branko holstered his .38. When the door closed, he said, "The colonel."

Mrs. Maxwell rubbed her arms. Her face showed pain. "Why don't you leave?"

"How'd you like to be an accessory to murder?"

She stood up and brushed past him, and he smelled her perfume. She walked to the French doors and stared out at the patio. When she spoke, her back was turned. "If I tell you, will you keep me out of it?"

"Depends."

"I've got to stay out of it. I want to leave town and go somewhere. I'm going to change my life."

"Tell me what you know about the colonel. Then we'll talk about you."

There was a long pause.

In his mind Branko saw an image of Cade, the colonel, Rubidoux, the big bearded guy, and the blonde in blue, all armed and all converging on a red, white, and blue target on an enlarged map of Newport Beach. At the center of the bull's eye was Reverend Terry O. Williams, alone, waving a cross as if it were the American flag.

Mrs. Maxwell sighed and hugged herself, pulling the gown tight across her back and shoulders and waist. "All right. The colonel I know is named Devane. Robert Devane. He joined the Foreign Legion and then the U.S. Army. After that he was a mercenary. Jordan said he fought mostly in Africa. He hates blacks, all minorities. Apparently, he's killed thousands. Devane and Jordan did some money deals, Ministry Beach, things having to do with oil, and when Jordan got the idea of running Reverend Williams for Congress, Devane wanted in. I heard them arguing about the primary. Then Jordan died, and that was that."

"Did Devane know Douglas Cade?"

She nodded. "Yes."

Branko exhaled. Cade knew Devane. Devane did business with Jordan Maxwell, who supposedly hired Cade to bring the reverend's campaign into the black. Devane hired Rubidoux to shoot the reverend. Cade knew that, up in the Tower. The reverend figured it out. Now they'd taken Lissa to. . . . "Where is Devane?"

"Sierra Monte, the tourist village near Lake Elsinore. He has a sort of . . . compound."

"Have you been there?"

There was a pause. "A few times."

"Is there a gate? A fence?"

"Yes. It's very tight security."

"How do you get in?"

She turned and stared at him. "You can't go there!"

Branko shook his head wearily. "How many people are out there?"

"On the weekend, twenty. Perhaps twenty-five. This is insane, Sergeant. The house is like a fortress. There are guns everywhere."

"Where do the weekend warriors come from?"

"I've seen men from Sierra Monte, deputies. Otherwise, I have no idea."

He asked her again. "How do you get in?"

"I have to call ahead. There's an automatic gate hooked up to an alarm system. The system has to be turned off. I tell him which car I'll be driving."

"You drive up to the compound, or what?"

"No. There's a tunnel, part of an old mining operation, from the gold days. I park near some rocks and walk underground."

"How long does it take?"

"Ten minutes. Perhaps twelve."

"Get some paper. Draw me a diagram."

Mrs. Maxwell found paper and a pencil and sat at the rosewood desk, drawing a rough diagram of the compound where Devane lived. There was a fence that stretched for several miles. Then there was the main compound. She drew a square representing the house, and then three other buildings. One was a barracks for the weekend warriors. One was a garage. The third was a warehouse.

"What does he keep in the warehouse?"

"I'm just guessing, but I think he sells guns."

"Who to?"

She shrugged, and he smelled her again. "Any fool who wants to be king."

"How does he transport them?"

She stood up, brushing the hair away from her face. "I am not his partner in crime, Sergeant. I really have no idea."

He grabbed her arm. "We're going out there."

"Now?"

"Yes, now."

"What about the fog?"

"We'll drive slow."

"It would be smarter to wait until tomorrow. I have to call ahead anyway, and even if we made it over the mountain, we couldn't get in. No one gets in at night."

"There's no time. Get dressed."

She stepped closer, staring at him with her direct blue eyes, and he felt the pulse of her sex appeal. "Look, Sergeant, I'll help you all I can, but we need to think this through."

He pointed upstairs with his .38. "Get dressed."

She dressed in her walk-in closet in the bedroom. Their love-making earlier seemed years away, a picture fading among the yellowed pages of a book. He could hear the rustle of silken things. She emerged in ten minutes, wearing a brown jump suit and running shoes. She had applied lipstick and eye makeup.

"You insist on going now?"

"Yes."

"We'd better take my BMW. It will be less suspicious."

They walked downstairs to the garage. The BMW started right away, its engine purring. Mrs. Maxwell drove. Branko sat in the passenger seat, running through possible scenarios. It took them fifteen minutes to crawl through the fog down off Spyglass Hill, and then another fifteen minutes to drive along Jamboree to the San Diego Freeway. The freeway itself was impossible and they kept running off the road, onto the shoulder. Once, she almost collided with a slow-moving truck. At El Toro Road, Branko told Mrs. Maxwell to exit and they registered in a motel. He asked for twin beds and put it on his credit card. In the motel room she looked around with an amused expression and said, "How sordid, Sergeant. California grunge."

He took her car keys and her purse and used his handcuffs to lock her left wrist to the bed near the inside wall.

"Handcuffs. You know how to turn a girl on."

Branko said nothing. She unlaced her running shoes with her right hand, pulled the blanket up, and watched him with cat's eyes until he turned off the light.

"We should have brought the brandy, Sergeant."

"Get some sleep."

As he drifted off to sleep, Branko wondered what kind of guy Jordan Maxwell had been.

312

Chapter Eighteen

BRANKO woke at six on Monday morning and went out to check the terrain. The rest of the world lay asleep, and the fog hung thick and gray as he jogged to a pay phone. He made two calls. The first was to Matt Murdock, a private eye and Special Forces veteran who possessed an impressive private arsenal. After four rings, Murdock's answering machine clicked on with the message that Murdock was not available. Probably on a case, Branko thought. Very bad timing. He could have used Murdock today.

His second call was to Zeke Torres, a carpenter and handyman from Santa Ana. Branko knew that Zeke was an all-night poker freak. It took five calls to locate him. Branko identified himself and told the gruff voice on the other end of the line what he wanted—a handgun, fifty rounds and two spare clips, and some explosives with detonators.

"I was just heading out for San Diego," the voice said. "When do you need this?"

"In an hour."

"Two hundred to rent the piece. Two hundred for the plastique."

Branko checked his wallet. "How's fifty on account?"

The voice laughed. "Okay, Sergeant. I need a favor."

"Name it."

"My cousin Mario's in the pokey in Santa Ana. See what you can do to get him out."

Branko wrote it down. "What's Mario done this time?"

"Hasn't done nothing, man. The charge is B and E."

"I'll do what I can."

The fog was still thick. They agreed to meet at a Texaco station at the junction of the Ortega Highway and the San Diego Freeway at seven-thirty.

313

At Denny's restaurant Branko bought two large cartons of coffee and some breakfast Danish. Walking back to the motel, he thought fondly of his thermos, which was in his Volvo, which was back at Mrs. Maxwell's on Spyglass Hill.

Zeke Torres was waiting at the Texaco station on the Ortega Highway when Branko drove up with Mrs. Maxwell. Branko signaled, and they motored east through the fog to a deserted roadside park to make the exchange. He took the car keys and left Mrs. Maxwell behind the wheel. The handgun was a flat-blue automatic. Zeke, a slight Latino with the sparkly eyes of a movie star, wore faded jeans, a Western shirt, boots, and a concho belt.

Branko hefted the pistol, which lay heavily in his hand. "Matchmaster?"

"Yeah. An M-S Safari Arms. It's a nine millimeter, seven-shot. This baby retails for seven hundred, so consider it a rental."

"Ammo?"

Zeke handed over a clip and a box of shells. "I could only find one spare clip, so here's fifty extra rounds. This is a sweet piece of machinery, Sergeant."

"Good, because on this shoot I need leverage." Branko handed over the fifty dollars.

Zeke grinned. "You need help on this?"

Branko could have used a professional like Murdock. Mrs. Maxwell was an amateur. So was Zeke Torres. One amateur was enough. "Stay out of trouble, Zeke."

Zeke climbed into his pickup, made a U-turn, and zipped back toward the freeway. The plastique was a gray lump in a wooden box. Branko stored it and the .38 in his tennis bag in the trunk of the BMW. He put Zeke's automatic in his shoulder holster, the extra clip in his jacket pocket. Zeke had included two timers, some blasting caps, and a length of primacord detonating fuse.

"Who was that man?" asked Mrs. Maxwell.

"A friend from the past."

"He looked like a movie star, someone famous."

314

Branko laughed. "Zeke would love that."

They headed up the hill, into the gray mountain fog. "Where did you meet the merc?"

"Funny, I never really thought of him as a 'merc.' A lord of the manor, perhaps. Or a soldier of fortune." She bit into a sweet roll. "We met in Hollywood, at a party."

"How long ago was that?"

"Four years. Or five. It was the holidays, I remember, and he and Jordan got talking about Arab oil. Then the next thing I knew Jordan had invited the colonel to dinner. He arrived with a gorgeous female in tow."

"Where was Devane born?"

"Texas, I think. He uses his redneck accent to fool you into thinking he's a dumb hick. He fooled me. I think he even fooled Jordan."

Branko nodded and sipped his lukewarm coffee. "What was your husband planning, once the reverend got into office?"

"He wanted to own a congressman."

"Just like that?"

She shrugged and went on chewing. "Jordan was very persuasive. He could use you and make you enjoy it. Once, when he bought a Rolls from an Arab, he took me along as a diversion. He asked me to wear short shorts and a skimpy blouse. The buyer was a greedy little man with hairy arms. He couldn't keep his eyes off me. Jordan saved seven thousand dollars on the car and paid me a commission of three thousand for my help."

"You didn't object?"

She finished the sweet roll and wiped her mouth with the back of her hand. "Don't be silly, Sergeant. It's the way of the world."

"When we were in bed yesterday making whoopee, did you know about Colonel Devane and the Balboa shooting?"

"How could I?"

"You're smart, that's how. You read people. You put things together."

"Sergeant, you put it together *for* me. Last night, with your probing questions." She rubbed her arms. "I have bruises where you grabbed me."

Branko slowed down for a slow-moving truck. They were near the crest of the hill. The dashboard clock read 8:32. "Did you have sex with this guy Devane?"

She smiled at him and shook her head sadly, her eyes as hard as California flint. "Why must men always think like men?"

There was no way to get around the truck due to the fog. Outside Sierra Monte, they stopped at a roadside stand, where a sleepy fruit vendor sold them four grapefruit from the lush Coachella Valley. In the small tourist town, across from the bank, Branko stood next to Mrs. Maxwell in the phone booth while she phoned Devane. His nerves were on edge and he kept checking his wristwatch.

"Roberto? It's Susannah. I'm in town, dear. Twenty minutes away. Yes, I know. Yes. But I must see you. It's about—" She paused and turned her blue eyes on Branko. "It's about Douglas. He left something in my safe that's rather, well, incriminating."

He could hear a man's voice on the other end but could not make out the words.

"Well," Mrs. Maxwell said, "It's just some evidence, Roberto. A few things in writing. A cassette recording. It ties you to the events of Friday. And I know you wouldn't want me to say too much more on a public telephone. What's that? Well, for starters, I want the paper from your nasty little man at the bank."

She nudged Branko with her hip and smiled. So, the lady had her own ax to grind with the colonel. She hung up. There was a pale sheen of sweat on her forehead and upper lip when she was finished and her eyes were bright with the fire of battle as she stepped out of the booth.

"What was that all about?"

"A deal the colonel made with my husband."

"What kind of deal?"

"Money and real estate. He owns the bank across the street. The bank controls a note signed by my husband."

Branko grabbed her arm, the same place he had bruised her last night. "Damn you. What else haven't you told me?"

She stared at him, eyes burning. "I can get you inside, Sergeant. The rest is up to you."

"Is Cade there?"

"He didn't say."

"I have to make a call. Will you wait here or do you need the handcuffs?"

"I love handcuffs."

He kept an eye on her while he dialed Tommy Osterhaus at the Newport Beach station. The dispatcher patched him through right away. Tommy's voice was cheery. "Francisco? You taking a day off, or what?"

"I found the bastard who iced Roscoe."

"Colonel Big Time? Where?"

"Lake Elsinore. He's holed up in a merc compound in the mountains."

"Correct me if I'm wrong—Elsinore's in Riverside County, right?"

"I don't have much time, Tommy. The merc's holding Lissa Cody, my reporter friend. And maybe the reverend."

"Francisco, are you there now?"

"Twenty minutes away."

"It's not your jurisdiction, Francisco. Back off."

"No time to argue, pal. Alert your pals in the CHP—and maybe the Marines. Alert the chief, but don't tell the Archer or the FBI or the sheriff's station in Sierra Monte."

"Dammit, Francisco. This could be the end of a brilliant police career. Have you forgotten I'm retiring soon!"

Branko grinned. Reading from his makeshift map, he repeated Mrs. Maxwell's directions. "I need backup, Tommy. Sirens and copters, the works. This guy's a merc, weekend warriors, Ku Klux Klan mentality. He needs killing."

Tommy's sigh was audible. "Please, Francisco. Wait for some help—"

Branko hung up before Tommy could wish him luck. This one was for Roscoe.

They got back into the BMW, and Mrs. Maxwell clawed the skin off a grapefruit. The meat was bright pink. Juice dribbled down her chin and she smiled wickedly at Branko.

They turned right, heading out of town toward the brown mountains. He could reach out and touch her, grab her wrist, lock on the handcuffs. He could caress her honey-gold skin and make wild and memorable love to her. But he would never know what she was thinking, or what made her tick. Yesterday afternoon in her bed was a magic moment out of time, gone now, already fading from memory. Sunday with Mrs. Maxwell had been like that Zen parable about sticking your toe in the river. You could revisit the spot on the riverbank where you put in your big toe, but you could never find the same place in the water, because it was charging downstream, forever changing.

"Grapefruit, Sergeant?"

"No."

"It's quite lovely meat, pink, full of sweetness."

"No thanks."

They drove on. She asked him about the case and, heading uphill with the BMW in second gear, he told her about Benny Rubidoux and the woman who called herself Rachel English.

And as he talked, he knew for sure she had slept with the goddamn merc.

What an actress.

When the phone buzzed, Robert Emory Devane was having a late breakfast on the veranda. The sun was out, but patches of wispy fog still hung in the bushes like spiderwebs. Devane's guest was Brigadier General James Jack Jessup, one of the king-pins of Pentagon Special Operations and Devane's main channel for kickbacks from the huge budget allocated to the Department of Defense. Jimmy Jack poured himself another cup of coffee and looked across the sparse yellow grass to the loading area, where men in dungarees worked. An olive-drab forklift was hoisting a wooden case onto a railroad car.

A satchel sat on the wood floor at Devane's feet. The satchel was made of black leather, worn with age. It contained nine mil-lion dollars—one-third in Swiss francs, one third in German marks, and one third in U.S. greenbacks. Devane was happy the deal was going through. The Lard-Ass Caper was finished, over, done with. It had been a long shot, like Ministry Beach. The cost, including two dead shooters and Cade and a half million in running expenses, would be a million two hundred thousand. The next order of business was to eliminate Phoenix, the mole in the LAPD. And then find another congressman.

Robert Emory Devane did not give up easily.

Devane was wearing his jungle fatigues. The Bren Ten automatic pistol was in his shoulder holster. Jimmy Jack was wearing tan slacks with a stretch waistband and a pale yellow shirt with no tie. Devane's old buddy was twenty-five pounds overweight. Most of the excess showed in his face and belly. J. J.'s hands were soft, pudgy from deskwork. He was not armed. To Devane, an unarmed man looked naked.

"How much extra weight you packing these days, J. J.?"

"Ten pounds, twelve. Nothing I can't handle."

"You should cut down on the groceries while you're flying a desk."

"Blazes, Bobby, I try. I really do. I eat to soothe my nerves." Jimmy Jack speared a last fried potato and popped it into his mouth. "When will my materiel get rolling?"

"Midday. It's Monday and I lose seventy percent of my cadre during the week. If you black-bag assholes had gotten on the stick, your guns would be at sea, sailing south."

J. J. chewed, then swallowed. "You could have trusted me, Bobby. For old times' sake."

"Teach your grandma to suck eggs."

J. J. blanched. To change the subject, he aimed his fork at the plaque on the wall next to the front door. The motto on the plaque read, "If your a turd, go lay in the yard." The metal frame showed signs of rust. "Your spelling's off, Bat Shit One. That pronoun needs an *e* and an apostrophe."

"I like it that way."

The phone buzzed and Devane reached to the wall to answer. It was Suze Maxwell, with some bullshit about Doug Cade. He listened to her bullshit and then told her to come on in. He hung up the phone and went into the War Room to shut off the gate alarm. The camera at the tunnel entrance was fuzzy, so Devane turned a dial, trying to refocus, but the goddamn picture stayed fuzzy. His technician, a troop named Bradshaw, had gone home with the Cadre. Have to wait until Saturday, he told himself, when Bradshaw came back for weekend duty.

Devane walked back through a long hallway without windows to check on Cade and company. He unlocked the door of a small storeroom and stepped in. The three prisoners were hog-tied, ankles roped to hands. Doug Cade was asleep, snoring. His face was pale, and dried blood streaked his shirt.

Lard-Ass and the newspaper gal were awake and whispering, probably planning an escape. They broke off talking when the door opened. Devane said nothing as he checked their bonds. He had already decided to execute all three of them and bury them in some hard ground to the southeast of the compound. For a while, he'd thought of shipping the girl to Macao, to a Chinese slaver named Hop Chin. He owed Hop Chin and could use the redhead to work off his debt. In Macao, red-headed pussy brought top dollar. But it was too much trouble getting her there, not like the old days.

"I am warning you, sir," Lard-Ass said. "Release us or know endless wrath."

Devane laughed and re-locked the door. As he walked back to join J. J. on the veranda, he thought back to the first time he'd seen Suze Novak. Chicago, in the early seventies. Watergate. Nixon about to be out on his ass. The Arab oil embargo. Devane was just back from a big-money coup in Umbala. He'd come to Chicago to peddle some statues and shit taken from the Umbala treasury. He'd asked around for a call girl and come up with the name Nightingale Enterprises. He'd made the date by phone, using the names of three customers as references. Nightingale tricks were expensive, three hundred for a night, six hundred for a weekend. But the girls were said to be special. At seven on Friday, there was a knock on the door of his suite. . . .

She stood there wearing college-girl clothes, tall, lean as a snake, blue eyes, pale lipstick on her mouth, knee socks, boots, a plaid skirt under the big heavy coat. He sensed smoky sex, the irony in her eyes flashing like a silver dagger. A smart-ass if he ever saw one. Her hair ran in a ponytail down to the middle of her back. She was carrying a brown leather suitcase. Around her neck was a thick red muffler. Her eyes clicked on Devane, the room, the money on the table, then back to Devane.

"Colonel Devane?"

"That's me, kid."

"I'm Susie Novak, Nightingale Enterprises."

"Pleased to meet you."

She shook his hand, then set the suitcase down and moved to the sofa. She sat down, crossing her long legs and allowing the plaid skirt to lift up, showing smooth knees and dusky shadows underneath. She acted like a princess who wasn't about to sleep on a pea. Her eyes were shrewd and knowing, like the eyes of the statue of Shakti, an Oriental goddess, that Devane had sold to a collector in Singapore for $250,000. The statue had been gold, ten inches high, part of the swag from a raid on a princely state near the Golden Triangle, in Burma.

"Are you CIA?" she asked.

Devane laughed. "No. Why do you ask?"

"You feel like CIA."

"Oh, yeah?"

"It's the eyes. They're shrewd, like a priest's eyes. They're just about to laugh. But they don't."

"How many CIA guys have you known?"

"Three." She held up three fingers.

"You're kidding."

"Chicago is the hub of the country, Colonel. Here, we get all kinds."

"You like that?"

"Government types tip well."

"Well, I'm not a government type. Not anymore."

She was still wearing the big coat. Now she unbuttoned it, revealing a tan college-girl mohair sweater with a crew neck. She didn't take the coat off, just sat there with it open, a real pro. She re-crossed her legs. He indicated the money on the table. "You didn't pick the money up yet."

She arched her eyebrows. "Is it going somewhere?"

Devane grinned. She was fighting him for control of the situation, negotiating. She would sit there and spar with him for as long as it took, crossing and re-crossing her sexy legs, letting the skirt hike up, shifting her position on the sofa like a serpent out of the Bible. Her face was lean, like a magazine model's, and it made him want to see what the rest of her looked like. Her hands were graceful, the fingers long. Her neck was still wrapped in the red muffler. Where had she learned to handle herself? Devane was amused, irritated, turned on. She stared at him and wet her lips. He wanted her and she knew it.

"Drink?"

"Um."

"What will it be?"

"Rum on the rocks, with two limes, please."

There was no rum in the bar, so he ordered from Room Service. While they waited, Susie Novak unwound the muffler from her neck, revealing a throat that was delicate, as slender as a flower stalk. She asked him about his work, but he didn't know her well enough to talk. Not yet. He shifted the conversation to her life. She was a student at a local cow college in Illinois and she talked easily about her favorite subjects—political science, psychology, consumer behavior, marketing, literature.

"Tell me about your business, Nightingale Enterprises."

She crossed her legs. "You're a soldier, aren't you?"

"Yeah."

"You lead men. You shoot guns. You kill people."

"Sometimes."

"You sleep in a tent in the bush and invite buxom native women to share your blankets."

Devane laughed.

"How do they smell, the native women?"

"Like the earth."

She stared at him, the color rising along her throat, and he felt his own face getting hot. There was a knock on the door and he opened it to an old guy with a tray. On the tray was a rum bottle, a bowl of limes, and one of those little pewter squeezers you saw in bars. The old guy had sad, rheumy eyes. He told the old guy to put it on his tab and tipped him five dollars. When he turned back to the room, Suze Novak was no longer sitting on the sofa. The red muffler was there. So was the big navy coat. There was one knee sock on the arm of the sofa. The other knee sock lay on the floor, near the bedroom door. The three hundred was gone from the table.

Devane grinned. His offer had been accepted. Now they had a contract, him and the little college gal smart-ass bitch.

322

The bedroom door was ajar and Devane moved to it, heart pumping, the way it did before battle. He opened the door and walked in. The plaid skirt lay on the floor. A few feet farther was a half slip, white, feminine. With one part of his mind, he admired the way women operated. Smooth skin, slick silky underwear, straps so thin they were pure ornament, pure window dressing. The other part of his mind was occupied with tactics. He saw each woman as territory to be invaded. Set 'em up. Spread their legs. And then conquer.

He heard water running in the bathroom. Then the toilet flushed. Maybe she wanted to stall him, take a bath, soak her body all night. Maybe he would join her. Now that she had taken the money, anything was possible.

Still holding the tray from room service, Devane crossed the carpet to the bathroom. He started to push the door open, then thought better of it and rapped.

"Room service," he said.

The door opened wide enough for her to put out her left hand. In her palm was a Canadian quarter. "For your trouble, my good man." She spoke with a hoity-toity, upperclass accent, the kind used by British phonies. He smelled perfume. "Would you mix the drinks, please."

It was a game. He took the quarter. "Yes, miss."

"Call me Your Highness, please," she said through the opening.

"Yes, Your Highness."

He set the drink tray down on the table and built two drinks with ice and a splash of rum and the juice from two lime wedges. The bathroom door opened, and she waited a moment before stepping into the opening. Susie Novak, the college girl, stood leaning against the door frame, both hands behind her. Her lips were pale, glistening with fresh lipstick. She was wearing only the sweater and the brown boots. One knee was bent and the sole of her boot rested against the door frame in a model's pose. He would destroy her. The boots and the sweater only made her legs look more naked, bare thighs flowing in a sweet line to flaring hips, surprising on a woman so lean. Her bush was

323

the same golden color as her hair. The way she was standing, knee bent, pelvis out, seemed to mean business. But he couldn't tell for sure because she wore dark ski glasses.

"What's with the glasses?"

"Address me as Your Highness."

Devane grinned. He walked toward her, intending to take her into his arms and get on with it, but she met him with an outstretched palm. "Say it. Say Your Highness." Her voice was a husky whisper. She was a great game player, this one, and he understood now why she could get six hundred for a weekend. She was worth twice that. Three times. Control was the only thing he respected besides soldiering.

"I call you Your Highness. What do you call me?"

Her arm still held him off. "Odysseus. Hannibal. Nero. How about Ike. Or Tricky Dick."

Devane grinned. "Call me Zapata."

"Zapata. Yes."

"Now, Your Highness."

He knocked her outstretched hand away and cupped her naked bottom with both hands and pulled her roughly toward him. The boots brought them eye to eye. He yanked the glasses off. He watched as her pink tongue flicked over her white teeth. The two front ones had a tiny gap between them that he hadn't noticed until now. Her neck when he bit into it was buttery soft. He wrestled her onto the bed, onto her belly, and jacked her hips up high. She squirmed and told him not to, but once he was in her she writhed like a snake.

Later that evening he told her about his soldiering and she told him about Nightingale Enterprises. The second time he saw her was that spring, when he taught her to shoot. She wasn't much with a handgun, but with a shotgun on a skeet range she was hell on wheels. With a shotgun, the college gal could hardly miss. . . .

Devane found Jimmy Jack in the War Room, sitting in his granddaddy's wooden chair, snooping. The fuzzy screen showed Suze parking her BMW and getting out.

"Goddamn you, Bat Shit One. That is some visitor."

"Vacate the chair, J. J.!" Devane pulled out his silver-plated Bren Ten and aimed it at Jimmy Jack.

Jimmy Jack vacated the chair. His eyes were wary as he scurried out of the War Room. Devane followed him. His back was to the screen as the other door of the BMW opened.

The way out of town led up a country road, with signs announcing the boundary of the Cleveland National Forest. There was a turnoff and the road became gravel. Branko stopped fifty yards from a storm fence with a gate and they changed positions. Behind the wheel, Mrs. Maxwell looked as relaxed as a jungle cat. She opened the gate with an automatic device and they rode a mile and two-tenths before rounding a curve. How would Tommy and the backup find this place? Branko wondered. He saw a rock outcropping and a few scrub pine trees, and then slid below window level while she brought the car to a stop.

"The tunnel is there, in that rock crevice."

"Park up close."

She maneuvered a few feet closer. "How long before you get inside?"

"I'll be right behind you. A minute. Ninety seconds."

"I'm nervous, Sergeant."

She did not look nervous. "Think of retiring that bank note."

The sun was hot now and Branko sweated heavily on the floor of the car as she left it.

He gave her time to enter the tunnel and then opened the door and ducked around the side of the car to the trunk. Then, carrying the tennis bag that held his .38 and the plastique, he ran after her. The Matchmaster hung heavily in his shoulder holster. Twice he stopped to check Mrs. Maxwell's diagram with his pencil flash. The buildings on the edge of the compound seemed to be about three-quarters of a mile away. If the tunnel curved the way Mrs. Maxwell's diagram showed, it would pass within a few feet of a corner of the warehouse. What if the tunnel did not intersect the warehouse? he wondered. What if there were no explosives stored there? Tough. He had no other choice.

He remembered that there were about seventeen hundred yards in a mile, which meant about thirteen hundred in three-quarter's of one. He counted thirteen hundred steps and then he stopped and placed his charges. Two minutes had passed by the time Branko finished. Figuring he was four minutes from the end of the tunnel, he set the first timer for four minutes, the second one for five. His throat was tight and his hands trembled as he started on up the tunnel.

Devane was back on the veranda when Suze arrived. Her hair needed attention and her smile looked frozen as she shook hands with J. J. She was wearing a cute little jumpsuit and running shoes, and J.J.'s eyes bugged out when he saw her. Devane wasn't surprised. She was a real show-stopper, especially with the front of her blouse unbuttoned halfway to her navel.

"Coffee, Suze?"

"Yes, thanks. Is there something to put in it?"

Devane laughed. The bitch was as edgy as a cat in a roomful of rocking chairs. "Brandy inside. Top shelf in the kitchen, to the right of the sink."

"I'll get it."

She slid back inside and J. J. whomped Devane on the thigh. "Godalmighty damn, Bat Shit One. That is some female!"

"Yeah."

"What brings her all the way out here, anyway?"

"Money," Devane said. "The gal was born poor. She never got over it."

"Whatever she costs, it's worth it."

"Yeah." Devane waited, listening. Ice clinked at the bar. A cork popped. Devane estimated a minute had passed, maybe more, before he walked toward the kitchen. Suze wasn't there. A brandy bottle was open and ice cubes were melting in the sink. He heard noises from the War Room and grinned. The bitch was after the loan note. He moved through his living area to the War Room. The door was half open. Inside, Suze Maxwell was pulling drawers open with both hands, a frantic look on her face.

"Need some help?"

She looked up and kept searching. Any other female would have stopped dead in her tracks. Not Suze Maxwell. She kept on, her eyes wild. Devane grabbed her wrists and stared at her.

"Damn you, Roberto! I want that paper."

"Gonna cost you, Suze." He forced her to her knees.

326

She didn't have a chance to say anything as an explosion rattled the hacienda right down to its railroad-tie foundation. "Goddamn!" He dragged her to the door as an alarm buzzer went off. Smoke billowed out of the library, out of the Rumpus Room.

The tunnel.

"Goddammit, woman. What did you do?"

"Police, Roberto. An army of police."

J. J. came in from the veranda looking green around the gills. "What the hell is it?"

"World War Fucking Three." Devane pulled his Bren Ten and headed for the Rumpus Room. "Watch her, J. J."

J. J. stared around, eyes wide as saucers, as Devane hunkered past him, with the Bren Ten pointed up at seventy degrees. The explosion had blown up the wall separating the library from the Rumpus Room. His copy of *On War* was there, along with the sack of diamonds. In sixty seconds, his men would hit the door. He could hold off an army for sixty seconds. Still, he was pissed. No one fucked with his tunnel. No one.

He picked up a hand grenade from where it hung on a hook on the wall and kept going.

Remember Dien Bien Phu!

Branko hated combat.

He liked tracking down bad guys. He liked running down leads and putting the details together and doing his endless what-ifs. But combat made him edgy. It was crazy cave-man stuff, mindless, savage, prehistoric. If your reflexes weren't on, you needed luck. If your luck ran out, you were dead.

He climbed three steps from the dirt floor of the tunnel to a door left ajar by Mrs. Maxwell and found himself in a closet full of military uniforms and a dozen pairs of boots, all with a high polish. Seven zippered gun cases stood upright against the wall. On the shelf, boxes of ammo.

He could hear voices from another part of the house. Mrs. Maxwell had been right about the windows. They were four feet high and only six inches wide.

More voices, a man's, Mrs. Maxwell's.

Working quickly, Branko packed his last bit of gray plastique against the wall of the bedroom closet, underneath the ammo boxes. He clipped off a piece of primacord, attached it to the plastique, and lit it with a match. Ten seconds until the blow. He settled behind the big bed to await the blast and started counting. Thirteen. Fourteen. Fifteen. Damn. He had mistimed it. Maybe the fuse had gone out. Sixteen. He was just about ready to double-check when it blew. Plaster dust filled the room and there was a muffled throbbing as the explosive backfired down the tunnel. Branko figured thirty seconds until the big one, outside. The smoke made him cough.

Footsteps. Voices. Someone cursing.

He was behind the bed when the merc tossed in a hand grenade. It hit the top of the bed and rolled to a stop four feet from his head. Shit. Moving fast, he grabbed the grenade and tossed it into the closet and at the same time a gun went off with a loud report and Branko felt a bullet tear into his shoulder, spinning him around and down. The grenade exploded with a soft *whoosh*. Branko fired at the doorway. He couldn't see anyone and he knew he was outclassed on the merc's home turf. It was like playing Spider Longo at Le Club. Bullets tore into the mattress. Branko stayed low. Would he ever find his own turf?

"Hey in there," a voice called. "Come on out and let's parley."

"Are you the colonel?" Branko called.

"I been called worse."

"You murdered a friend of mine."

"Shit." There was a pause. "Who?"

"Roscoe Smith. He was on Balboa Friday afternoon."

"Tough titty, boy. You—"

The colonel's sentence was cut short by a second explosion, outside the house, and then by several smaller detonations. "You craphead!" the colonel howled. "You blew up my tunnel!"

The merc came through the door firing, the gun held in one hand, cowboy style, his face twisted by anger. Branko had a glimpse of steel-blue eyes and gray hair, a lean face, a whipcord body in jungle fatigues. An old merc, blasting away at the enemy with a flashy silver automatic.

Steadying Zeke's Matchmaster on the mattress, Branko shot the merc in the chest, a heart shot, spinning him around and slamming him against the doorjamb. Branko's ears rang from the noise. He waited for a count of twenty, his breath coming harshly now. He knew he should get up and check the colonel's pulse and assess the situation before reinforcements could arrive, but all he wanted to do was sit there and try to keep himself from shaking.

Finally, he crawled around the edge of the bed. The merc lay sprawled near the doorway, blood gushing from his heart. His eyes had the glassy cast of death. Branko kept crawling. When he reached the merc, he shoved the muzzle of his weapon under the grizzled jaw. The face was tanned from years under a tropic sun and there was a scar running diagonally for a couple of inches across the right eyebrow, to his hairline. The white hair was thick and the pale-blue eyes were open, staring at Branko in a dead man's curse.

Then Branko heard men shouting. He stood with difficulty, pulling himself up by using the wall. His left arm was useless, and blood ran from the wound in his shoulder. Where was Lissa?

He stumbled toward the doorway. The grenade had blown a hole through to the next room, a library where books were smoldering. He remembered a library on Mrs. Maxwell's diagram. Where was Mrs. Maxwell?

A man appeared in the doorway, wearing jungle fatigues and carrying an automatic weapon. His face was grim. Branko shot him in the leg and the man went down. He rolled himself backward through the doorway and past a table and two chairs. Outside, on the veranda, Branko saw a table, plates, food, a coffeepot. Brunch at Devania. Through the door, he could see a wide field with yellowing grass, two buildings beyond, some railroad flatcars, and three Army trucks. Flames licked at the roof of one of the buildings, where a big burly man with blond hair and a red face was handing out weapons. Branko counted at least eight men, plus the leader.

He holstered his pistol and swung the big door shut. Mrs. Maxwell appeared from a door behind him. Her face was cut and bleeding and the blouse of the jumpsuit was ripped open in front. Today she was wearing a white brassiere. She carried an automatic rifle with open sights.

"Can you use that?"

"Yes."

"Who else is in the house?"

"Some man. He says he's from the Pentagon."

"Where is he?"

"In here."

There was the sound of heavy pounding on the door. Mrs. Maxwell led the way into a control room packed with enough electronic gear to monitor the stock exchange and three ICBMs. A heavy man in civilian clothes sat slumped against a wall. His face was bleeding and he was holding his crotch with both hands.

"What did you hit him with?"

"One sharp knee and a rifle butt."

"Nice work."

"Thank you, Sergeant."

"I've got backup coming, but I don't know when. Can you shut down the windows while I hunt for Lissa?"

She smiled at him like a foxhole buddy. "Of course."

Carrying the rifle, Mrs. Maxwell left the control room. Branko used his handcuffs on the wrists of the heavyset man, running the cuffs through the arm of a heavy wooden chair. Then he went looking for Lissa.

He found her in a storeroom near the back of the house. Cade and the reverend were there, too. Beyond the wall, he could hear the sound of digging. Crazy mercenaries out there, he thought, chipping away.

"Frank! Thank God!"

He used his knife to cut the ropes around her hands and feet. Then he cut the reverend loose and handed the knife to Lissa. "Can you shoot?" he asked the reverend.

"A little."

A bullet whizzed through a window slot and smacked into the wood above their heads. Lissa sawed through Cade's bonds, and Branko led them out into the windowless corridor. The sound of digging was louder now.

330

"There are guns in the bedroom closet, at the front of the house. Get up there and return their fire. Lissa, go into the control room and call for help. Call the CHP and the sheriff and the Marines. I counted eight guys out there, minimum. Some of them are trained soldiers. They're trying to come through the wall. Any questions?"

"What happens to the mad colonel?" the reverend asked.

"He bought the farm."

"What a pity."

Branko spent the next few minutes dodging bullets as he slammed the shutters closed on every window he could find. In the rear, near the storeroom, the digging had stopped but he could hear machinery working, the roar of a big engine, causing the house to shake. When he looked through the narrow shooting slot, he saw a big truck backing up as it maneuvered itself into position for a second ram. Lucky thing they didn't have a bulldozer or they'd have been through the wall already, he told himself.

Back in the living room, Mrs. Maxwell was standing at one window, coolly firing her automatic rifle. The reverend stood at another, jerking his shots badly as he fired a pistol. Douglas Cade was crouched in a corner, behind a chair, holding his hands over his ears. Not a bad idea, Branko thought. He finished checking the windows and went into the control room. Lissa was sitting in the only chair, talking to someone on the phone. The arm of the wooden chair was smashed. There was no sign of the fat man from the Pentagon.

"Are you getting through?"

Lissa nodded. "They're coming." Her cheeks were stained with tears as she reached out to touch him.

Branko took her hand. "How long?"

"Twenty minutes. A half hour."

Branko shivered. "Tell them to hurry."

The house shuddered as the truck rammed it again. Branko left Lissa and jogged back along the narrow corridor. The truck was attacking a spot near the corner of the house in a room full of packing boxes. The wall was already badly caved in. Two of the boxes were full of hand grenades. Branko holstered his weapon and picked up two grenades. He needed his other hand. The shoulder wound burned.

The house shuddered again, followed by the sound of wood splintering and someone shouting, "Heybo, sonofabitch, we done it." The wall collapsed as the heavy front bumper of the truck shoved through. A piece of roof came down. Branko squatted down and pulled the pin on a grenade with his teeth. The truck backed up, pulling away chunks of drywall and timber and dusty adobe brick. The hole was three feet high and maybe six across. Branko waited until the voices were close. Then he let the safety up on the grenade, counted to six, and rolled it through the hole. There was a scurrying sound and someone cursed. The grenade went off, *blam*. A man screamed, "I'm hit!"

Branko duck-walked away from the doorway as automatic weapons spewed lead into the storage room. A fire started in one of the boxes, the flames crackling. When they reached the grenades, there would be another explosion. Branko shoved the box of grenades closer to the fire and headed back for the front of the house. In the living room, Lissa was bent over Cade. With her help, Branko pulled a table into a blocking position at the end of the narrow corridor. The hacienda, he realized, had been built for sector defense.

Branko stationed Lissa in the library with his .38 and instructed her to poke it through the hole and pull the trigger. He told Mrs. Maxwell to rove between the bedroom and the kitchen. He kept listening for sounds of the attackers coming through the hole made by the truck.

His mind was racing with adrenaline, but the loss of blood was making him dizzy and he wished Tommy Osterhaus was there to give him precise instructions.

Running footsteps in the corridor meant they were coming. Branko laid down a pattern of fire into the corridor and heard someone grunt and then tossed his second grenade and squatted down behind the thick table. That's for Roscoe. And that. The grenade exploded with a *whuff*. Mrs. Maxwell appeared from out of the smoke, firing her automatic weapon like an Amazon. They fought side by side for a minute, two. Branko saw the action in slow motion. Bullets whipped through the room. Someone pounded on the front door with a sledgehammer, slowly cracking the stout wood with a heavy rhythmic action. Across the room, the reverend stopped to reload. His eyes were lit with a fanatical fire. Branko guessed he'd hit nothing but dirt with his bullets.

From the rear of the house came the sound of a huge explosion, the box of hand grenades being ignited by the fire. Smoke drifted down the corridor as footsteps hurried away.

From the library, Branko could hear the pop of Lissa's revolver. He left Mrs. Maxwell to guard the corridor while he checked the kitchen. A truck bumper protruded into the wall near the stainless steel sink. Branko was out of hand grenades. The truck backed up and gears were ground in preparation for one more assault on the house. Branko had nine rounds left in the Matchmaster. He fired two rounds through a window slit in the kitchen. One round blew a tire on the truck, which kept moving forward. If he didn't stop it, the kitchen wall would be breached.

Then, suddenly, the attack stopped.

The truck didn't make its ultimate charge. The sound of gunfire faded. Then there was the steady *whop-whop* of helicopter rotors as a whirlybird lifted off from the heli-pad outside.

Mrs. Maxwell was the first to speak. "I hear a siren."

She walked into the library and Lissa came out. The two women smiled at each other, temporary comrades in arms. A strand of red hair hung down across Lissa's forehead and there was soot smudged on her cheek. Branko moved to take her in his arms. Behind her head, he could see Mrs. Maxwell on her hands and knees in the library, hunting for something.

"I see a police car," the reverend said. "Should I open the door?"

"Wait until we see some identification." Branko spoke into Lissa's ear. "You okay?"

"Yes. How did you get here?"

"How did you get here?"

She put a finger on his lips. "Reporter's hunch, what else?"

"Sergeant? Would you come here, please?"

Branko walked to a window-slot and looked out. A black-and-white panda from the California Highway Patrol sat parked on the yellow grass, between the house and the burning warehouse. Two officers in CHP khaki were hunkered down behind the car with their revolvers out. The officer on the right was holding a blue bullhorn. A sheriff's vehicle was coming through the gate, siren drowning out the bullhorn.

"They're acting like cops," Branko said.

The siren died.

"Hello in the house," said a voice over the bullhorn. "This is the police. Come out with your hands—"

Before the officer could finish, his voice was drowned out by Lissa Cody, speaking from the control room on a giant loudspeaker. "Hello out there. This is the house. We need some identification."

"Who are you?"

There was a pause. "My name is Lissa Cody. I'm a reporter for the *Orange County Tribune*. The policeman in charge in here is Sergeant Frank Branko, of the Newport Beach Police. Reverend Williams is with us. And Mrs. Susannah Maxwell. Who are you?"

Branko grinned. The girl reporter was already setting the stage for her big story. It was Pulitzer time for Lissa Cody. He left the Reverend and walked into the library. Mrs. Maxwell was on her hands and knees in the corner, her back to the door. As he entered, Mrs. Maxwell turned to him, her fingers busy buttoning a pocket on her jumpsuit. The automatic rifle was leaning against the wall.

"You okay?"

"Yes." She stared at his wound. "You need a doctor."

"Find what you came for?"

Someone was banging on the door, calling for them to open up inside.

Mrs. Maxwell undid a button and brought out a manila folder she'd tucked into her waist. "Mission accomplished, Sergeant."

"I got my ass shot off for a piece of paper."

"You're the original avenging angel, dear. Now you'll be crowned a hero."

The banging on the door was more insistent. Above the noise, he could hear Lissa's voice echoing across the compound on the merc's loudspeaker.

Mrs. Maxwell moved toward him. Her face was close to his and he got a good whiff of her perfume. She brushed her body against his, at the same time grazing his lips. "Come and visit," she whispered. "You're welcome at my house any time."

Branko said nothing as she left the library and walked straight to Reverend Williams, who was still standing at his window-slot, staring out at the world beyond the hacienda. She put a hand on his shoulder, turned him around, and handed him her automatic rifle. At the same time, she took his revolver.

Simple exchange.

Mrs. Maxwell led the reverend to the front door. Together they lifted the heavy bolt. Branko watched from the library. His shoulder burned like crazy. Lissa reentered from the control room carrying a tape recorder and looking business-like. There was a noise in the bedroom—a voice calling for help. The front door opened to admit two CHP officers and a deputy in green.

"What's going on here?" asked one of the officers.

"One perp escaped." Branko motioned them to the bedroom door. Let somebody else take some heat for a change, he thought.

Guns drawn, the deputy and one CHP officer entered the bedroom. They emerged a couple of minutes later with the fat man in civilian clothes still wearing Branko's handcuffs. His hands and face were caked with filth from the tunnel and the dust was making him wheeze. The fat man had tried to escape, but the tunnel was blocked.

"Who's this fellow?" the CHP officer asked.

"Some hotdog from Washington."

"A Fed?"

"Why not?"

The CHP officer grinned. "What went down here?"

"He'll fill you in." Branko motioned across the room to where the reverend was talking to Lissa Cody. Mrs. Maxwell handed a glass of water to Douglas Cade, who still had his right hand cupped over his ear. Cade's eyes were glazed with madness. It would be a while before he tiptoed through the numbers on a spreadsheet, Branko figured.

Mrs. Maxwell sauntered back to the kitchen. "Anyone for a beer?"

"Here," Branko said.

"Two here, if you please, my dear," the reverend said.

"Holy shit," said the CHP officer, staring at Branko. "You're bleeding bad, buddy."

Branko sat down heavily on the gnarled sofa and waited for his beer. His mission was over. Roscoe Smith had been avenged.

He was lying on the sofa getting medical attention when Agents Moore and Friedkin arrived, looking spiffy in their suits. Agent Moore spoke to the CHP officer in charge while Agent Friedkin talked in whispers to the fat man. The handcuffs stayed on as they marched the fat man out and put him in a brown Ford and drove away.

CHAPTER NINETEEN

TUESDAY dawned clear and sunny and by noon the temperature had reached 92° in the inland valleys and 80° along the beaches. Traffic was jammed up on Balboa Boulevard, on the coast highway, and on the Newport Freeway heading southwest toward the beaches. Because of the summer heat, election watchers predicted a lower-than-normal voter turnout.

Then Lissa Cody's story hit the newsstands.

It filled the front page of the *Orange County Tribune* under a banner headline:

NEWPORT COP, PREACHER WIPE OUT HORNET'S NEST

The photo covering the top half of the page showed Frank Branko in the War Room at Devania, his arm in a makeshift sling. The reverend, holding an automatic rifle, stood on

Branko's right, holding up two fingers in a victory sign. Lissa Cody was to Branko's left. Mrs. Maxwell, the eye-catcher, stood on the reverend's right, holding a revolver. In the background were computers and electronic communication devices. The caption above the photo, white letters on a black field, read: "Happy Foursome: Picnic at White Supremacist's Mercenary Hangout at Devania."

A second headline read: KIDNAPPEES TURN TABLES ON MERCE-NARY DEVANE.

By one-thirty, action at the voting booths had picked up.

Early ballistics reports showed that the automatic rifle the reverend was holding in the photograph had accounted for three enemy casualties. Branko's bullets had wounded two of Devane's people. He'd wounded another with a grenade. Mrs. Maxwell's revolver hadn't hit anything. Neither had Lissa Cody, who'd been using Branko's .38.

There was no mention in Lissa's story of the fat man in civilian clothes. There was no mention of Agents Moore and Friedkin of the FBI, who had arrived at the hacienda at noon to take the fat man away. Agents Moore and Friedkin did not reappear on Tuesday for the postmortems and follow-ups.

An accompanying story on page two gave two columns to the life and works of the white supremacist and ex-soldier of fortune, Colonel Robert Emory Devane. The chronology in the sidebar told only part of Devane's story:

1933—born on a farm outside Amarillo, Texas
1949—booked for criminal assault on a black preacher; served six months at Cal Farley's Tascosa Boys Town
1950—dropped out of high school to join the French Foreign Legion
1954—escaped from Dien Bien Phu
1956—joined U.S. Army, posted back to Vietnam
1960—field commission, Special Forces
1962—promoted to captain
1963—promoted to major
1964—promoted to colonel
1968—resigned Army commission to form Devane's Raiders, a mercenary squad

1969—Africa, coup
1971—Cambodia, drug running
1973—Central America, fighting communists
1975—Israel
1976—Middle East
1977—Africa
1979—Central America
1981—Africa
1983—built Devania; purchased bank of Sierra Monte
1984 to present—sold guns to old acquaintances
1988—death of a mercenary, Sierra Monte, California, in the
    Santa Ana Mountains

Photos accompanying the story showed men with shovels standing over an unmarked grave and the decayed remains of three unidentified corpses. An excerpt from the story read:

A preliminary coroner's report conjectures the discovered bones might belong to three male Chicanos who disappeared in the spring of 1985. As of this writing, a massive and intensive search continues for more unmarked graves in the bare, scraped earth of the Santa Ana Mountains near the Cleveland National Forest. Authorities will not estimate at this time how many corpses might be found eventually. In a related search, a Riverside County bulldozer unearthed a gold cache with a possible exchange value of several million dollars. The disposition of the money will be decided by the courts.

One inset box had a brief story about police capturing two of Devane's men when their helicopter was forced down outside National City, California, south of San Diego, near the Mexican border. A second box announced an investigation of the office of the sheriff of Sierra Monte.

Tuesday morning, Newport Beach Homicide Sergeant Frank Branko killed four dreary hours answering questions from the FBI, the DEA, Treasury, the IRS, and the CHP. The IRS was present due to the discovery that in his thirty-odd years as a working adult, Robert Emory Devane had never filed an income-tax statement. Devane was an American citizen with a military record, but he had no Social Security number. His passports—there were four of them, in different names—were impeccable and legal. The IRS people said it was impossible, then phoned Washington for advice.

While he answered questions, Branko was thinking mostly about his aches and pains. Pain pills made him groggy, and his left shoulder where Devane's bullet had gone through burned steadily. The black sling that cradled his arm felt tight and uncomfortable. It was lucky for his tennis game that the left arm was his ball tossing arm. The doctor had said six weeks, minimum, before he could play again. Branko planned on four weeks, max. Watch out, Spider Longo.

Chief D'Agostino backed him up all the way. There was a minor flap about Branko being out of his jurisdiction, but the chief got on the phone to Riverside and Sacramento and smoothed things out. The chief loved heroes and good PR. For the moment, Branko was the fair-haired boy of the department. Lieutenant Archer fumed in his office. Maybe he had a secret lunch date with the IRS and DEA.

Branko called Lissa Cody at home and at the *Tribune* during a break in the questioning, but got no answer. The lady was working. He understood. It was her hour of power. He understood, but he missed her.

He broke loose from the station at twelve-thirty and drove to the hospital to check on his wounded officers. Randy Whitson had temporarily placated his wife with an offer of a trip to Hawaii as soon as he was able to travel. Officer Jamie Duncan had broken the hearts of three interns and a beefy resident named Horowitz who was going through a nasty divorce. Jamie, pretty in a blue bathrobe, was beaming from all the male attention. She gave Branko a sisterly kiss. The room where Roscoe Smith had spent his last hours on earth was now occupied by a lady with blue hair and a voice strident enough to clean fish. Branko left the hospital and drove home.

That afternoon they had a memorial service for Roscoe Smith. The service was held in Marcie Deegan's church in Costa Mesa. Branko sat next to Marcie and thought about the years he'd shared with Roscoe. Hearing his friend eulogized dulled his senses and made his eyes water. His necktie chafed, made him feel suffocated. After the service there was a gathering of friends at Marcie's condo in Costa Mesa. Branko shook hands and spoke to people. When he started crying for real, he walked out without saying good-bye. His tears tasted of salt and sweat.

So long, Roscoe.

At home, he stripped off his coat and tie and opened a beer and sat on his narrow deck, soaking up the sun. When the beer was finished, he went inside and flipped on the television and there was the reverend, talking from his new election headquarters at the Cote d'Azur Hotel in Newport Beach. The reverend's subject was biblical revenge, an eye for an eye. "On Friday, while making a political speech on Balboa Island, I was shot by an assassin. I was only wounded, but my bodyguard died, as did a police officer. In the ensuing days, more blood was spilled. My son was wounded, my family threatened, and I vowed revenge. The trail led to a devil incarnate, a modern-day Satan in the garb of a mercenary soldier, an evil white supremacist named Colonel Robert Emory Devane. With the help of a courageous reporter and a brave policeman and a very good friend named Susannah Maxwell, I survived my sentence in the dungeons of this madman. Now he is dead. His legions are routed to the ends of the earth. And I have no wish to profit from the pools of blood. That is all I have to say."

The reverend's face tried to smile, a reflex sharpened by a public life spent facing the cameras. He shut it down with difficulty.

A newsbreak consisting of a photographic summary of events beginning with the Balboa shooting and ending with the assault on Devania followed. There was a ninety-second spot on Promontory Chapel, with color footage of the fire-damaged Tower of Prayer. In the lower left-hand corner of the screen, an election box showed the reverend trailing Sherwood by only seven percentage points.

The phone rang. It was Tommy Osterhaus, calling from the station. "Francisco, did you hear about Dink Carruthers?"

"No. What about him?"

"He didn't come in for work today. A neighbor heard a

gunshot in Dink's place in Santa Monica and called it in. They found him in front of his television with the back of his head blown off. The gun was on the floor. There was a note."

Branko felt a chill on his neck. "Are you sure it was Dink?"

"They're sure. Thought you'd want to know."

"Thanks, Tommy."

"The note admits he was tied in with Devane."

Lissa's instinct had been right. "How?"

"They're not sure how deep it goes, but there's a good chance he tipped Mendoza and the Mace on the Cosmos' shooting."

"I'm having trouble digesting this."

"Yeah. It sounds bad. He was living high on the hog. Two cars. A condo that would have cost him five years in salary. I'll keep you posted."

"Thanks."

"Oh, one more tidbit. The lady shooter has been identified as Amity Jane Pitcairn, twenty-nine, sometime pianist, born in St. Louis, no known place of residence in the U.S. And one of our fraud guys knows a diamond dealer who thinks that rock we took off the lady shooter could be worth two hundred thousand. It's Siberian, rare as hen's teeth."

"Fancy that," Branko said.

He stared at the wall after Tommy hung up. Then he opened another beer and went into his bedroom and lay down on the bed. He was asleep before he'd finished half the beer.

It was a troubled sleep.

The Reverend spent a glorious, electric Tuesday morning speaking to reporters and television people. He had taken a suite at the Cote d'Azur Hotel overlooking the water in Newport Beach. Susannah Maxwell was paying for everything. Dear Susannah, always so generous. Harrison Wakefield was still in the hospital, and to fill the void she had taken over the burden of campaign planning. She was marvelous. And beautiful. And wealthy.

Today, the events of yesterday seemed like a dream. There were images in the reverend's mind of himself aiming and firing, aiming and firing. In his heart, he knew he hadn't done much damage out there. Thanks to Susannah, however, his legend was growing. In the legend, evil people fell and the reverend emerged victorious, clutching an automatic rifle. He loved watching himself on the television, hands wide, beaming into the cameras as he handled reporters.

"Reverend Williams, could you tell us again how you found out about Colonel Devane? How did you know he was implicated in the Balboa incident?"

"Simple deduction. I overheard Douglas Cade conspiring with the killer who had taken us hostage. This conspiracy took place in my church, Promontory Chapel, in the Tower of Prayer. When I saw my son was out of danger I paid Cade a visit. He was terrified that I knew, so he volunteered to guide me to this man Devane."

"Did you threaten Cade?"

"I prefer to view it as ministerial persuasion."

"What about Lissa Cody? Did she volunteer to come along?"

That was a weak point in his story. But so far, Miss Cody had seemed more interested in writing her own story than in charging him with kidnapping. Smart girl. "As a witness, yes. As an objective observer."

"And then when you arrived, Devane took you prisoner and threw you in a cell. Is that right?"

"Quite right. The place was an armed camp, bristling with mercenaries. We were surrounded. They bound our hands and feet and locked us up. If Mrs. Maxwell had not arrived with the policeman, there is no doubt in my mind that I would not be standing here today."

"Where is Mrs. Maxwell?"

The reverend smiled. "She will be along shortly."

"And your family? Will they be here?"

"My son is recuperating from a bullet wound to the stomach. At last reports, Terry Junior is mending nicely. Mrs. Williams, as you know, has been stricken ill and will not appear. My daughter, Delia Sue, is with her mother but has promised to come here sometime after lunch."

"Do you expect to win this primary, Reverend? You're trailing sixty-forty in the percentage vote."

"Only the voters can decide whether I win or lose."

"What about God?" a reporter called. "Will he help?"

"I hope you capitalized He," the reverend said.

Laughter from the reporters.

"God was on my side yesterday." He held up his cane in a victory gesture. "I am here today. That is the proof."

"What about now? Is God on your side today?"

The reverend decided to temporize. There were atheists out there. There were Jews, agnostics, Christ-haters, unbelievers, scoffers of every ilk. Each scoffer had a vote. "Only time will tell."

There was scattered applause from the crowd of reporters and the reverend beamed a smile into the cluster of cameras and for a moment the arrangement of camera lenses reminded him of the beatific rose from Dante's *Paradise*, with choirs of angels singing. He cleared his throat. A hand was up. "Sorry. I missed the question. Would you mind repeating it?" The questions kept coming and he felt stronger with each passing moment. His leg wound was healing quickly, and the pain almost gone. He was surprised he was doing this well without Winona Lee. He had only spoken to her once, over the telephone late Monday, when he had called to ask her to pack some clothes and send them over to the Cote d'Azur.

Susannah Maxwell appeared at election headquarters at three o'clock, looking beautiful in a simple white dress and a wide white hat and gloves. The reverend was pleased to note that the neckline of her dress was modest, indeed, almost chaste. Reporters swarmed around her and Susannah smiled into the cameras, captivating her audience. Her time with the press gave the reverend a chance to rest. He was too excited to sleep. His life was changing in a great sweeping arc that curved from spotlight to spotlight across a gigantic stage in front of thousands of worshipful voters, from Promontory Chapel to the hushed and hallowed corridors of the nation's Capitol. And the trumpet shall sound. And the dead shall be raised.

Susannah rapped on his bedroom door around five o'clock and he called for her to come in. She stood silhouetted in the doorway, hands holding her purse, posed, poised. With a whisper of silken clothing, she sat on the edge of the bed. He smelled her perfume. It was glorious, heady.

"You were marvelous out there, with those newspersons."

"We're a pretty good team," she said.

His wildest dream. "Where are they?"

"I sent them away."

"And they went?"

"Yes."

The phone rang. It was Winona Lee. Her voice was raspy, testy. "Is she there?"

"Is who here?"

"The Jezebel of Spyglass Hill."

"She's here." He took Susannah's hand.

"The congressman called. He waits for your withdrawal statement, husband. I wait for your return to the church."

On the television screen, the reverend was trailing by only eight percentage points. "I'm waiting for the election results."

His wife's voice was frantic. "I have prayed to God. He has instructed the flock to vote for Sherwood."

"Good-bye, Winona Lee."

"I shall display those photographs to the elders."

The reverend hung up.

Susannah's weight shifted on the bed. "The reason the reporters went was because I invited them over later. To Spyglass Hill, my house, for a victory drink. Reporters love to drink. I was hoping you'd be there."

"I wouldn't miss it for the world."

Susannah's hand pulsed with heat as she patted his head. She left the room and he turned up the volume on the television. He was watching himself on the screen when the door opened and Delia Sue came in. His daughter looked different. She was wearing a dress without holes or chains. Her hair had been dyed back to its original color, a dark brown. The black eye makeup was gone from beneath her eye. Delia Sue sat on the edge of the bed and let her red backpack drop to the carpet. She gave her father a hug. The reverend felt his heart fill to bursting.

"Are you all right?"

"Yes. Are you?"

"Oh, yes, yes. I passed Susannah on the way out and she invited me to her house tonight. Everyone will be there, she said. Rod Whitten, Billy Archibald, Rick Tango."

Two movie stars and a rock musician. Rick Tango was the latest rage among teens, with his stark white face and blue hair with a green streak. He dressed in rags, chains, heavy boots. The reverend sighed. "I hope to meet him, to shake his hand."

Delia Sue hugged him again, then fished into her red backpack and brought out a plain brown envelope, which she handed to her father. It was sealed with masking tape.

"What's this?"

"Fun pix." His daughter was smiling a naughty, knowing smile.

The reverend tore off the tape and withdrew a stack of photographs. They showed a hefty blond man committing fornication with a tanned woman. The woman was Helen of Troy. The man resembled the reverend's father, Odell Macaulay Williams. At the edge of one of the photos was a pale blue dress, folded, on a chair. "Where did you get these?"

"Mommy's drawer."

The reverend blushed. "Did you look at them?"

"Oh, sure." She shrugged.

"And?"

"Begat. Begat. Begat, Daddy. Just like in the Bible. Mother's old-fashioned about sex."

"Does your mother know you took them?"

His daughter shrugged again and changed the subject as if she had turned the dial on a television set. "Daddy, do you really think Rick Tango will be there tonight?"

"It's possible. Susannah knows a lot of people."

"I love Susannah," Delia Sue said. "She's really *exciting* to be around. I just love the way she *dresses*."

By six o'clock, Reverend Terry Odell Williams was neck and neck in the primary with his opponent, Jumping Jimmy Sherwood. By seven o'clock, two of the networks, working through their affiliate stations in Los Angeles, had predicted that Laguna Beach artist Lonnie Chevron would win the Democratic primary for the Fiftieth District over Solomon Steinberg, the wealthy lawyer from Irvine. With only eleven percent of the vote counted, however, no affiliate would predict a win in the Republican primary.

By eight o'clock, when the polls closed, Sherwood had eased ahead by two percentage points on CBS. But on ABC and NBC, the reverend was ahead.

One definition of democracy is diversity of point of view. The party at Susannah Maxwell's house on Spyglass Hill was growing. There were reporters from Los Angeles, San Francisco, Riverside, San Diego, Santa Barbara, all of Orange County. The Reverend spoke briefly to Rigby Benford, from the *L.A. Times.*

"I looked for the *Tribune* lady, Lissa Cody," Benford said, "but I don't see her."

The reverend looked around. It was difficult keeping his mind on anything except the television screen, where he was now leading Sherwood on a chart of red, white, and blue by four percentage points. Excitement boiled in his veins. "No. I haven't seen her either."

Benford bored in with his intense brown eyes. "There are a couple of points I wanted to clear up, Reverend, if you've got a minute. For example, the fact that you were a crack shot is not well-known and I was wondering how you . . ."

Benford's voice faded as the reverend noticed Susannah striding like a queen across the room. She was wearing a blue dress tonight, a silken affair with a slightly more daring neckline. Helen of Troy had sailed back into his life from her distant sunset isle. The reverend shivered.

"There's someone here," she whispered, gripping his arm. "Someone to see you. They just arrived. From Washington."

At that moment the new arrivals stepped into the room, three men, one in the lead, two flanking him and slightly behind. They wore quality three-piece suits, gray, summer-weight. The man in the lead was Frederick X. O'Brien, the senior senator from California and a major force on the Republican National Committee. "Good Lord!" the reverend said. "It's Fred O'Brien!"

Susannah leaned into him, pressing him firmly with her hip. Her voice thrilled with excitement. "The man on the senator's right is Benjamin Winters. He's the chairman of the national committee. The man on the left is Gerald Naseby. I think he simply coins money."

Benford, the *Times* reporter, was forgotten as the reverend made his way with Susannah at his side to greet the newcomers. Senator O'Brien had a polished winner's smile and the gleam of political intelligence in his eye. His handshake was professional, a close clasp, warm, intimate, masculine. There was much to learn in this new arena, the reverend reminded himself.

"Reverend, allow me to introduce myself. I'm Freddy O'Brien. This is Bud Winters. And this fellow with the sad accountant's eyes is Jerry Naseby." The senator looked around at the house admiringly, then cut his his eyes once more toward the television screen. "ABC's predicting a winner."

Silence gathered in the room like a pair of huge wings folding together as all eyes turned toward the jumbo-sized screen. Anchoring for Channel 7, Roberta Robertson ran down four congressional districts before she came to the Fiftieth. "In that race down in Orange County, between incumbent Jimmy Sherwood and Reverend Terry Odell Williams, with nineteen percent of the vote counted, ABC Election Central is projecting Reverend Williams as the winner."

Cheers exploded in the room. The senator pumped the reverend's hand. Susannah kissed him lightly on the mouth, and for a moment he thought he felt the tip of her tongue against his teeth. He thought he saw a definite promise in her blue eyes. It had not been a chaste kiss. In that moment, he felt young again, like a muscular bronzed lifeguard on the beach at Malibu. Champagne was handed around. The reverend drank gratefully. Reporters clamored for a victory statement. A few moments later the senator ("You gotta call me Freddy, Reverend. What do they call you? Terry? Good ring to it, Terry Williams. Name like a winner") took him by the arm and walked him to Susannah's library.

Susannah followed, with Republicans Naseby and Winters close behind.

Once they were inside, the senator took charge and asked everyone to sit down. Susannah brought out a bottle of excellent

Scotch and poured everyone a drink. The glasses were Waterford, exquisite. The senator proposed a toast. "To our next congressman from District Fifty."

"Hear, hear."

They drank. The senator looked at his watch. "I've got a call coming through, Mrs. Maxwell. Thought it would be better to take it in here. Hope you don't mind us commandeering your lovely home."

"Of course, Senator. Should we leave you alone?"

"No, no. This concerns—" He paused, his look marked by a winner's confidence. The senator didn't have to run this year; his term had four years to go. "This concerns all of us."

The phone rang and the senator answered and it was clear he was talking to someone in power. The reverend's mouth was dry. Could it be—?

"Yes, sir," the senator said. "He's right here. Yes, sir." The senator smiled at the reverend and motioned for him to take the phone. "Terry?"

"Me?"

The senator nodded as he handed over the phone.

"Hello?"

"Reverend Williams, I presume?" The voice was deep and pleasant, a farm-boy voice right out of the American heartland.

"Yes."

"This is Charley Donnelly, Reverend. I'm calling to welcome you into the fold."

The voice sounded like Daddy's, and sent chills up his spine. He stared at Susannah, who was sitting on the edge of an armchair, swinging one lovely leg and smiling back at him, nodding. "Thank you, Mr. President. I don't know what to say."

"Win, goddammit," the president said. "You've won today. Now win in November. That's what my daddy used to say. Get your ass out there on the line and win. He was a football coach at Purdue."

President Donnelly was a hard-charger and the Donnelly football legend was well known. "That's very good advice, Mr. President."

"Let's get together this summer in Houston, at the convention. My people will set it up. I want to hear a play-by-play of how you wasted that bastard Devane."

"Yes, Mr. President."

"And bring that Mrs. Maxwell with you. Christ, that's the best thing that's happened to this country since Marilyn Monroe stood over a sidewalk air vent with her skirt around her ears."

"Yes, Mr. President."

"What do your friends call you? Terry?"

"Yes, Mr. President."

"Okay, Terry. I'm Charley. And I plan to win in November. How about you?"

The reverend took a deep breath. "I plan to win, sir."

"Charley, remember?"

"I plan to win, Charley."

"Goddamn right you do. See you in July then. And take care of that leg. That cane is a nice touch. FDR used a cane. It was a helluva touch."

"Thank you, sir."

The reverend said good-bye and hung up. They drank one more toast before they went out to join the other guests. On the way out, the senator took the reverend aside. "Did he talk about religion?"

"No, Senator."

"He wouldn't, but I will."

"What is it, Senator?"

"Know how old I am, Reverend?"

"No, I don't."

"Sixty-seven. I didn't have to run this spring, or I might not be here today. California's a young state, always has been. It's the goddamn—pardon my French—it's the goddamn future of this country, westward ho, the Pacific Rim, all that monkey shit. California votes young even as the population as a whole gets older. We'll need someone to step in when I step down, someone with backbone, someone to ace the liberals and sob-sisters. That someone could be you, Reverend."

The reverend's eyes watered, and yet the idea was not so far-fetched. In just four days, a bullet in his leg had catapulted him into a phone conversation with the chief executive himself. In two years, perhaps he would be ready for the U.S. Senate. He decided to play it modest. "You'd better let me get to Washington first."

The senator dug him in the ribs. "Hell, you're running against a fag artist. You can't lose this one. We'll get you to Washington on a railroad handcar if we have to. But listen up, Terry." The senator's eyes bored into him. "Do your job back there in the District of Columbia. Keep your nose clean. Handle this business with your wife. My first wife was a white-eyed albatross, and I know one when I see one. Keep those kids close. Nothing more sympathetic than a father with two brave kids. Attend church, but steer clear of the lunatic religious fringe and that spooky Armageddon crap. Vote the party. Keep your cock out of the headlines. You've got a great set of teeth and a bull of a voice. Let charisma do its work."

The reverend was only partially shocked at the locker-room language. More than anything, he wanted to be part of the club. "Thank you, Senator."

"One more thing."

"Yes?"

"If you're going to hang around Mrs. Maxwell, you'd better marry her—or I will. What a magnificent female. What a magnificent smell she has. I feel I've known her somewhere, but can't seem to recall the exact time and place. Well, that's what happens when you get old. Your goddamn memory turns into Swiss cheese. Now let's join that party. I need to wet my whistle."

Leaning lightly on his cane, the reverend walked side-by-side with Senator O'Brien back to the party, back to where Susannah waited, smiling, suffused in unrelenting brightness.

Marry her? What a lovely idea. He wondered what she would say.

Branko was watching television when the doorbell rang. The picture was *Casablanca*, starring Humphrey Bogart, Ingrid Bergman, Claude Raines, and Paul Henreid. Branko's favorite actor in the movie was Raines, the smirky Vichy police inspector who always landed on his feet. Raines had a pussy-cat smile that

350

was impossible to imitate. The picture had been shot in black-and-white, just right for giving the feel of those early war years.

He wobbled when he stood up to answer the door and his stomach rumbled. Beer cans were lined on the edge of his coffee table. At number six, he had stopped counting. His head felt fuzzy and there was a bitter taste in his mouth. But the beer had put a wall between himself and the nightmarish events of Monday at Devania.

Was it really only yesterday?

He opened the door to find Lissa Cody standing there, purse slung over her shoulder. In one hand she held a flat box marked Roma d'Italia. In her other hand was a straw-covered bottle of Chianti. Seeing Lissa, he felt a sudden warm excitement. The bandage was gone from her cheek and her bruise was healing.

"Are you alone, Branko?"

"Sure. Who did you expect to see?"

Lissa brushed past him into the room without answering and he knew from her vibrations she suspected something. "Did you vote?"

"No. Did you?"

"Yes. I'm a registered Democrat. In this county, we always vote."

"Who did you vote for?"

"All the Democrats, including Lonnie Chevron."

Lissa went into the kitchen and came back with a paper grocery sack. She tossed the empty beer cans into the sack, then took the sack to the kitchen, where she deposited it with a resounding noise. The reason for the noise, he figured, was to tell him he was a lousy housekeeper. Lissa came back with wine glasses and a serrated knife. She used the knife to open the pizza box. "I got pepperoni, bell pepper, mushrooms, black olives, and anchovies."

The pizza smelled wonderful. He hadn't eaten since early this morning, a piece of too-sweet Danish. "I hate anchovies."

"Then I can have yours. Aren't you going to open the wine?"

"Sorry."

He walked into the kitchen, where he rummaged in a drawer until he found a cork screw. This one was yellow, with the words Lambert Bridge Winery on the side. It was a souvenir from a trip to the wine country with his ex-wife Karen, three summers ago. He walked back into the living room with it. "Want to go to the wine country with me?"

"When?"

He opened the wine and filled their glasses. "Soon. I've got some time off coming. We could drive up. Takes a day. We could see a couple of wineries where I know the owners."

Lissa plucked off the anchovies before handing him his slice of pizza. The cheese was still warm as he bit into it. They clinked glasses. The Chianti tasted of grapes and alcohol and rusty nails—the real Chianti taste.

Lissa sat on the sofa next to him. She kicked off her shoes and her skirt rode up over her knees and she made no move to pull it back down. The legs of Brenda Starr, girl reporter, he thought. There was a different mood in the room with her there. Her green eyes looked smoldery. She still hadn't answered him about the wine country.

She eyed the beer cans. "What did you do today, Branko?"

"Slept. Answered questions. Visited the hospital. Went to a funeral. Called you. What did you do?"

"Wrote my follow-up story. It's tomorrow's front page, all about white supremacy and political conspiracy and how politicians and preachers are alike. There are some marvelous photos of Devania and a couple of you that are heroic. Three photos show the reverend, shooting. The gun in his hand is a revolver, of course, not an automatic, so they won't use those. There are two photos of Mrs. Maxwell firing the automatic rifle she handed to the reverend after it was over. There's one of Douglas Cade with his hands over his ears, a symbolic warning to timid accountants who get mixed up with mercenary soldiers."

"When did you have a chance to take photos?"

"When I reloaded." Lissa sniffed and cut two more slices of pizza. "They cut the part about James Jack Jessup."

"Who's he?"

"The fat man you put into handcuffs. His name's James Jack Jessup, Jimmy Jack to his pals. He's a brigadier general, works at the Pentagon. This pizza's not bad. I had a coupon that was good until the end of the month, twenty percent off if you ordered four toppings, and even though this is the beginning of the—"

Branko stopped her with a finger on her lip. "What do you mean, they cut that part?"

"My editor. He took it to the publisher, who conferred with legal counsel. When he came back, the stuff about Brigadier Jessup was gone. And how he was spirited away by two federal agents, along with a black briefcase that I did not have a chance to look into."

"What happened to freedom of the press?"

Her face was hollow with irony. "It's their paper. Their explanation was they had space problems. They cut the part about the brigadier and about the Spyglass Hill Gang. They cut everything about CASS and my involved tie-in with Ministry Beach."

"I hear it's a total shutdown out there."

Lissa refilled his glass with Chianti. "Good finish for my book, still-life at a construction site. What do you think of my body, Branko?"

"What?"

She gave him a straight stare. "I'm not as obvious as slinky Mrs. Maxwell in her open front jumpsuit, but then she's *so* rich and *so* perfect and *so*—"

He grabbed her wrist. "What's up, Cody?"

"You two made a cute couple out there, shoulder to shoulder, guns blazing. Dazzling Duo at Devania. They're certain to cast you as the lead in the movie."

"If you had time to watch, Cody, you weren't holding up your end."

She leaned over to give him a kiss. With her kiss, she asked questions, serious questions. With his kiss, he tried to answer. Behind her lips lurked intensity, promise, mystery. When she broke away, Branko's heart was hammering.

"Hmmm," she said. "Not bad, Branko."

She reached into her leather purse and brought out a plain white envelope. She popped open the envelope and dropped three stones into Branko's hand. They were rough diamonds, like the one found on Rachel English, a. k. a. Amity Jane Pitcairn, Shooter Three.

"Where did you find these?"

"The library at Devania." Lissa smiled. "'The Library at Devania.' That sounds like a title for a television soap."

"Where were they?"

"Scattered around, as if from an explosion. One was buried in a seat cushion on a chair. Any idea what they're worth?"

"Half a million. Maybe more."

Lissa whistled. "That much?"

Now he knew what Mrs. Maxwell had been hunting for on the floor of Devane's library. Diamonds—yet another reason for her trip. How many stones had she found?

Lissa handed him a stone. "This one is yours."

"Why me?"

"Hero's reward. You came after me like the white knight out of fairytales. The white knight always gets his reward."

He handed the stone back. "I got pizza and Chianti. And a kiss full of promise. That's enough."

Lissa set the stones on Branko's coffee table, then moved into his bionic chair and sat in it, testing. "I want you to take a trip with me. As my bodyguard."

"Where to?"

"Amsterdam. My God, this chair is wonderful. What is it?"

"Bionic chair. Why are we going to Amsterdam?"

"Amsterdam is a diamond town. We can get an appraisal, sell a stone, hop down to Zurich and open a numbered account. I love this chair. Where can I get one?"

"Roll backward. Kick your legs out and up."

Lissa set her wineglass down and rolled backward. "Unbelievable. I would kill for this."

"You'll have to. The chair stands between me and madness."

Lissa closed her eyes. "A friend told me to go to Amsterdam and do three things. One, ride a canal boat on a tour of the city. Two, drink the local gin. Three, eat a sandwich of raw herring to go with the gin."

"They call it *genevre*."

"Your accent is terrible, Branko. In Amsterdam, we might find someone to cut these for us."

Branko picked up the middle stone. "How do they grade diamonds?"

"The four Cs. Color, Clarity, something, something. Will you go?"

"Why not? I'm bushed. The chief wants me to take some time off. Amsterdam's only a few short hours from the wine country. What about your editor?"

"After what he did today, my editor doesn't count. I'm taking a leave. Or quitting. I'll write my book and leap onto the best-seller lists and talk learnedly on the Carson show."

"How is the weather in Amsterdam this time of year?"

"It's raining, fifty-three degrees. I checked in the paper before I came here bearing pizza." Lissa rolled forward in the chair, to an upright position.

"Umbrella weather."

"Um. And knee boots."

"You own knee boots, Cody?"

"I bought some on sale in January. Haven't had a chance to wear them yet. Reason number four for Amsterdam. Knee boots."

Branko stood up and walked to the telephone.

"Who are you calling, the IRS?"

He dialed. The phone rang at the other end. "Pan Am."

"At this time of night?"

Someone with a musical voice answered the phone. "This is Pan Am, Arla Watson speaking, how may I help you?"

"Information on flights from LAX to Amsterdam, please."

"One moment, please."

Branko covered the phone by holding it against his ribcage and said, "Knee boots?"

Before Branko could stop her, she was out the door, moving in her stocking feet down the front steps. Branko let the phone drop and hurried after her. Behind him as he went out the door he heard the voice of the Pan Am rep. Still musical.

He caught her in the courtyard and turned her around to face him and she came into the circle of his good arm willingly. He nuzzled her cheek and she pressed into him with newfound intimacy.

"You came after me."

"Yes."

"Thank you for saving my life, Branko."

They kissed for a long moment, bodies pressed tightly together. "Want to know what they called me back in high school?"

"Yes." Her lips were cool and feathery against his throat. "What did they call you back in high school?"

"Birdman." His secret was out.

She giggled, moving against him. "Birdman?"

"Yes. Branko, the Birdman of Beloit."

"Why?"

"Tell you later." He blew in her ear.

"Tell me now."

"Later. Where were you off to in your stocking feet?"

She murmured against him. "Knee boots."

"Where?"

"In my car. I wanted to model them for you."

"With umbrella? Or without?"

"Do you own an umbrella, Birdman?"

"Sure do."

"Then it's with. Definitely."

He kissed her then full on the mouth and she kissed him back and then they put their arms around each other and walked back up the stairs.

Here's a taste of *MERRY CHRISTMAS, MURDOCK*, on sale from Delacorte Press in November.

The phone rang again, but I kept on slicing the onion, five cuts along the grain, then nine cuts the other way, starting from right to left, the chef's knife winking in the light. *Aida* was playing on my vintage RCA stereo, Maria Callas belting out a hefty Italo-Egyptian love tune, and I hummed along, pushing back the December chill with a bottle of good Mondavi Red.

It was Wednesday, four days before Christmas, and I was making soup to fight off the holiday gloom. I learned to make soup from my mom, who made it to feed my dad, the Sergeant, who was career Army. Winter and summer, Mom kept soup stored in our fridge. The Sergeant had a way of appearing in the doorway by surprise. Honey, I'm home, babe, the tired old foot-soldier, home from the wars, starved as a POW, thirsty as Gunga Din, so what's for dinner, hey?

In five minutes my mom would have hot steaming soup on the table, corn bread, Tabasco, carrot sticks, black olives, real butter, and an iced mug of Schlitz beer. The Sergeant's favorite soup was goulash, which he claimed was an ancient Celtic recipe stolen by the Viennese. My mom's favorite was bouillabaisse, with gazpacho a close second. Whatever the type, she made eight quarts at a time to feed my friends and the Sergeant's bachelor buddies, dragged along to our place for a home-cooked meal. When she died, my mom willed me her soup tureen, a lovely curved piece made in Dresden, inherited from her German grandmother.

So when the phone rang I was in the first stage of creating Minestrone à la Murdock: You braise the beef. You slice four onions. You peel six garlic buds. You pack the beef, the onion, and the garlic into a pot, where the magic is. I paid $17 for Cal, my pot, after finding him at a garage sale in peaceful Irvine. Cal stands for Calphalon, the gray-flannel wonder metal, swirled at the factory for memorable taste and easy clean-up. You add beef stock, Italian spices, a bay leaf, crushed black pepper, and a pungent Neapolitan clove. You simmer for an hour, maybe two, while you watch sports on television. You cool the brew overnight, while the grease floats like magic to the top. Stage two begins next day when you . . .

My answering machine clicked on, the red light winking like a gnat's eyeball. I poured in the beef stock and set the fire on simmer and turned down the volume under Callas and sipped red wine while I waited for the message. Some old flame, I thought, happily married, inviting me over for a chummy family Christmas. Or some Scrooge of a bill collector, grousing at me to pay up or else. Or maybe a rich client. Merry Christmas, Murdock.

"Lancelot," said the voice of Wally St. Moritz. "Wally here. Are you monitoring, dear boy?"

I picked up the phone, heard that hollow echo of the recorder bounding back at me. "Hey, Professor. I'm on. Where are you?"

"El Toro General."

"Ten days too early for your annual blues," I said. "So they must be treating your tennis elbow."

"Ho-ho-ho, as Santa says to greedy little mall monsters. Can you motor down here? I think I've unearthed a client."

"One with money?"

"And trouble." Wally paused. "All it needs is your presence. Your inimitable persuasive powers."

I stirred the soup. "Who's the client?"

"A state senator from Texas, with a wounded child, who is most impatient with local police procedure."

"I identify with the impatient part. What kind of wound?"

"A hit-and-run."

"Ouch. Where'd it happen?"

"Xanadu Mall, in the parking lot."

"What time?"

"Last evening, nine-ish."

It hadn't been big enough to make the evening news. "Xanadu's in the sheriff's jurisdiction. What are they doing?"

"Not much. That's why I'm calling you."

"Does the Senator know? Or is this your idea?"

"The Senator became interested when I explained you knew people on the inside."

"Used to know."

Wally sighed. "Be resourceful, Matthew. I assured the Senator you could help."

It didn't feel holiday hopeful. Josh McBride, my deputy pal inside the sheriff's office, had retired to Idaho, where he was running a fishing camp for the tourists. The deputies I'd met on the street were aging jock hot dogs who still hugged dreams about making the jump into pro ball.

I eyed my soup and took another sip of wine. Inside, it was warm and toasty. Outside, it was nasty, cold, and wet. Problem: I needed the work. I'd had a gritty six days in San Diego, doing reference checks for Tritonics, Inc., a software company that was hiring a vice president for marketing at a base salary of $120,000, plus perks and fringes. Out of four candidates, three had come up dirty as Hell's Angels at an Oakland beer bust. The dirtiest had been handpicked by the Tritonics comptroller, a tight-ass named Binder, who was busily seeding his little dukedom with fawning supporters. Tritonics owed me two grand for my work, but since checks had to be signed by Binder, it would be Easter before I saw the money. Meanwhile, I had $104 in the checking account and Christmas was closing fast.

Would the Senator be my Santa?

I filled the kettle with water for coffee and turned on the fire.

"Are you there, Matthew?"

"Yo."

"When shall we expect you?"

I needed the work. "Half an hour."

Wally told me the hurt kid was on the fourth floor. We hung up. The rain hammered my roof and I shivered as I tugged on my boots. Bugging the sheriff was not my idea of a hot case. I yawned. Damn Binder. Damn all tight-ass comptrollers.

Boots on, I spent three minutes deciding about the shoulder harness. Yes. No. Yes. No. They still wore guns in Texas. Was the Senator a hunter? Would hardware impress? I filled the thermos with travel coffee, antidote to Mondavi Red. Drink that on the way. I checked my face in the mirror. Would you hire this man? Circles under the eyes, a broadening swatch of gray in the beard, my mom's straight teeth, the Sergeant's suspicious frown.

With a last look around, I turned *Aida* off, cut the fire under my minestrone, shrugged into my Eddie Bauer rain parka, and walked down the stairs carrying the thermos and the shoulder harness. The rain slapped down onto the puddles outside my apartment. The pier was deserted. The wind was cold off the sea.